TWIST AND SHOUT

Merseybeat, The Cavern, The Star-Club & The Beatles

by Spencer Leigh

TWIST AND SHOUT
Merseybeat, Hamburg, The Cavern and The Beatles

First published in Great Britain in 2004 by
Nirvana Books
5 Mayfield Court, Victoria Road,
Freshfield, Liverpool L37 7JL

Some of the matrial in this book appeared in Spencer Leigh's
'Let's Go Down The Cavern' published in 1974 by Vermillion.

A catalogue record for this book is available from the British Library

ISBN 09506201-5-7

Printed and bound by T. Snape & Co. Ltd., Preston, Lancs.

BOOKS BY SPENCER LEIGH

Paul Simon – Now and Then (Raven 1973)

Presley Nation (Raven 1976)

Stars In My Eyes (Raven 1980)

Let's Go Down The Cavern (with Pete Frame) (Vermillion 1984)

Speaking Words Of Wisdom: Reflections On The Beatles (Cavern City Tours 1991)

Aspects Of Elvis (edited with Alan Clayson) (Sidgwick & Jackson 1994)

Memories Of Buddy Holly (with Jim Dawson) (Big Nickel 1996 U.S. only)

Halfway to Paradise: Britpop 1955-62 (with John Firminger) (Finbarr Int. 1996)

Behind The Song: The Stories of 100 Great Pop & Rock Classics (with Michael Heatley) (Blandford 1998)

Drummed Out: The Sacking Of Pete Best (Northdown 1998)

Brother Can You Spare A Dime: 100 Years Of Hit Songwriting (Spencer Leigh Ltd. 2000)

Baby That's Rock 'n' Roll: American Pop 1954-63 (with John Firminger) (Finbarr Int. 2001)

Sweeping The Blues Away – A Celebration Of The Merseysippi Jazz Band (Liverpool University 2002)

The Best Of Fellas – The Stroy Of bob Wooler, Liverpool's 1st D.J. (Drivegreen 2003)

The Walrus Was Ringo: 101 Beatle Myths Debunked (with Alan Clayson) (Chrome Dreams 2003)

Puttin' On The Style: The Lonnie Donegan Story (Finbarr Int. 2003)

Coming Soon:

1,000 No. 1 Hits (with Jon Kutner) (Omnibus 2005)

*"Don't talk to me about music.
I could have been in the fucking Beatles."
(Tommy in Willy Russell's 'Breezeblock Park')*

ACKNOWLEDGEMENTS

In 1980 and 1981 I conducted interviews for what became a series of 12 one hour programmes on BBC Radio Merseyside called *Let's Go Down The Cavern*. That led to a stage musical, *Cavern Of Dreams*, written by Carol Ann Duffy and directed by Bill Morrison for Liverpool Playhouse.

No one had written a book on Merseybeat and I thought that the interview material would make an entertaining prospect. Somehow I acquired an agent and the book, also called *Let's Go Down The Cavern*, was published by Vermilion, an imprint of Hutchinson, in 1984. The publishers sold their run of 5,000 copies in the first year, but decided not to reprint. Since then, the book has acquired a cult status and I have seen copies at Beatles Convention for sale at £30 or £40. Bizarrely, a brochure incorporating some of the text and illustrations and distributed without charge for the opening of Cavern Walks fetches even more inflated prices.

The rights to my book were returned to me some years ago, but I never got round to doing anything about it. It is difficult to work on more than one book at a time and there has, I am glad to say, been a steady flow of new projects.

Ron Ellis, who writes the Johnny Ace detective stories that invariably relate back to Liverpool in the Sixties, wanted to reprint the book, but I knew it would need updating. Although the book concentrates on the years up to 1966, the commentary on their later lives (and, in some cases, deaths) needed amending. Also, and perhaps more significantly, I had done scores of radio interviews and articles over the last 20 years with both the existing interviewees and characters I had not interviewed before. I had plenty of new material and, hopefully, insights as I had also undertaken research into various aspects of Merseybeat which intrigued me, notably the Cunard Yanks. I knew the book could not be published without a radical overhaul.

Around the same time, I saw the film about Britpop, *Live Forever*, with its highly opinionated comments from the Gallaghers, Damon Albarn and Jarvis Cocker. It was hilarious and I realised that *Let's Go Down The Cavern* was equally funny. Parts of it are sad, but like Britpop, it is the story of young lads having a great time. When *Live Forever* was released on DVD, the commentary from the director, John Dower, and the producer, John Battsek, was even funnier than the film's original soundtrack. I realised that this book could have a writer's commentary as the background to some of these interviews is hilarious. I've incorporated some of this in the text.

Over the years, I have written books on my own and books with other authors, but this is the first time I have written a book with myself. I have taken my 20 year old text and expanded it to create what is definitely a new book, *Twist And Shout*. At times, I was surprised by my naïvety - I had tended to think that interviewing one person in a group could give me the full picture - and now I think the conflicting reminiscences add to the fun and sheer *joie de vivre* of the book.

My 1984 thanks go to Brian Bowman, Jenny Collins, Philip Collins, Lynda Davis, Carol Ann Duffy, Pete Frame, Jonathan Harradine, Susan Hill, Pete Hogan, Ian Judson, Rob King, Andrew Lauder, Chris Leigh, Mark Lewisohn, Nicky Mackay, Paul Mercer, Colin Miles, Bill Morrison, Jim Rimmer, Frank Sellors, Gerry Stubbs, Digby Wolff and Pamela Wolff. In 2004, I add Geoffrey Davis and Ron Ellis. Thanks to all the musicians who have lent material for the illustrations.

In 1984, I thanked my wife, Anne, saying that she "now knows more about Merseybeat than she could ever have wanted to know". Now, by osmosis, it could be her specialist subject on *Mastermind*.

Spencer Leigh
Liverpool
June 2004

TWIST AND SHOUT
Merseybeat, The Cavern, The Star-Club & The Beatles
by Spencer Leigh

CONTENTS

FOREWORD BY RON ELLIS

Merseybeat

Without Merseybeat, a sound that started in Liverpool in the late fifties and peaked with the triumph of The Beatles, pop music today would be very different. Merseybeat was the fountain from which sprang the British beat boom of the Sixties and led ultimately to the development of what came to be known as Rock. Yet there has never been a complete history of this unique movement.

Old copies of Bill Harry's *Mersey Beat* paper change hands at £100. Beatles Fan Club magazines are much in demand at auctions. Various books on the Sixties grudgingly devote a chapter to the Liverpool scene but none of them give the full picture.

The nearest anyone has come to capturing the spirit of Merseybeat is Spencer Leigh, with his 1974 book 'Let's Go Down The Cavern' which chronicled interviews with Merseybeat musicians on his BBC Radio Merseyside show, *On The Beat*. This has long been out of print and has become a much sought after collectors' item.

Now Spencer has revised the work and added another 40,000 words, bringing the story up to date. There is lots of new information within these pages, a big section on the important Hamburg scene, a full index and an update on what has happened to the Merseybeat personalities over the passing years, as well as a large selection of photographs and illustrations, many of them never before published.

Strangely, major publishers have been reluctant to commit themselves to commissioning a book about Merseybeat, invariably claiming it is of interest only to a minority readership. Therefore, I am very pleased to have the opportunity to publish it under the Nirvana Books imprint.

To understand Merseybeat, it is necessary to survey the popular music scene at the end of the Fifties.

Distorted by the rosy glow of nostalgia, the Fifties seems to have been an idyllic time to be a teenager in Britain. Pleasures were simple, life was carefree, there was no crime and vandalism like we have today and our avuncular Prime Minister, Mr. Macmillan, told us we'd never had it so good.

All lies.

Life had actually been far more exciting in the Twenties, in the age of Jazz, flappers, and ragtime, a social scene that became known as The Roaring Twenties. The proliferation of dance combos formed to cater for the demand for jazz music, and the first generation of gramophone records, mirrored the situation in the sixties when the beat group boom exploded.

By contrast, the Fifties were dull. After the War there was poverty and uniformity as Britain bore the cost of rebuilding its cities. Bomb sites were everywhere. Food was rationed and there was little choice in the shops. Cars were black and money was tight.

The transition from childhood to adulthood was instantaneous. Children wore the same clothes as their parents and often followed the same hobbies.

The Second World War was a great dividing line. Boys of 18 were called away to do National Service. When they returned, they were men and expected to forget the pastimes of their adolescent years. They got a job, found a nice girl and settled down.

Not a recipe for excitement.

Even the music was stale. The Big Bands of the Thirties had given way to smaller units, partly because of economics. Also, with the improvement of microphone technology, the bands' vocalists had assumed greater importance leading to the cult of the crooners.

Singers like Bing Crosby and Frank Sinatra became more popular than the bands themselves and their voices dominated the airwaves.

Even newer 'pop' singers in the early fifties like Johnny Ray and Guy Mitchell were performing material that hadn't changed much in twenty years.

In the dance halls, ballroom dancing still held sway and young people had to learn the waltz, the quickstep and the foxtrot in imitation of their parents.

A night at home meant listening to the BBC's light orchestral music on the wireless.

Few people owned a radiogram and even fewer had a television set. A gramophone was something you had to wind up after each 78 rpm shellac record was played, and you probably had to change the needle as often.

The Top Twenty charts were determined by sales of sheet music not records.

Ther teenager had not yet been invented.

America in the Fifties

The music scene was the same in most of America but in the Deep South, things were different and it was from there that the New Music came.

After the Depression in the Thirties, thousands of rural farmworkers emigrated to Northern cities looking for work, many of them ending up in the stockyards and factories of Chicago. The old blues singers changed to a new, urban style using electrified instruments and this was the music being played on the black radio stations. They called it rhythm and blues or race music. Exponents were artistes like Fats Domino, Muddy Waters, Elmore James and Big Joe Turner.

Meanwhile, the old folk music of the Southern whites was becoming more sophisticated and calling itself Country and Western. Hank Williams songs were reaching audiences that dismissed the old hillbilly music. Western Swing outfits, led by people like Bob Wills and Bill Haley, were filling dance floors across the South. The local radio stations preferred Lefty Frizzell to Vic Damone.

In the early fifites, Sun Records in Memphis were releasing many rhythm and blues material by black artistes and the owner, Sam Phillips, noticed how many white kids were becoming interested in this music. He realised that if he could find a white teenager who could sing like these black singers, he could have a star on his hands.

He didn't realise how big. He found Elvis Presley. The teenager from Memphis with the smouldering good looks recorded Arthur 'Big Boy' Crudup's 'That's All Right Mama' and immediately became the excuse white teenage girls needed to buy what were now termed rock'n'roll records, a music that fused black rhythm and blues and white country. And, even better, he appealed to males as well.

A host of imitators followed. Sun themselves had Carl Perkins and Jerry Lee Lewis; Lubbock, Texas spawned Buddy Holly and the Crickets whilst Chuck Berry, Little Richard and Fats Domino were black singers whose music hadn't changed but who were now accepted by mass audiences.

Film-makers jumped on the bandwagon with movies like *Don't Knock The Rock* and *The Girl Can't Help It* while Bill Haley's 'Rock Around the Clock' featured in *Blackboard Jungle* became forever the archetypal song of the era.

Rock'n'roll had arrived.

The Rise and Fall of Rock'n'Roll

In Britain, the impact was just as big and we tried to create our own rock'n'roll stars to match the Americans. Tommy Steele was the first one to be launched but, like Wee Willie Harris and Screaming Lord Sutch after him, he was more music hall than rock'n'roll.

Johnny Kidd & The Pirates and Vince Taylor were Britain's only genuine contenders in the 1950's although Cliff Richard looked promising with 'Move It' until he was turned into a boy next door teen idol.

But then, 'boys next door' were happening in America too. The music industry had retaliated by absorbing the wildness of rock'n'roll and regurgitang it in a watered down form.

The record that heralded the movement was Buddy Holly's version of the Paul Anka song, 'It Doesn't Matter Anymore'.

Holly's manager, Norman Petty, recorded it in New York using Dick Jacob's string section to play a pizzicato backing to augment the usual Crickets' guitar and drums accompaniment.

Shortly afterwards, Leiber and Stoller recorded black doo-wop group The Five Crowns, using a full string section. Re-named The Drifters after Clyde McPhatter's defunct group, their first single, 'There Goes My Baby', topped the American charts in June 1959.

Around the same time, another classic doo-wop group, The Skyliners from Pittsburgh, scored with their own composition, 'Since I Don't Have You' which also featured soaring strings.

Thereafter, hardly a record was released that didn't sound as if the entire Philharmonic Orchestra had strayed into the session.

In Britain, Chuck Berry was forgotten as fans queued to buy records by ex-paper boy Adam Faith who copied Buddy Holly's pizzicato strings (courtesy of arranger John Barry) to perfection. Faith even tried to emulate the American singer's peculiar enunciation but succeeded only in producing a sound not unlike that of a tone deaf sheep with a cleft palate.

It was a sound that sold several million records.

Suddenly, the Bobby Era was upon us. By 1962, the likes of Bobby Vee, Bobby Rydell, Fabian, etc. in the States and Craig Douglas, Marty Wilde & Co. in Britain, had taken us back almost to the days of the crooners with their emasculated Tin Pan Ally songs.

But there was a backlash on the way and it started in Liverpool, England.

The Liverpool Sound

After the War, the two main venues for dancing in Liverpool were The Grafton Rooms in West Derby Road and the slightly more upmarket Rialto in Upper Parliament Street.

The Rialto was destroyed in the Toxteth Riots of 1988 but The Grafton Rooms are still going strong today.

The bands that played these halls in the early fifties represented the cream of British jazz and swing. Ken Mackintosh, Chris Barber, Oscar Rabin, Harry Gold and Joe Loss all appeared regularly between 1952 and 1957. Other halls opened up including The Locarno next door to the Grafton, Blair Hall in Walton, Holyoak Hall in Smithdown Road and Garston Baths.

In the late fifties in England, trad jazz had taken a hold before Lonnie Donegan came out of the Chris Barber Band to create the new craze of skiffle. Now, any kid with not much money, and no musical training, could buy a cheap ukulele á la George Formby, and strum out a tune, accompanied by a washboard, double bass and, possibly, a drummer. Do-it-yourself music had arrived but skiffle soon gave way to electric guitars and rock'n'roll.

The movement began in youth clubs in church halls where Dansette record players, playing the latest hits on 7" 45rpm vinyl discs instead of old 78's, were replaced by embryonic rock'n'roll groups learning their trade.

They graduated to the interval spot at dance halls and soon superceded the bands and trad jazz groups as the ballroom dancers made way for the jivers.

But in Liverpool, things were different. When the rest of the country was listening to The Shadows and Tommy Steele, Liverpool groups were apeing the rhythm and blues sound of the American South. Their heroes were people like Chuck Berry, The Coasters, Larry Williams, Carl Perkins and the Tamla Motown stars who at that time were still unknown in England.

The docks were in terminal decline, jobs were scarce, so playing in a group was an attractive alternative (and in many cases supplement) to the dole for many teenage boys.

Soon dance clubs opened up all over the city, many of them like The Cavern, unlicensed. The music was what mattered. An order for American albums written by John Lennon in 1963 included LP's by Dr. Feelgood (the American blues singer a.k.a. Piano Red), Bobby Blue Bland, The Olympics, James Ray, Rufus Thomas, Inez and Charlie Foxx which showed the hard-edged R'n'B direction his tastes were taking.

After The Beatles hit the big time, taking a few other lucky bands on their coat tails, the scene moved to London and Merseybeat became history. There had been over 300 groups in the city and well over 200 of them were left behind. And not always the worst ones. Some drifted into cabaret and others pursued fame elsewhere but most went back to their day jobs. Some are still going strong today, sixty year old men reliving their youth, although a surprising number have already sadly passed away. All of these people and many more are the unsung heroes of Merseybeat and deserve to be remembered.

People like George and Jim Blott who ran the Peppermint Lounge Club above Sampson and Barlow's in London Road and ran the Peppermint Agency with ex-Merchant Taylors pupil and TV script-writer, Geoff Leack, who was manager, and later husband, of Irene Green who sang as Tiffany with, first, The Thoughts and then The Dimensions. The 'Pep' became Dinos, was eventually demolished and George Blott bought a mansion in Gloucester where he hosted Northern Soul weekends in the grounds.

Nearby Southport had a scene of its own. Rhythm'n'Blues Incorporated, were managed first by Ronnie Malpass ('the best chef in the North West', owner of the Mocambo Club and later a children's entertainer) and then by impresario Jim Turner who got them a record deal with Fontana. Their version of 'Louie Louie' reached the lower reaches of the charts, the first Southport band to have a hit record. Lead guitarist Barry Womersley went on to win Opportunity Knocks with Inner Sleeve and currently plays with Kingsize Taylor. Drummer Alan Menzies has been with The Bootles for over a quarter of a century although they are now based in Denmark. Lead singer Pete 'Kin' Kelly has a recording studio in London and is half of the duo Soul Mates with his young girl friend.

Vocalist Pete James wrote 'Doreen The Spaceman's Delight' and went through rock'n'roll, soul, psychedelia and punk in various bands. In the 80's, he changed his name to Eddy Vincent, shaved his head and joined Ugly's Agency who gave him a lot of TV work. He is now a DJ at a Llandudno entertainments complex.

Other Southport groups included The Teenbeats, The Smokestacks, The Berry Pickers, The Jokers, The Zeniths, The Toledo Four, The Mersey Boys, The Diplomats, The Original Principals, Syrian Blue, The Blue Chips, Little Gene and The Outlaws, The Rave-Ons, Stella and The Rondels, Fender Ray and The Gems, The Tudors, The Upset, Nuclear Magenta, etc.

Behind the scenes were club owners like Tommy Barton who had The Chequers in Seel Street and now owns Toad Hall and The Sands in Ainsdale and runs a computer business. Bodybuilder Roy Adams at various times owned The Pyramid, punk venue Erics and The Cavern (he was the last owner) in Liverpool, Shorrocks Hill in Formby and The Kingsway in Southport. Ex-Mr Universe, Terry Phillips, ran Pickwicks and The Wooky Hollow whilst his brother, Sonny, had the Yankee Clipper and still sings on the folk circuit. Neil English ran The Sink Club and The Rumbling Tum.

Among the early agents and promoters were Doug Martin, Brian Kelly, Ralph Webster, Mike Birchall and myself who gave work to numerous groups in the Northern end of the city.

Today, with The Beatles assuming the mythical stature of The Brontés and Shakespeare, Liverpool has become a world famous venue for music lovers. With the city gaining the European Capital of Culture of 2008 accolade, this will grow.

All these people, and many more, were part of that exciting scene known as Merseybeat that was the start of a legend.

In the 60's, RON ELLIS started out as a dance promoter, manager and agent for Merseybeat groups, eventually taking to the road as one of the North's first mobile D.J.'s.

In the 70's, he was appointed Promotion Manager for WEA Records and went on to set up his own company arranging promotion tours for visiting pop stars.

In the 80's, he conducted over 100 interviews for Albert Goldman's controversial best selling biography, *The Lives of John Lennon*, and had a hit himself in the new wave charts with the self-composed punk anthem, *'Boys On The Dole'*, recorded under the name of Neville Wanker and the Punters.

In the 90's, he lectured on *The History of Popular Music in Britain 1940-80* for The University of Liverpool and wrote songs for P.J. Proby.

Currently he writes the popular series of crime novels, published by Allison & Busby, featuring Liverpool private eye /radio DJ, Johnny Ace, and contributes regular articles to the music press.

1   INSTANT KARMA

I. Liverpool then
II. Liverpool redux

"Welcome to Liverpool, Home of the Beatles."
(Street sign at entrance to city, 2004)

"So this is where western civilisation got fucked up."
(Paul Kantner of Jefferson Starship on playing the Cavern in 2004)

I. Liverpool then

In 2003, straight after it had been announced that Liverpool would be the European Capital of Culture in 2008, Alan Coren on Radio 4's *News Quiz* remarked, "This is good news for Liverpool. Now it's got five years to find some." A witty remark and typical of the way Liverpool has been portrayed in the media. You know the jokes: "What do you call a Scouser with a suit?" "The accused." Very funny but a bit tiresome and we're hoping that, after being the Capital of Culture, the city will no longer be the butt of jokes.

Alan Coren had a point. It underscored the fact that Liverpool's bid was considerably helped by both football and rock music being considered cultural. If the selection process had been made a generation earlier, football skills and songwriting ability would not have played a part and Liverpool, I am sure, would not have reached the short list. With rock music in the package, what chance did Birmingham have? How could Ozzy Osbourne compete with the Beatles?

A year before the Capital of Culture festivities, Liverpool will celebrate its 800th anniversary. King John knew what was happening north of Watford as he granted Liverpool its charter in 1207. It was a harbour for sending supplies to Ireland, but because of strong tides, it did not develop as a port for several centuries.

The links between Liverpool and the Irish have continued to the present, with many Liverpool-Irish families living in the city. Its slogan for 2008 is "The world in one city". The multi-cultural aspect of Liverpool is crucial to its development although, by way of contrast, Merseybeat is the territory of white, teenage males.

In the end, Liverpool's location proved to be perfect: it was situated at the mouth of the Mersey: there was a direct link to Manchester and the surrounding Lancashire towns and what's more, Liverpool looked out to New York. With the industrial revolution and the development of manufacturing industries in those towns, Liverpool became a major port in the 18th century. Liverpool merchants imported raw materials and then exported finished goods from the mills – King Cotton, as they say. The link between Liverpool and Manchester's cotton market was very strong and both cities prospered as one.

There is a dark side, a very dark side, to Liverpool's history and that is the slave trade. This enterprise had begun in London but Bristol and then Liverpool wanted some of the action. In the so-called triangular trade, the ships would take cooking utensils and liquor to the west of Africa where the goods were exchanged for slaves. The slaves were transported to the West Indies and the southern states of America, where they were sold for cargoes of rum, sugar or cotton for the journey home. Almost as objectionable as slavery were the press gangs who would force young men to work on the ships and indeed the appalling hours and cramped conditions in Lancashire's cotton mills.

The MP, William Wilberforce, called for the trade to be outlawed and, over 20 years, he became the figurehead for the abolitionist cause. When his bill came before Parliament, 64 petitions against it were received from Liverpool merchants in contrast to only 12 from Bristol and 14 from London. These merchants feared bankruptcy and unemployment for themselves and their workforces and to be fair to them, they may not have appreciated how barbaric these practices were. In 1807 it became illegal for British ships to carry slaves and for British colonies to import them. There had been over 2,000 voyages from England and over 300,000 slaves had been transported.

Nowadays there is a rewriting of history in Liverpool as though the city stopped slavery as opposed to promoting it. Several of the streets in Liverpool 8 are named after slave traders and there have been moves to rename them: it might be better if the names stood with a plaque stating who they were. During the Derek Hatton era, I remember one crusader holding forth in Liverpool high streets and saying that the actions of our ancestors had brought this upon us.

The abolition of slavery did not affect the city's prosperity as the city could still import produce from existing plantations: indeed, its volume of trade was second only to London. One dock after another was built, all of them outstanding achievements and none more so than the combination of water and warehouses at the Albert Dock. Queen Victoria's husband, Prince Albert, opened the Albert Dock in 1846. The buildings reflect the confidence that people had in the city. The gigantic Stanley Dock, now the site of a Heritage Market, was built at the entrance to the Leeds and Liverpool canal in 1848. Ships were built across the Mersey in nearby Birkenhead. Liverpool was booming. The population grew from 200,000 in 1831 to 600,000 in 1891.

In 1845 some local businessmen decided that the premium rates for marine insurance by the London companies were excessive, and set up their own company, Royal Insurance. Its magnificent Head Office in North John Street is unoccupied today but it is listed and hopefully sooner rather than later, a new use will be found. This is typical of Liverpool today where there are plenty of splendid buildings looking for new users.

Another major insurer, Royal Liver, was formed in 1850. This started as a society to provide burial funds for its members, and, like the Prudential, it became famous for its door-to-door collections. It became so successful that it built its own impressive Head Office on the waterfront in 1910 and in so doing, established the city's emblem, the Liver Birds. The birds, close cousins to cormorants, stretch back into history and are reputed to have given the city its name, although the pronunciation is different. It is said that the city will fall when the two birds fly away. No chance of that.

The buildings in Liverpool are wonderful, worthy of the Capital of Culture accolade on their own. There is the 18th century elegance of the Town Hall and the Royal Liver Building is grouped with the Cunard and Port of Liverpool buildings to form the Three

Graces. When Liverpool is featured on television, we are shown its waterfront which includes the Three Graces. It is a reminder that Liverpool first came to prominence as a seaport.

Liverpool was described some centuries ago by Lord Erskine as the Venice of the North, and both Mr. Moby Dick and Mr. Robinson Crusoe, Herman Melville and Daniel Defoe respectively, praised the city in their travel writings. Judging by *Notes From A Small Island*, Bill Bryson would be hard pressed to endorse their opinions. "I took a train to Liverpool," he writes, "They were having a festival of litter when I arrived." My favourite story by Ramsey Campbell, a Merseysider noted for his horror fiction, is about someone trapped in St. John's Market at night and pursued by huge balls of rubbish.

The psychoanalyst, Carl Jung, described Liverpool as "the pool of life", and this remark is often repeated as a lavish testimonial. Untrue. Jung never visited the city and his phrase, none too original either, came to him after a dream.

In the 19th century, some remarkable public buildings were built. Liverpool Museum and the Walker Art Gallery are adjacent in William Brown Street and opposite them is St. George's Hall, an unlikely combination of concert hall and assizes. Its architect, Harvey Lonsdale Elmes, did not see the building until it was too late: by which time, it had been built back to front.

George Stephenson wanted to create journeys by steam train and he started in the north-west, creating the 30 miles of track between Liverpool and Manchester. This was no easy task as the line had to cross bogland and the workers had to cut through rocks. The line was opened with much ceremony in 1830 with the Prime Minister, the Duke of Wellington, travelling in a carriage on the first train to Liverpool. The day was clouded by tragedy. The Liverpool MP, William Huskisson, was so excited that he ran on the track and was run over.

The French dictator, Napoleon Bonaparte, who had been defeated by Wellington, went into exile in 1815 and a Liverpool businessman, Joseph Williamson, created work for those returning from the wars. No one knows why he could not have given them gainful employment, but he ordered them to carve out underground tunnels and chambers beneath the city. One day his men, digging away, came across Stephenson's team, digging another tunnel. Stephenson was invited to view Williamson's work, one of the few outsiders to do so. Nobody stopped Williamson or even asked him why, but surely the residents in the houses above must have complained. When Williamson died, the tunnels became a dumping ground for rubbish and worse.

James McKenzie matched Williamson for eccentricity. The businessman liked gambling and one evening he played poker with a Mr. Madison. When he lost all he had, Madison suggested that they had one more game for his soul. McKenzie lost again but Madison said, "Don't worry. I shan't collect it until you are dead." McKenzie was so petrified that he demanded to be buried above ground, sitting at a card table and holding a winning hand. He felt that as long as he was above ground, Mr. Madison (aka the Devil) could not claim his soul. He died in 1871 and the tomb, shaped like a pyramid, is in Rodney Street, and why has nobody written a country song about it?

The Royal Liverpool Philharmonic Society began in 1840 and, despite the lack of a huge arena today, the city has a reputation for attracting high quality productions and performers. My favourite moment occurred in 1874 when the organisers of the Liverpool Festival invited Franz Liszt to play. He wrote back, "You are presumably unaware that for 26 years I have altogether ceased to be regarded as a pianist." Oops.

The Grand National has been run at Aintree since 1838 and has been known by that name since 1847. The country's most famous racehorse, Red Rum, won the National three times and in a radio poll in 2003, it competed against humans to become one of the city's greatest Merseysiders. It came in a very commendable 15th, the winner being Ken Dodd. When the Grand National started, battles were still being fought on horseback: in 2004, the nearest we will ever see to a cavalry charge is the start of the Grand National.

A football club was formed by St. Domingo's Sunday School in 1878 and the next year it became Everton FC and quickly grew in stature. In 1888, the club became a founder member of the Football League and it won the title in 1891. Their home ground was at Anfield, but, after quarrelling with the landlord, they moved to Goodison Park in 1892. To avoid an unused ground at Anfield, Liverpool FC was formed. In 1959 Bill Shankly began his tenure as manager of Liverpool FC. The club won the Cup for the first time in 1965. Not to be outdone, Everton, who had been league champions in 1963, won the Cup in 1966. The intense rivalry between the teams is well-known, so much so that the plan to share a new stadium, by far the most practicable solution, has been a non-starter, and yet how many Scousers appreciate that Anfield was once Everton's ground?

There is even stronger rivalry between Liverpool FC and Manchester United, which many see as an enmity between Liverpool and Manchester itself. I find it incredible that two Councils in the late 20th century, one for Liverpool and for Manchester, should sign a document amidst much hoo-ha that the rivalry between the cities was over and that they would work together in future for the good of the north-west. What a load of bollocks, and the alarming thought is that previously they had been at each other's throats. Let's make **Graham Nash (1)** from the Manchester group, the Hollies a councillor: "I didn't sense that inter-city rivalry between Manchester and Liverpool too much and I certainly had nothing to do with it myself. I always thought that there was a lot of great talent in both cities, which should really go without saying."

Liverpool did not go into the 20th century a cathedral city, but it now has two, linked, rather poignantly, by Hope Street. The Anglican cathedral, designed by Giles Gilbert Scott, took 70 years to complete and it is the largest place of worship in the country, completed in an imposing and austere Gothic style. The Roman Catholic Cathedral is contemporary, a huge tent-like structure in the shape of a crown. It is known affectionately as the Mersey Funnel or Paddy's Wigwam, and again, note the Irish reference. This is not a city that does things by halves: two football teams, two cathedrals, two Mersey Tunnels. two radio stations.

In between the cathedrals is the art deco glory of the Philharmonic Hall, one of the best concert halls in the world and the home of the Royal Liverpool Philharmonic Orchestra. My criteria for a good concert hall is being able to pick out the individual instruments of an orchestra – you can do that very easily in the Phil. On the other side of the road is another glorious building, the Philharmonic pub. It houses the most grandiose public toilets in Europe. As I said, the city had confidence then.

Lime Street Station was built in 1870. Growing up in the 1950s, I only remember Lime Street Station as being grubby and grimy – there's a line of Leonard Cohen's, "I feel as dirty as the glass roof of a train station": spot on, Lenny – but the steam trains have gone. The station has been modernised, and keeps on being modernised, although the process has brought anonymity. Still, the entrance into Liverpool station is as impressive as ever: you can't fail to be stunned by the huge cuttings made in the rocks by the navvies.

The Adelphi Hotel on Lime Street is unique, and deliberately so. Many cruises departed from Liverpool and the passengers would travel to Liverpool on the day before the boat was due to sail. The Adelphi's rooms were built like staterooms so that passengers could acclimatise to life aboard ship.

Perhaps more than most cities, Liverpool is often associated with tragedy. However, despite what many believe, the Titanic was not built here. It was built in Belfast but the ship was registered by the White Star line in Liverpool. The cruise liner hit an iceberg on its maiden voyage in April 1912 and 1,500 passengers and crew perished. In what was seen as an act of both cowardice and selfishness, the Chairman of White Star secured a seat in one of the lifeboats, and he was criticised for the remainder of his miserable life.

In 1960 there was a major fire in Henderson's department store in the centre of Liverpool. Eleven people perished and many more were injured but when I went to the site to seek information from the plaque, I could find nothing. Why have these people been overlooked? Still, the fire had one positive outcome: it became mandatory for large stores to have sprinkler systems.

The most notable tragedy in recent times took place at the 1989 FA Cup semi-final between Nottingham Forest and Liverpool at Hillsborough when 96 people were crushed to death. The official report complained of a "failure of police control" and to add to their grief, the victims' families have been campaigning for criminal charges.

II. Liverpool redux

Jazz originated in America and by most accounts, it arrived in Britain when the liner carrying the Original Dixieland Jazz Band arrived in Liverpool on April Fool's Day, 1919. If they had performed in the city, it would have represented the first professional performance by an American jazz band in the UK. Instead, they moved to London for a season of variety with George Robey topping the bill. With their tiger rags and ostrich walks, they introduced jazz to Europe. Many reviewers were approving, but others sound like the critics who denounced rock'n'roll in the Fifties, "I can see clearly that if I can rattle on any old tin, my future will be made."

Several Beatle books tell you that John Lennon was born in the midst of an air raid. There were no strikes that night in October 1940, but the bombers over Merseyside did untold damage, especially in May 1941. The recovery was slow. The hardship continued with rationing and a bombed-out church has been left untouched at the top of Bold Street as a permanent reminder.

In the early 50s, everybody seemed old – at the earliest opportunity, youngsters dressed like their parents. That there was nothing for teenagers is illustrated by the BBC's broadcasting hours. There was a children's hour in the late afternoon and then the station shut down until the adult programmes at 7pm. The mould was broken with a show aimed specifically at teenagers, *6.5 Special*. With the advent of rock'n'roll, teenagers had their own music. "It was possibly the best-ever time to be a teenager," says **Marty Wilde (2)**, one of the UK's first rock'n'roll stars, "We had money; we had jobs; there were no drugs; conscription was abolished, and we could enjoy ourselves at coffee-bars without wanting to drink. Most of all, we had the music. The music of the late 50s and early 60s was so original and so wonderful."

The population of Liverpool and its suburbs was over a million, and maybe 20 per cent of the work force was on the docks, but employment was readily available in the early 60s. As you will find out, many of the Merseybeat musicians had no qualms about leaving a job, certain that they would find another when they wanted to. Nowadays the UK seems to run on Lottery money and in the 60s, the equivalent to the Lottery was the football pools and both Vernons and Littlewoods were based on Merseyside. John Moores was the true pools winner and he became a most successful entrepreneur with his nationwide stores. His recipe for making a million, "Do it now": in other words, don't think about doing it, do it, and that philosophy is shared by Paul McCartney. He is also associated with the best in contemporary art as his name is given to the John Moores Exhibition in Liverpool.

Liverpool was still the busiest port in the UK, and although the dockers were known for industrial unease, it was also one of the friendliest cities. The wit was everywhere, and no matter how depressed the city has been, there has always been warmth and wit. **Ken Dodd (3)** calls the area 'Mirthyside' and said, "We have the soil that talent can grow in. Liverpool people encourage talent and that's why the best comedians, the best entertainers and the best football teams come from Merseyside. Liverpool is a tremendously exuberant city. There's a great life-force here with no respect for dignity. Ask a Merseysider what his favourite subject was at school and he'll say, 'Playtime'. One reason is that Liverpool's always been a very cosmopolitan city. There's an ethnic mixture of Welsh, Irish and Scots, as well as the English. We had a Chinese quarter before San Francisco."

The saying that you have to be a comedian to live in Liverpool is probably true. The Beatles brought Scouse wit to popular music, while the long list of Liverpool comics includes Dan Leno, Robb Wilton, Tommy Handley, Arthur Askey, Ken Dodd, Jimmy Tarbuck and Alexei Sayle. Fred E. Cliffe (Clifford Howcchin), who wrote many lyrics for George Formby's innuendo-driven comedy songs, was a Scouser. The cartoonist, Norman Thelwell, was at the Liverpool College of Art during the war years, almost 20 years before John Lennon.

Cavern DJ **Bob Wooler (4)** reveals his Liverpool wit at the same as he denies it: "I have reservations about the famous Liverpool humour. A lot of British humour such as *Monty Python's Flying Circus*, *Fawlty Towers* and *The Goon Show* has nothing to do with Liverpool. However, Stan Boardman would have you believe that Liverpool is at the heart of the nation's humour. Ken Dodd says that you have to be a comedian to live here – but he should come to Lark Lane – there are plenty of miserable people around. Ken Dodd himself is very funny and the Beatles' natural humour was a significant part of their charm. It is true that you will find a comedian in every pub, but that is true of other cities as well. Liverpool was a seaport renowned for its ocean-going liners, and now it's renowned for its one-liners."

When the Memory Man Leslie Welch appeared at the Liverpool Empire in the 50s, he requested questions from the audience. He should have known better. "Okay, Mr. Welch," said one wag, "Where will you find an England cricket cap, a England football medal and an England rugby shirt in the same place?" The Memory Man thought hard but had to admit defeat. "All right," he said, "What's the answer?" "The pawn shop in Lodge Lane," he was told.

John Lennon told *Rolling Stone* in 1970: "We were the ones that were looked down upon as animals by the southerners, the Londoners. The northerners in the States think people are pigs down south. Liverpool was a very poor city but tough. People have a sense of humour because they are in such pain. They are very witty, and it's an Irish place. It's where the Irish came when they ran out of potatoes, and it's where the blacks worked as slaves or whatever." I don't think we had slaves in Liverpool but you know what he means.

Lennon added, "America is where it's at. I regret profoundly that I was not an American and not born in Greenwich Village." This surprising quotation has been conveniently overlooked in all the John Lennon celebrations in Liverpool. John Lennon was a man of contradictions and we prefer to remember that he kept a trunk of memorabilia marked 'Liverpool' in the Dakota.

Many entertainers have loved the city so much that they haven't sought national fame. For example, Hank Walters has been performing country music on Merseyside for fifty years, before, during and after the Beatles. William Ralph Walters was nicknamed Hank by his workmates at the docks. When he was still working at the docks, **Hank Walters (5)** said, "Although I'd like to see the world, I'd sooner live on dry bread than leave Liverpool. It's my home town and all my family's here. I wouldn't want to leave and make new contacts. In fact, it's a hell of a job getting me out of Liverpool for a booking. It's bloody hard work driving home in the early hours knowing you've got to go to work. As it is, I put in a ten-hour day on the docks, go on to the stage and only get two or three hours sleep a night."

Another Liverpool musician, **Bernie Davis (6)**, says, "You can't imagine country music in Liverpool without Hank Walters. His way of playing is a one-off and he does so much comedy that he might only do four songs or five songs in his set. The show is as much about Ralph as it is about country music."

In 1953, the torch singer, Lita Roza, became the first Liverpudlian to have a No.1 record and indeed, the first British female to have a No.1. She had no interest in the song and her comments display a Liverpool stubbornness. **Lita Roza (7)** says, "After 'Allentown Jail', Dick Rowe, who was my A&R man and chose the material, asked me to sing 'How Much Is That Doggie In The Window?' and I said, 'I'm not recording that, it's rubbish.' He said, 'It'll be a big hit, please do it, Lita.' I said that I would sing it once and once only and then I would never sing it again, and I haven't. The only time you'll hear it is on that record."

Liverpudlians have pride in their city, and this is noticeable in the music of the 60s. The Animals, from Newcastle, recorded 'We Gotta Get Out Of This Place', while the American songwriter Paul Simon described how dreary he found Merseyside in 'Homeward Bound'. There are no comparable songs from Liverpool performers. The Beatles are jumping for joy amidst urban debris on the cover of their *Twist and Shout* EP, and John Lennon wrote 'In My Life' about his love of the city. Paul McCartney made a suburban shopping street sound magical in 'Penny Lane' and Gerry Marsden's 'Ferry Cross The Mersey' has become an anthem.

Cilla Black's version of the Stan Kelly song 'Liverpool Lullaby' was only released as an album track and as the B-side of her single 'Conversations', and yet it is better known than many of her hits. On 'Liverpool Lullaby' **Cilla Black (8)** becomes a Scouse mum. "It annoys me when people say I put on an accent. I am a Liverpudlian and I come from Scotland Road, so why shouldn't I have an accent? The members of my family have much thicker accents than me and I've had to smooth mine down a bit so that I can be understood. I've got more things to worry about than my accent. The Queen has one, so why shouldn't I?"

Liverpool author **Paul Du Noyer (9)**: "The Beatles were the first to make Liverpool famous and the first to establish the value of coming from Liverpool in the first place. If they did trade upon it, that's okay. It was they who made it a place worth trading upon. It is also intriguing that the adoption of 'You'll Never Walk Alone' by the Liverpool crowd was uncanny in its timing. It coincided with the rise of Merseybeat, so you had Merseybeat as a music phenomenon and Liverpool as a footballing phenomenon at the same time." The escape routes for working-class kids (football and music) also saved Liverpool.

The Beatles were brilliant ambassadors for Liverpool but the "four lads who shook the world" failed to move some influential Merseysiders. When Howard Channon wrote his lengthy *Portrait of Liverpool* in 1970, he only included two passing references to the Beatles and one more to the Cavern. His attitude was shared by the city fathers, who were reluctant to praise the group, and indeed, my own father, who thought, like many of his generation, that they were a disgrace to the city. Labour councillors in the Sixties were highly critical of the Beatles lifestyle. Fortunately, the officials now in charge of the city grew up in the Beatles era or later and appreciate their worth.

Never A Yes Man, the biography of MP Eric Heffer, indicates his generation's disinterest in the Beatles, whilst, at the same time, appreciating their vote-catching potential. He admits to singing "If there's anything that you want" from 'Please Please Me' on the hustings and he says of the 1964 election, "There is no doubt in my mind that the astounding Merseybeat boom had a big effect on the outcome of the general election. The groups were young, vibrant, new. They were in tune with the desires of the people. They asserted working-class values, they looked to the future. I believe the Beatles made a powerful contribution to Labour's victory without recognising it."

But they did recognise it. On the eve of the election, Brian Epstein sent the Labour leader Harold Wilson, a telegram, "Hope your group is as much a success as mine."

Most people have affection for where they come from, but it is particularly noticeable in Liverpool. Most Scousers love being Scousers. There is a genuine pride in the city and at times, perhaps because we look out to sea, Liverpool feels like a separate state, isolated from the mainland. Noël Coward wrote 'London Pride' in wartime and similar sentiments are reflected in Pete McGovern's 'In My Liverpool Home', which was written in the early 1960s to comment on the completion of the cathedrals. The song, made popular by the Spinners, has many, many verses (and they are still being written by McGovern as well as by others) but the most pertinent one relates to the city's independence:

"So raise up our flag overhead the Town Hall,
Red and blue stripes with a rampant football,
We'll annex the shops, the factories and the banks
With a Merseyside customs post on the East Lancs.

In my Liverpool home, in my Liverpool home,
We speak with an accent exceedingly rare,
Meet under a statue exceedingly bare,
And if you want a cathedral, we've got one to spare,
In my Liverpool home."

The jazz singer and commentator **George Melly (10)** states, "I am a Liverpudlian and I was brought up here until I was 20. I don't have an accent, I was always posh, but it is a city that never really lets you go. You meet people from other cities such as Birmingham or Manchester and you may not know for a couple of years where they come from, but Liverpudlians let you know at once. Two Liverpudlians together can be insufferable as they can just say the names of streets and burst into tears or laughter. The city has produced a remarkable amount of talent – comedians in great quantities – Arthur Askey, Ted Ray, all that lot but also many musicians, poets and painters." Thanks, George, I was forgetting about George Stubbs.

The port prospered in the eighteenth and nineteenth centuries with, first, the slave trade and then cotton. More recently, a slackening of commerce has led to unemployment, but, after a shaky start, the new-look container port, which requires much less labour, has worked out well for the city. For its population though, Liverpool did not have enough manufacturing industries to fall back on and the industrial estates created at Kirkby and Speke have had problems. They also lack the sense of community which was recognised in one of Jacqui and Bridie's songs from the early Sixties:

"Don't want to go to Kirkby,
Don't want to go to Speke,
Don't want to go from all I know
In Back Buchanan Street."

Although it was not tackled perfectly, the slum clearance programme did a lot of good. The childhood disease, rheumatic fever, which often left its victims with damaged hearts, was eliminated. Billy Fury was one of those who suffered and he was surprised to make 40.

From time to time, comparisons link Liverpool to New Orleans. Both cities are ports and both cities have shameful pasts through the slave trade, but, as a result, both cities are now cosmopolitan. Jazz began in New Orleans in 1895 and Merseybeat in Liverpool in 1962. The world's most successful jazz musician, Louis Armstrong, came from New Orleans and the world's most successful songwriters, Lennon and McCartney, came from Liverpool. There is one major difference: one city was embracing jazz and the other rejecting it.

In the 1980s, the Mayor of New Orleans wrote to the Lord Mayor of Liverpool suggesting a twinning of the cities. It was an apt suggestion but nothing came of it. However, in 2001, both New Orleans and Liverpool renamed their airports after one of their musical sons – namely, Louis Armstrong and John Lennon. It is not yet possible to fly direct from Louis Armstrong to John Lennon or vice versa, but the time may come. I'd love to know what Paul McCartney really thinks when he flies into the John Lennon airport.

Since the 60s, like many northern cities, Liverpool has been battered socially, economically and politically, but Liverpool was named as the centre of the black economy. What was *Brookside* but a series about thieving scallys? Manchester life was depicted more warmly in *Coronation Street*. In the 70s, economic and political troubles brought Liverpool unwelcome publicity. The riots in 1981 in the black community of Liverpool 8 (Toxteth) focused attention on inner-city deprivation. The city was seen as the prime example of the threat posed to the Labour party by the Militant Tendency, particularly while Derek Hatton was deputy leader of the council. (Not even leader, you note.) To the outsider, Liverpool was seen as a working-class city full of troublemakers.

Derek Hatton did his best to bring down the Thatcher government, but did he need to damage Liverpool's reputation with his crusade? It took many years to rebuild the city's confidence, leading now to the accolade of the Capital of Culture, and hopefully 'The Leaving Of Liverpool' becoming the leading of Liverpool. When I wrote the original text of *Let's Go Down The Cavern* in 1984, it was like a giant obituary: now there are feelings of vibrancy and energy about the city.

Ken Dodd (11): "Liverpool exports more entertainers than any other city in the world and, whatever else Liverpool entertainers do, it's always done with tremendous enthusiasm. People in Liverpool live their lives in higher gear than most people. We're very enthusiastic people and the Beatles were four young men with a tremendous desire for life and with the typical Liverpool trait of not caring what they said. They ad-libbed everything and they personified life and brought a lot of credit to Liverpool."

Despite being the owner of the Cavern, **Bill Heckle (12)** is even-handed when he says, "The Cavern didn't make the Beatles because you could have the same argument for the Hamburg clubs. There are lots of different factors, but the Fifth Beatle was always Liverpool. It is more pertinent to say that Liverpool made the Beatles. There were so many elements of them that were typically Liverpool: you could put them 20 or 25 miles away in Wigan or Widnes and they would not have been the Beatles. Liverpool, I am certain, had a huge input in making the Beatles. The Cavern was a venue like the other venues where they learnt the trade. If there hadn't been a Cavern, they would have played somewhere else." Similarly, as we shall see, the Beatles didn't make the Cavern. It was a marriage of convenience but both parties were to benefit.

Liverpool's saving graces have been tourism and education, which have much in common. There is a need for a good night out and so the city is awash with clubs and pubs, and students, it seems, are everywhere. For a time, Cream was the coolest club in the UK. The annual Summer Pops concerts in the green and yellow striped Big Top at the King's Dock are enormously successful and Elton John, Tony Bennett, James Brown and Ray Charles have been among the star performers. The high ticket prices show that there is now money on Merseyside. Indeed, I was sitting next to a couple of ladies who had spent over £500 on tickets during the year's festival.

Liverpool is, in the jargon of the day, a cool city, and it is being reinvented for the 21st century. The city with a past is going forwards and one new hotel follows another. The Duke of Westminster promises to reconstruct the city's centre by 2008 and he has to keep his word as nothing would be worse than the city looking like a building site during the European Capital of Culture festivities.

Even more important, the city has to obliterate its gangland culture and drug-related crimes. Come on, make the city so great that no one wants to take drugs. This sounds a ridiculous thing to say but it's not. How many people take drugs because they feel abandoned? The quickest way out of Liverpool should not be drugs or alcohol, for that matter.

The leader of Liverpool City Council, Mike Storey, has said, "We are still a poor city with some appalling pockets of poverty and if you're living in a rundown tower block or maisonette with no hope, you might be thinking 'Capital of Culture, so what?', but it is going to improve the city's prosperity at all levels. It is a great achievement both culturally and economically." I hope he's right.

In 2004 Liverpool, through its council, attached itself to the celebrations in Memphis for the fiftieth anniversary of rock'n'roll. The rebellious nature of the music is diluted by such patronage, but after all, it was 50 years ago. The date is a tad tenuous as relatively few people heard Elvis Presley singing 'That's All Right (Mama)' in 1954, but, from 1956, his music reverberated around the world, the biggest impact being on Merseyside. This book is a celebration of that.

2 UNDERNEATH THE ARCHES

I. The Cavern as a jazz club
II. Skiffle and rock'n'roll
III. NEMS
IV. The Morgue
V. Discovering Carroll Levis

"John Moss, cabinet maker, 8 Mathew Street
Peter Clark, customs officer, 8 Mathew Street
Robert Deardon, bill poster, 9 Mathew Street"
No entry for 10 Mathew Street.
(Gore's Directory of Liverpool, 1857)

I. The Cavern as a jazz club

Alan Sytner was the son of a docklands GP, Joe Sytner. Joe wanted his son to follow him into the medical profession, but his earlier generosity prevented it. He had taken out an insurance policy for Alan when he was a baby and it matured when he was 21, giving him £400. In 1956 Alan started the 21 club at 21 Croxteth Road, close to the city centre. **Alan Sytner (13)**: "I was doing okay with the 21 and enjoyed it but I realised that if I had a better place, a more interesting place, I could open two or three or four nights a week, perhaps for different sorts of jazz including modern jazz. I realised that if I rented a property, it would work out far more economically and I would have my own say as to when I opened and what I did. I went looking for a property that could be turned into a jazz club. I looked at lots of sites but nothing was of any great interest."

Alan Sytner (14) had an idea of what he was looking for: "I had spent most of my school holidays in France, and I had spent most of that time in Paris, so that I could go to jazz clubs and witness the bohemian life. I was only a kid, 14, when I first went, but I was dazzled by it and it was all part of the glamour of Paris after the war. They enjoyed listening to jazz in Paris, which dates back to the 1920s, and they liked real music and not muzak. Even today the background music in a supermarket could be Charlie Parker or Dexter Gordon."

Mathew Street is just off Liverpool's city centre, but no shopper would have ventured there in the 1950s. The narrow street was little more than two rows of seven-storey warehouses, and lorry-loads of fruit and vegetables were unloaded throughout the day. Number 10 Mathew Street was typical: the basement had been used as an air-raid shelter during the Second World War and was then used for storing wines and spirits and after that, for eggs and Irish bacon. In 1956, the building was being used to store electrical goods, but the basement was vacant. **Alan Sytner (15)**: "An estate agent, Glyn Evans, told me he knew of an old cellar which was full of arches and derelict. I got the keys and went down a rickety ladder with a flashlight. Glyn Evans didn't realise that he was showing me a replica of Le Caveau and that is where the name came from.

Mathew Street looked like a little narrow street in the Latin Quarter in Paris, so I felt I was bringing the Left Bank to Liverpool."

The first job was to clear the site and Alan sought volunteers. An architect friend, **Keith Hemmings (16)**, helped out. "I was a very good friend of Alan's and we used to go on holiday together. He had this great idea of having a jazz club in Liverpool and he found the place and I was going to be his partner. I drew up the plans and with a few friends, we knocked the walls down, put toilets in and built the stage."

Alan Sytner (17): "The place had been reinforced to make an air-raid shelter, and these brick reinforcements had to be removed with sledgehammers as we couldn't get a pneumatic drill in. Well, we didn't even know where to get one. We did it by hand and we were left with a lot of rubble. That was the ideal foundation for the stage, which was made of wood and just went over the bricks. It did a great job of balancing the acoustics, and the acoustics in the Cavern were terrific, absolutely brilliant."

Most surprisingly, considering he is an out and out jazz enthusiast, **Alan Sytner (18)** thought of starting with rock'n'roll. "I didn't like rock'n'roll but the initial plan was to launch Bill Haley and his Comets at the Cavern. They were coming over on a liner and the *Daily Mirror* thought it would be a good idea if their first appearance was at the Cavern. It was a mad scheme that never happened. There would have been no point in putting on rock'n'roll at the Cavern. There were no local bands to speak of and hardly any in London. Tony Crombie, who was a good jazz drummer, formed a rock'n'roll group in order to make some money, but I saw them at the Pavilion and they were awful."

Meanwhile, the Merseysippi Jazz Band, which was formed in 1949, was growing disillusioned with its residency at the Temple. **John Lawrence (19)**: "The licensee, realising that he was on to a very good thing, decided to charge us a lot of money for the room. We were rather annoyed and moved to the Cavern. The Cavern was opened by Alan Sytner, who had found this dirty old cellar in Mathew Street. I was going to say he decorated it, but that would be an overstatement. It was rough and scruffy but it had atmosphere."

Missing the Christmas and New Year trade, the Cavern opened on 16 January 1957. The opening bill featured the Merseysippi Jazz Band, the Wall City Jazzmen, the Ralph Watmough Jazz Band and the Coney Island Skiffle Group. The guest of honour was to be the 21 year old drummer, the Earl of Wharncliffe. **Bob Azurdia (20)**: "The queue stretched all the way down Mathew Street and into Whitechapel. Prior to the Cavern, the Temple was the only evening venue for jazz in the city and it opened only on Sunday nights. Life was very different in those days. The only other places you could go to were a cinema, a palais for strict-tempo dancing or a coffee bar. Young people tended not to go to pubs, which in any case closed at ten without any drinking-up time. The Cavern was therefore very welcome."

I wondered what the Earl of Wharncliffe was doing on the bill for that opening night. **Alan Sytner (21)**: "The Earl of Wharncliffe had nothing whatever to do with jazz or blues: he had a very iffy rock'n'roll band which only got PR because he was an earl. However, I was keen to make an impact and there was a jazz promoter in Liverpool who had a monopoly on the main jazz bands so I couldn't hire any of them. I couldn't get Chris Barber, Ken Colyer or Humphrey Lyttelton for the opening and I had to do something to make an impact. I was a member of Liverpool Press Club and one of the boys suggested the Earl of Wharncliffe and said they would write about it. In the end, he didn't show up because he was at Cirencester Agricultural College and he'd had an ultimatum – Stop doing gigs and go back to college or get expelled. He was hauled back but he didn't bother to inform me. Eventually I got a call when everybody was in the club. I had to announce that he wasn't coming, but nobody was the least bit bothered because having got into the Cavern on the opening night, everybody was thrilled to be there. We had lots of good bands on and everybody had a great time. The fact that the Earl never showed was much better than if he had. He did gigs all over the place so his not showing was a national story."

Ralph Watmough (22): "We played on the opening night of the Cavern. The Cavern was an old bonded warehouse and someone had limewashed the walls. The unexpected din from the musicians caused the limewash to flake off. The Wall City Jazz Band from Chester played the first set and they came off looking like snowmen. They were covered from head to foot and Alan Sytner had to do something to stop it happening again. The Cavern must have been a fire officer's nightmare. There was only an entrance and exit combined and it was down a very narrow steep flight of steps. There were no toilets to speak of and conditions like that could never exist these days."

Roger Baskerfield (23) of the Coney Island Skiffle Group: "I played on the first night. I was also here when Lonnie Donegan came down to have a look at his skiffle club one lunchtime. Before Lonnie came on the scene, everybody used to listen to music. When Lonnie came around, everybody bought a guitar and everybody played music. It was so hot on the opening night that I fainted in the dressing room. When I opened my eyes, I found four girls undoing my shirt, so I quickly closed them again."

Keith Hemmings (24): "Right from the first night, I knew the Cavern was going to be a tremendous success. There was such a spirit in the place – it was so vibrant and exciting. I was going to be Alan's partner, but we fell out and I disappeared from the scene about a fortnight after it opened. I went into the family business and I have forgotten about my involvement with the Cavern, to be honest with you."

Many Beatle books have them entertaining over 1,000 fans at the Cavern but that is impossible. **Alan Sytner (25)**: "The maximum ticket sale that we had was 652, and that was on the opening night where we turned more away than we let in. Only a third of the people got in. We had mounted police to control the queue which stretched for half a mile, but, unlike today, there was no trouble when they told people to go home. We got very close to 652 on several other occasions, but it got very heavy when it got to 600. It's good to say 'Sorry, we're full' when you're in the entertainment business. We didn't get to 600 that often, but when we did, we would say, 'That's enough'."

Roger Planche (26) of the Coney Island Skiffle Group: "I think we performed pretty well when our set came. We received £4 between us for our efforts and as it was impossible to get out before the last train to the Wirral, it was all blown on a taxi."

The doorway was lit by a single bulb. 18 stone steps led down to the cellar which was divided by archways into three long, dimly-lit barrel vaults, each a hundred feet long and at least ten feet wide. The walls were covered with emulsion and there were no curtains or decorations. The entrance to the first vault was used to collect admission money and there was also a cloakroom. The second and largest area contained the stage and a few rows of wooden chairs. All the lighting was concentrated on the stage, and there were no coloured bulbs or filters. There was only dancing – the Cavern stomp – when there was room to move.

Given the circumstances, it was an excellent arrangement, but the lavatories were appalling, the band room tiny and the air-conditioning non-existent. Most people smoked and within minutes of opening, the Cavern could contain hundreds of sweaty bodies. Condensation would cover the walls and drip off the ceilings.

In March 1957 the public health inspector blew up some football bladders at the Cavern to obtain air samples. Outside it was 52 Fahrenheit and inside 82, a remarkable difference as there was no heating in the club. The public health inspector lacked the powers available to environmental health officers today and had to rely on persuasion. Nevertheless, a ventilation shaft was installed, but as it extended only 30 feet up in a narrow passage between two 110-foot buildings, the air coming into the building was stagnant. Electric fans were installed to circulate the air but, being warm, it was already fetid.

What does **Alan Sytner (27)** think? Should he have improved conditions at the Cavern? "I didn't have the finances to do that and anyway the places in Paris were pretty stark. I knew that if I fancied it, they would fancy it, simple as that. I was 21, a little more sophisticated than the average Scouse 21 year old, but nonetheless, I was a 21 year old Scouser and I knew that they would like it. The Cavern was bigger than the places I'd seen in Paris, which were also licensed and charged more for admission. Their clubs had an ambience and I knew how to get that at the Cavern."

In a move that would have far-reaching effects, **Alan Sytner (28)** decided against a liquor licence for the Cavern. "I wasn't anti-booze but my heart wasn't in it and I didn't think that I could meet the requirements for a liquor licence. I was going to get a lot of young people in the place and so it wasn't a good idea to have booze there. They could always get a pass-out and go to the White Star or the Grapes, where incidentally they might find me."

John Lawrence (29): "I can't remember what triggered the Cavern's instant success as I can't remember Alan doing a lot of advertising about the Cavern. I thought that we were taking a bit of a chance by moving from a moderately comfortable pub to a damp cellar, but it was the best thing that ever happened to us. They came flooding in every time we played there. The stage was just about big enough for an eight-piece band, but the piano was hanging over the edge. Acoustically it was very good as there were three long tunnels – the outside tunnels were full of benches and chairs and the centre tunnel with the stage at the end was acoustically just right. It was a long room with hard surfaces, brick and a stone floor, which is always good. If you play in a room full of curtains and thick carpets, you can blow your teeth out trying to make the sound right."

Steve Voce (30): "Acoustically, the Cavern wasn't brilliant but we were all much younger and our hearing was much more acute. I can't remember any problems in hearing bands there. If you'd had a few pints, it was a good place to hear jazz but then I don't think I ever tried to hear it without having a few pints."

Valerie Dicks (31): "I was a student nurse at Sefton General and I used to wear my uniform on the bus because the bus conductor wouldn't take the fare and I never had enough money to pay the fare anyway. Everybody has somebody who is sick sometime and maybe a nurse looked after your mother or sister, so we didn't get charged. It was a shilling to get in at the Cavern and I would get in for half price because of my uniform. I would go into the toilets and change into my clothes and put my uniform in a bag. The water ran down the walls: you went in with straight hair and you ended up with curls. One side was for those who hadn't done much educationally and the other side was for the ones who went to grammar school, and we kept to our sides. Thelma ran a coffee bar at the top end and would dish out Cokes and hot dogs. When the pop groups came on, who were the fill-ins for the jazz groups, we would go to the White Star or the Grapes with a bottle of Coke from Thelma. We would empty the Coke down the grid and come back with Cherry B and cider in the Coke bottle, drinking it through a straw. Thelma often wondered why we were so happy at the end of the night. I would put my uniform back on and go back home on the bus."

Despite being dry (even if the patrons smuggled drink in), the Cavern's membership reached 25,000 in two years, and as well as nightly jazz performances, the club organized riverboat shuffles on the Mersey in the *Royal Iris*. The membership figures are surprising in view of the dinginess of the Cavern and the fact that it confined itself to jazz. However, jazz encompasses a wide variety of sounds and special evenings were given over to blues and modern jazz. The beatnik and bohemian set favoured traditional jazz (trad), which was the New Orleans jazz then played by British bands, notably Acker Bilk and Kenny Ball.

Alan Sytner (32): "There were very marked demographics according to the night of the week and what was being put on. On Thursdays I put on modern jazz to please myself and again I got a very hip, very cool audience – crew-cuts, button-down collars and little skinny ties. They thought they were massively superior and cleverer than everybody else. These were people who had their own cars and so we could stay open a little later. Sunday was the Merseysippis' night and they attracted a very middle class audience with lots of people from the Wirral and Crosby. These people didn't cause any trouble, and as they formed the majority, nobody else did either. Friday night was completely different. We used to get kids from the top end of London Road. There were quite a few gangs and they used to love making trouble, similar to football hooligans today, and they were the same sort of people. If I'd had any sense, I would have closed on Fridays. On Saturdays you got a cross-section. If there was a band with a strong appeal, you would get a nice audience. If it was a so-so band, you would just get whoever was out on Saturday night and going to the Cavern for want of anywhere else to go."

Steve Voce (33): "Jazz was still being polarised between modern fans and traditional fans, and Ronnie Scott and Tubby Hayes would never have had a platform in Liverpool if it wasn't for Alan Sytner. The barriers broke down when Humphrey Lyttelton dragged them together very slowly by having a band which combined the best aspects of both"

Alan Sytner (34): "Some of the modern jazz musicians were really laid-back and terribly unpunctual. They took playing seriously but they didn't take making a living seriously. They were all pros, but they were very hard to deal with. Tubby Hayes, the little giant, was the worst. Once he came to Liverpool on the train and he drank 28 bottles of Worthington Green Shield between Euston and Lime Street. He was all right, he was an amazing bloke, but he wasn't *that* all right. He still played. Another night he turned up at 10 o'clock for an 8 o'clock gig. He was full of apologies and said he would play until one in the morning, knowing full well that we had to close at 11.30."

The gospel singer Sister Rosetta Tharpe was backed by the Merseysippi Jazz Band in Manchester and then by the Wall City Jazzmen at Cavern. She voiced her doubts about appearing at the Cavern by saying, "You might wonder what a woman of God like me is doing in a place like this. Well, our Lord Jesus went down into the highways and the byways and if it's good enough for Him, it's good enough for me." By not being licensed, the Cavern was not wayward enough for Tharpe's husband, who was known as Lazy Daddy. **Steve Voce (35)**: "The licensing laws baffled all Americans except Lazy Daddy, who had a complete working knowledge of opening hours within 20 minutes of stepping off the boat."

Alan Stratton (36): "I went to the jazz nights with the bigger bands – Acker Bilk, Cy Laurie, Tubby Hayes. They had a Thursday night modern jazz which I loved, but they also had the Merseysippi and Sister Rosetta Tharpe. She was wonderful 'cause she had this gold-top single coil Les Paul guitar. Sonny Terry and Brownie McGhee came and T-Bone Walker. They were playing guitar like you never heard guys play here. People could play little solos for maybe 15 seconds but they were going for a minute or a minute and a half with wonderful chords. That to me was the best thing about it. Ray Ennis of the Bluegenes used to play solos too and I used to think, 'How can a guy play all those notes and know what's coming next?'"

Local talent included the Swinging Blue Jeans, then called the Bluegenes. **Ralph Ellis (37)**: "The front line of a normal trad jazz band would be clarinet, trombone and trumpet, but we had three guitars, and Ray and I used to play harmony on our guitars. That was the sound we had – a rock'n'roll front line with a trad jazz rhythm section. We had double bass, drums and Tommy Hughes and then Pete Moss playing driving banjo, which you can hear on our demo of 'Yes Sir That's My Baby'." Many private recordings of the Bluegenes exist, which reveal that they were magpies, often putting all their influences into one song. In the course of a single track, you can hear trad, rock'n'roll and music hall as well as their own lively personalities.

Ray Ennis (38): "As a skiffle group, we were heavily influenced by the jazz bands and we used to play with the best of them on Sunday nights at the Cavern. We watched them closely and we tried to do with guitars what they were doing with brass, using lots of harmony guitar. We did the jazz songs that we liked and we didn't want to do Elvis songs as we felt that we were being different. We would not have got the Cavern gig if we were rock'n'roll because Alan Sytner hated it and the audiences would boo anyone who attempted it. We got booed ourselves as we played on the same bill as Ken Colyer. He had such a fanatical following that his fans hated anyone else."

II. Skiffle and rock'n'roll

Skiffle became popular in the mid-1950s. The king of skiffle was Lonnie Donegan and, indeed, nobody else came close. The craze started in 1956 with 'Rock Island Line', which **Lonnie Donegan (39)** made when he was playing banjo for Chris Barber's Jazz Band and recording an album for Decca. He recalled, "It was felt that the album should contain a vocal track for variety, but the producer thought so little of it that he went for a cup of tea while it was being recorded. I was paid £3 10s (£3.50), which was the standard session fee, and although it didn't make me any money, it did give me a career. Decca never thanked me for that record, yet it sold enormously in America at a time when British records hardly ever made the charts. 'Rock Island Line' sold three million copies worldwide in six months and Decca didn't bother to put anything else out. It wasn't entirely their fault because the whole British record scene was a cottage industry. There were three big companies, and their prime purpose was to make American records available here. No one knew what to do when a British artist started selling."

Lonnie Donegan encouraged fans to make their own music. Skiffle was simple, energetic music, and a group could get by with a guitar, a washboard and a tea-chest bass. **Pete Shotton (40)**: "Lonnie Donegan was the Messiah. Up to then, you had to have professional tuition and had to learn the chords. Lonnie comes along and says, 'You can all play music. Get a drum and bang on it, get a tea-chest bass and twang the string, get a washboard: it doesn't matter whether you're good or bad, just enjoy it.' He took the music from the professionals to grass roots, street corner stuff, which was brilliant."

As he did in many cities, Lonnie Donegan opened a skiffle club in Liverpool. It was at the Cavern, and the weekly sessions were organised by **Mick Groves (41)**, later a Spinner but then part of the Gin Mill Skiffle Group: "I was the first washboard player to join the Musicians' Union. I had a nice letter to thank me for joining, but saying that they didn't think that they would be able to place a lot of work my way."

Alan Sytner (42): "There were hundreds of skiffle and blues groups in the country, the Lonnie Donegan factor was mega, so on Wednesdays I put on a competition for local talent. It encouraged kids who were learning to play, and I would have a couple of more accomplished groups who could play. These kids did the Lonnie Donegan, Dickie Bishop and Johnny Duncan repertoires and they were all pretty awful. Talent night was no talent night as far as I was concerned but I wasn't being altruistic as skiffle was very commercial."

Steve Voce (43): "We disliked skiffle with almost the same contempt that we disliked rock'n'roll. I didn't like Lonnie Donegan in the least, but he saw an opening and seized it. The only reason that skiffle was tolerated at the Cavern was because it made some money for some jazz musicians whom we were sympathetic to. The genuine skiffle music – Big Bill Broonzy, Blind Lemon Jefferson, the people from the 20s – was marvellous, but the later thing was a fraud."

A pianist, **Roger Planche (44)**, who was studying at the College of Building in Clarence Street, was inspired by Lonnie Donegan: "It didn't take long to convince several boys that it was very easy to make music in this idiom. One made a tea chest bass and another learned to play a few chords in C on an old guitar. A Roman Catholic pal had his own set of drums and we had to persuade the vicar to allow him into our Church of England hall to play with us. Since we were four C of E lads with one RC, we called ourselves Four Saints Plus One, really after another band called the Firehouse Five Plus Two. When we got on a bus with our equipment one night, a passenger sang 'O Happy Band Of Pilgrims' and we became the Pilgrims. We asked a banjo player called Barry Chesworth to join us. He claimed to carry a gun because people were after him. We didn't believe him but he produced it one night and fired it in the air. In no time at all, there were three skiffle groups in Heswall, one in Irby and several in Hoylake, and in far off New Brighton, there was the Gin Mill Skiffle Group."

Skiffle was a homemade music incorporating cheap makeshift instruments, which were as likely to come from a chandler as a music shop. It did not catch on in the States because American teenagers had more money. Hence, the Beach Boys could be electric from the start. Skiffle, and then Merseybeat, were working class – hence, the lack of money – and so it is ironic that the one Merseybeat musician who called himself a 'working class hero' was John Lennon. He was the most comfortably placed of the Beatles and I don't know of any other Liverpool musician who lived in better circumstances.

Roger Planche (45) promoted the UK's first open-air pop concert. "In the summer of 1956, I thought of staging a concert in Heswall's municipal grounds. There was a high grassy bank looking down on four tennis courts and a bowling green, and there were good toilets as well. The father of a pal of mine was the chairman of Wirral UDC and so I persuaded him that it would look good if he did something for local youth and that with our limited equipment, there would be little noise. Probably thinking of his OBE, he let us have the courts for a nominal fee of £5. We asked six local skiffle groups to play and we charged two shillings a head (10p) for entry. We borrowed a couple of vans that were used in elections and so we had a PA system. It was a sunny day and there were 400 people dancing on the tennis courts. Unfortunately, there was a competition on the bowling green and none of the players could concentrate. We didn't stop and they sent for the village bobby. He sent for his sergeant and fortunately for us, his daughter was one of the dancers. He gave us until five o'clock to stop. The shops sold out of ice cream, crisps and lemonade and at the end of the day we had £30 profit. I should have realised the potential of what I'd done, but I had to study hard at the College of Building. If you failed, you would be conscripted, surely the best-ever way of ensuring good results. Your national service couldn't be deferred forever and I went in the army in June 1958. National service was responsible for the break-up of most of the skiffle groups."

Alan Stratton (46): "I knew the Black Cats when they started in 1956 and they were the first rock'n'roll band to play the Cavern. Alan Sytner said that he would only have rhythm bands or skiffle bands and if you were playing in a rhythm band, you were something like a steel band. They were semi-jazz and they called themselves the Black Cats Rhythm Group so that they could officially play there. They did what they considered blues, 'St. Louis Blues', 'Guitar Boogie' and 'Frankie And Johnny', and I saw them and was made up."

John Lennon's Quarry Men made their debut at the Cavern on 7 August 1957 and appeared again on 24 January 1958. **Alan Sytner (47)**: "Skiffle was a breeding ground for musicians – one or two of them became jazz musicians, but more ended up doing rock'n'roll. Lennon and McCartney were there, I know that because I had a girlfriend at the art college who was in the same class as John, and she persuaded me to let them play and they were diabolical. I knew John Lennon quite well as we lived in the same area: he lived 400 yards up the road from me. They were 16 and arrogant and they hadn't got a clue, but that was John Lennon, and no doubt Paul McCartney caught it from him. John Lennon was considered a huge personality at the art college by all the kids and Ann told me that he would like to play. They'd only been playing for a short while so you wouldn't expect them to be any good but they became world class, the best. At the time, they couldn't play to save their lives and all I can remember is their cheek and their chat."

Colin Hanton (48), drummer with Quarry Men: "We did some skiffle numbers to start off with at the Cavern but we also did rock'n'roll. John Lennon was passed a note and he said to the audience, 'We've had a request'. He opened it up and it was Alan Sytner saying, 'Cut out the bloody rock'n'roll.'"

Kingsize Taylor (49): "Our first gig at the Cavern was about 1958 or 1959 and we were on with the Merseysippi Jazz Band and they thought that we were still skiffle and they weren't amused when they learnt that we were rock'n'roll so we only did one spot and that was it. They wouldn't have us back on as it was still a jazz club."

John Johnson (50): "My brother Kenny said he wanted to start a band and I said, 'People don't do that where we come from.' He insisted and we went out to see another skiffle group, the Connaughts, watched them and said, 'We can do that.' We sat down, talked about it and decided to have a go. Brian Evans lived next door, and Ronnie Cole lived further up the road, and they had guitars. I decided to opt for the tea-chest bass. We got a tea-chest from a local factory and with a pole off me mam's brush. I would put the pole under my arm and the tea chest under the stairs on the buses and away we'd go. Sometimes the conductor would say, 'If you can't pay your way, you can give us a song.' We would pretend that the open window was our audience. We were practising a few songs one night, we knew about three songs then, and there was a knock on the door and some chap wanted a word with us. It was a bloke from a local club and he wanted us to do a few songs because their artist hadn't turned up. So we went up to the local club for our first gig. God, I was nervous, there were people there who knew me as a kid. The Connaughts put a lot of comedy into their act, but Kenny said right from the start that we were doing it seriously. We did skiffle and country songs. Hank Williams was very popular with the generation before us and 'Window Shopping' always went down well."

Tommy Hughes (51) from the Swinging Blue Jeans: "We went to play in Kirkby at a youth centre and they had music on when we arrived. It was just records and they announced us and we looked at the audience and there were hard-looking blokes there, bit of a gang, and they walked to the front and they were shouting, 'Records, records, records'. We were skiffle you see, and they wanted rock'n'roll. Another time Ralph made some joke on stage at the Cavern and this bloke said, 'We'll get you afterwards.'

We went back in the bandroom and we were soaked in sweat 'cause it was that hot, and these girls came in and said, 'That's Harold Hughes and his gang. If they say they're going to get you, you've had it. You'll be mincemeat outside.' We stayed in the Cavern 'til half-past four in the morning. Fortunately, there weren't there when we left."

Rod Davis (52): "Unless you bought the record, you wouldn't know the words. When the record came up on the radio, which wouldn't be very often, you would shout for a pen and start scribbling the lyrics down, or you could go to a booth in a record shop until you got thrown out. John Lennon would fill in the missing words and that's how we got the bit about the penitentiary in 'Come Go With Me', which scanned and fitted in with the themes of skiffle songs. I remember him rewriting 'Streamline Train' as 'Long Black Train', but John didn't make lyrics up on the hoof. He thought about the changes he was going to make."

Eric Griffiths (53), also from the Quarry Men: "We started with skiffle songs like 'Rock Island Line' and 'Maggie May'. The songs were easy to play and were very acceptable to audiences but fairly soon after we started, we were playing the early Elvis Presley tunes, 'Blue Moon Of Kentucky', 'All Shook Up', 'I'm Left You're Right She's Gone'. They were more difficult musically but skiffle had enabled us to go onto that."

Rod Davis (54): "The Quarry Men was definitely a skiffle group but we played a few rock'n'roll numbers, depending on which venue we were at. The Cavern was a traditional jazz venue and as skiffle had grown out of trad, that was perfectly acceptable as an interval entertainment. No problem, but rock'n'rollers and jazz fans were daggers drawn, and one sure way to get beaten up was to play the wrong music at the wrong venue. You could get torn apart, so if we played a jazz venue, it was prudent to stick to skiffle."

It's said that none of the Beatles wanted to tell Pete Best he was being sacked, but John Lennon had, five years earlier, sacked his washboard player, **Pete Shotton (55)**: "You have to realise the circumstances in which that washboard was put over my head. I was telling John that I didn't want to be in the band any longer. I had taken a long time to do this, John was my best mate and I felt that I was letting him down. We played this gig in Rosebury Street and I was totally embarrassed, I didn't like it, and we were having a beer together on the floor and I said, 'John, I am sorry about this, mate, but I just can't do this anymore. I want to leave the band.' John picked up my washboard and smashed it on my head, the inserts came out and it left the frame around my shoulders. He said, 'Well, that solves that then, Pete.' I didn't realise that he was having the same problem. He realised that I wasn't musical and he wanted to form a real band. This solved the problem beautifully and we ended up laughing with me having the frame of the washboard round my neck."

Taking your instruments to a booking could be a problem as few groups had their own transport. **Johnny Guitar (56)**, who played with Rory Storm and the Hurricanes, described a typical day: "Our transport used to be the 61 bus to the Stanley Road junction where we would meet Ringo standing by the roundabout with a snare drum or a washboard. We'd all jump on the L3 bus to St Luke's Hall. We'd have problems fitting the tea-chest with the broom-handle under the stairs. When we got there, the stars of the show, we'd have to disgorge ourselves from the bus, complete with tea-chest bass and snare drum."

Later, Ringo befriended a bus conductor and was allowed to leave his drums overnight in the Ribble bus station in the city centre. **Dave Lovelady (57)** of the Four Jays, later the Fourmost, found that not all bus conductors were so sympathetic. "One conductor was very loath to take our tea-chest bass on the bus. After we pleaded with him, he agreed to let us stand it on the platform, right on the edge. As we were pulling off from the next stop, a chap came running at full pelt for the bus. He made a frantic leap for the platform but grabbed the broom handle instead of the pole. He went sprawling into the street and the tea-chest bass went all over the road."

Jim Turner (58): "I started off at 17 playing a tea-chest bass for Rory Storm in his skiffle group. There were no vans in those days and we had to take the bus to the gigs. The Blue Jeans would get on the bus at Twig Lane and another band at Page Moss and the conductor would end up shouting, 'No more instruments – there's no room for the paying public.'"

Ken Baldwin (59), the banjo player with the Merseysippis: "We were playing at the Cavern in 1958 and this guy came through the door. It was Clinton Ford but we didn't know him and his face was hidden by a pair of sunglasses. I thought he was a poser – you don't wear sunglasses in a cellar – but there was a reason for this as he had two black eyes. He had just finished a summer season at Butlin's in Pwllheli. He sang in the bar every night and he had become friendly with one of the girls who worked there. He had taken her to his chalet but she happened to be the chef's young lady who sussed out where she was. The chef duffed him up and he still had the shiners when we saw him. He didn't create a good impression at first but as soon as he sang with the band, things were different. We realised he could sing. He knew a few jazz numbers and he had a good voice. His first love was country music which he does very well and then in the nightclubs, he'd be doing 'Fanlight Fanny'. We love playing with him and we know a lot of his numbers."

Clinton Ford (60) settled in Liverpool and played with the Merseys when other work, usually at Butlin's, wasn't available. "I had a little bedsit in Canning Street for fifteen shillings a week. It was a marvellous little place. Ron Rubin, who's worked with everyone, had a bedsit opposite to me, but his was smaller than mine and only ten shillings a week. Somehow he got a piano up there. I played my guitar in my room and did write some songs there. I recorded one of them, 'Now That You've Gone'. I liked playing the Cavern with the Merseys but it's hard to convey how squalid it was. When it was packed, the moisture would rise and settle on the ceiling. It would condense and drip down your neck. It was an awful place but we loved it."

The Cavern had skiffle evenings on Wednesdays, modern jazz on Thursdays and trad at the weekends. Although the club had started successfully, it was running into trouble by mid-1959. Skiffle had lost its novelty appeal, modern jazz had only an élitist following, and the trad fans were switching their allegiance to a new and much plusher jazz club, the Mardi Gras. Furthermore, Alan Snyter had married and was now running the operation from London.

Ray McFall was a 32 year old clerk who worked for the accountants who dealt with the Sytners' finances. **Ray McFall (61)**: "The Cavern featured traditional jazz and it also featured modern jazz plus various singers and so forth. Skiffle came in, mushroomed enormously and then went out equally quickly, all in the space of 18 months. Alan promoted modern jazz, which he liked but it was foreign to me and was an acquired taste. It was loss making. Of the five days he was open, two were taken up with skiffle and modern jazz and the other three were traditional jazz, so he then retained Friday, Saturday and Sunday for traditional jazz. Attendances declined and Alan went to London where he went to see if somebody wanted to acquire an interest, and his father looked after the place. Dr. Sytner had enough to do and he wanted to dispose of it, so we came to an agreement. The deal was done and the club reopened, if you could ever say it closed, on 3 October 1959."

Ray McFall bought the Cavern for £2,750 and stated that he wanted to "put Liverpool on the map as the leading jazz centre in the country outside London". He also said, "I have long felt that something needs to be done to draw off the excess heat when the club is full." Fine words, but, as it turned out, the second intent was as difficult as the first.

The powerfully built **Paddy Delaney (62)** was asked to be a bouncer: "I said I'd do it for £1 a night. The dress of the day was then a big fluffy pullover with corduroy trousers and rope sandals, but I dressed in a tuxedo, cummerbund and diamond studs. Ray McFall told me that the club was ruled by hooligans and there were fights every night. I told him that I could clean the place up, but it would take three months and I'd need more men. That's the story and I never looked back. I was there fifteen years."

The first Liverpool Jazz Festival was held in January 1960 and guest musicians included Acker Bilk and Terry Lightfoot. Among the local groups were the Bluegenes, still playing traditional jazz, and Rory Storm and the Hurricanes, whose drummer was Ringo Starr. Rock'n'roll was still banned from the Cavern and Rory was reprimanded for breaking into 'Whole Lotta Shakin' Goin' On'. **Johnny Guitar (63)**: "The jazz brigade was all duffle-coats and they were into trad jazz and would just about accept the Blue Jeans, who did a lot of jazz numbers. We did skiffle, which was okay for a while, but we saw the way things were going with rock'n'roll. Our set list included 'Maggie May' and 'Hi-Lili, Hi-Lo' and we said, 'To hell with it, let's do some rock'n'roll.' We didn't know many numbers but we knew 'Great Balls Of Fire' and 'Whole Lotta Shakin' Goin' On', and Rory said we would throw them in. We did 'Whole Lotta Shakin'' first and I don't think we reached the second one because the atmosphere was deadly. People were whistling at us and shouting disapproval. Then came a barrage of pennies and I was ducking as those old pennies used to hurt you. The stage was covered in copper coins, and I went round later and picked them up and it came to more than our fee. When we went to get paid, it was the time of the Jazz Festival, and Ray McFall said he was fining us 10 shillings (50p) for playing rock'n'roll and he said, 'We are not going to tolerate that music down here,' and he came to regret those words because rock'n'roll did come in. I liked jazz but I knew that rock'n'roll was coming in and that was more my style."

The jazz festival was not a success, and the club sustained losses of £3,000 in Ray McFall's first year. Ray had noticed that rock'n'roll nights were popular in the suburbs but there was no outlet in the city centre. So on 25 May 1960 the Cavern held its first beat night, featuring Cass and the Cassanovas (who later became the Big Three) and Rory Storm and the Hurricanes. It attracted a new audience and its success led to a complete change in policy at the Cavern. Nevertheless, the club still had a full house for the chart-making trad band, the Temperance Seven.

The first rock'n'roll groups to be booked for the Cavern were wary of the compliment. **John Cochrane (64)**, drummer with Wump and His Werbles, recalls, "The first time we played the Cavern we were terrified because it had a reputation that if the audience didn't like you, you got pulled apart. There was no back exit so the groups had to leave through the front. If you hadn't gone down very well, you would have to hide in the back until everyone had gone."

And what happened? **John Cochrane (65)**: "It was a total complete disaster. One of the band members rang Ray McFall and said, 'This brilliant new band is available for one night only.' We had played about three gigs. He said he would fit us in and we were totally out of our depth. We emptied the place. We must be the only band that has emptied the Cavern. I was in a group that I hoped people would forget about. Unfortunately, because of that ridiculous name, it keeps coming up all the time."

III. NEMS

Beat music in Liverpool didn't originate at the Cavern. We'll have a look at where the music *did* come from in the next chapter, but the role of the record shops, in particular, NEMS is crucial. Even if Brian Epstein had not managed the Beatles, his role in stocking significant American R&B recordings is important. He, or rather his father, had two shops in the city centre – one in Whitechapel, one in Great Charlotte Street – and he was the only record retailer to stock every new release. In other shops, you would have to order the more obscure ones, but not in NEMS. The Whitechapel branch in particular was fantastic: classical music was on the ground floor and pop in the basement, and the basement ceiling was covered with LP sleeves, which looked great and was Brian's own idea.

Alan Stratton (66): "Brian Epstein always dressed immaculately and spoke immaculately and I used to buy my records off him. I always wanted the original record of, say, 'A White Sport Coat', and I would look at the charts in America and buy the Marty Robbins' version. I have the 10-inch Johnny Burnette LP which is worth a fortune and it still has the wrapper on it 'Purchased at NEMS' because he had these polythene bags with NEMS stamped on."

Mick O'Toole (67): "I went into NEMS with my sister to buy *Songs For Swingin' Lovers* and Eppy just said to her, 'SP 463' or whatever the number was. I said, 'Do you know the numbers of all the records?' And he said, 'Quite a few,' with a big smile on his face. He was very pleased that someone had noticed his talent."

Alistair Taylor (68), who worked in NEMS, recalls,: "One of the biggest sellers was the soundtrack of *South Pacific*. At Christmas 1960, Brian ordered 500 copies. I said, 'Brian, you will have this on your hands forever.' We ended up just before Christmas being the only record store for miles around with *South Pacific* and we sold the lot. Incredible. Pop management's great gain was record retailing's great loss. He was brilliant."

Mick O'Toole (69): "When I was 15, I had a Saturday job on a game and poultry stall in St. John's Market and that financed my record buying. I could normally buy two records on a Saturday. I would go along Great Charlotte Street to the bus by the Adelphi and by the time I'd finished, it was well after six, and although NEMS had shut, Eppy would be there doing the books. One night I was desperate for some record and I knocked on the door. He invited me in and served me. I told him that I wasn't paid until after six, and he said, 'No problem. Any night you're passing and you see me, just knock on the door and I'll be only too happy to serve you.' This became the norm for me. I would finish at twenty past six and I would scamper round and knock on the door. I didn't know anything about Epstein at the time and I was taking a bit of a chance really."

And **Alan Sytner (70)** throws some fresh light on Brian visiting the Cavern: "The famous story of Brian Epstein coming down into this murky gloomy place and having his mind blown by the Beatles is absolute crap. He had been to the Cavern lots of times previously. He came down on Sunday nights, he was a very middle-class boy and so were his friends. Brian Epstein asked me to arrange a band for his twenty-first birthday party, and I told him that the Merseysippi Jazz Band would cost about £25. He asked if there was anything cheaper, and I said, 'Yes, I can get you the Blue Jeans for £12.'"

IV. The Morgue

You've heard of the Jacaranda, the Cavern, the Casbah, the Iron Door and the Tower Ballroom, but what of the Morgue? Until I started researching this book, I'd never heard of it and yet it played a crucial role in Liverpool beat music during its short life: it opened in March 1959 and closed the following month.

Johnny Guitar (71): "The Beatles first appeared with us at the Morgue Skiffle Cellar in Oakhill Park and it was John, Paul, George and they didn't have a drummer at the time. We started that club off in a Victorian house and it closed a few weeks later because of complaints about people frolicking in the garden, and we had put a lot of work into that cellar too. The atmosphere was good but it was small."

Tommy Hughes (72), then with the Pinetops Skiffle Group: "Rory Storm knew a nurse who worked in Broadgreen Hospital and she was staying at this house with a lot of other nurses, and they converted the cellar to the Morgue. The Bluegenes were there with Martini label shirts and we went on as the Pinetops Skiffle Group. Right afterwards, Bruce McCaskill asked me to play for the Bluegenes, but I would have to buy a Martini shirt. He said that they got plenty of bookings and I was made up. Next night it was teeming down with rain and there was a knock on the door and Bruce was standing there in a duffle coat, dripping wet, water pouring off his head, and he said, really excited, 'We're playing the Cavern', which was the jazz place that had only just opened. I went down to play with them and I didn't even know the tunes they were going to play but I did my best to join in.' With the Bluegenes being half a jazz band – the banjo, bass and drums – no, Norman Kuhlke was playing a washboard, I think – we were a big hit and the jazz fans accepted us as a good little band."

Colin Hanton (73) of the Quarry Men: "John, Paul and Eric Griffiths were the three guitarists and I was on drums. Eventually we were playing at the Morgue in Old Swan, which was run by Rory Storm, and it was a real dump. It was a condemned building and the whole thing was illegal and never advertised. It was a large terraced house and that is where we met George Harrison. Somebody asked him to play something. I thought it was 'Guitar Boogie' but everyone else reckons it was 'Raunchy'. A few days later Ivan Vaughan told me that Paul and John wanted George to join, but Eric would have to leave as they didn't want four guitarists. I knew I was on borrowed time as they were running the group. I got fed up in the end. I had carted my drums around on a bus for two years as none of us had cars. There were a lot of talent contests where we came second – we were always the bridesmaid and I'd had enough."

Rory Storm's sister, **Iris Caldwell (74)**: "The Morgue was under a nurse's home around Oakhill Park. We had the cellar, which was all black, and we painted it with skeletons and used ultra-violet light, which was so trendy at the time. We had the Beatles on there for 30 bob (£1.50) on a Saturday night, but George Harrison wasn't with them then. George was my boyfriend: we were kids but we were seeing each other. You couldn't charge entrance money as we had no permit. Instead, they would charge people for a bottle of Coke or orange as they went in. I was 13 and I desperately wanted to go although Rory did let me go one night. I was not well developed and so I got a lot of cotton wool and shoved it down my bra and thought I looked older and off I went. Just as big brothers do, Rory announced that there was Iris at the back and she had cotton wool down her bra, and that broke my heart. I ran out of there sobbing and George chased me right round Oakhill Park and gave me my very first kiss when he caught me. The only thing between us was cotton wool."

V. Discovering Carroll Levis

Right from the start, the groups wanted some national recognition. **Johnny Guitar (75)**: "I used to write off to the radio stations and Jack Good's *Oh Boy!* and I would be trying to get on. They would say, 'Get lost.' Nobody was interested in any bands from Liverpool, but we were the first Liverpool band to play on the radio show *Skiffle Club* and we did 'Midnight Special'."

In June 1957 the Quarry Men played the Empire Theatre, the biggest venue in Liverpool. **Rod Davis (76)**: "It was the Carroll Levis discovery show. The preliminary heat was on a Sunday, and my mother wouldn't let me go. The rest of the band went without me and got through the heat. On the show itself we only got to play one number, which was 'Worried Man Blues'. Another skiffle group had come from North Wales with their coachload of supporters and they beat us hands down on the applause meter. All credit to them though. They were leaping all over the stage and the bass player was rolling on his back. They gave a real show. We were just standing there, expecting people to appreciate the music."

Colin Hanton (77): "We had gone from someone's front room to the stage of the Liverpool Empire. It was unfair on the night as the last group on had an extra three minutes. They did two songs and were the winners. When Carroll Levis called us back on the stage and was lining us up, he said, 'I might have been a bit unfair there, lads, but you were quite good so keep at it.'"

Bobby Kaye (78): "When we had this vocal group, the Crescents, we went on the Carroll Levis show at the Empire and the Darktown Skiffle Group was on with Ringo as their drummer, and we won it. We sang vocal harmonies with one guitar. We were along the lines of the Four Aces and the Four Lads. We went on television and sang 'Little Darlin'' just as it was released and I remember the girls in NEMS saying that people were asking for our version of 'Little Darlin''. We hadn't done it: it was the Diamonds. We did three Sunday nights from Blackpool on a TV show called *Meet The Stars*. Three television shows on a Sunday night would make you stars now, wouldn't they? And then, probably my fault, I got promoted at work and moved out of town and the group broke up, and then the whole thing hit Liverpool like the Big Bang."

Karl Terry (79): "We were on a talent contest at the Pavilion in Lodge Lane. We came on with our backs to the audience and I had 'Karl Terry' across my back and they had 'The Cruisers' on theirs. We got through four or five heats but we were beaten an 84 year old lady who sang 'Ave Maria'. We got a fiver between us and I bought a Ricky Nelson EP because I wanted the song, 'It's Late'."

After failing a Liverpool audition for the ITV show, *Opportunity Knocks!*, in 1959, the Remo Four tried their luck with Carroll Levis. **Harry Prytherch (80)**: "We passed the audition and we were on the show on a Tuesday night and there was us and a snake dancer, one of these guys who used to put sand on a mat and do dancing, moving his body and arms like a snake, and he beat us. We did the Jerry Keller number, 'Here Comes Summer', and as soon as they announced us we went into the song and after about 20 seconds, the amp blew up, and we only had one amp between three of them. One amp in the Empire Theatre! Carroll Levis came on from the wings and said we could have another chance. Derry and the Seniors were on that show with Howie Casey and they got through to the finals."

3 MUSICAL YOUTH

I. American Rock'n'Roll in Liverpool
II. Tuning up
III. Liverpool College of Art
IV. Roll with the Punches

"Let me get it out of my system, Mimi"
(John Lennon)

I. American Rock'n'Roll in Liverpool

Before the advent of rock'n'roll in 1956, dance bands were popular in America and Britain. Guy Mitchell, Frankie Laine, David Whitfield and Ruby Murray were the stars of the day. In 1955 Slim Whitman topped the charts for eleven weeks with 'Rose Marie', while Jimmy Young had No.1 hits with 'Unchained Melody' and 'The Man From Laramie'. It was predictable, uncontroversial music, the songs being the product of Tin Pan Alleys in New York or London. A good night out in Liverpool might be had doing quicksteps and tangos to live dance bands at the large, brightly lit Grafton Rooms in West Derby, about three miles from the city centre. **Paul McCartney (81)**: "My main roots are in the singalong stuff like 'When The Red, Red, Robin Comes Bob-bob-bobbin' Along' and 'Carolina Moon'. I didn't know the origins of songs like 'Milkcow Blues Boogie' and 'That's All Right (Mama)'. It's only later that I found out about Leadbelly, Arthur 'Big Boy' Crudup, and all the black guys."

Besides ballroom dancing with the likes of Mrs. Wilf Hamer, there was a thriving interest in country music in Liverpool. The city had been called the Nashville of England and a pub was named the Honky Tonk long before the term was generally known in the UK. Many people deride country music. Why, then, was it so popular in Liverpool? **Ken Dodd (82)**, who has recorded many country songs, explains, "Liverpool people get very emotional. They think with their hearts and not with their heads. Country music is emotional and dramatic and that's why it is so popular. You get earthy lyrics with a touch of philosophy. There's a story to the lyrics and that's why country songs are better than the average popular song. A popular song generally says 'I love you' while a country one says 'I love you because...'."

The hillbilly docker **Hank Walters (83)** ran the Black Cat Club near Lime Street station: "One time we did a show and John Lennon said, 'I don't go much on your music, son, but give us your hat.' I told him that I didn't think much of *his* music, come to that, and I didn't think they would get anywhere unless they got with it and played country." As it happens, the Beatles recorded Buck Owens' 'Act Naturally' and you'll find many country songs in the Discography. Country music was a significant influence in the development of rock'n'roll, and it was the rock'n'roll era that made such an impression on Merseyside's youth. John Lennon remarked, "Before Elvis, there was nothing." Wildly untrue, but a great quote.

Something happened in the mid-1950s to shake the record industry out of its stupor. The austerity after the Second World War was passing and many teenagers had money to spend. Something more exciting than ballads and dance-band records was called for. Traditional jazz, by its very name, was, well, traditional.

The first inkling of a change was the success of the American singer, Johnnie Ray. During his act, he would fall to his knees with emotion and he was dubbed 'The Cry Guy', 'The Nabob of Sob' and 'The Prince of Wails'. Johnnie Ray was gay and, in 1952, he married an eager fan, Marilyn Morrison, probably to allay probing into his sexuality. Marilyn was soon drinking hard and early in 1954, she filed for divorce in Mexico. Johnnie Ray told reporters, "Someday I plan to marry again. Every man wants a home and children", but what else could he say? His real feelings were made clear in 'Such A Night', where he yowls and yelps as he responds to sexual excitement. It was the frankest exposition of sex put on record. 'Such A Night' was banned by the BBC but it still went to No.1. Seeing Ray in concert was something else again as Ray would whip himself into a frenzy, drop to the floor and wrap himself around a piano leg. For all that, Ray wasn't pioneering a new form of music, just a very emotional variant of the old.

The break came with Bill Haley and His Comets and 'Rock Around The Clock', a No.1 in 1955. The song's sentiments and driving beat were aimed at teenagers, but Haley, a chubby family man, was no one's idea of a teenage idol. On personal terms, he couldn't compete with the charisma of the new breed of truculent cinema stars, James Dean and Marlon Brando.

Howie Casey (84): "I was born in 1937 and when I was 15, my cousin John Howard introduced me to Stan Kenton. It was a great, super powerhouse band with a fabulous brass section. I started to listen to other big bands and the other musicians I liked tended to be saxophone players Then Bill Haley came along and on his records there is Rudy Pompilli playing sax. I bought a sax in Frank Hessy's and I found I could honk along with people like Rudy Pompilli easier than the jazz things. That doesn't make jazz better than rock'n'roll – it simply means that it is more difficult if there are dozens of chord changes. There are wonderful sax players on all those New Orleans records by Fats Domino and Little Richard. Going in the army was a great grounding for me as I learnt to read music and learnt about arranging. I was playing all the time for three years. When I got out in 1958, I could do the military band stuff and I was a fine honking sax player. I went to Wilson Hall in Garston and saw the Rhythm Rockers with their bandleader, Frank Wibberly, who was a drummer who swung brilliantly. British records of the time had something missing, but Frank had it. I sat in with them and the kids were jiving with the girls dancing around their handbags. I lived in Huyton and I met the band, the Hy-Tones – well, the drummer was going out with my sister – and I joined them and started wearing silly jackets. It wasn't long before I'd formed a group with some really good musicians like Brian Griffiths and Jeff Wallington. We had a good singer called Ginger Jim but then we saw Derry Wilkie and he exploded across the stage and was a wonderful showman. We became Derry and the Seniors which was a nick off Danny and the Juniors. We were all a bit older than them, me being the grand old age of 21."

Stan Johnson (85): "They weren't silly jackets. They were red and black striped jackets which we bought from C&A. I was so broad-shouldered that they didn't have a jacket in my size and I was the odd one out for three weeks until they could get one in for me."

Karl Terry and the Cruisers was another of the first groups and Karl's love of Bill Haley and his Comets has never left him. **Alan Stratton (86)**: "Karl Terry always played undiluted rock'n'roll. He was always well regarded and was high in the polls and on the main shows, and he has never changed. In the 60s, people used to laugh when he did 'Rock Around The Clock' and 'Shake Rattle And Roll' because they weren't Merseybeat but now a lot of bands are doing those songs. He is still doing the splits and banging the cymbals, and it was always dangerous to be on stage with Karl as he would jump round and he would break things. He doesn't rehearse and some musicians say, 'I'll never play with him'. There is no warming up and he has a battered PA. There is no posing and he has kept live music going through all the karaoke and the electric pianos."

The film *Rock Around The Clock* caused riots and, in Liverpool, police chased hundreds of hysterical teenagers nearly a mile from the cinema in Lime Street to the Pier Head, where presumably they caught the ferries home. Rock'n'roll was associated with Teddy Boys and crime and so crepes and drapes were banned from many dance halls. *Violent Playground,* a film starring Stanley Baker and John Slater and shot in Liverpool in 1957 accurately reflected the tension in the city and can be seen as a precursor of *Z-Cars*. The film featured Freddie Starr as a young tearaway: he's the young lad perpetually wiping his nose with his sleeve.

Bill Haley was the first rock'n'roll star to come to the UK and he played the Odeon in Liverpool in February 1957. **Mick O'Toole (87)**: "Bill Haley was very disappointing. The first half of the show was the Vic Lewis Orchestra with Kenneth Earle and Malcolm Vaughan, and the management announced that if anybody danced, they would be ejected. There was another announcement to welcome on stage Bill Haley and his Comets. There was a long pause and they started the intro to 'Razzle Dazzle' and on the 'Go', the curtains flew back and there they were. They seemed a band of fat old men, though they were only in their late 20s. I was 14 and I had sagged school to buy the tickets to go to the Odeon in the first place. They looked terrible and they were doing corny vaudeville routines: the double-bass player was on his back and kicking his legs in the air and he had odd socks on, oh, very amusing. Somebody else would ride the bass as he was playing, and as they continued, I got more and more dissatisfied, but we were surrounded by three solid rows of girls who screamed from start to finish. We wondered what they were screaming at as Bill was like a fat old uncle. I was quite glad when they finished."

Eddie Amoo (88) of the Real Thing: "I absolutely loved 'Why Do Fools Fall In Love?' and I still do. My mam took me to a Frankie Lymon and the Teenagers concert in the Empire. I was about ten. It was my first concert and I was absolutely knocked out. I was absolutely thrilled, I had never seen anything so exciting in my life. I was mesmerised by them and I saw all the crowds waiting for Frankie's autograph. There were only a few coloured people in the audience, and I remember somebody pointing me out and saying, 'There's one of them, there's one of them', which was really funny. I said on the way home, 'That's what I want to do, that's what I want to be', and my mam was laughing and saying, 'Okay, son.'"

As luck would have it, a young truck driver from Memphis, Tennessee, Elvis Presley, combined the qualities of Haley, Dean and Brando and had a lot more of his own. Presley merged pop, country and blues music in an incredible onslaught of sound. He sang 'Hound Dog' as though his life depended on it, wallowed in despair on 'Heartbreak Hotel', and spoke for a generation in 'Blue Suede Shoes'. He had 19 different titles on the UK charts in 1956 and 1957 alone.

Newspapers attacked Elvis Presley and naturally something that was so reviled by the establishment endeared itself to teenagers. This tactic has subsequently been used by the Rolling Stones and the Sex Pistols. Despite his popularity, Elvis effectively had a cult following. His stance echoed the views of a generation, yet his records were rarely heard on the BBC. The broadcasting of popular music was very limited and even Top 10 hits were played only a few times a week. True, there was Radio Luxembourg, but reception in the UK was generally poor.

There was even less chance of seeing rock'n'roll stars on TV, assuming that you were lucky enough to own one. *6.5 Special* was a brave attempt to create a youth programme, and this was followed by *Oh Boy!* which was the only British show to capture the excitement of the music. However, most of the performers were British and there were few opportunities to see American stars. Their growing following indicated the need for their music and the importance of youth club and school grapevines.

British record companies made little attempt to cater for this new market. Most of the best American rock 'n' roll records were issued in the UK, but usually several weeks after the American release. Some classic rock'n'roll records received very little promotion. For example, Chuck Berry's only Top 20 hit in the UK during the 1950s was 'Sweet Little Sixteen'. This is surprising as Chuck Berry is now regarded as being second only in significance to Elvis Presley. On the other hand, Pat Boone became the leader of the bland with his milky version of rock'n'roll.

Liverpool had a direct shipping line to New York. For centuries sailors brought music from other countries back to Liverpool and after the Second World War, there was a society on the Wirral to listen to new American jazz records. As **John McNally (89)** of the Searchers recalls, "Most people in Liverpool had some relation who went to sea and could bring record imports in. My brother bought me Hank Williams records first of all, and I started from there, mainly because my mum and dad would go to the pub and say, 'Our John can play the guitar. We'll get him over for the last half hour.' I'd be playing Hank Williams songs and I learned the trade in the local pub. My brother then brought back the first Elvis ones, then Carl Perkins, then Buddy Holly long before they were released over here. I remember him coming over and saying he'd seen Elvis on the telly and Jerry Lee Lewis live."

Pete Frame (90): "When all the bands were starting in Liverpool, the records they were playing and getting excited about were by Jerry Lee Lewis and Chuck Berry, the Everly Brothers, Elvis, records made for the white American teenage market or the mixed American market as it was becoming that you couldn't segregate the airwaves.

They got the records over here and they sounded so much more exciting than the English records: English records at the time were very tinny. Americans think it is bad that they had to put up with Pat Boone and the Crew-Cuts, but we had to put up with the Billy Cotton Band Show and Ray Pilgrim with the David Ede Orchestra: absolutely rubbish versions which murdered the original records. We idolised American records, as indeed we idolised everything American. Their sports were more exotic, and we thought that they had better coffee and better candy and better architecture. They had the skyscrapers, the cars, the girls, the mountains, the rivers, the Grand Canyon, the cowboys, the gangsters and the movies. Everything about America was better than England. All our parents had had it really bad in the War but we were liberated from that and we just wanted to enjoy ourselves and have a great time."

Buddy Holly and Charlie Gracie were among the first American rock'n'rollers to perform in the UK and their performances in Liverpool gave heart to a lot of Merseyside lads. John McNally was impressed with Charlie Gracie's guitar playing, and **Mike Pender (91)**, another Searcher, recalls, in the spirit of St. Paul on the road to Damascus, Buddy Holly playing at the Philharmonic Hall. As it happens, I was speaking to Mike backstage at the Phil: "I've played here a few times over the years and I always think back to when I saw Buddy Holly. I was 15 and in my first job at Ray's Tugs, one of the Merseyside shipping companies. Somebody got me the ticket for Buddy Holly at the Philharmonic Hall, and Des O'Connor was the compère. They also had the Tanner Sisters on but it was really just Buddy Holly with music hall acts. The show was magical and Holly had his Fender Stratocaster. There were only three of them on stage but it was a big loud sound and the audience was on its feet. He had a white suit on and he looked terrific. From that night onwards, everything I learned, everything I played, was based on Holly. Groups now have banks of amplifiers and speakers all over the place, and most times they still don't get the sound they want. Holly went on stage with just a double bass, drums and one amplifier and he brought the house down. It was a magical night. I remember going away from the theatre thinking, 'I would like to do this for a living,' and I did."

Tom Earley (92): "I saw Buddy Holly live at the Philharmonic. That was the first time I had seen a Fender guitar and to see those three guys playing their records was just spectacular. There was a drummer and a bass player and I don't even think that the bass was individually miked. There was just one small Fender amp on stage and Buddy Holly's guitar was going through that."

II. Tuning up

The managers of the dance halls on Merseyside did not approve of the new music and its followers, but realised that they had to move with the times. A lot of older people did not want to go dancing if there might be trouble and hiring large dance bands was becoming uneconomic. Instead, they booked a few young musicians for next to nothing and hoped that rival gangs wouldn't attend.

One of the first rock'n'roll bands on Merseyside was led by a butcher's boy named Teddy Taylor. They were called Kingsize Taylor and the Dominoes. **Kingsize Taylor**

(93): "We started off as the James Boys in 1955. We just stood in a chip shop one night and Bobby Thomson was in the same chip shop. He had a guitar with him and I had a guitar with me. He said, 'How many chords do you know?' I said, 'Three,' and he said, 'I know four,' so we just formed a group, just playing Lonnie Donegan and stuff that was on television."

Their pianist, **Sam Hardie (94)**, says, "Dave Anthony had a resident band on at Litherland Town Hall and we were hired to play in the interval. Rock'n'roll was only just coming in and the big band scene was still very strong. People went to Litherland Town Hall for ballroom dancing. When we came on, the floor would empty. But we did our spot and we were given a meat pie and a glass of orange each."

In 1957 and 1958 the Dominoes made private recordings which testify that they were already a rock'n'roll group. They were recorded in Sam Hardie's lounge and, despite the primitive conditions and the drummer playing from the top of the stairs to get a better balance, the results are very enjoyable.

When the skiffle craze was ending, the groups had to determine their next move. The Gin Mill Skiffle Group turned into those yellow-shirted folkies, the Spinners, but most became rock'n'roll bands with a line-up of lead guitar, rhythm guitar, bass guitar and drums. Kingsize Taylor and the Dominoes and Gerry and the Pacemakers both had pianists, which was unusual. The invention of the electric bass guitar saved groups from having to hump huge double basses around.

The banjos had to go. **Rod Davis (95)** of the Quarry Men: "I had bought the banjo from my uncle and if he'd sold me his guitar, I might have been a decent enough guitarist to keep McCartney out of the band. I might have learnt guitar chords, I might not, and that was the big limitation really. McCartney could play the guitar like a guitar and we couldn't, and let's face it, a banjo doesn't look good in a rock group. I only met Paul on one other occasion after the Woolton fete and it was at Auntie Mimi's a week or two later. He dropped in to hear us practising. From my point of view, I was the person he was replacing – it's like Pete Best – you're the guy who doesn't know. Some things had gone on that I was unaware of."

Both John Lennon and his Quarry Bank schoolfriend, **Eric Griffiths (96)**, bought guitars. "We both went to a guitar-teacher in Hunts Cross. We went for one or two lessons but we decided that it was boring, trying to learn to play the guitar properly and not being able to get a tune out of it for some considerable time. John's mother, Julia, played the banjo so she re-tuned the guitar strings and we played in that manner until Paul McCartney joined the band. We were using four strings and the top two dead, tuned to the fourth string."

Billy Maher (97): "His mother knew these chords which were designed for a four-stringed instrument – a banjo has four strings, a guitar six – and so it would be easy for her to play the first four strings on the guitar. In other words, you wouldn't be using two of the strings. It would sound okay because guitarists sometimes play four-string chords today even though they have six strings. They would be very trebley chords, but they would sound all right."

Why, I wondered, was John allowed a guitar when Aunt Mimi frowned upon such things? **Eric Griffiths (98)**: "I'm not aware that Mimi frowned upon it that much. She frowned upon his dress and his behaviour at school, but I wasn't conscious of her frowning upon him playing the guitar and being in a group."

A beat group required more cash than a skiffle group. Many of the youngsters had hire-purchase agreements with Frank Hessy's, the leading shop in Liverpool for musical instruments. In Willy Russell's play *John Paul George Ringo...and Bert*, the Lennon character sneers that you get a free plectrum if you buy your guitar from Frank Hessy's.

Colin Hanton (99) of the Quarry Men bought a set of drums. "I was interested in the drums and I used to play on the furniture to jazz records. Once I was an apprentice upholsterer, my parents said that if I could pay for them, I could have them. I went to Frank Hessy's and bought a set of drums for ten shillings down and ten shillings a week for whatever it was. It was £34 in all. I was a drummer, or so I thought. Len Garry and I were what you could loosely call the rhythm section. You can get a loud thump out of a tea-chest bass as it does reverberate in that big box."

Chris Curtis (100): "I wanted to join a group as things were going to happen. I thought you didn't need any training to play the drums, you just have to bash hard, so I told my mum and dad that I wanted some drums and my dad signed for them at Frank Hessy's. They were very snazzy, all blue and shiny. One Saturday afternoon when I went to make my payment, I met Mike Pender, who'd been in primary school with me. Drummers were hard to find and he asked me to join them for a booking at Wilson Hall in Garston that night. My brother had a little Anglia and he took me with my drums scrunged in on the backseat and a big tom-tom on my knees. It was a bit like busking, but it wasn't difficult. They were doing songs I knew such as 'Oh Lonesome Me'."

Alan Stratton (101): "My guitar was a very cheap-looking guitar and I remember playing it once on the Iron Door and Tony Jackson was walking off. He too was poor and he had made his own bass guitar. He had modified it and it was a copy of a Fender, and I said to him, 'Where did you get those machine heads?' He said, 'From the violin department in Rushworth's', so I popped along and did the same thing. I got cello machine heads, and only about four people had the coffin-type amplifiers that Adrian Barber used to make and I was one of them. He used to get the circuits from Goodman's for the actual size of the cabinets and then he would build them out of chipboard. That marvellous deep bass sound was the secret of Merseybeat. It was the first thing that you heard, the deep bass as you walked outside the Cavern. The bass drum thumping away that was the essence of Merseybeat. Everybody tried to get the bass as deep as they could get it. They all wanted big cabinets and 18 inch speakers, just like reggae musicians later on."

Tommy Hughes (102): "Bruce McCaskill took an empty guitar case into Frank Hessy's and he was being shown all these guitars and when they got outside, he said to Colin, 'Not bad, is it?' He opened the case and he had a guitar in it that he had nicked. We had to throw Bruce out of the group. He would say, 'We haven't been paid for this booking' or 'I've got a cheque.' We knew that there was something going on when he asked for the money in advance for a gig at the Cavern. We told him that we wanted all the money he owed us, or off you pop. Sad really as he was the founder member and it was his van. We should have been suspicious when we did an early gig in Walton jail and someone shouted 'Hiya, Bruce' to him."

Peter Cook (103): "I used to follow Alfie Diamond and the Skiffle Kings around and my mum thought I must be interested so she bought me a guitar. I used to carry it with me, and because it was a good one, the lads from the skiffle group used to say, 'Let us use your guitar.' I had the guitar a year before I learnt to play anything. I learnt 'Diana' in C and once I had learnt to play it in C, I learnt to play it in D and next thing I could play it in every key, so I was way ahead of everyone else in the street. I didn't really like skiffle and I think the Top Spots were the very first beat band on Merseyside. There's a certificate from 1959 for the Wallasey Boys Club where we got the Dance Band, Rhythm and Swing Award. All the others were skiffle groups and we were more rock'n'roll. We were into Gene Vincent and Eddie Cochran and we had drawn away from the skiffle groups."

Jim Gretty (104) sold guitars for Frank Hessy's: "Lots of people used to come and listen to me. The guitar was selling left and right, but nobody could play it. I said, 'The best thing to do, Mr. Hessy, is to give free lessons to anyone who buys a guitar'. Mr. Hessy took another shop a little bit farther down Whitechapel and I used to get 30 to 40 people every Monday night from six o'clock to half past seven. I sold the Beatles their first guitars, and many other musicians as well."

That doesn't mean that every guitarist was a good musician. Veteran manager **Ted Knibbs (105)** saw one group at a social club. "I went one night to the ODVA in Orrell and this group of lads came on. After they'd done their turn this lad said to me, 'What did you think of us?' I said, 'What made you ask me?' and he replied, 'We've been told you're well up in clubland and we'd like your opinion.' I said, 'I'll just give you a bit of advice. Throw that blinking guitar away and just concentrate on singing because you can't play it.' That was Billy J. Kramer." When Billy went on stage without his guitar for his next performance, it was stolen from the dressing room. However, the advice stuck and from then on, Billy concentrated on singing. His Nibs, Ted Knibbs, became his manager.

John Gustafson (106): "I didn't know anyone who had a double bass and the part of Liverpool I was brought up in was not well off at all. Thing like that costs hundreds of pounds and bass guitars weren't around when I started. The first bass I played was just an ordinary guitar with bigger notches cut in the nut at the top. Lumps were cut out of it and bass strings put on. Adrian Barber made it for me. He cobbled it together as a Heath Robinson job, but there was no way I could have afforded a bass guitar on my £2.10s a week wage. I knew stand-up bass players played with their fingers but I thought that because it was called a guitar, it must be played with a plectrum. I had no other knowledge."

And then you had to rehearse. **John Duff Lowe (107)**: "I was at the Liverpool Institute with Paul McCartney. During one of the breaks, he asked me if I wanted to play piano with them. For about six months, we met every Sunday at his house, and George Harrison joined at the same time. The line-up was Paul, John, George and myself and we didn't normally have a drummer at the rehearsals as we were in a terraced house and the noise would carry. Jim McCartney wouldn't allow it, but when we could, Colin Hanton would play with us. We did Elvis and Buddy Holly numbers and I remember 'Mean Woman Blues'. Jim McCartney would be sitting at the end of the piano and he would be waving his arms if we got too loud. He was worried about what the neighbours would think."

Iris Caldwell (108): "It was Rory who gave Ringo his confidence introducing 'Ringo Starr-time' and getting him to sing 'Matchbox' and a few other things. They used to rehearse in our house and Ringo would put a cushion on his drums so that it wouldn't disturb the neighbours too much as it was only a semi. In those days nobody had a car and we used to go to the Orrell Park Ballroom on the bus. I was so happy that they took me, but the reason they took me was because if they missed the last bus home, they would have to hitchhike. I would stand in the road hitchhiking and when the car stopped, everybody would run in with their amplifiers. Ringo got a car but he drove it for a long time without a licence. He even gave a policeman a lift one night. Rory loved cars: he had a Cresta and his last car was a Chevrolet Impala, which was a massive big car. He liked a bench front seat with the gear stick on the steering wheel, not on the floor, so that he could make love on the front seat."

Sam Leach (109): "I opened the Cassanova club over Sampson and Barlow's in London Road. I know the spelling was wrong but I took the name from Cass and the Cassanovas, who were the resident band. I was stood there proudly one evening and this burly guy came in with a young girl who was obviously pregnant. 'Are you the owner?' he said, and I said proudly that I was. 'Well,' he said, grabbing me by the collar, 'Are you going to marry my daughter?' I managed to gasp that it wasn't me and his daughter said, 'You don't think I'd marry him, do you?' It was Cass they were after: he got so many girls pregnant that he had to leave town."

But the club didn't last. **Sam Leach (110)**: "One Saturday night the Assistant Chief Constable was walking past our club in London Road. The windows were open and the sound of the Beatles could be heard. Outside the club were two drunks threatening people with bottles and he didn't realise that they were from the Black Cat club, which was over our club. He rang Sampson and told him to close the club. We closed and the Black Cat stayed open, which really sickened me."

The Casbah opened in the basement of a huge old house in West Derby, about four miles from the city centre. It was run by **Mona Best (111)**, mother of Pete Best: "The boys had so many friends that the house was like a railway station. They asked me to open a club. We all got down to it, working all the hours that God gave us. When we opened, we had people coming from everywhere. I never thought that such a little seed would grow into such a big oak tree. We ended up with 2,950 members."

Sam Leach (112): "Kingsize Taylor and the Dominoes auditioned for me at the Cassanova Club and they were the best harmony band I had heard in Liverpool. Teddy, Bobby and John were brilliant together. I was going to pay them the standard £2 audition fee but they were so good that I gave them £10, and I can't think of another promoter who would do that. Teddy did more for Merseybeat than anyone on Merseyside because they were doing a lot of the American songs first and you could see the others with pens and paper, copying down the chords."

Although Kingsize Taylor and the Dominoes were competent, I'm surprised that they had many bookings. Guitarist **Bobby Thomson (113)** recalls, "We had a dreadful reputation with Brian Kelly, who used to give us bookings. One time he banned us from

Lathom Hall and Litherland Town Hall and a place he had in Skelmersdale. We got banned because we liked picking fights with the audience. I feel ashamed about it now, but at the time we thought it was clever. It was straight off the stage and sail into them."

Dave Lovelady (114) was playing drums for the Dominoes. "One great advantage of having Teddy Taylor in the group was that he was six foot five and 22 stone. There was a private function for Southport Rugby Club and there was some trouble over the money. The atmosphere got nasty and it ended up with Teddy Taylor hanging two rugby players on coat hooks. He just lifted them up, one in each hand, and hung them on the wall. And I remember a terrible fight breaking out in Knotty Ash Village Hall. Teddy threw five blokes through the window, real Clint Eastwood style, so he was very handy to have around. We always got paid."

I asked **Kingsize Taylor (115)** to confirm the rugby club story. "That was the manager, who was also a rugby player. He went missing and when he came back, we hung him up on the coat-hooks. We got our money off him of course and we just left him there."

Sometimes Kingsize could use his strength to extract a higher fee. **Pat Clusky (116)** of Rikki and the Red Streaks recalls, "The money wasn't too good and Kingsize Taylor and the Dominoes decided that they were going to strike for more. Teddy barricaded everyone out of Litherland Town Hall and said that nobody was going to play. We were on very little money or just some food and nothing else, and he was trying to get us all some money. We did get more. I got £1."

Joey Bower (117) played with Brian O'Hara in the Four Jays. They adopted a more subtle approach. "We'd been playing St. Luke's Hall in Crosby for about nine months and we were on £5 a night. We knew that Doug Martin liked us because we were on every other Saturday, but we couldn't get another halfpenny out of him. Well, Brian's very good at impressions, so he rang him up at home and said he'd seen this fabulous group called the Four Jays and he was thinking of having them every Saturday. The other end of the phone went quiet and, and when we saw Doug the next Saturday, he said, 'Listen, lads, I've decided to give you £7 instead of £5.'"

Dave May (118) of the Silhouettes remembers how tough it could be at St Luke's Hall. An accidental manoeuvre could start a scuffle. "We were playing on stage, and all of a sudden a fellow went down in the middle of the dance floor. The other guys piled on top of him and soon they're laying into each other. The whole floor erupted until the police came with the dogs. We found out later what had caused it. A guy was dancing and dislocated his knee. He fell down on one knee and the guy next to him immediately hit him because he thought he wanted a fight."

III. Liverpool College of Art

Nicholas Horsfield (119), a lecturer at the Liverpool College of Art, taught John Lennon. "A proper study should be made of the people who achieve noteworthy careers in popular music and other activities who start from the basis of an art school. Arnold Bennett had been at an art school and his literary sketchbooks are like an artist's sketchbooks: that is to say, brief notations of something seen or experienced. As far as

John Lennon was concerned, the art school gave him a year or two to relax and find himself. He was never under any real pressure to achieve art works. He was always held artistically on sufferance and finally he got the push. But that year or two gave him the opportunity to develop within himself."

Bryan Biggs (120), the director of the Bluecoat Arts Centre: "If you believe the history books, there was this enormous crossover happening in art schools. You could be a painter or you could be a musician, and some chose to go down one path and some the other. It has continued ever since. The reason that I think a lot of them went into pop music was because they were not very good as artists. The phenomenon that art school is the place where things could happen is very interesting. You could do what you wanted to do at art school, there was very little in the syllabus, and there weren't exams. You could do posters for the gigs."

Mike Evans (121): "Stu Sutcliffe and his girlfriend Astrid foisted the flat, moptop haircuts and the leather jacket look upon the Beatles, but, more interestingly and more subtly, Stu influenced John in artistic concepts such as surrealism and Dada. John was very much a primitive – you can either do it or you can't – whereas Stu was academic and articulate. Arthur Ballard, who taught them both in college, says that, before he knew Stuart, John didn't know a Dada from a donkey and his reading matter didn't get much further than the *Beano*. John was very much a primitive, intuitive person, which came out in rock'n'roll 'cause he did it off the top of his head."

Nicholas Horsfield (122): "There are always rebellious spirits in any college of art and that is a very good thing. I had to teach Lennon, or try to teach Lennon, objective life drawing. For me and to the academic school for centuries, life drawing is an essential core discipline in learning to be a painter. It involves observation and analysis, feeling, expression, and this sort of thing was sheer nonsense to John Lennon: he couldn't care a button. I was never able to get him to concentrate at all in the actual study of the model. I soon gave up trying. I would leave Lennon to doodle on his own until he chose to walk out. The academic discipline was completely meaningless to a person such as John Lennon and indeed the understanding of painting in the proper sense was meaningless to him. I remember after a boring art history lecture by me, I was going to pack up the projector and finding John Lennon stretched out sound asleep with several bottles on the floor."

Dave May was at the Liverpool College of Art with John Lennon and Stuart Sutcliffe, and I discovered that he taught Stu to play the guitar. Much has been written about Stu's incompetence in the Beatles, but **Dave May (123)**, being his teacher, doesn't think it's true. "I had a homemade guitar, which wasn't very good because I didn't know anything about the technical side. The Students' Union bought the Beatles equipment and Stuart had a Hofner bass guitar which was the bees' knees but he couldn't play a note. I always remember going over to John and Stuart's flat in Gambier Terrace. I said, 'I'll teach you to play 'C'mon Everybody' if you let me measure your guitar.' That was the bargain. I taught him to play the song – it's only three notes – and then measured his guitar. I then made my own guitar and Stu Sutcliffe played with the Beatles."

IV. Roll with the Punches

In the late 1950s John, Paul and George played regularly at the Casbah club as the Quarry Men, but they were not in the forefront of Liverpool groups. Sometimes they played at the Jacaranda coffee bar, which was run by Allan Williams. It was conveniently sited near the dole office. After many years of other uses, the Jacaranda reopened in 1984 and Stuart Sutcliffe's murals are still there in its basement. Allan Williams maintains that this is John Lennon's work but there is no supporting evidence, and if they were Lennon's work, they would hardly be unprotected. (Come to think of it, if they are Stu Sutcliffe's work, why are they unprotected?)

The beat poet **Royston Ellis (124)** came to Liverpool in 1960 for a reading at the Jacaranda: "I had had my own TV spot and had appeared on a documentary, *Just For Kicks*, so they knew of me. John would bombard me with questions about London. I mentioned that the latest thing was to buy a Vick inhaler, open it up and chew the wadding. It was a minor high compared to later, and presumably this led to other things. We had a conversation one night about what we wanted to be. I'd had some poetry published and I told them that I wanted to be a paperback writer. The phrase stuck in Paul's mind and became part of a hit song, although I haven't seen Paul since 1963 to confirm it."

More importantly, **Royston Ellis (125)** makes this claim: "John Lennon said, 'A man appeared on a flaming pie and said unto them, "From this day on you are Beatles with an A".' I am that man. When I was staying with them, I was doing the cooking and providing the food as they had no money of their own. One day it was chicken pie but I burnt it, hence the pie reference. They were calling themselves the Beetles with an E at the time, so I suggested that as they liked beat poetry and they played beat music, they should become Beatles with an A."

Allan Williams (126) was responsible for promoting the show which first brought the Liverpool beat groups together. The American rock'n'rollers Eddie Cochran and Gene Vincent had played at the Liverpool Empire in March 1960, and Allan arranged for Eddie and Gene to play a further date at the Liverpool Stadium in May. Then came the car accident outside Chippenham, which killed Eddie and injured Gene. "I was shattered by the death of Eddie Cochran," says Allan, "Gene Vincent was also badly hurt and I phoned Larry Parnes about a week later and said, 'I take it for granted that it's all over.' He said, 'No. Gene Vincent has gone back to the States but he's returning to England and would like to do it.' So I thought I'd put on Liverpool groups to supplement the show – Rory Storm and the Hurricanes, Bob Evans and the Five Shillings, and Cass and the Cassanovas. Bob Wooler came to the Jacaranda and suggested I have Gerry and the Pacemakers. I went along to Blair Hall and was knocked out by them, and so we went ahead with the first ever Merseybeat rock 'n' roll show.'

Gerry and the Pacemakers were one of the most versatile groups on Merseyside. **Gerry Marsden (127)** says, "From 1955 to 1960 we used to do every one of the Top 20 in our show and that got us around a bit. We were one of the few groups in Liverpool that used a piano, so we could do the Jerry Lee Lewis ones and Fats Domino ones better than most of the other bands." But his brother, Fred, adds, "The stadium was a strange place to play. The sound got lost."

Mick O'Toole (128): "The Stadium show was a total madhouse. With its seating, the stadium wasn't set out like the Empire and people were dashing about all over the place. There were no marshals or stewards and no discipline amongst the crowds. It was a very unsettled night. It was a difference in attitude. If you went to the Empire, you behaved yourself but this was a boxing stadium and it was a shambles."

The Beatles weren't considered good enough to be included.

Perhaps it was just as well. **John Gustafson (129)** was playing with Cass and the Cassanovas: "Larry Parnes was at the stadium and he saw me and thought, 'Star quality', or something like that. He took me to London and I did a recording test in Denmark Street which was a shambles, me singing 'Money Honey' on an electric guitar, which was not even plugged in. (Laughs) He treated me very well, but I was very wary about him – my dad had given me a lecture before I went. He bought me some clothes and I was a 17 year old being showered with gifts. Things turned sour because I didn't go along with his grand plan. I returned to Liverpool and carried on as before."

What was this grand plan? **John Gustafson (130)**: "Oh, you want the nitty gritty. Larry Parnes had a flat off Oxford Street and he took me there after picking me up from the railway station. He said, 'Do you want to get freshened up before we go to dinner?' and he offered me a bath or a shower. We didn't even have a bath at home and, in my poverty, I used to go to the public baths. I ran the bath and climbed in and on the wall there was a huge mirror, almost floor to ceiling. There was an armchair as well, and I thought that was very odd. Why would you have an armchair in a bathroom? Larry wandered in while I was having my bath and sat down in the armchair. It started to dawn on me what was happening. I said, 'Would you mind waiting outside?' That didn't bother him – the mirror was double-sided and he simply went to a little room round the corner and watched. Things turned sour because I didn't go along with the scheme of things, his grand plan. I returned to Liverpool with promises of something later, maybe. That fell apart then and I just carried on in Liverpool then."

Relatively few people had heard of Crosby before the 1981 by-election that swept Shirley Williams to victory, but 20 years earlier it was a base for many Merseyside groups. Those eight miles to the centre of Liverpool can seem a long way as **Ian Edwards (131)** of Ian and the Zodiacs discovered: "The biggest decision of our musical career was whether to branch out into the city. We had an offer from Sam Leach to play at the Iron Door. We had HP commitments and we didn't want to lose steady work at St. Luke's Hall, which paid £3 10s (£3.50) a night between five of us. But in the end we decided we'd go into Liverpool."

In 1959 Mark Peters was Liverpool's first DJ, working at the Locarno Ballroom. Mark had a group called the Cyclones and they merged with Ken Dallas and the Silhouettes. **Rod McClelland (132)** of the Silhouettes recalls, "We all liked Buddy Holly and Bobby Vee, and I was much more impressed by the Remo Four than by the Beatles. Like them, we were very good at instrumentals."

Ian and the Zodiacs were often compared to Gerry and the Pacemakers. Bass player **Charlie Flynn (133)** remarks, "The two groups were very similar in style. I didn't care for the more melodic Bobby Vee numbers which we played. I'd been playing with Kingsize Taylor and I was all for rock 'n' roll."

The Fourmost's comedy talents were never developed on record. **Dave Lovelady (134)**: "As far as I know, we were the first group to do impressions. We did them long before the Barron Knights and the Rockin' Berries. Brian O'Hara was doing impressions of Gracie Fields and Chick Murray in the Cavern days."

Brian Griffiths of the Big Three points out that the Liverpool venues, particularly Wilson Hall, could be as rough as any in Hamburg. A terrible fight broke out at the Iron Door one night. Hutch was playing the drums with one hand because he was pushing people off the stage with a chair with the other. But even so he still played loud.

Harry Prytherch (135): "By August and September 1959 – we were starting to get into dance halls and we were regularly getting £3 and £4 a night. In the early 60s, the beat clubs were starting to open like Wilson Hall in Garston. If anyone has played there and lived to tell the tale, I'd be very surprised. It was the most notorious club I have ever worked in. Wilson Hall was near the docks, and on a Saturday night, which was usually when we played there, all the black sailors used to come to the dance hall as it was the only one in the area. All the girls would be on the floor dancing and their boyfriends would be on one side of the dance hall, all the sailors would be on the other side, and round about half-past ten, everybody would be piling in and it was a free-for-all. The police used to be outside in a Landrover but they would usually wait until it was throwing-out time. One night it got so bad that we stopped playing and ran into the dressing-room. We put our shoulders behind the door until I realised that my drum-kit was still on stage. I opened the door and managed to drag some of my drums in, but it was rough."

John Duff Lowe (136): "John Lennon was certainly a rebel who didn't care what anyone thought. He would strut down the road on a Sunday to Paul's house. We would see him walking down the road, coming through the gate, strumming away, completely oblivious to anyone who might have been walking past. At one time at Wilson Hall, he had a cold and couldn't sing: there was virtually nothing coming out. A tall, drainpiped Teddy Boy took him by the scruff of the neck and told him to sing 'Mean Woman Blues', something that required a considerable amount of sound, and John was going, 'I can't do it, I can't do it'. We got through it but it could have got quite nasty."

Harry Prytherch (137): "Wilson Hall was right in the centre of Garston, opposite the baths. It was so notorious, and you knew that there would be a fight there. It was run by a lovely man called Charlie McBain and he had a whistle tied round his neck on a piece of string. He would leave the fighting for so long but when it got out of hand, he used to run to the door and blow the whistle and the policemen in the Landrover outside, waiting for it, used to come running in the dance hall and would throw everyone out. The bobbies in those days were big men, big bobbies and on a Saturday night they were looking for some exercise."

The rule of thumb is one bouncer for every 100 patrons, so a dozen bouncers for a hall that held 400 seems excessive. **Wally Hill (138)** ran Holyoake Hall in Wavertree: "When we had a riot and we had a few riots in our time, you needed bouncers – you are protecting yourselves and not just the dance hall. They took Blair Hall to pieces. Luckily by different methods we managed to hush it up as otherwise we would have been thrown out. The odd knife was thrown and we found out what a docker's hook was. There were branches pulled off trees and milk bottles, but you get acclimatised to it and it becomes a way of life. The adrenalin would flow and if we didn't have much trouble, we would think 'It's a bit boring tonight.' It was quite fun and, except for a few occasions, we were in the strongest army."

When wasn't Wally in the 'strongest army'? **Wally Hill (139)**: "Two guys were having a fight outside, so stupid me or big-headed me, whichever way you think of it, went to break it up. One of the guys goes to the pub and comes back with his mates. We had just closed the dance hall and I was walking down the stairs and they cornered me and they gave me a right going-over, but apart from that, no problems."

Adrian Barber (140): "I've forgotten where it was but we heard that two or three teams of teddy boys were going to come to this hall and kick the shit out of the bands. They picked a bad night as three real hard bands that were on that night – us, Kingsize Taylor and the Strangers. They kicked at the door, which we had barricaded, and then they came in at the windows. That was the worst tactical mistake that they could have made as it narrowed their forces down to two individuals and we were throwing empty beer bottles at them as they came through the window. The guys behind are going 'Kill'em' and the guys in front are trying to get away from the glass that's hitting them. There was blood and glass everywhere. The bands won."

Harry Prytherch (141) continues, "We did the Cabaret Club in Upper Parliament Street and it was a late night place with a group called the Delacardoes. That was the first black band we had seen, they were playing jazz and Afro-Caribbean music. I'd never seen any black groups at all, even when we played at Wilson Hall, there were no black groups. Somebody came on stage and put his hand over the microphone and told us to stop playing. He said that he was a police officer and this was a raid. The doors opened and these policemen confiscated everybody's drinks and put labels on everything. Don and Colin were still at school and we had a problem that night trying to explain what they were doing there. We were there 'til three in the morning."

John Duff Lowe (142) adds, "We used to play at Wilson Hall and a couple of working-men's clubs. I remember going to auditions and talent contests at the top of Smithdown Road, Lodge Lane possibly. We would get tuned up, go on, play six or seven bars and the organiser would say, 'Thanks, lads, that's enough. Next please.' At least half a dozen organisers missed signing the Beatles. Most of the time, we were filling in during the interval, doing a quarter of an hour or 20 minutes. Everybody had to tune up to the piano, and John Lennon hated doing that. He would have his guitar tuned perfectly when we arrived. The piano would be a semitone out, one way or the other, and they would have to start retuning, and they weren't as adept at tuning as they later became. The pianos generally had notes missing and were out of tune – they were awful."

Alan Stratton (143): "We had our own guest nights at the Iron Door and we were on with Johnny Dankworth and the pianist would not play the piano 'cause it was so bad. Tommy had to organise a coal lorry with Bruce and they went and got the piano from Tommy Hughes' house on the lorry and brought it to the Iron Door. The bass player had a little door in his bass and he would open it and the whiskey would be there. He would swig it and put it back in the cupboard."

Bobby Kaye (144): "I remember being on a club in Rainford and I was in the dressing-room which was a little pokey hole. The compère went on stage and said, 'You'll notice that there's a seat empty in the front, well, Nellie, who has been with us all these years has died. We say cheerio to Nellie as we say hello to the Crescents.' I thought, 'Are we going to die here as well?'"

Sam Leach (145): "My first big promotion was at St. George's Hall on 1 April 1960. It was the week that Bobby Darin, Duane Eddy, Clyde McPhatter and Emile Ford were appearing at the Empire opposite. I left tickets for them and asked them to come over after their show. Around midnight one of the bouncers told me that the doorman had realised I was on a fiddle. We had printed two lots of tickets with the same numbers – the capacity was 1,250 and we had printed 2,500. When I got to the door, I found that Bobby Darin, Duane Eddy, Clyde McPhatter and Emile Ford were outside in the rain. The doorman would not let them in and he had no idea who they were. I asked Bobby to sing for him and he did 'Singin' In The Rain'. Nothing. Then Emile sang 'What Do You Want To Make Those Eyes At Me For?' and he said okay and let them in. As they filed past, the old guy said, 'Emile Ford's all right but that Bobby Darin is rubbish.' We had great fun in the VIP dressing-room. Darin did a take-off of Little Richard which is one of the funniest things I've seen."

4   GERMANY CALLING

I. St. Pauli – Sex And Drugs And Rock And Roll
II. Schlager You Than Me
III. The Indra and the Kaiserkeller
IV. 27 December 1960

"We forgave the Germans and then we were friends."
(Bob Dylan, 'With God On Our Side', 1964)

I. St. Pauli – Sex And Drugs And Rock And Roll

"I had expected Hamburg to be grimmer – a sort of German Liverpool," writes Bill Bryson in his travel book, *Neither Here Nor There* (1991), but he is pleasantly surprised. I expected Hamburg to be a German Liverpool too when I went in 2001, but that would be a compliment in my eyes. I expected this because the Liverpool groups had fitted so snugly into the city, and many musicians spent several years there.

Situated on the Elbe River in northern Germany, Hamburg is Germany's second city and largest port, now a container port but still with an enormous volume of trade. The director of the Museum of Hamburg History, **Dr Ortwin Pelc (146)** told me, "The people in Hamburg feel separate from Germany and also from Saxony or Bavaria. They won't say, 'We are German, we are Bavarians.' The Hamburgers say, 'We are from Hamburg.' That is not just in the twentieth century. It has been that way for hundreds of years." Sounds familiar? Already you sense the pride that links the people of Hamburg and Liverpool.

There is a tendency for Scousers to claim that Liverpool people invented everything and in my short time in Hamburg, I noticed a similar tendency. Several people told me that the word 'hamburger' came from Hamburg, though why anyone should want to claim that beats me. It appears that the Americans saw the German immigrants frying steaks and discovered they were very tasty: hence, hamburgers were born. I'm not convinced. Frying meat involves no great thought and surely several communities were doing it at the same time. Maybe 'big fries' comes from the Grosse Freiheit.

Dr Ortwin Pelc (147) senses that Hamburgers are not like other Germans: "Maybe it is a different humour but there are a lot of parallels between England and northern Germany We have some people working here from Vienna and Austria: they don't understand our humour and we say, 'Well, there is a kind of English humour here.' We have very close connections to London. We have a ferry from here to Harwich. We have an English theatre here and we have British clubs here."

Hamburg espouses freedom, and all manner of behaviour is tolerated in its St. Pauli area. There are elegant department stores and beautiful town houses elsewhere, but St. Pauli is a working-class district down by the docks. The thoroughfare is Die Reeperbahn, which means 'Rope-making Street' and provides another link to the ships, and the Star-Club was in Die Grosse Freiheit, which means The Great Freedom. Some centuries ago, the Reeperbahn was divided from the rest of the city by a wall, and the prostitutes, gypsies and beggars would live there. On the whole, St. Pauli is a cosmopolitan area, created for the needs of sailors (and we all know what sailors want), and hence, there is nothing especially German about it.

Günter Zint (148): "The Grosse Freiheit goes back 400 years. Hamburg was Protestant and there you could be of any religious persuasion. You could attend a Catholic church, and we had six churches in St. Pauli in the seventeenth century. If you had a profession and you were not in a union, you could go to Grosse Freiheit and work as a shoemaker, for example. It was just outside Hamburg, so everything that was new or funny or anti-establishment was there."

Henry Heggen (149): "The Reeperbahn is where they let it all hang out. They made the ropes for the ships and then they established the dives, so it became the place to get drunk and be with a woman. The equivalent would be Las Vegas where prostitution is legal, but it doesn't have the tradition the Reeperbahn has. It is 100 yards to the harbour so over the centuries sailors have been going there for a good time."

Dr Ortwin Pelc (150): "The history of the Reeperbahn has so much to do with sex because it is the second biggest harbour in Europe. When the sailors came here in the Fifties and Sixties, they stayed in St. Pauli with the music, the sex shops and the sex shows. The authorities in Hamburg would like St. Pauli to have a better image and you have got a theatre which is staging *Cats* at the moment. If you are in St. Pauli at night, you will meet people that you would prefer not to meet. The harbour isn't so important for the sailors. The ships are only here for two or three hours and the sailors do not have time to go to the Reeperbahn. The clubs are more for tourists and the people in northern Germany. When the Berlin Wall fell in 1989, a lot of people came from East Germany to look at the Reeperbahn."

Oh yes, there is culture in St. Pauli. When I was walking round the Reeperbahn, I came across a museum – a museum devoted to erotica. The entrance looked supremely unerotic. What, I wondered, was in it? Inflatable dolls from the 30s, sex aids from the 19th century? If you didn't get a hard-on, could you ask for your money back?

It was seven at night and 10 girls propositioned me within a hour – if I had said yes to them all, I would have been worn out. A blonde with pigtails put my hand on her breasts to assure me that they were real. I didn't doubt it but I wondered about the rest of her as she wore a red miniskirt and fishnet stockings, which appears de rigueur for a Hamburg prossie, or indeed anywhere else for that matter. Still, I liked the idea of a free sample from a good-looking girl, but who would want to shag someone who had already been shagged six times that day? Not to mention the possibility of theft or Aids: the best time to steal your wallet must be when your trousers are round your ankles. Most of the prostitutes were good-looking: you'd have to be to compete for the business, I suppose, but a couple did look as though they had been around at the time of the Beatles. Perhaps I should have asked for an interview.

There appear to be no regulations regarding what sex shops can show in their windows and all manners of dildos and condoms are on open display. One shop's centrepiece was a gigantic, erect penis. Who on earth buys the inflatable dolls, especially the ones with three orifices: would the purchaser ever admit it and wouldn't you feel like Benny Hill as you cuddled it? I found the answer at the Tate Gallery at the Albert Dock in

2004. One artist had two sex dolls on display and I asked if he had made them himself or had simply purchased them. He bought them at a German airport, I was told, and it is an example of Found Art. I think I will become a Found Artist.

I should add that these dolls can have other uses. When Phil Spector was married to Ronnie from the Ronettes, he was concerned about her driving alone around Los Angeles, so he installed an inflatable doll in the front seat. This is taken as a sign of his madness but it might indicate his consideration. Of course, it would be far better to have darkened windows or to tell her to lock the doors, but there you are. Surely an inflatable doll in the front seat would only dissuade short-sighted muggers.

I walked past the sex shows, scores of them, some of them offering nude photographs of artists who would definitely not be appearing there – Demi Moore and Madonna, for example – but at least you might be intrigued as to what was inside. Others had such unappetizing pictures out front that you would have to be desperate to go in and even then, you might prefer to take a chance on Demi Moore. When the Liverpool groups appeared in St. Pauli, did they put photographs of Elvis Presley outside the clubs?

In Liverpool, such posters would have been riddled with comments, but there is surprisingly little graffiti in St. Pauli. I didn't feel intimidated when I was walking around. I didn't come across any beggars, nor anyone selling the German equivalent of *The Big Issue*. Walking round St. Pauli at night is less menacing than walking in the centre of Liverpool. You do have to be wary of cyclists in Hamburg though: cycles are everywhere and very often they are being ridden on the pavements.

200 years ago sailors would come to Liverpool and find the prostitutes on Lime Street (Maggie May means Maggie will) and the aptly-named Paradise Street. They are still there, though the prostitutes have moved to Liverpool 8. As well as being accosted by prostitutes on the Reeperbahn, there is a whole street of them about 100 yards away in the Herbertstrasse. Walls have been built at each end of the street to hide it from public view. You walk through the entrance and there are terraced houses on either side.

Gerry Marsden (151): "John was at the Kaiserkeller while we were at the Top Ten. They would finish at 2am like us, and we would have a drink together. John was my best pal as you know, and he said, 'Let's go down the Herbertstrasse.' This was a street of terraced houses: the windows were like shop windows and sitting behind the windows were young ladies who couldn't afford many clothes. John said, 'Let's go in.' I said, 'No.' So we knocked three times on one of the doors and this German geezer said, 'Ya vol, vot?' I said, 'Can we come in please?', and he said, '80 Deutschemarks' which was a lot of money. John had about 20 and so did I, and I said, 'Is 40 any good?' He shouted at me, something to do with sex and travel, and we offed. John said, 'Let's go in next week', and so next week, same house, knock, knock, knock, same big man. I said, 'Here's the money', and he said, 'Danke schoen.' He said, 'Back in a moment', and he came back three minutes later with the biggest woman I have ever seen. She looked like a brick shithouse. I looked at John and he looked at me, and we jumped up and ran out of the door. I said, 'What a waste of money, John: 80 Deutschemarks and we got nothing for it.' He said, 'I did. I got the shock of me bloody life.' God bless him. We were kids and we enjoyed it."

Lee Curtis (152): "You didn't have to be anybody special to go there, and the Herbertstrasse was available to anybody over 18. It had gates on the end, a little maze that you could walk through, and, because the wall was ten foot high, you couldn't look in from outside. Otherwise, it could be a cobbled street in England. They were little terraced houses, about 14 on either side, and sitting in the windows were almost any woman of any style or design that you could ever want – young girls, old girls, thin girls, fat girls, the schoolteacher, the secretary, the office type, in leather, in lace, in underwear, in suzzies and some of the most beautiful women in the world – in every window was a different type of woman. If you were interested you would tap on the window and they would open it. When you had done a deal, the window closed, the curtain was pulled across, the door opened and in you go. When you went in, you always had to buy champagne, the extras came first. There would be the waitress to serve the drinks. It was fascinating to go round the back. There was a passageway as the houses were all attached and the madams were looking after the needs of the girls."

Ian Edwards (153): "The girls of the night in the Herbertstrasse would see us if we walked down there and say 'Ah, die Beatles.' It didn't matter who it was, if you had long hair, you were a Beatle. You couldn't take a lady down there. I walked down there with my wife, to show her what it was like, and she was insulted something terrible. All it said outside was 'No servicemen and no under 18s.' There was nothing about ladies."

"I have sat in those houses," says **Lee Curtis (154)**: What, I say, offering yourself for sale? "No, I have been backstage in those houses. The girls became great friends of the bands, they loved the musicians and they would come into the Star-Club in their free time. They would invite us for drinks. The girls around the Star-Club would spoil you bloody rotten. They bought you everything – meals, drinks – if you didn't have it, you got it. If you didn't have a woman, they gave you one. They tried to make you happy." Very happy, it would seem.

In the middle of an all-purpose store, Aladdin's Cave, I came across a gangster's paradise selling guns, knives and handcuffs, opposite the kiddie's videos as it happens. I hung round for a few minutes looking at postcards but hoping I might witness some exciting purchase: just how did thugs choose their knives, but nothing happened. Isn't there a danger that a customer may say, "Yes, I'll take this gun. Don't bother to wrap it and, by the way, hand over your takings as well." The store was very close to the police station – the very police station in which Paul McCartney and Pete Best were charged with burning down the Bambo Kini. I should think the policemen are kept busy.

Günter Zint (155): "My wife has grown up in St Pauli and it is more dangerous to walk in other parts of town at night because in St. Pauli, it is business and they do not want to scare away the customers. If somebody is talking shit to her, she says, 'Okay, it costs 1,000 marks' and he runs off. (Laughs) She feels safe here but the problem is the traffic. It is such a crowded place. We have 60,000 people living on four square kilometres. It is so expensive to live or work here. In the end, I was only making enough money to pay the rent and so we moved away. When we want to go to St. Pauli, we jump on the train and we are here in 15 minutes."

Maybe the Hamburg authorities prefer the less salubrious night life being concentrated in one area. In 2002, legislation was passed that made prostitution a business like any other. Prostitutes pay taxes and are entitled to social benefits like any other worker.

Presumably they can claim any surgical enhancements against tax. I was told that the unemployment rate was high in Hamburg, but I don't know whether sex workers were included in the statistics. **Bernd Matheja (156)**: "Today the Reeperbahn is just a place for tourists. There are more music clubs and restaurants than in the Sixties and not so many sex clubs. It is the only place in Germany that looks like that, even today. Neither Berlin nor Cologne has a red mile like the Reeperbahn. The authorities have raids from time to time, but they have never wanted to close it down because they make money out of it. Many people live in the smaller streets off the Reeperbahn, and school-children walk along there in the morning."

II. Schlager You Than Me

In the mid-Thirties, bunkers were being added to the houses in Hamburg as if the authorities and the residents were expecting something to happen. **Dr Ortwin Pelc (157)**: "The Nazis prepared for war from 1935 and that was exclusive to Hamburg. They had training for bombardments in the town because Hamburg is in northern Germany: it is not far from England and they expected some retaliation. They built battleships in Hamburg because of its big harbour. It should have been obvious to anyone that Germany was preparing for war."

Sadly, it wasn't obvious until it was too late. Hamburg was one of the last German cities to be convinced by Hitler's rhetoric and it suffered badly in the bombing raids.

Intriguingly, there was a movement against Hitler, centred on music. **Ulf Krüger (158)**: "Even in World War II, you had Die Swing Jugend, the Swing Youth, the young boys who loved swing music and mostly listened in private because it wasn't allowed in public. Some of them were prepared to go the concentration camp for their love of it. Their idol was Glenn Miller."

This seemed amazing. You could be put in a concentration camp for simply liking Glenn Miller. Could this possibly be true? **Kuno Dreysse (159)**: "Don't take this too far: it was simply that Glenn Miller was the music of the enemy. It was not allowed. Today you have the internet and you can't stop any message getting through but in those days it was forbidden. You couldn't sing German schlagers on the streets of Britain, so it's the same thing." One German bandleader, Hans Carstoe, took a chance as he took the American tune, 'Joseph, Joseph, Won't You Name The Day?' and had a very successful record under a German title.

And everyone sang 'Lili Marleen'. While I was in Hamburg, I bought a CD featuring 20 different versions of 'Lili Marleen' including Lale Anderson and Marlene Dietrich as expected, but also Eric Burdon and the New Vaudeville Band. **Clive Garner (160)**: "It was originally recorded in 1939 by Lale Andersen who was a Danish born artist. It didn't become popular until 1941 when the Germans invaded Yugoslavia. Wherever the Germans went they set up a broadcasting station, specifically for broadcasting music to their troops. The radio station in Belgrade didn't have a large stock of suitable songs. They got a lot of fairly recent, older records from a shop in Vienna, and en route to Belgrade, a lot of these 78rpm records were broken, thanks to the poor state of the roads. One of the ones which survived was 'Lili Marleen', and the station was forced to play it over and over again. It became popular with their troops. Our soldiers, also tuning in to music from the German stations, heard it and it became popular on both sides of the lines. One of the most popular versions was by Marlene Dietrich, but many Germans regarded her as a traitor because she had become an American citizen. Years later, a lot of Germans objected when she was used to publicise the German airline, Lufthansa." In Berlin, I found a superb Film Museum with a special section devoted to her: nobody else was there. Nearby is Marlene-Dietrich-Platz.

When the British beat groups visited Hamburg in the Sixties, they had grown up with a background of war films and humour about the Germans. **Astrid Kirchherr (161)**: "We had this big guilt we carried around because of what our parents did in the war, and meeting English people was very special for us. They thought we were the krauts with big legs and eating sauerkraut all the time. It was unusual for teenagers from different countries to meet then and they would joke, 'We won' and we got used to that."

Lee Curtis (162): "I don't think that the war was a taboo subject but I rarely heard it mentioned. They wanted to forget it. They were genuinely ashamed of the things their parents had done, but most of it was done in fear. That young lad in *The Sound Of Music* offers a great insight into it: he joins the Hitler Youth Movement and he is frightened. He becomes a total stranger to his family and nobody trusts him. You had to do your duty and if your duty was to shoot someone, then so be it."

In the 1950s, there were jazz clubs in Hamburg. **Chris Barber (163)**: "We went to Germany and we found that a tune that we had recorded in Denmark in 1954 called 'Ice Cream' had taken the young generation by storm. We were the most popular thing since sliced bread in Germany – in Hamburg and Berlin in particular." Indeed, the fans used to call Hamburg 'Freie Und Barber Stadt' instead of 'Freie Und Hansestadt'.

By 1960, the Wall had divided Berlin. Hamburg, with a total population of around 1.7m, was the second biggest city in German and it became the most important centre for music. Several record companies had their head offices in Hamburg and made their recordings here. Schlager was the term for the popular music of the day but the term goes back further than that. **Bernd Matheja (164)**: "Schlager is an Austrian term found in a magazine around 1862 and it means 'It's nice, it's great, it's a hit.' We had Freddy Quinn, Peter Kraus, Ted Herold and Peter Alexander and they were performing lightweight material but very successfully. A lot of songs were written for them by German composers, but most of the time they sang cover versions."

The German lyrics for the UK and US hits came from the same writers. **Bernd Matheja (165)**: "It was a group of 10 to 15 people, nearly all men, all born in the 1920s, who wrote the German lyrics. It was a closed circle and they wouldn't let anybody in. They translated everything. They often changed the meaning of the song completely. They were not always interested in using the original text and if it didn't fit, they would do something else. Dave Coleman was an Englishman who worked with Casey Jones and the Governors, and when he left, he worked as a schlager singer. He did a song in German called 'Alaska Quinn' and it was Bob Dylan's 'The Mighty Quinn'. The German song is about a park you can walk to and there is somebody running round clad like an Eskimo. If Bob Dylan had heard a re-translation, I think he would have killed him."

Considering their wild lifestyle in Hamburg, I am surprised that John and Paul never allude to it in any of their songs – you'd have thought that it would have led to a succession of songs. Surprisingly, I couldn't find many songs about Hamburg. Lale Andersen sang 'Unter Der Roten (Under The Red Lantern At St Pauli)', which is about a soldier bidding his girlfriend goodbye and the red light is not emphasised. The German actor, Hans Albers, had some success in the Thirties with 'Auf Der Reeperbahn (On The Reeperbahn At Half Past Midnight)', which was performed by many other artists. Freddy Quinn, who was marketed as 'the singing sailor', recorded a schlager single in 1962, 'Homesick For St. Pauli', a curious reversal as most sailors would be visiting St. Pauli.

Ulf Krüger (166): "I can appreciate why schlager was popular. That generation had lost the war and they wanted tunes that looked forward to better times. Going to Italy for your holidays was, for example, better times – sitting in the sun, having a nice drink, swimming and so on. There are a lot of German songs about Italy, supplying people with dreams."

Frank Dostal (167): "Schlager did not have anything to with reality: it was all, how about you and me getting together in Hawaii. The songs were about the mountains, the beauty of nature and going very far away. It was all so corny and we would never have dreamt of singing it when we were in the Rattles."

Although James Last and his Orchestra play schlager to this day, generally it is made by singers with a small group. An example of reverse schlager, if you like, would be Elvis Presley singing in German in 'Wooden Heart'. **Tommy Kent (168)**: "I am a schlager singer, yes. You sing for all the people, for families, and it is light music, middle of the road. My name is Guntram Kuhbeck but in 1959 the record company said that it was not a good name for a singer. Bert Kaempfert said, 'I think Tommy is good for you, you look like a Tommy. Take these singles and go to your hotel and pick one to sing.' There were about 100 records and I went through them and found 'Susie Darlin'' by Robin Luke. We tried it the next day and it was a big success. Bert Kaempfert was not famous at the time but he made 'Susie Darlin'' with me and it sold a million. I was selling in Germany, Switzerland and Luxembourg and I was a big star in Austria. I was No. l there for six weeks with 'Alle Nachte (All Night)'. Bert became a big name producer and I was a star. My next song was Elvis Presley's 'I Need Your Love Tonight'. It was a big success in Germany but not as big as 'Susie Darlin''. Then 'Personality' and both of them sold 250,000. I made about ten records with Bert Kaempfert but I could never repeat the success of 'Susie Darlin''. The sales went down to 100,000 and then when they were only 30,000, the record company said, 'That's enough.' (Laughs)"

Bernd Matheja (169): "You have to learn English in school. I was nine years old when I started English and then later on French. I always listened to English records and I always wanted to understand what they were singing and so, yes, I tried and tried and practised. The young people did not like schlager: they wanted the English and American beat and rock'n'roll. They did not know the words so they were interested in learning English. German lyrics for English songs are never satisfactory because the words are longer in German. Look at a book. If a chapter in the English original is four pages, it will be five in the German translation. It is always longer."

"Hideaways"—A Group With Promise

AT the Winter Gardens "Meet the Beat" dance on Saturday were the Hideaways, one of the most promising rhythm and blues groups in Liverpool.

The group drew plenty of screams from the girls in the Winter Gardens crowd.

With the group were Ray McFall, owner of the Cavern Club, and Bob Wooler, compere of the club, who had come along to listen to the group. Ray told me that he sees a lot of potential in the group, and that they have improved tremendously in recent months.

I was suprised to learn that the Hideaways have only been formed for five months, and after only two months they were signed by the Cavern Agency.

Members of the group are: Ozzie (lead guitar, vocals), of Childwall; John (drums, vocals); Dave (bass guitar, vocals), of Huyton; Frank (rhythm guitar), of Anfield; Judd himself plays harmonica, tenor sax, piano and sings. He comes from Fazackerley.

They refuse to disclose their sur-names.

They have played on the same bill as John Lee Hooker, Memphis Slim and Alex Harvey, and Judd has sat in with Alexis Korner. Judd's favourite harmonica players include Sonny Terry, Cyril Davies and the harmonica player in the Sheffields. The rest of the group likes "most blues men."

"We were talking," said Judd, "to Brian Jones and Mick Jagger, of the Rolling Stones. They said they were trying to put over more blues to the audiences . . . to go further out, Manfred Mann is doing the same."

"Blues is coming—and it's going to be very big," chipped in Frank.

"Very big," continued Judd. "Mind you, I thought Liverpool audiences were poor till we played out of town. Then I realised how good they were for rhythm and blues. In some places they just won't take it, you know what I mean? Manfred Mann can get away with it—that's about all. When we played in Scot-land the other groups were doing "Do Wa, Diddy Diddy" about three times in two hours. Man!"

"We did go down well in Scotland, though," said Ozzie. "The audiences are good."

Ozzie said that rhythm and blues was bigger in the North of England than down South. Judd agreed.

"Everyone says that the London scene is fantastic," continued Judd. "Believe me, it isn't."

"We were talking to Alexis Korner at Hope Hall, and he told us just how good London is. He says that there's real feeling for the blues up North—that's why he's come up here."

So there are the Hideaways. Five 17-year-olds caught up in a web of blues. To improve; to be accepted; or perhaps to be rejected. But quite excited abouyt it all—and quite exciting too.

From the Crosby Herald, September 11th, 1964

**MARK PETERS
and THE SILHOUETTES**

Tommy Quickly

THE ESCORTS

Representation : Jim Godbolt Agency
145 Wardour Street, London, W.1
Regent 8321-2

Management : Jim Ireland
Mardi-Gras, Mount Pleasant, Liverpool 3
Royal 4448-3401

*Terry Sylvester
John Kinrade*

*Mike Gregory
Pete Clarke*

Roy Orbison (centre) with (l-r) Les Braid, Norman Kuhlke, Ray Ennis, Ralph Ellis

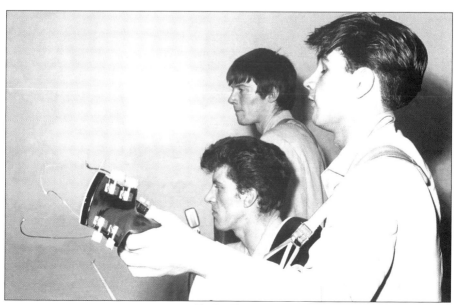

The Big Three ~
This line-up features Johnny Hutch, Johnny Gustafson and Brian Griffiths, 1962

Pete Best at The Beatles Convention, 1994
(photo by Steve Hale)

Cass & The Cassanovas
(l-r) ~ Adrian Barber, Brian Casser,
Johnny Gustafson
with Johnny Hutchinson at the back

Kingsize Taylor & The Dominoes, circa. 1961
(l-r) ~ Sam Hardy, Kingsize, Bobby Thompson, Dave Lovelady

The Liverbirds, 1964

The Mersey Four
(l-r) ~ Eric Wright, Ray Marshall,
Alex Paton, Russell Peart

The Tabs ~ winners of the Liverpool Show talent contest, 1964,
lead singer Dave Crosby, 4th from left

Bill and Virginia Harry

*Bill Haley with Les Chadwick, Les Maguire and Gerry Marsden of The Pacemakers
at the Star Club, Hamburg, 1962*

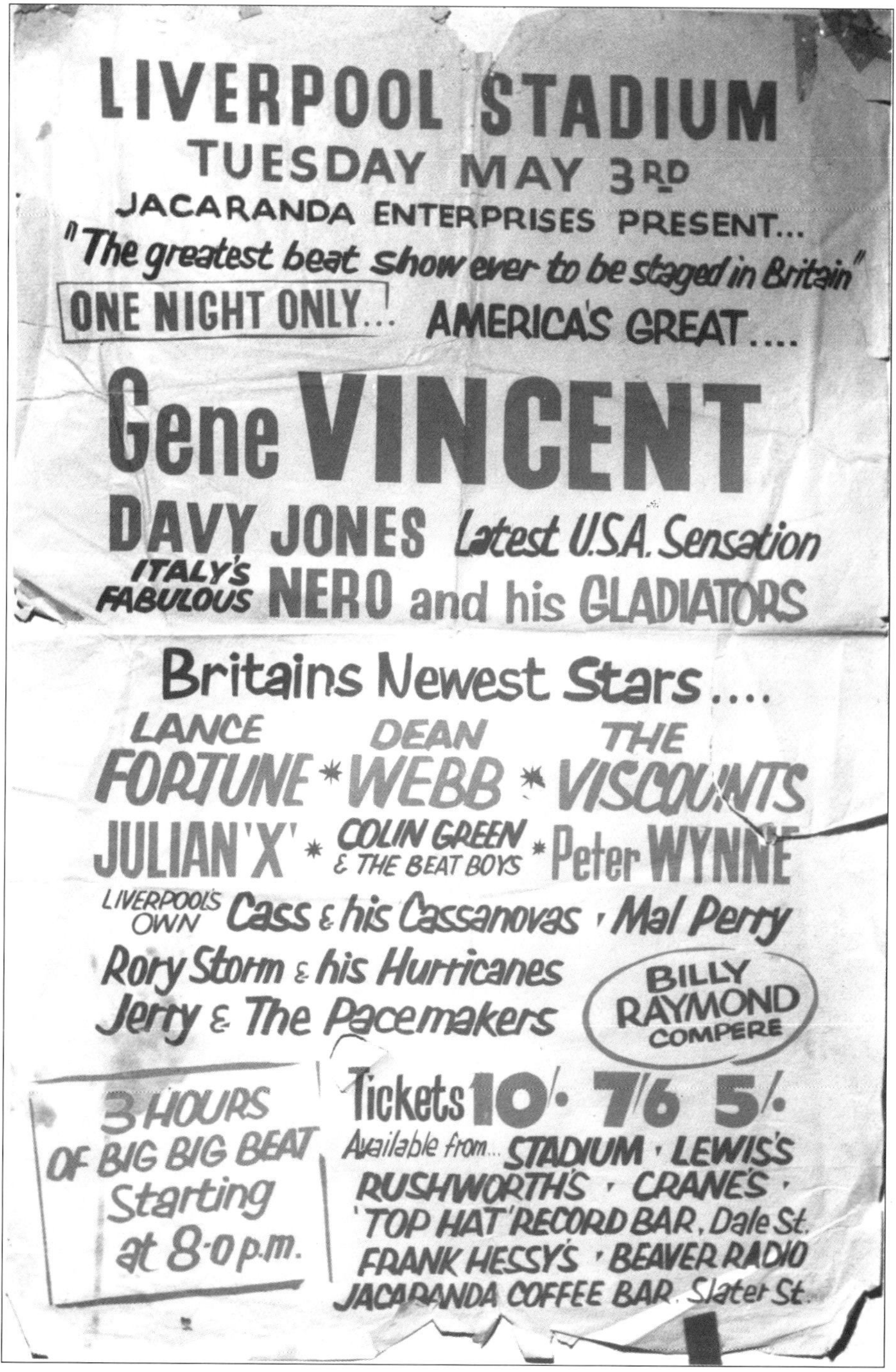

Poster from 1960

Sheet Music

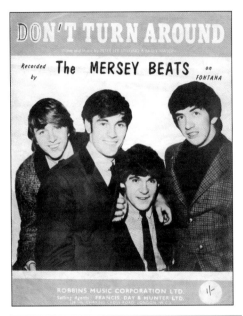

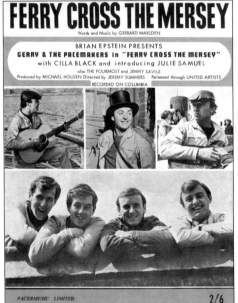

As a special offer to our regular patrons this ticket will admit 2 for 7/6 (Pay at door) to

Operation Big Beat 6th

Tower Ballroom, New Brighton
Friday, October 19th, 1962
7-30 p.m. - 1 a.m.

10 Groups — Starring — 10 Groups
Their first appearance following an extensive tour of Europe

Johnny Sandon
with the fabulous Remo Four

The Undertakers

Rory Storm and The Hurricanes

Billy Kramer with The Coasters

The Strangers - The Mersey Beats
plus four other genuine top groups
Also the grand finals of The all Merseyside
Jive and Twist Championship—£10 in Prizes

Licensed Bar until 12-15 a.m.
LATE TRANSPORT ARRANGED
WIRRAL
all areas Wallasey, B'head, Ellesmere Port,
Brombro'., Bebington, Heswall, Neston, Moreton,
West Kirby, Hoylake, Leasowe etc.
LIVERPOOL — all areas
Coaches leave St. John's Lane-Lime Street
7-30 - 8-30 p.m.

Please don't waste this—
your friend may want one

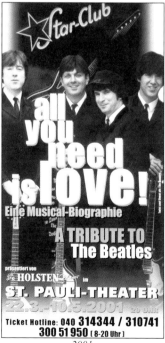

2001
A Beatles Tribute Show
'The Beatles' return to St. Paul's

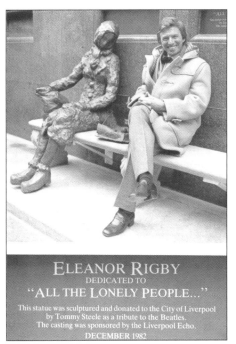

ELEANOR RIGBY
DEDICATED TO
"ALL THE LONELY PEOPLE..."

This statue was sculptured and donated to the City of Liverpool
by Tommy Steele as a tribute to the Beatles.
The casting was sponsored by the Liverpool Echo.
DECEMBER 1982

*Tommy Steele poses beside his
statue of Eleanor Rigby*

*The infamous
trouser-splitting tour*

Germany welcomes The Beatles

1962

Liverpool Echo, May 1962

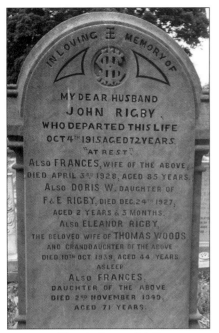

(Photo by Spencer Leigh)

(Photo by Spencer Leigh)

The Quarrymen excavated in the 21st Century
(Rod Davis, Len Garry, Eric Griffiths, Pete Shotton)
(Photo by Spencer Leigh)

Howie Casey, 2002
(Photo by Spencer Leigh)

Kingsize Taylor at the Cavern Club, April 2004
(Photo by Ron Ellis)

The Beatles
(l-r) ~ George Harrison, Pete Best, Paul McCartney, John Lennon at The Cavern, 1962

A rare photo of Southport's top group, Rhythm & Blues Inc.
(l-r) ~ Barry Womersley, Pete Kelly, John McCaffery, Alan Menzies

*Pete James and Maria Woods
performing as The Upset*

*Wump and His Werbles
Singer: Steve Day, Drummer: John Cochrane*

*Bernard Jewry (aka Shane Fenton and Alvin Stardust) marries Iris Caldwell on August 30th, 1964.
Her brother, Rory Storm stands next to Duffy Power and Johnny Guitar*

*George Harrison offering sartorial advice to Billy J. Kramer backstage at
The Liverpool Empire, December 1963. (Photo by Ron Ellis)*

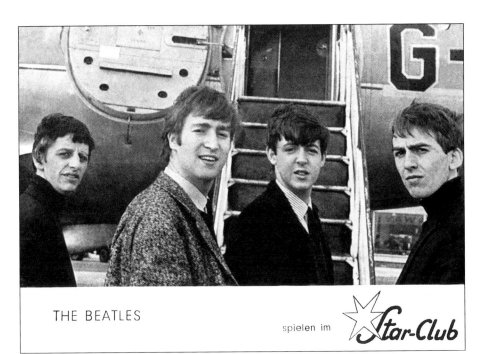

Promotion photo for The Star Club, Hamburg, January 1963

Kuno Dreysse (170): "English is the language for popular music, it doesn't matter which period it is – you can go back to the 20s, to the swing era or the blues and you will find English is the language. I am a German but I don't like German singing as much as English singing. I used to be in a band in the Sixties as well and we would sing in English. We loved singing harmonies like the Hollies."

This chapter is going to look at the significance of Hamburg. Is **Bill Harry (171)** right when he says: "Hamburg's importance has been exaggerated by nearly every author. Liverpool is far more important. When the Beatles went over to Hamburg, there was the Indra, the Kaiserkeller and then the Top Ten. It wasn't until 1962 that the Star-Club opened. There were only two venues open at the same time. In Liverpool you had every kind of venue, town halls, village halls, swimming baths, ice rinks, cellar clubs, and it was a thriving scene with 400 groups. In Hamburg, you didn't have anything. We had watch committees so Liverpool was dead on Sundays. Strip clubs were not allowed and there was no drinking after ten o'clock. The groups loved Hamburg because booze was available 24 hours a day and it was completely uninhibited. This is why they have so many stories about Hamburg, but the music scene was virtually nothing."

Kuno Dreysse (172): "I am not so big-headed as to call the Liverpool sound the Hamburg sound but all the Liverpool bands came here to work hard and find their style. The Beatles changed when they came to Hamburg, but what really happened? They got older. If you are 16, 17 or 18 years old, every year is a long time. They came with their guitars and they had to work every night. The Beatles played eight hours a night seven days a week. If you have some talent, then you must get better. If not, then you have to finish your musical career. The Beatles were good and they found themselves in the red light district where they could get drugs, where they could get girls, where they could get anything they wanted, so what did they do? They took their chance and they become world stars."

III. The Indra and the Kaiserkeller

Welcome to an incredible cast of characters. The owners and managers of the Hamburg beat clubs had wonderfully onomatopoeic names – Bruno Koschmider, Manfred Weissleder, Horst Fascher. You're scared before you've even met them.

In 1950 Bruno Koschmider, who was born in 1926, had opened a strip club, The Indra, at Grosse Freiheit 64. It was a small club, much smaller than the Cavern, with a bar and with tables around a raised stage. The stage was higher than usual at two feet so that the patrons could get a better view of the strippers.

In October 1959 Koschmider opened the much larger Kaiserkeller, literally 'King Cellar', at Grosse Freiheit 36. This was a cabaret club so the stage was only 18 inches high. The club could take 700 patrons and it was designed for sailors as the décor was nautical and the seats were like rowing boats. The bouncers were led by another guy with a splendid name, Willy Limper, although it was presumably the victims who were the limpers.

One of Allan Williams's ventures was to open Liverpool's first strip club. Attention from the police meant that the club did not last long, but it was a start and Allan thought he would see how things were properly (or improperly) done in Hamburg. It was a sea-port too and, more to the point, the St. Pauli area had a notorious reputation. While there, Allan Williams thought he would sell the Liverpool groups to Bruno Koschmider. **Allan Williams (173)**: "Koschmider was a horror, he was a gay, deformed homosexual and a trapeze artist who had broken his leg in a fall which left him with a permanent limp. The first time I encountered him was when I went over with Lord Woodbine to discuss the possibilities of getting work for Liverpool groups. I went to the Kaiserkeller because I heard rock'n'roll music being played by an awful German band and, in the interval, everybody danced to Cliff Richard's records. One of the waiters took me in to meet Herr Koschmider and while I was doing my sales pitch for Liverpool groups, somebody shouted, 'There's a fight,' and I could see this feller on the marble floor. Herr Koschmider gets a truncheon out and beats the feller to a pulp. That's the type of personality he had."

Allan Williams convinced Koschmider of the merits of British music, but Koschmider signed a London band led by Tony Sheridan from Norwich. Sheridan, a fine but maverick performer, had had some success in the UK appearing on the ATV show, *Oh Boy!*, but his manager, Larry Parnes, found him unreliable. He went to Hamburg with his group, the Jets. **Tony Sheridan (174)**: "There was nothing when we got there. The aftermath of Adolf Hitler was a big void and there was no German musical scene to speak of. We shocked everybody with our music and they couldn't believe it. Lots of people flocked in to see us and it was wonderful."

Being in an uninhibited area like St. Pauli suited Sheridan fine, but, with little thought to the consequences, he transferred to a new club, the Top Ten, which was opened by Peter Eckhorn at Reeperbahn 136, in July 1960. This was a large cabaret club that could take 1,000 patrons. Eckhorn was only 21, but he was supported by his gangland family and as his minders were tougher than Koschmider's, he did not fear retaliation. Instead, Koschmider came to London to find more British acts.

Meanwhile, Allan Williams had arranged some auditions in Liverpool for backing musicians for Larry Parnes' acts, musicians who would be more reliable than Sheridan. As a result, the Beatles did a short tour in Scotland with Johnny Gentle, and Cass and the Cassanovas with Duffy Power. Derry and the Seniors were expected to back Dickie Pride (another splendid name and chosen by Larry Parnes and Russ Conway – say no more!) on a summer season in Blackpool, but it fell through. **Howie Casey (175)** of Derry and the Seniors: "Larry Parnes was looking for cheap Liverpool bands to back his stars. We got the gig to back Dickie Pride, but it was cancelled at the last minute. Allan Williams said he would drive us to London and we could perform at the Two I's coffee-bar instead. We followed an instrumental band and Derry went into his wild thing. Bruno Koschmider was in the audience and he told Allan he was looking for a band for the Kaiserkeller to replace Tony Sheridan, who had gone to the Top Ten."

There is a possibility, although he would never admit it, that Allan Williams never went to Hamburg until he went with the Beatles in August 1960. Brian Casser of Cass and the Cassanovas might have set up the contacts with Bruno Koschmider, but, not having his own telephone, he was using the one at the Jacaranda. Allan Williams may have known of this and taken over. Unfortunately, for reasons unconnected with beat music, Brian Casser has had nothing to do with the scene for years and has been keeping the lowest low profiles. In other words, I haven't a clue where he is. A great pity as it would be intriguing to interview him about this aspect of the Hamburg story.

Derry and the Seniors had a horrendous train journey to Hamburg. Neither Williams nor Koschmider provided work permits, but they managed to bluff their way into the country. **Howie Casey (176)** remembers it vividly: "In the doorway of the Kaiserkeller was a huge notice painted in all sorts of colours. It had 'The Seniors' in big letters and underneath '*mit der Neger Sänger Derry*.' We were looking at it, thinking it was great, when Derry pipes up from the back. 'Hey, la,' he says, 'what's all this about a Nigger singer?' I knew *Neger* meant Negro in German, so I assured him that they weren't having a go. Bruno Koschmider showed us round. It was a huge club, bigger than anything we'd seen in Liverpool, beautiful décor and a big stage. We asked about our accommodation and were shown two little rooms which contained only two single beds, a couch and a few chairs. There was no bedding and we used coats for blankets. I found a huge Union Jack to cover myself with and so I used to lie in state every night. We were paid £16 a week each, which wasn't bad as my dad was only earning that much. We had to feed ourselves and clean ourselves, although we didn't worry too much about that, but our clothes had to be clean. Drinks and cigarettes are important and we spent money on girls to show off. Before the end of each week we were totally broke and were living on scraps, and, of course, there were doctors' bills for certain illnesses."

Derry and the Seniors enjoyed Hamburg's night life. **Howie Casey (177)**: "Rory Storm was taking over from us at the Kaiserkeller. We wanted to stay and Derry got a job with a German dixieland band, would you believe. The American navy was coming to Hamburg on a goodwill visit, a huge aircraft carrier and a few battleships, so someone made contact with the really tatty Casanova Bar on the Reeperbahn. This was a strip joint with little booths where people did dodgy things to one another. We played background music and the strippers would have particular songs to strip to. Every one of them wanted 'It's Now Or Never'. We would play quietly in the background, and there was a stage with a chair that the strippers stood on to get on it. The Americans would be giving them drinks, and they would be pissed sometimes and go arse over tit. They were charged exorbitant prices, but once the fleet left port, we were out of work again. I had two saxes with me and one was an expensive baritone sax that I had bought on hire purchase when I was in the army. A pawnshop on the Reeperbahn asked me to play it to prove it was mine and I sold it for the equivalent of £17. It was worth £400 so some lucky German got a cheap baritone. I kick myself for that."

Koschmider was having such success at the Kaiserkeller that he decided to have beat music at his other club at the dark end of the Grosse Freiheit, the Indra. Allan Williams was asked to send over more groups, but most musicians had day jobs. Not the Beatles however. There was a drawback – they lacked a permanent drummer – so **Pete Best (178)** was invited to join. "My mother took a phone call from Paul McCartney. He said that they'd had an offer to go to Germany and needed a drummer. George Harrison had seen me play and knew that I had a drum kit. He thought I might be interested in joining. I went down to Allan Williams' house and auditioned. Two days later, I was a Beatle."

Geoff Hogarth (179): "The Iron Door was a drinking club then and the customers wanted us to be open on Sunday afternoons. I said okay but we would try something different. I thought about the cha cha cha but Harry Ormshire booked Johnny and the Moondogs. They didn't sound bad but they weren't musically adept. They said to Harry, 'Don't introduce us as the Moondogs: we are the Silver Beatles now' and they had sprayed some silver on their clothes. Stu Sutcliffe had a floppy cowboy hat and I asked him about some more bookings. He said, 'There's no point. We're going to Hamburg on Thursday.' I didn't care for John Lennon, who was definitely the leader. He would be giving me abuse but that's the way he was. He didn't change when he was famous."

The long hours on stage gave the Beatles the opportunity to experiment. They developed a raucous style and made a big impact. They had never met a musician like **Tony Sheridan (180)**: "If you play 'Blue Suede Shoes' 2,000 times, you have got to find ways to do it differently and this is when innovation happens – you put in sevenths, and ninths and elevenths. That is what Hamburg can do for you – you become something else, but I believe that the only way to be is spontaneous. All those guys who plan their shows are not being creative. Of course, I had bad nights, but there were nights when I turned myself on and turned everybody else on."

Allan Williams (181): "It was not Liverpool that made the Beatles, but Hamburg. Bob Wooler used to say to me, 'Okay, smart arse, if it did that for the Beatles, why didn't it do it for Gerry and the Pacemakers and Howie Casey and Rory Storm and all the other groups?', but they were established acts before they went. The Beatles were a bum group before they went. They only had done a few gigs in Liverpool and they hadn't got their act together, and that is where they learnt the trade. Howie Casey sent me a letter when I told him I was sending the Beatles over. He said, 'Allan, you've got a good thing going over here. If you send that bum group, the Beatles, you're going to louse it up.' I had enough confidence in the Beatles to know that they were good enough, and history has proved me right. They went for three months which was extended for another two, so they were out of Liverpool for five months, working outrageous hours seven nights a week. That would either make or break a group and it made the Beatles."

Howie Casey (182): "I knew all the other bands at the Larry Parnes auditions – Cass and the Cassanovas, Rory Storm and so on. I had never seen the Beatles before and they borrowed Johnny Hutch and he was one of the great drummers of the time. He sat in with them, but I wasn't impressed and I wasn't the only one. When I was at the Kaiserkeller, Allan Williams sent me a letter saying he was going to send over the Beatles to play in the Indra, which was a little bar up the road. I wrote back immediately to say, 'Don't send the Beatles, you will ruin the scene. Send Rory Storm instead.' The Beatles arrived and we went to see them on their opening night as they started earlier than us and they finished earlier at 11. They kicked off and my jaw went to the floor. There was such a difference from what I had seen at the auditions and we were buddies from that point on. They were jealous that we were playing in this huge club and it was a proper rock club too and they would come down and jam. We had some great nights."

Hans Olof Gottfridsson (183): "It was a tough job. You can see from their letters home that they constantly had problems with their voices. The standard for performing for so long was set by the Jets. They were told to play three hours and have a break but they wanted to play for one hour and have a break. The Jets were professional musicians who were used to performing. The Beatles had just left school. It must have been murder for them."

The German youths were impressed, notably **Herbert Hildebrand (184)**, who was to form the Rattles: "In 1960 the Beatles appeared at the Indra and we were street boys from the red light area, so we became close friends and we showed them around and we asked them to get us records by Chuck Berry, Jerry Lee Lewis and Little Richard. They encouraged us to perform and when we appeared at the Star-Club it was a big success."

Jurgen Vollmer (185) was an art student, who took that famous photograph of John Lennon in a St. Pauli doorway: "It wasn't so much the Beatles: it was the whole atmosphere in that district. It was a very rough and tough area where only rockers went. I had just finished art school and types like us wouldn't go to those places. When we went, we were so fascinated by the atmosphere of it and by the Beatles who were rockers themselves. They looked like the audience with their leather jackets and their hair, the pompadour, Elvis-style, and their ducktails. They attracted us because they were so menacing-looking, and they were something that we hadn't seen before. It was the look that inspired me: John's cool, arrogant, above-it-all rocker look. He isn't that way, but he projected that image. Marlon Brando in *The Wild One*, a popular movie at that time, had that image, and John perfected that image, but he wasn't at all like he looked. The rockers were provoked very easily and for someone with my arty look, it was dangerous. Other friends of mine who had the same look were beaten up on different occasions, but for some reason I escaped that."

Ulf Krüger (186): "When the Beatles arrived here, they wore their little jackets, drainpipe trousers and winklepickers and then came the influence of Astrid Kirchherr and her gang, who wore black leather. It's cool. Astrid wore leather first and then Klaus Voormann wore a leather suit that Astrid had specially made for him. The Beatles couldn't afford a thing like that so they bought cheaper stuff on the Reeperbahn."

Astrid Kirchherr (187): "Our philosophy then, and remember we were only little kids, was wearing black clothes and going around looking moody. We knew of Sartre and we were inspired by all the French singers and writers as that was the closest we could get. England was far away and America was out of the question. We dressed like the French existentialists. We wanted to be different and we wanted to look cool, although we didn't use that word then."

Hans Olof Gottfridsson (188): "Paul made more in Hamburg than his father did or his teachers at school and they bought new clothes and new instruments, but when you're a teenager, money tends to roll away fast. They got 35DM a week and this was more than an average German worker. They earned more in Hamburg than they did in England and they played every night in Hamburg, something they did not do in Britain.

Before they went to Hamburg, they were looking for jobs. They had some gigs at the Grosvenor Ballroom, but they had problems getting work. Going to Hamburg was a big break for them."

Derry and the Seniors were replaced by Rory Storm and the Hurricanes at the Kaiserkeller. **Johnny Guitar (189)** recalled, "Allan Williams sent us out and Bruno Koschmider booked the Beatles into the Kaiserkeller with us. It was a twelve-hour stretch split between two groups. Each group did an hour and a half on, an hour and a half off. When they give you a contract in Germany, you've got to stick to it. If you deviate in any way, they take away your work permit. If Koschmider says that a five-piece group is to appear on stage, then a five-piece group must appear. It doesn't matter that one might be a singer and doesn't sing all night. Koschmider would rush up and say, 'Where is the fifth man?' The singer might have gone to the toilet but he'd tell us to get him back."

The residents complained of noise at the Indra and even though Koschmider shut it early, the authorities told him it must revert to being a strip club! He decided to present Rory Storm and the Hurricanes with the Beatles every night at the Kaiserkeller. **Johnny Guitar (190)** remembered some collusion between the Hurricanes and the Beatles. "Germans like you to *mach schau*, which means 'stamp your feet and clap'. The rickety stage was very dangerous, so we came to an arrangement with the Beatles that we'd wreck it. First, they'd go on and stamp their feet and then we'd go on and jump up and down. Koschmider would say, 'Very good, boys, you *mach* good *schau*.' Little did he realise that this was a deliberate effort to destroy the stage. The club was packed one Saturday night when Rory got on top of the piano for 'Whole Lotta Shakin' Goin' On' and the whole stage collapsed. The orange boxes supporting the planks couldn't take the strain. Koschmider went berserk and dismissed Rory for breach of contract. Rory was wandering about Hamburg like a waif because he had no money. At that time, the Beatles were sleeping in a room by the side entrance to a cinema and we were living in the luxury of the seaman's mission down by the docks."

Günter Zint (191): "Bruno Koschmider did not like to spend much money and the stage was very old. The microphone stands and the drums sometimes fell off the stage because it was so rotten. One night they said, 'Now we make such hard music and we stamp with our feet on the stage and we will break it.' They did that, and that, I think, was the night that the beat was born."

Brian Griffiths (192): "One Saturday morning at about eight o'clock we were sitting in a bar after we'd been paid at the Kaiserkellar. A guy came by with a wheelbarrow and dumped a pile of old clothes in the street. We were pretty high so Lennon, myself and Derry Wilkie dressed up and went jigging around the streets. The Germans thought we were weird with the rock'n'roll and now they thought we were crazy."

There was trouble after the Beatles had jammed with Tony Sheridan at the Top Ten. When Peter Eckhorn asked them to leave Koschmider and join him, Koschmider was furious. **Allan Williams (193)**: "When the Beatles decided that they were not going to play for Koschmider and go to a competitor, he turned nasty and tried to get them into jail. He said that they had set fire to the cinema and that they didn't have permits but fortunately for me, he was supposed to get the permits. That's how we got into

Germany the second time. The contract said that they could not perform within 70 miles of Hamburg within six months, and because he didn't give me my commission, didn't put the lads in decent accommodation and never got them work permits, the German Embassy gave me the work permits. It was harder to get them into Germany the second time because they had been deported the first."

Well, it sounds as though the embassies were kept busy. **Howie Casey (194)**: "Allan Williams and Bruno Koschmider hadn't got us work permits. Allan said, 'Just tell them you're tourists' and when Peter Eckhorn offered us work at the Top Ten, he told us to go to the Embassy and get them. They took our passports off us and we were repatriated. We had the shame of being skint and dishevelled, dirty and tired and getting this piece of paper in place of passports. We had no money for food and we were treated like scum on the way back. When we did get back to Liverpool, we were seen as returning heroes. It sorted the group out – the ones who said, 'Bugger that, I'm not doing that again' and the ones who wanted to be musicians and would keep on being ripped off."

Still, even if the Beatles had not been allowed back, there were plenty of other groups to choose from. They were now prepared to give up their day jobs. **Allan Williams (195)**: "The first group that went over was Howie Casey's and when they came back and told everybody what Hamburg was like, they all wanted to go over there. I was the kingpin, 'Get us over to Hamburg, Allan.' Gerry Marsden kept calling me in the Jacaranda and asking me if Hamburg had been fixed up."

IV. 27 December 1960

The Beatles returned early from Hamburg in December 1960, but it should not have been a problem. Allan Williams had opened his own Top Ten club in Liverpool. He had asked Bob Wooler, a railway employee, to give up his job and become the full-time manager and organiser. **Allan Williams (196)**: "The first group who played at my Top Ten club was Howie Casey and the Seniors and they blew the place apart. The only snag was that it was in a tough area known as the Four Squares and the locals said it was their club. I didn't want that, and I don't know how it would have developed, whether they would have grown weary of it. The premises were fantastic. It was like a barn with big thick wooden beams and we had to write notices, 'Please mind your head'."

Bob Wooler (197): "It was in 1960 that I decided to go pro. I would say to my fellow clerks on the railway, 'This is not my station in life', and so on, and they would say, 'Wooler's gone off the rails.' All very funny, but they couldn't believe I would pack in my job for the precarious business of disc-jockeying. I was given a job at the Top Ten club in the roughest area in Liverpool. Allan Williams, who launched the club in Soho Street, took the name from a similar establishment in Hamburg. It lasted five days and then someone got careless with the Bryant and May's. At one Beatles Convention, I said it was a torching job and I glared at Allan. He said, 'What are you looking at me for?' I was to learn about incinerations as that was not the only place in Liverpool to go up in smoke." Indeed not, I was in a pub with a Merseybeat group a few years back and one of them said to me, "That's Tommy the Torch. He's done more damage to Liverpool than Adolf Hitler." However, in this instance, although the insurance company was suspicious and took Allan Williams to court, the allegation was not proved.

Allan Williams (198): "I had absolutely no reason to burn down the club and it loused up my plans. I had even selected Bob Wooler as the right person to run it. I had persuaded him to give up his day job, and five days later the poor feller was out of work. History would have been altered if the Top Ten had not caught fire. That would have been my Cavern club. The Cavern was only doing jazz at the time and there wasn't a venue in the centre doing rock'n'roll. Still, I opened the Blue Angel and that was a luxurious night club." Strangely perhaps, I find myself agreeing with Allan Williams. He had no reason to burn down the place.

Bob Wooler (199): "Allan was preoccupied with the demise of his Top Ten club and the opening of his new club, the Blue Angel, which wasn't for beat music. The Beatles would have played the Top Ten on their return but, in the event, they had come back early with no work on offer. Allan said to me, 'You get them work. Try Brian Kelly. He has a string of dance halls and you have some connections with him.' The Beatles asked me about bookings and they didn't want to play Allan's coffee-bar, the Jacaranda. I agreed with them – it was a former coal cellar and had no stage, no lights and no microphones. It was totally unsuitable for showcasing a group. It was also very small, and I doubt if you could get 50 people in there. On the other hand, Litherland Town Hall, Lathom Hall, Aintree Institute and Hambleton Hall had stages and there could be some impact in sweeping the curtains open and saying, 'Here they are, the Beatles.' Presentation is very important."

A turning point in the Beatles' career was an appearance at Litherland Town Hall, on 27 December 1960. **Bob Wooler (200)** continues: "You can write your entry for *Who's Who* and Paul McCartney has written, 'Made first important appearance as the Beatles at Litherland Town Hall near Liverpool in December 1960.' Mona Best had given them some work at the Casbah but she couldn't sustain them with a residency and I am pleased to say that I got them onto Brian Kelly's circuit. The first booking was on 27 December 1960 when they were added to the bill of a BeeKay (Brian Kelly) dance. Brian Kelly nearly collapsed when I asked for £8 because he was a tight-wad, but most of the promoters were. He offered me £4 and we compromised on £6, which is a £1 a man, five Beatles, and £1 for the driver. I didn't take my 10 per cent."

Tony Bramwell (201): "George Harrison worked as a butcher's delivery boy in Hunts Cross on Saturday. He delivered our meat and he used to borrow our records as I had two older brothers who had a fair collection of rock'n'roll. Gerry Marsden went out with Pauline, who lived about four houses away and to get into the dances, I would carry Gerry's guitar for him. I got on the 81 bus one day to go to Litherland Town Hall and I saw George Harrison with his guitar. He said, 'We're playing Litherland Town Hall' and I said, 'Can I carry your guitar so I can get in for free?' He said, 'Sure' and when I got there and saw 'Direct from Hamburg – The Beatles', I said, 'You're not from Hamburg' and he said, 'Of course not. It's a cock-up in the adverts.' I carried George's guitar around until Neil Aspinall got his van. When I saw them, I recognised John because he was a teddy boy – he had set fire to the roof of our local hall once and I kept away from him. I found that the Beatles were playing the stuff that I had lent to George."

Bob Wooler (202): "They were billed as 'Direct From Hamburg' but too much has been made of this. There wasn't any deceit in trying to present them as a German group, although I did mention they'd been playing in Hamburg when I announced them. It was an amazing night. When I did hear the Beatles, I was fab-ergasted. Other groups were playing what was in the charts – they felt reassured that way. The Beatles liked obscure R&B stuff. They were only on stage for 30 minutes, but they put everything into their performance and rocked the joint."

Although there was by now a healthy beat scene on Merseyside, most groups had a matching-tie-and-handkerchief approach and played versions of the pop hits of the day. Opening the show was Kingsize Taylor and the Dominoes. **John Kennedy (203)** sang with them. "We used to open and close those shows. We'd do our spot and then go to the pub for a few pints. We never got to the pub that night. We'd just reached the door when the Beatles started off and that was it. We stayed there all night and watched them. They were brilliant. There was something raw and animal about them."

Another Domino, **Bobby Thomson (204)**, also remembers that night. "The place went bananas. I've never seen a reaction like it. You could see that they were going to be big and I wanted them to be big. It was a funny feeling for blokes to want that. You can understand hero worship from girls, but the blokes felt the same. Everybody loved them."

Joe Fagin (205): "My first sight of the Beatles when they came back from Germany amazed me. Prior to going, they were just another band but now they had a totally different drive, much tighter guitar licks and a format that really worked. Both John and Paul were wonderful singers and I had the impression that Paul was the biggest influence on the band at the time. They were much better without Stuart Sutcliffe because he didn't contribute anything musically."

Dave Forshaw (206): "I couldn't believe how loud they were and that they wore leather jackets and jeans. Most venues on Merseyside would not allow jeans as they were seen as cheap working man's gear. In most places, you had to wear a tie. Everybody looked at them, everybody listened to them. We couldn't believe that they had so much confidence. I loved what they were doing and in spite of what Bob Wooler says, I had no trouble in getting into their dressing-room and booking them for three dates. It was £6.10s. (£6.50) for the first night and then £7.10s (£7.50) if they were all right. Lennon did the most talking and he was the one who would answer back."

Tony Sanders (207) played drums for Billy Kramer and the Coasters. He saw the Beatles a few days later. "A friend of mine told me about this fabulous group at Litherland Town Hall. He said, 'They're all German. They wear cowboy boots and they stomp on the stage.' A week later, we were coming off stage at Aintree Institute and saw these guys coming on next. Lennon wore a leather jacket and McCartney had a jacket that looked as though he'd been sleeping in it for months, but when they kicked off, it was unbelievable. They were all smoking cigarettes and that tickled us because it went right against convention. They were so cheeky with it. Instead of trying to look good, they didn't give a damn. They played 'Wooden Heart' with Pete Best on bass drum and hi-hat. He was only using one hand and he was smoking with the other. We thought this was tremendous. We were all smoking the next time we went on stage, but it didn't go with our short haircuts and clean boy-next-door image.'

Sam Leach (208): "I had seen the Beatles as the Silver Beatles before they went to Hamburg and I didn't think they were very good. I was coaxed into seeing them after they came back at Hambleton Hall. There was a lot of fighting and I was going to go but then I heard Bob Wooler say, 'It's the Beatles' and they played 'The William Tell Overture'. I thought, 'Why are they wasting classical music on this lot?' I could not believe what I was seeing – I was hooked immediately. John did 'Slow Down', Paul 'The Hippy Hippy Shake', George 'I'm Henry The Eighth I Am', Stu 'Wooden Heart' and Pete 'Matchbox'. I followed them into the dressing room and told them that they would be as big as Elvis. John said, 'We've got a nutter here, Paul' and Paul said, 'Yes, but a nutter with bookings.' I booked them for 12 gigs at £10 a time which was top money at the time." The record used to introduce the Beatles was 'Piltdown Rides Again' by the Piltdown Men.

Peter Cook (209) of the Top Spots: "In the early days, I played with the Beatles virtually every week at the Grosvenor Ballroom in Wallasey. Paul was on rhythm then and he used to have a Lucky 7 guitar. They were a very very average band and I used to think that we were far better. Paul did have a brilliant voice for singing 'Good Golly Miss Molly', but they were nothing special. They went away to Germany and then there was a buzz going round, 'Have you heard the Beatles?', and I pooh-poohed it. We then played Lathom Hall and the Beatles were on and I was with my arms folded on the dance floor, thinking, 'Let's see how good you are', and the curtains opened and they started off with 'Lucille' and they were so tight and so good that every hair on my neck stood up. It was a completely new sound and I had never heard anything like it. I know now that they had the drums miked up, they had a mike in the bass drum, so I know what the secret was. I was in awe of them."

Harry Prytherch (210): "Anybody who has played at Blair Hall will remember that the stage was on a slope. I had some string which I tied to my bass drum pedal and then tied to my drum seat so my weight would stop the drum from sliding. The first time we saw the Beatles was at Blair Hall and the curtains opened and this awful mighty sound came out. Pete Best hit his bass drum eight to the bar and really hammered it, and the first time he did that, the bass drum started sliding and I could see he was going to be in trouble. I ran backstage and I took the string off mine. He was hanging onto his bass drum with one hand and playing it with a stick in the other and between us we wrapped the string around his bass drum pedal and around his seat and every time he played at Blair Hall, he took a piece of string with him."

Alan Stratton (211): "The Beatles were the first band to have harmonies and they would change the lead vocalists – John would sing one, then Paul and then George. It was interesting to watch as a lot of the bands only had one singer. They also had that deep throbbing bass with Pete Best. The exciting thing for me with the Beatles was watching Pete Best set up his drums. They knew exactly what they were doing. They would speak to the audience a lot, and if they snapped a string as Paul did once, he would smile and continue playing: he wouldn't go off and change his string."

Not everyone was convinced that the Beatles were a change for the better. **Don Andrew (212)** of the Remo Four nursed doubts: "We were shocked that they had such an attraction and commanded such a following when they looked dirty and made such a horrible deafening row. We were intent on making our guitars sound as nice as possible and Colin Manley changed his strings religiously. He got the real Fender sound out of his guitar and they came along with big amplifiers and a big throbbing noise."

Colin Manley (213) recalled, "We were flabbergasted at what we saw, but I wasn't impressed musically. They improved when they went down to four with Paul on bass, but it was a long time before I could appreciate what they were doing."

Sam Leach (214): "George was playing 'Moonglow' and it was romantic with the lights down. I saw that Stu's jack was on the floor and he was bashing away but nothing was coming out. I stuck the jack in and a sound like ten cats being run over by a lorry came out. Paul leapt across and yanked out the plug. He said, 'You're a fool, Leachy, don't you know he can't play?'"

Lewis Collins (215): "My favourite memory of the Cavern is of steam coming off the ceiling and watching the original Beatles. The sound used to vibrate off the walls and they all wore leather gear. To this day I have in my possession Paul McCartney's leather jacket from the original Beatles. I'm very proud of it. I suppose some mad American might want to buy it." So now we know where it is. Portions of Paul's leather jacket have been offered for sale for years and if they were all genuine, he would have been the size of the Incredible Hulk or Kingsize Taylor.

Every group realised that things would never be the same again. **Johnny Sandon (216)** was the lead singer with the Searchers. "We thought we were near the top of the heap and we were pretty popular around Liverpool. Gerry and the Pacemakers were the leading group and Johnny Sandon and the Searchers weren't far behind. We were doing a show at St. John's Hall in Bootle and we'd heard about this group called the Beatles who'd come back from Germany. We were copying Cliff Richard and the Shadows and they were doing something new altogether. As soon as they started playing, I knew it was the beginning of the end for us."

John McNally (217), also of the Searchers, recalled, "This was the first time I heard a drummer playing fours on a bass drum. It was a wall of sound and these were the days before you had your big PAs. They did rock'n'roll stuff just like the Americans, but with more rawness to it and in a Liverpool accent. There was no way we could follow them effectively with our tinny sound."

These groups had not yet been over to Germany and so they had no understanding of what had caused this transformation.

5   LUNCHEON BEAT

I. Mersey Beat newspaper
II. Raymond Jones
III. Gigging Around
IV. The Eppy-Centre
V. I Call Your Name

"The man that hath no music in himself,
Nor is not moved with the concourse of sweet sounds,
Is fit for treasons, stratagems and spoils."
(The Merchant Of Venice, William Shakespeare)

"Our next production will be The Merchant Of Widnes."
(Ken Dodd at the Liverpool Playhouse)

I. Mersey Beat newspaper

In February 1961 the Swinging Blue Jeans (then still the Bluegenes) started their 'Guest Nights' at the Cavern. The visiting guest group on 21 March 1961 was the Beatles. This was their début at the Cavern, though they had been there as the Quarry Men. Shortly afterwards they returned to Hamburg. In July 1961 they made a triumphant return for a 'Welcome Home' appearance and a residency on Wednesday nights. **Ralph Ellis (218)** of the Swinging Blue Jeans recalls, "Their singing was very rough and their guitars were out of tune. We rehearsed a lot to get our sound right and we weren't too happy to see the Beatles going down so well with something they'd only rehearsed five minutes before."

Ray McFall (219): "Bob Wooler had told me about the Beatles and I had become aware of the Beatles earlier when Pete Best's mother, Mo, phoned me to say, 'My son is in a wonderful group, they do very well, so why don't you book them?' My response was, 'I'll let you know.' When it came to beat music, Bob was the expert and I relied on him to select the groups. He told me that the Beatles had come from Hamburg and he was at Litherland Town Hall and saw their return, and he said, 'You've got to have them.' Brian Kelly, who ran Litherland Town Hall, booked them for all his shows, which were all on a Wednesday. I couldn't have them on Wednesday, I wasn't open on Thursday or there would be modern jazz, and the weekend was traditional jazz, and so I decided to book them on a Tuesday. This was the Blue Genes guest night, and they wanted good, well-organised, clean beat groups, ones that weren't too loud and wild, and they would suggest groups to me. The Blue Genes would play and then introduce the guests, and they'd play again and then introduce the second guest, and then they would close the show. I told them that the Beatles would be playing, and the club was full. Afterwards, three of the Blue Jeans tackled me in Mathew Street and they were most upset. As far as they were concerned the Beatles didn't have the musical talent or the appearance, they weren't clean, fresh and well-organised. I said that if the place is full, there are a lot more people watching the Blue Jeans. We parted on reasonable terms and the irony is that the Blue Jeans were eventually awarded a recording contract and they did one of the Beatles' numbers, 'Hippy Hippy Shake', and they replaced their double-bass with an electric one."

Wally Hill (220) was promoting dances in Garston and Walton. "Bob Evans and the Five Shillings were a popular group and they asked us if we had used the Beatles yet. We said no and we asked what they were like. Bob Evans said, 'Don't touch them, they don't wash their hair and there's a fight every night.' There was a fight every night anyway, so that didn't mean anything. We wrote to them in Hamburg and they signed an agreement that they would play for us every Saturday and Sunday at a tenner a night, which was big money then. They played a few times and we increased it to £12 and then one night they came along to Blair Hall, Walton, and Paul said, 'We are not going on unless we get £15.' There was a bit of haggling and in the end we decided that they weren't worth it. (Laughs) We parted company. They didn't play that night and the kids were disappointed and we never had them again. I made a mistake there."

I asked **Adrian Barber (221)** if they had got rid of Cass so that Cass and the Cassanovas could become the Big Three. "No, we had the hottest band in Liverpool, so what would we want to get rid of Cass for? He was a show-biz guy, an all-round entertainer, and he jumped up and down. Cass said he was leaving the band and going to London because Liverpool was a Dead End Street and 'you guys don't like me anyway.' We said that wasn't true but Hutch also said we would keep going as a trio: we'd be like Johnny Burnette's Rock'n'Roll Trio so that validated it. I thought of the name the Big Three, which was Roosevelt, Churchill and Stalin, who met at different conferences to divide up the world. We played the gigs as the Big Three, and we got harder and harder and harder. I made a bass cabinet for Johnny Gus's bass and that sounded really good. Hutch wanted to kill me every night and man, if there was ever anyone who could scare you to death, it was him. We never had a good personal relationship but he could play drums like the black American records. He used the back of the sticks for a harder sound. He dragged me to his house one day to listen to a record and it had the most amazing vocal I had ever heard. It sounded like the guy was tearing his throat out and the riff was so unusual, and it was 'What'd I Say' by Ray Charles. Your performance of that song was to define you among the Liverpool groups. If you didn't do a great 'What'd I Say', your other stuff went right in the toilet. We had it beat, we were too hard for a lot of the girls, but there was nobody who could hold a candle to us as far as hardcore rock'n'roll was concerned."

The competitive spirit among the groups encouraged them to improve. **Kingsize Taylor (222)**: 'We were getting records in Liverpool from the American boats before you could buy them in the shops. If the Liverpool groups had gone down to London at the start of the Sixties, they'd have ripped them up because they were still playing old crummy stuff down there. Everybody up north was playing songs by Chuck Berry and Fats Domino and Little Richard. People in London would have thought they were brands of cigarettes." Come on, Kingsize, don't over-egg the pudding.

This repertoire applies to some groups on Liverpool (and, indeed, to some in London) but most were still playing chart material. John Cochrane, drummer with Wump and his Werbles, kept a list of what other groups were performing in order that his own band would not duplicate numbers. It's a remarkable document. The list dates from early in 1961 and, considering the groups together, the Shadows' material appears 44 times and Cliff Richard's 31. Elvis Presley heads the American rock 'n' rollers with 21 appearances, while Gene Vincent and Buddy Holly both have 11. **John Cochrane (223)** comments, "The groups did a lot of Gene Vincent's songs and this was because they were easier to play than Chuck Berry's. The Shadows' tunes were dead easy to play. They must have been. They'd release a record on Friday and every group would be playing it by Saturday night."

Chris Curtis (224): "There were so many groups living in each other's pockets when it came to songs. I remember when Roy Orbison came out with 'Dream Baby'. Within a week, everybody was doing it, and I do mean everybody. Paul McCartney did it best. He was really right for the song."

The Beatles' repertoire is the most distinctive and it draws on a wide range of sources. John Cochrane listed 19 of their songs - the Beatles were ultimately to record only one of them, 'Boys', for Parlophone. Rock'n'roll is represented by 'C'mon Everybody' (Eddie Cochran), 'Twenty Flight Rock' (Eddie Cochran), 'Mean Woman Blues' (Jerry Lee Lewis), 'Lucille' (Little Richard) and 'New Orleans' (Gary U.S. Bonds). Buddy Holly is featured with two of his lesser known songs, 'Crying, Waiting, Hoping' and 'Mailman, Bring Me No More Blues'. Rhythm and blues is there with two Ray Charles songs, 'Hallelujah, I Love Her So' and 'What'd I Say.' Turning to country music, there's Hank Williams' 'Hey Good Lookin'' and Bill Monroe's 'Blue Moon Of Kentucky', which had previously been rocked up by Elvis.

The Beatles' ballads are 'Love Me Tender' (Elvis Presley, and Stu Sutcliffe's solo vocal with the Beatles), 'Red Sails In The Sunset' (already an oldie, and the Beatles' version predates Fats Domino's rock'n'roll treatment), 'Over The Rainbow' (presumably taken from Gene Vincent), 'Corrina, Corrina' (an early Phil Spector production and a US hit for Ray Peterson) and 'Don't Forbid Me' (a mawkish hit for Pat Boone). Also on the list are the Shirelles' 'Will You Love Me Tomorrow?' and Elvis Presley's 'Wooden Heart'. This No.1 record contained a passage in German, which would amuse German audiences.

Overall, the list suggests that the Beatles repertoire wasn't as rough and tough as some have imagined, although, to a certain degree, it ain't what you do, it's the way that you do it. It is certainly more imaginative than the repertoire of other groups. Here are a couple of examples:

Gerry and the Pacemakers: 'Ginchy' (a Bert Weedon instrumental), 'Skinny Minnie' (Bill Haley), 'You'll Never Know' (Shirley Bassey) and two songs shared with the Beatles, 'What'd I Say' and 'Will You Love Me Tomorrow?' Johnny Gus called Gerry "the human jukebox" because he knew so many songs.

The Swinging Blue Jeans: 'Easter Bonnet' (Irving Berlin standard), 'Calendar Girl' (Neil Sedaka), 'I Love You' (Cliff Richard), 'Wheels' (String-a-Longs), 'Samantha' (Kenny Ball) and, like the Beatles, 'Wooden Heart'.

Terry Sylvester (225): "I loved seeing Gerry and the Pacemakers because it was so unusual to hear a pianist, and a very good one too. I remember the Beatles doing 'Apache' with the Shadows walk. They weren't sending it up either unless I didn't see the humour in it. I thought the Big Three were the best of the lot but they were unreliable and you didn't know if they would appear. They would set off for a gig and not get there. We heard stories of them going into a pub and getting smashed and going back home."

Geoff Hogarth (226): "I would mark out each group according to what they played. I had a colour like blue for Buddy Holly and so on and I would put the names of the groups alongside. In that way, I could put a blue band with an orange band and be fairly sure they wouldn't be duplicating the songs. If you did an all-night with 14 groups, I wanted people to say as long as possible so that I could sell wagonloads of Pepsi-Cola and orange juice, and one way to do that was to have 14 groups with some variety."

Denny Seyton and the Sabres added some variety. **Dave Maher (227)**: "We were at the Peppermint Lounge and we were doing a comedy routine for 'Along Came Jones'. I was holding up signs that said 'Clap', 'Boo' and 'Hiss'. We had to fire a cap gun and when it didn't go off, I remember saying, 'For Christ's sake, fire'. We also did 'Rhythm Of The Rain' with water pistols and wearing sou'westers."

The American blues singer Muddy Waters had played in Liverpool, but surprisingly, his music was not featured by any of the groups. He exerted a great influence, however, on the Animals in Newcastle and the Rolling Stones in London. **Pete Frame (228)**: "The blues didn't have the excitement as they had a down-home feel and they were still being aimed at the black, adult audience in the clubs of Chicago or wherever, and so they were not very exciting compared with these teenage records that were coming out. I was never very interested in the Fifties in listening to Muddy Waters, but they weren't really available anyway, and it wasn't until the Sixties when we heard John Lee Hooker records and Pye and EMI were releasing albums that we started hearing them in a different light. Merseybeat music was moulded on the late 50s and was based on all Buddy Holly-type influences."

Indeed, you don't really hit the blues until you come to a second-generation group, the Mojos. **Stu James (229)**: "The Nomads played R&B, the twelve-bar stuff. We played songs by John Lee Hooker, Little Walter and Jimmy Reed. We were one of the first bands on Merseyside to play real loud R&B and so we quickly made a name for ourselves"

Whatever the music that was being played, the beat scene on Merseyside was thriving. **Bill Harry (230)**, another student at the Liverpool College of Art, launched a fortnightly magazine. "I was trying to get backers for a jazz magazine I'd designed, but I'd got so involved with the Beatles that I decided to do a rock'n'roll mag instead. I borrowed £50 to start the paper and thought of the name *Mersey Beat* and June 1961 was when the Merseybeat scene officially began. The music didn't have a name before. When I started *Mersey Beat*, I got together with Bob Wooler and we came out with a list of over 400 bands covering the area from Liverpool to Southport and over the water. I knew that there was no other scene like this in the entire country, probably not in the whole world, and I thought it was very like New Orleans at the turn of the century when jazz began.'

Bob Azurdia (231) wrote for *Mersey Beat* and was proud to have been involved. "Without *Mersey Beat* the whole explosion wouldn't have happened in the same way.

Mersey Beat reported the trends and told you where the groups were playing. *Liverpool Echo* only had paid advertisements and they were generally for the major halls, rather than the clubs. *Mersey Beat* was more important than has ever been recognised. Bill Harry should be congratulated for his vision."

Mersey Beat had several novel features. Bill Harry encouraged musicians to write about their lives and he included bulletins, somewhat sanitized, from Hamburg. John Lennon was a regular contributor and he supplied witty copy reminiscent of the work published later as *In His Own Write*. **Bill Harry (232)**: "John Lennon came to the office and gave me these photographs that had been taken in Hamburg. He was on stage with a lavatory seat around his neck and in another he was reading a newspaper on the corner of the Reeperbahn in his underpants. When Brian Epstein signed them, John came rushing into the office, 'Bill, can I have those pictures please? Brian says I have to have them back."

Brian Epstein wrote record reviews and also sold the publication in his family's record shops, NEMS. It is thought that he hadn't heard of the Beatles until late 1961 when he was asked for a copy of their German single, 'My Bonnie'. But surely he read *Mersey Beat*, to see his own reviews if nothing else, and he would have noticed the Beatles' name? Furthermore, the Beatles used to hang around NEMS wanting to hear new records in the booths and he *must* have known who they were, if only to chase them out.

Alistair Taylor (233): "NEMS was the finest record shop in the north-west because Brian Epstein was a brilliant retailer. If a record was available somewhere in the world, he could get it for you – not 'could' but 'would', It might take six months but he would get it. He had an incredible stock control system – GOS, general overstock – which meant that we were never out of stock of anything we might sell. Dobell's in London was the only other store in England with the whole catalogue of the Blue Note jazz label in stock. He could spot hits and the only time I can remember him being wrong was when he overstocked on the Everly Brothers' 'Muskrat'. He took 250 between the two shops and they hardly sold at all."

John Johnson (234): "I went to NEMS and to Pat and Gerry Allen for country music in Lark Lane. NEMS was superb – the other shops were grotty compared to NEMS which was sparkling and brand new. They had booths so you could listen to records before you bought it. You couldn't fail to buy a record. They had a good cross section of everything including skiffle, country and jazz."

Bill Harry ran a *Mersey Beat* popularity poll, with results published in January 1962. The Top Twenty was:

1	The Beatles
2	Gerry and the Pacemakers
3	The Remo Four
4	Rory Storm and the Hurricanes
5	Johnny Sandon and the Searchers
6	Kingsize Taylor and the Dominoes
7	The Big Three
8	The Strangers

9	Faron's Flamingoes
10	The Four Jays (later the Fourmost)
11	Ian and the Zodiacs
12	The Undertakers
13	Earl Preston and the TTs
14	Mark Peters and the Cyclones
15	Karl Terry and the Cruisers
16	Derry and the Seniors
17	Steve and the Syndicate
18	Dee Fenton and the Silhouettes
19	Billy Kramer and the Coasters
20	Dale Roberts and the Jaywalkers

Billy J. Kramer is only at No.19 and the Swinging Blue Jeans, who hadn't yet switched to rock'n'roll, weren't even placed.

Dave Lovelady (235) has fond memories of Rory Storm and the Hurricanes. "One night at St. Luke's Hall was an absolute sensation. Rory Storm came in with Wally who had the first bass guitar in Liverpool. There was always a bass on American records, but we'd never seen one, and here was Wally with a Framus four-string bass guitar. The groups crowded around in amazement, and when they opened with 'Brand New Cadillac', this deep, booming sound was tremendous."

Jim McIver (236) promoted dances at St. Luke's Hall in Crosby. "Rory used to jump from the floor onto the piano. He'd practically do the splits on the piano and pour lemonade over himself. He'd jump from the piano and do a somersault back to the mike. Those mike stands had heavy bases, but he did tricks with them."

Another local promoter was **Ron Appleby (237)**. "Rory was years before his time. He'd be immaculately dressed in pink suit and pink tie, and in the middle of his act he'd go to the piano, get out a very big comb, and comb his huge blond quiff. He was very fit and often he would run home from gigs. One day a porter at Bootle station caught a chap writing 'I love Rory Storm' on the walls. It was Rory himself."

Having Ringo Starr for a drummer is Rory Storm's main claim to fame, but his group was essential to the development of beat music on Merseyside. **Faron (238)** says, "Rory Storm and the Hurricanes was the first band I ever saw and they got me interested in music. Rory was the greatest showman you could ever see. Twenty years ago he was doing what Rod Stewart is doing now, right down to the gold boots."

Iris Caldwell (239): "One night he wore an orange suit for a gig and when he came back in later, he was hysterical. It had been St. Patrick's Night and he was performing in a Catholic club. They'd thrown chairs at him and Ringo was on his knees, still trying to play the drums."

Rory Storm wanted to make an impact at that pollwinners concert. **Ray Ennis (240)** of the Swinging Blue Jeans recalls, "If Rory had got the breaks, there wouldn't have been any Gary Glitter. Rory would do anything for a publicity stunt. He hired Graham Spencer, who was doing the photography for pop magazines, for the *Mersey Beat* Pollwinners Concert at the Majestic Ballroom in Birkenhead. He said, 'I want you to come along tonight because I'm going to jump off the balcony.' The Hurricanes were on stage and Rory went upstairs to jump off the balcony. He did jump but he broke his leg. Graham Spencer was laughing so much that he never got the picture."

That list is exclusively male. Merseybeat was a male-dominated sound. Cilla Black and Beryl Marsden were the best-known female performers, but rather than form their own bands, they sang with established groups. **Beryl Marsden (241)** says, "There weren't a lot of female singers around because they couldn't associate themselves with the songs. The majority of female singers that had made the charts were the Susan Maughan types, pretty songs and party clothes, but in Liverpool you had to be one of the boys."

Geoff Hogarth (242): "I went to the Kardomah in Dale Street for a coffee one day and coming back, I heard this powerful voice wafting through the huge fan at the Iron Door. It was Cilla Black. Sam Leach was putting on an all-night session at the Tower Ballroom and I said, 'You should put her on' which he did. She had an easy passage really as she went straight from playing a few gigs into making records. Beryl Marsden was very talented but she was a giggler. I don't think I ever heard her finish a song."

Despite Liverpool being a cosmopolitan city, the only black performer on the list is Derry Wilkie, who worked with white musicians in the Seniors. The black groups included the Chants, the Sobells, the Conquests and the Poppies. The Chants were a male harmony act, backed by several Merseyside groups including the Beatles. **Eddie Amoo (243)**: "I met up with Joey and Edmund Ankrah, Alan Harding and Nat Smeda and we formed the Chants. We met in the cellar of Joey and Edmund's house, and their dad was a church minister, he played organ and had his own church, and he taught his two sons very simple harmonies. Joey handed out the harmonies to us and the song was 'Don't Gamble With Love', a Paul Anka song, and we couldn't believe the sound we came out with, it was absolutely terrific. We ran up to Stanley House which was a youth and social club at the time in Princes Park, everybody in Toxteth used it, and we stood there singing it and nobody could believe it. We learnt more songs and we met up with Paul McCartney and we went down to the Cavern one lunchtime to do an audition for them and we rehearsed two songs with them, 'Sixteen Candles' and 'Duke Of Earl'. We did them that night. Joey used to come on first going, 'Duke, duke, duke'. We would then walk on, clicking behind him, while he was doing the bass part, and the audience had seen nothing like that. They went mad. The Beatles were made up, but Brian Epstein said, 'No, you can't appear with the boys as it hasn't been sanctioned by me.' Bob Wooler got him to change his mind. We did about six shows with the Beatles. Then we formed a group called the Harlems and they became our backing band."

I asked **Eddie Amoo (244)** what he thought of white Liverpool groups performing songs originally recorded by black acts like the Drifters and the Coasters. "Not too good, as most of the groups were pretty weak vocally. That's why we made such an impact. We were the first group to sing the songs pretty much as they were meant to be sung."

Sam Leach (245): "I took them to the Blue Gardenia Club in Soho, which was owned by Brian Cass. George and Pete were away with two girls but John and Paul got up for a couple of numbers. The locals could not believe what they were hearing and that was their first warning of what was to come."

II. Raymond Jones

For many years fans and commentators have argued about the role of Raymond Jones in the Beatles' story and whether, indeed, there was even a Raymond Jones. Did he turn Brian Epstein on to the Beatles, or was it just a good story? Living in Liverpool, I determined to reach the truth about this matter and in so doing, I encountered the Pinocchio-like problems relating to any story about the early years of the Beatles.

In 1961, while the Beatles were in Hamburg, they recorded 'My Bonnie' with Tony Sheridan for the German label, Polydor. The single made Number 32 on the German charts, but it was not released in the UK. **Pete Best (246)** recalls, "If my memory serves me correctly, we gave a copy of 'My Bonnie' to Bob Wooler and asked him to play it, either at the Aintree Institute or Litherland Town Hall. It sounded good to hear our record coming out of the speakers alongside the American stuff." Local fans would hear the record – and want to own it. A key element in the Beatles' story is that an 18 year old called Raymond Jones went into Brian Epstein's record store, NEMS, in Whitechapel in October 1961 and asked for 'My Bonnie', which would have to be imported. There are conflicting accounts about what happened.

Alistair Taylor worked for Brian Epstein at NEMS as his personal assistant. He wrote his autobiography, *Yesterday – The Beatles Remembered*, in 1988 and he doesn't identify himself as Raymond Jones in that. In 1997 Raymond Jones was listed as one of the guests at the Penny Lane Beatles Festival, and who should stand up but Alistair Taylor and say, "I am Raymond Jones." Alistair has repeated this on several occasions, notably on the Brian Epstein *Arena* special on BBC-TV. According to Alistair, the public was asking for 'My Bonnie' but Brian wouldn't order the record until he had a definite order with a deposit in the stock-book. Alistair claimed, "It was me. I ordered the Beatles' record and put down the deposit." Alistair didn't know the Beatles and there was no valid explanation as to why he should do that.

I was at that Penny Lane Festival with Bob Wooler, who said, "Let's all do this. Let's do an 'I am Spartacus' and all claim to be Raymond Jones." "Why are you so sure he's wrong?" I said. "Because I knew Raymond Jones," said Bob, "and I can assure you that I wasn't talking to Alistair Taylor."

Sam Leach's book, *The Rocking City*, was featured in the *Mail On Sunday* in March 2000. Sam claimed he was the one who told Brian about the Beatles, but Brian didn't want to acknowledge his presence. Sam said, "If I was the reason Brian went to see the lads for the first time, he would never have admitted it. He would invent a fictitious character instead and my own opinion is that Raymond Jones was a figment of Brian's imagination." That's credible but wrong.

Raymond Jones was first mentioned in Brian Epstein's autobiography, *A Cellarful Of Noise*, in 1964, and he does exist. He owned a printing company in Burscough, which is now run by his son and daughter, and he has retired and lives in a farmhouse in Spain. I spoke to him and learnt that he was a shy person who has never been interested in Beatles Conventions and he is disgusted that people are claiming to be him. **Raymond Jones (247)**: "I never wanted to do anything to make money out of the Beatles because they have given me so much pleasure. I saw them every dinner-time at the Cavern and they were fantastic. I had never heard anything like them. Everybody had been listening to Lonnie Donegan and Cliff Richard and they were so different. A friend of mine, Ron Billingsley, had a motorbike and we would follow them all over the place – Hambleton Hall, Aintree Institute and Knotty Ash Village Hall."

How did **Raymond Jones (248)** come to be talking to Brian Epstein? "I used to go to NEMS every Saturday and I would be buying records by Carl Perkins and Fats Domino because I heard The Beatles playing their songs. My sister's ex-husband, Kenny Johnson, who played with Mark Peters and the Cyclones, told me that the Beatles had made a record and so I went to NEMS to get it. Brian Epstein said to me, 'Who are they?' and I said, 'They are the most fantastic group you will ever hear.' No one will take away from me that it was me who spoke to Brian Epstein and then he went to the Cavern to see them for himself. I didn't make them famous, Brian Epstein made them famous, but things might have been different without me."

By the way, this Raymond Jones should not be confused with another Raymond Jones, a Manchester guitarist who played with the Dakotas. Brian Epstein knew the Beatles' name through the banner headlines in *Mersey Beat*, but he had not shown any interest in them before. Although Raymond Jones was heterosexual, no doubt Eppy was entranced that such a good-looking boy should be following the Beatles and he determined to find out about them for himself.

Raymond Jones had spoken to Brian Epstein at his NEMS shop in Whitechapel. So many Beatle sites have been turned into shrines, but not NEMS. There is nothing to suggest that it was even there. It is now a branch of Ann Summers which, considering Eppy's sexual tastes, is one of the best jokes in Liverpool. Almost as good as the gents toilet that the council built under Queen Victoria's monument. Quite appropriate too – once customers asked for 7, 10 and 12 singles and now they ask for 7, 10 and 12 inch vibrators. Oh, and it's right by Beaver Radio.

III. Gigging Around

If there had been a poll to find the top beat club on Merseyside, the Cavern would have won. Certainly other clubs were very popular, but even groups who were resident elsewhere realised that there was something special about the Cavern. It was an honour to play there and it was some time before the Undertakers got a booking. **Brian Jones (249)** of the Undertakers explains: "The Beatles had their strongholds and we had ours. We used to play at the Iron Door and they used to play at the Cavern. We had our first booking at the Cavern in 1962 and lots of people came out of curiosity. There was a queue down Mathew Street, round the corner, past Frank Hessy's, and round another corner by the Kardomah. A few months later there was a photograph of the queue with the caption, 'This is the queue for the Beatles at the Cavern'. If you looked at the picture closely, you could see *our* van being unloaded."

Ray McFall (250) thinks that the Cavern's apparent limitations were part of the attraction. "It was all the inconvenience that drew people. There was the condensation, the sanitation, the tobacco fumes, the crowded atmosphere, and no lighting to speak of. Everything militated against comfort, but nobody cared."

Dave Jones (251): "There was no alcohol, so you had theoretically a sober audience. People of course were tanked up before they went in or smuggled it in. In the 60s people were going there to listen to the bands, so it was a different mentality. That was the focal point, to watch a particular band. I didn't go there until 1964, but even in my own experience, you would go down to watch a band and when it had finished, if you hadn't copped off with someone, you went home."

Bill Heckle (252): "People like crowds. People may say it is jammed but they go away and tell people how great the atmosphere was. If the concert had been a quarter full, people wouldn't go away with those feelings of being somewhere special. The Cavern was special because it was a relatively small place and it used to pack out."

Even worse there were no facilities for the disabled at the Cavern, although that that didn't stop **Arthur Davis (253)** and his wheelchair. He played drums for the Four Just Men. "It took most people a couple of minutes to get down the steps and it took me half an hour. (Laughs) I fell down the stairs at the Cavern quite often. I would plonk myself on a little alcove and I would stay there all evening. I wouldn't move, watching all the drummers and seeing what they were doing. John Banks of the Merseybeats was my favourite."

Fred Marsden (254): "The hardest thing was taking the bass drum into the Cavern as it was very difficult to negotiate round the little tight bend at the bottom of the stairs. If there were a lot of people there, you had to lift the case above your head and work your way through the dancers. I don't think it would have worked if they had one drum-kit permanently there as everybody had their own adjustments, especially with the snare drum and cymbals. I never liked playing with anybody else's drums, but the Cavern was brilliant for sound as there was no echo and it was a dead sound so you could hear exactly what you were playing. I enjoyed every minute that I played at the Cavern, every dinner-hour, every evening, because it was always packed and we always got a good reception. The worst place to play was the Tower Ballroom in New Brighton because they never had a piano that was decently tuned. If you have a piano that's out of tune, there's nothing you can do about it."

Clubs were springing up everywhere and among the most popular was the Iron Door, only a few hundred yards from the Cavern, where the Searchers and the Undertakers frequently appeared. **John Johnson (255)**: "The sound in the Iron Door was very poor, not as good as the Cavern. It was a smaller place and it was wider from side to side. The Cavern was long, and the bands in the Iron Door were playing to a wall, five yards across and the wall was there. I would take Kenny there and he would set his PA up and I would be stood against the wall trying to balance him up. It was an awful place to get things balanced."

Sam Leach (256): "I put the Beatles on at a Wednesday afternoon session at the Iron Door and Ray McFall had already booked them at the Cavern for lunchtime. He gave the Beatles an ultimatum, either you play for me and not Sam or you don't play for me again. Terry McCann, a mate of mine, got some stink bombs from the Wizard's Den and flung down the steps at the Cavern." Did anyone notice?

Chris Finley (257): "I had a gig with the Runaways in a dive off London Road in 1963. There was no fee as it was called an audition. We needed a piano and so we ended up taking our sash window out to get our piano into the street and then into a van. We had to carry it down 15 stairs and then we had to get home when everybody had gone."

The DJ Bob Wooler organized the bookings at the Cavern, and although he worked at several other venues, he was particularly noted for that connection. Born in 1926 (but he said 1932), he was older than the group members and he gave them advice. He had cards printed saying, "Bob Wooler – Rock 'n' Roll Consultant". He can be heard on some live recordings and his best-known quip is "Remember all you cave-dwellers, the Cavern is the best of cellars." If you can imagine a hip version of Leonard Sachs, the presenter of the BBC's *The Good Old Days*, you'll have an idea of his style. **Terry Sylvester (258)**, then of the Escorts and later a member of the Hollies, remarked: "I think Bob Wooler is one of the best DJs in the world. I've listened to a lot of DJs travelling around the world and I still rate Bob. It's very odd that he's never made it to the top. I don't think he wanted to leave Merseyside."

Alan Sytner had introduced lunchtime sessions at the Cavern in November 1957. The club is close to the business quarter of the city so office staff would come along in their lunch breaks. These people would be quite smartly dressed as the publicity stated "Persons in dungarees not admitted". **Cilla Black (259)** worked in one of the offices and helped out in the cloakroom: "It used to be packed and I got five bob an hour for hanging the coats up. It knocks me out when I read that I was the 'hatcheck girl' at the Cavern. People only wear hats in Liverpool when they go to church."

Only the 'fully pro' bands could play the lunchtime sessions because setting up equipment, playing and taking it down took about three hours. **Gerry Marsden (260)**, who made his debut at the Cavern in October 1960, remembers, "We'd go in of a morning when it was empty to put the gear on the stage and there was a pong of disinfectant. I can still smell it. We'd finish a show and it'd be all heavy and sweaty. We'd go out and come in again and, bingo, there was the disinfectant."

Sue Johnston (261): "My heart was not in the civil service and I used to shoot down the North John Street to the Cavern in my lunch hours. Its smell and slimy walls used to get into my clothes. Everyone would know where I'd been. Willy Russell's play *Stags and Hens* reminded me of the toilets in the Cavern. A few of us were in there, backcombing our hair, when a rat ran along the top of the toilet doors. Even if it had been infested with rats, I still would have gone to see the Beatles. When they were on, I used to get as close to the stage as I could and I was excited by new sounds and new stages in their development. I can remember them putting 'Twist and Shout' into the act and it was always special when they introduced a new composition. Pete Best was very handsome but he seemed distant, sitting at the back, and he never looked as though he belonged with them. I wasn't that bothered when he left. Ringo had the right personality, if not the looks.'

The Beatles were very different from Gerry and the Pacemakers. They had an aggressive, surly approach, while Gerry always played as though he was having the time of his life: Tommy Steele with a hard edge. **Fred Marsden (262)**, Gerry's brother and drummer, recognised this: "The Beatles appealed to a different audience to us. They had more of a beatnik following. There was always friendly rivalry between us. Despite their rawness, Paul McCartney used to get a great reception for the sentimental ones like 'Over The Rainbow' and we thought we'd have to get a song that would go over just as well. We tried 'You'll Never Walk Alone' a few times and it went down excellently. We'd be playing rock'n'roll and all of a sudden, we'd stop and do 'You'll Never Walk Alone'."

Robbie Hickson (263): "I went to a lunchtime session and the Beatles sang 'Over The Rainbow' – I thought, 'A rock band doing that?' But the way they did it was brilliant and it went down a storm. It was a number that we would never have considered doing. It was square, but when you heard them do it, it was tremendous."

Fred Marsden (264) had no doubts that the Beatles were good. "We used to play the Cavern and the Iron Door of a dinner-time. I was waiting outside the Iron Door one day and two ladies came along. I asked if I could help and one of them said, 'I'm looking for John Lennon.' She was very upset that he'd been skipping classes at the Liverpool College of Art. I said that John would make more money out of playing with the Beatles than he ever would with his pictures. This was quite a long time before they'd made a record so I feel pleased that I was such a prophet."

Freda Kelly (265) ran the Beatles' fan club from start to finish and saw many performances. Her favourites were the lunchtime sessions. "The Beatles would be on three days a week and Gerry and the Pacemakers would do Tuesday and Thursday. The following week they'd do Tuesday and Thursday and Gerry would do Monday, Wednesday and Friday. We had our regular seats at the front and we used to shout up for them to do 'Besame Mucho' or 'Three Cool Cats'. They would play it there and then. The fans who came along afterwards never really saw the Beatles at their best. I loved all their records, don't get me wrong, but the lunchtime sessions at the Cavern were the best."

Cynthia Lennon (266): "I don't think that I ever heard of John speak of other Liverpool bands as being rivals. He didn't mention anyone being a rival until the Rolling Stones."

Fred Marsden (267): "We played the Cavern a lot because only the Beatles and ourselves were full-time professionals in those days. The Beatles didn't have any jobs as they were art students and the like. We packed our jobs in to go to Germany so we were professional musicians. Our parents didn't mind: they had faith in us and my dad used to come round with us. I think he was quite impressed. I was only earning £4 a week before I packed it in so it wasn't much to lose."

The promoter **Dave Forshaw (268)** has kept his diary of the amounts he paid bands to play at Litherland Town Hall or St. John's Hall, Bootle. "By March 1962, the Beatles had gone up to £17 and the Searchers were on the same night for £6. The other fees were the Four Jays £7, Earl Preston and the TT's £6, The Cyclones £5.10s (£5.50), Karl Terry and the Cruisers £5 and the Dennisons £1.10s (£1.50). Karl Terry was good value as he would bring about 25 girls who worked with him at the Gorgeous Bra factory in Linacre Lane, and they would shout and scream for him. We could hire a policeman to stand outside the door for three hours at £2.3s.9d (£2.18). I'd be pleased if I made £10 profit on the night, but I could lose as well."

Billy Hatton (269): "After the lunchtime sessions at the Cavern, I would go back to our little terraced house in the Dingle with George Harrison for a cup of tea and a bowl of soup. My mother would give George long, drawn-out looks, sort of 'Who is this thing in a leather jacket? What is he doing playing guitars with my son?' Once they became international stars, she was telling everyone what a lovely lad George was and how she loved him coming round to the house."

Paul McCartney (270): "A lot of people came down to the Cavern in suits but it was usually the natty three-button Italian jobs. The Cavern was great: it was more like a party than an impersonal audience. I'd love to have a residency now where I could build up an audience and have them handing in requests. What we did was more like a live DJ show, you know, 'This one's for Joey from Speke'. We'd do commercials too – things like (sings) 'If you want a lot of chocolate on your biscuit...' Because the condensation got into the amps, the power would go off from time to time so we'd do 15 minutes acoustically. Liverpool and Hamburg taught us how to deal with people."

Neil Foster (271): "I find it so incredible that the kids were impressed by the Beatles, who were total crap. There was one guy who was always raving about them and saying he had never seen a group like the Beatles. We went to the Cavern and tried to see what all the fuss was about, and we had to agree with him: we too had never seen a group like the Beatles. We had never seen a group so scruffy, so unpractised and so arrogant. I still don't know how they got away with being such terrible performers. They didn't give a damn about anything and it was like they were laughing at the audience, 'You suckers, you're paying to watch us practice.' Brian Epstein put an end to that, he tamed them down and made them a marketable commodity."

Tony Crane (272) recalled the first time he saw the Beatles. "I was very surprised. I'd gone down the Cavern to see what it was like, and it was so scruffy and dirty. Then this group came on who were just as dirty and scruffy as the Cavern. I was in a trance for days. Paul McCartney had a guitar which he didn't play slung around his neck and wore leather trousers which were hand-sewn to make them tighter. They finished with 'What'd I Say' and McCartney was madder than any time I've seen Mick Jagger. He danced all over the place. It was marvellous."

John Booker (273): "I was a fairly regular customer at the Cavern and the thing that made the Beatles different from the other bands was that they were true to the music in a way that none of the other bands were. Although they messed about on stage sometimes, they were still true to the music. They were sincere in a way that other bands weren't and very straight with the music."

Also at the Cavern was **Willy Russell (274)**, who wrote the award-winning play *John Paul George Ringo...and Bert* in 1974. "It's a shame they never recorded 'Some Other Guy' because it was their song and I remember them doing it more than any other. They generally started off with it. I don't think that the recording industry could cope with the weight of beat that the Beatles were capable of in those days. I find it interesting that people say that the Stones were *the* rock 'n' roll band: for me, the Beatles' beat section, the bass and drums, was much stronger live than the Stones'"

'Some Other Guy' and 'Money (That's What I Want)' were originally recorded by American performers Richie Barrett and Barrett Strong respectively. They weren't exclusively covered by the Beatles as **John McNally (275)** of the Searchers explains: "One band would see another band do a song and they'd ask for the words and go and do it their way. The Beatles did 'Some Other Guy', we did 'Some Other Guy', the Big Three did 'Some Other Guy'. Everybody did 'Some Other Guy', but if you listened to all the recorded versions of 'Some Other Guy' or 'Money', you'll find that no two versions are the same. That was a good thing about Liverpool."

Mike Pender (276): "'What'd I Say' was a classic song. Most people could do their own version of that song because it was so good. The lines were good, the chords were good and if you had a piano, you were made. We had to rely on guitars, but we still made a good job of it."

Chris Curtis (277): "Whenever we needed new material, I would get hold of soul records by the Coasters and the Clovers and we'd Blanco them up. We were white boys' voices singing black man's soul and it worked. 'Sweets For My Sweet' of course and 'Goodbye My Love', which is an even better example. The story about the Cunard Yanks bringing the records in is a load of bollocks. How would the sailors know to buy records by the Clovers? Some of them brought country records in, but that was about it. There was a second hand shop on Stanley Road by the Rotunda and I would go from Swift's in Stanley Road, where I was selling prams, by bus to Young's in my lunch hour, and they would watch me going through boxes of 45s and I would buy things like Bobby Comstock's 'Let's Stomp'. I think he had a supplier in America 'cause they were always in good nick. I was always looking for things – I found 'Love Potion No.9' in a second-hand shop in Hamburg when we were at the Star-Club. I thought, 'I've got to have it, it's such a weird looking record.' I took my little portable electric record-player to Germany and I played 'Love Potion Number 9' and I thought, 'This is excellent.' I remember coming across 'What'd I Say' by Ray Charles at a shop in Bootle and I wasn't sure about buying it because both sides were the same – 'What'd I Say (Parts 1 and 2)'. When I got it home, I found they were different and I played that brilliant riff over and over and over. I decided to sing it myself and we used to finish every show with it."

Pete Frame (278): "Groups like Russ Sainty and the Nu–Notes and the Barron Knights would play in Luton. They were very good for what they did but it was in the twist and Bobby Darin era, so they would play 'Lazy River', 'The Fly' and lots of Elvis and Cliff Richard. I was staggered when I saw my first Merseybeat groups – the first one was the Swinging Blue Jeans at the Majestic in Luton and they would say things like, 'This is another song by Buddy Holly. We think Buddy Holly is great' or 'This is another by Chuck Berry. We think Chuck Berry is gear.' I had never heard live versions of songs by Buddy Holly and Chuck Berry and I was overwhelmed and astonished by the proficiency of these guys – Ralph Ellis was giving it the old solos and doing it well. I had seen all these banana-fingered guys trying to do it. The Barron Knights were very good at harmony and had a professional show but the Swinging Blue Jeans took it into a new dimension – such excitement, such exuberance and such skilful playing. They could replicate these amazing American songs. The southern groups weren't playing that kind of material – they had forgotten about Buddy Holly and Chuck Berry. Much later, Jerry Leiber and Mike Stoller told me that the Merseybeat groups resurrected and resuscitated their catalogue. Their songs had been recorded and gone down the river, like yesterday's newspapers – but the groups brought them back again and the

Searchers took 'Love Potion No.9' into the Top 3 in America. That's when they first got the inkling that these songs could become standards. They weren't trite, ephemeral rock'n'roll hits that had past their day – these songs were going to last forever. It was the Liverpool groups that did it."

The Big Three developed from the 1950s group, Cass and the Cassanovas. Bass player **John Gustafson (279)** recalls, "We got rid of our rhythm guitarist and we wanted to stay together as a trio, mainly because it was a newish thing to do. Nobody had done a loud trio before, and Adrian Barber concocted some loudish amplifiers which were nicknamed coffins. They were only 30 to 50 watts each but in those days that was quite powerful."

Gus, Hutch and Adrian played hard and rough. **John Gustafson (280)** explains: "We played with violence and attack, and our drumming was loud and raucous. There was much bashing of cymbals and all this was combined with the obscure R&B material that we chose. We were the first in the field with 'Some Other Guy' and 'Money'. We were a rowdy R&B band and I suppose that, had we compromised, we'd have got more gigs."

Allan Clarke (281) of the Hollies recalls, "We played at the Cavern on a bill with the Beatles, but the Big Three were the stars for me. I idolized that group. Griff played a Guyatone guitar with rusty strings and he made it sing. Johnny Gus was a marvellous bass player. They did songs that nobody had ever heard before and it used to make my back tingle."

Johnny Gustafson (282): "Griff and Hutch were so individualistic, Hutch was a maniac, he never stuck to the pattern and he was always playing all over the shop, I took a free hand and Griff was the same. We never rehearsed in the Big Three. We never ever went to a rehearsal room and said, 'This is a rehearsal.' We would turn up at the gig and somebody might have a song, 'Let's try this, I know the chords', and we would do that night, mistakes and all. The audience wouldn't know it anyway so it didn't make any difference. When we did learn things, we never bothered to rehearse an ending. We would just stop when the words ran out. That's enough, splang! (Laughs) Hutch would do a roll and it would be all over. Chaos really, but part of our charm, I suppose."

By way of contrast, **Kenny Johnson (283)** aka Sonny Webb were well rehearsed: "We used to do Buddy Knox's songs like 'I Think I'm Gonna Kill Myself', 'Party Doll' and 'The Girl with the Golden Hair'. We also did a few Chuck Berry songs and Del Shannon's 'Runaway'. We were into Carl Perkins long before the Beatles. We liked 'Pointed-Toe Shoes' and I remember George Harrison asking me for a tape of 'Pink Pedal Pushers' and 'Sure To Fall'."

Once he had some money of his own, John Lennon was into gizmos and it was no surprise to learn that he had one of the first portable jukeboxes. *The South Bank Show* on John Lennon's Jukebox was exceptionally good, although you did wonder why he simply didn't have one of his minions carry round a box of records and a record-player. We had his choices from 1965 and many of them found their way into his songs – compare the intros of Bobby Parker's 'Watch Your Step' and 'I Feel Fine', for example. **Tim Riley (284):** "The Beatles did outdo their exemplars, and a very interesting question is what attracted a macho guy like John Lennon to these New York girl groups? It's very interesting to play the Shirelles' original of 'Baby It's You' as Shirley Alston sounds just like Yoko Ono." Was this what attracted John to Yoko?'

Jackie Lomax (285) from the Undertakers: "We were looking for obscure songs by people we liked and if we did them, we didn't want other bands copying us. We were into doing more obscure material and we guarded what we had. If someone asked us who did a song originally, we would give them the wrong information so that they would be looking in the wrong place. We even implied that we had written some of the songs." This contrasts with the experience of London blues musicians where John Mayall allowed them to look through his large record collection.

George Melly (286): "In 1964 I went along to a literary party given by the publishers of John Lennon's book, *In His Own Write*. It was a literary party with people like Kingsley Amis there. I was a bit drunk and so was John. I said to him, 'Of course I can tell that you admire the great black artists, in particular Chuck Berry.' 'Yeah, he's great.' 'Well,' I said, 'it must be extraordinary to be such an enormous success when they're not because these black artists are much better than us.' I was thinking of myself in relation to Bessie Smith and of himself in relation to Muddy Waters and Chuck Berry. He wouldn't have any of it. He said, 'I could eat Chuck Berry for breakfast' in a real wide-boy, arrogant Liverpool way. I was shocked by his response and got terribly cross and we had quite a shout-up about it."

Barney Kessel (287): "The Beatles handled their career very well and they used some brilliant recording techniques, but I find that, both individually and collectively, their music is very ordinary. It has very little to offer anyone except young children and people who like to hear white boys play black man's music. It's like being given the carbon copy instead of the original. I applaud their success and I think it's wonderful to have made so many people happy, but even if they were playing across the street, I'd have no desire to go and see them."

Kim Fowley (288): "I asked John Lennon what the secret of his success was when he was in Toronto in 1969. He said, 'Well, we liked Canned Heat but we thought they were humorless, so we wrote 'Why Don't We Do It In The Road?' which was our message to Canned Heat to put more humour in their music.' He said, 'The Beatles were based on one idea – to improve our record collection. We would take favourite records and then we would make better versions of them. We stopped being a group when we stopped trying to improve on records we liked.' They blame the wives for the breakup but I like that idea. Maybe they stopped going to record stores and they stopped listening to other stuff as an inspiration to do one step better."

Paul Du Noyer (289): "John Lennon liked to stay close to his roots which were in Fifties rock'n'roll, very powerful, simple music. The only time he strayed was during the psychedelic era where everything became multi-layered and more complex. John felt that as long as he didn't stray too far from the music he loved, he wouldn't go far wrong."

The Beatles were trendsetters: they couldn't care less about playing the latest chart hits and, like them, other groups started covering R&B records from the early Sixties. But when did the Beatles start performing their own material? Some of their songs (e.g. 'One After 909') were written in their early days, but they weren't among their Cavern favourites. **Earl Preston (290)** also claims, "We were one of the first groups to do a self-penned song on stage. It was called 'Sweet Love' and it was in a Cliff Richard vein. We were on the same bill as the Beatles and Paul said, 'Very good, I like to see somebody do something a bit different' I said, 'Why haven't you done anything like that? You must have the ability.' He said, 'We've written one or two but we don't think they're up to it.'"

Johnny Gentle (291): "The first time I met the Beatles was half an hour before we went on stage in Scotland. We did a quick rehearsal of well-known songs and we went on stage together. It worked well as the chemistry was right between us. They did their own spot as well and I told Larry Parnes that they were better than me. I can remember playing John Lennon a song I was working on, 'I've Just Fallen For Someone'. I couldn't work out a middle eight and John came up with something that seemed to fit (sings) ''We know we'll get by / Just wait and see / Just like the sun tells us / The best things in life are free.' It flowed well but I thought it was out of order 'cause I'd been writing songs for a year. I recorded it for Parlophone under the name of Darren Young but there was no question of him getting a songwriting credit as we all helped each other in those days. It's one of his first record compositions, if not the very first."

Billy Kinsley (292) heard some of John and Paul's early songs on stage: "I remember 'Tip Of My Tongue', which Tommy Quickly recorded, and 'I'll Be On My Way', which Billy J. Kramer recorded. Pete Best sang 'The Pinwheel Twist". Pete got off his kit, Paul went on drums, George played Paul's left-handed bass right-handed and Pete sang."

Billy Kinsley was interviewed the day after he'd been at a firework party at Mike McCartney's house. Mike was about to light a firework and he turned to Billy and said, "Pinwheel Twist?" The song is still remembered. **Pete Best (293)** couldn't recall the words: "Paul wrote the song and asked me to do it. He coupled it with Joey Dee's hit 'Peppermint Twist'. I used to get up and do the twist on stage and Paul played my drums. It was a novelty and it went down well with the fans."

Ken Dodd (294): "I agreed to do a charity show at the Albany Cinema, Maghull one Sunday afternoon in October 1961. I got there about 3 o'clock and there was chaos. People were walking out in droves because some idiots on the stage were making the most terrible row. I said, 'You've got to get these fellers off, they're killing the show completely', and they said, 'Okay, we'll have the interval and then we'll put you on.' So they had the interval and while I was changing one of these idiots came in and said, 'Somebody told me that if we gave you our card, you might be able to get us a few bookings.' I threw the card away. Two years later my agent said, 'How would you like the Beatles on your radio show? You can have them for two dates.' I said, 'I'm not sure, what do you think?' He said, 'I think we should just have them for one show because they're going to be one of those groups that fade overnight.' We brought them in for one show and Paul McCartney said, 'We've worked with you before, Doddy.' I said, 'No, you've never worked with me, lad.' He said, 'Yes, we did, at the Albany, Maghull.' I said, 'That noise wasn't you, was it?' He said, 'Yeah, we were rubbish, weren't we?' I said, 'You certainly were. I had you thrown off.'"

Because there were so many groups on Merseyside, a beat evening would normally involve three or four groups. The promoter Sam Leach ran a series of *Operation Big Beat* evenings which would feature eight or nine local groups, including the Beatles, for 5s (25p) admission. Sam was notorious for his 'audition nights' which would feature several groups, but for which they received little, if any, money.

Tony Crane (295) recalls, "We were resident on Mondays at St. John's in Bootle. We only got paid £6 a night but we could pick whom we wanted as guests and we had the Beatles one night. In the Liverpool Echo, it had 'THE MERSEYBEATS' GUEST NIGHT' in capitals and, in little letters underneath, 'This week's guests: The Beatles'."

Some groups became local heroes while stars who visited Merseyside could find it an assault course. **Ray Ennis (296)** says, "Gene Vincent was appearing at the Tower Ballroom in New Brighton and he went to the front of the stage to lie down for one of his numbers. There weren't any bouncers and a gang of Teddy boys were all over him. He got up and fell over. He got up again and fell over again. Some yobbos had undone the bolts in his caliper and the poor guy couldn't stand up. He was lying there for ages, but he kept on singing. The management had to carry him off."

Stars who visited the Cavern fared little better. In January 1961 **Colin Manley (297)** as part of the Remo Four was on the same bill as the Shadows. "They arrived in the afternoon and set up their gear, brand new amplifiers and all that. They had a sound check, which was unheard of at the Cavern. The club was packed that evening and their sound balance was completely wrong. It's totally different when the place is full. The crowd thinned out when we went on, but we were loud and could be heard. People were coming up and saying, 'Oh, you're much better than them.'"

Hank Marvin (298) steps out of the Shadows: "It was one of our first gigs independent of Cliff and it was a very difficult stage to perform on. Since we'd been with Cliff, we'd been used to concert halls and theatres where we had room to move and perform. Going to the Cavern was like going back to the Two I's with the audience looking up our nostrils. Jet Harris had consumed vast quantities of alcohol and could barely stand up, let alone play. He fell forward at one point, stiff as a board, and the front row caught him and pushed him back up again. I made an excuse about Jet not being well and some Scouser shouted, 'He's pissed.' We were a four-piece band, and the bass and the drums was our anchor. When the bass player is out of time and playing wrong notes, it doesn't make things easy. I've no doubt that the Remo Four were a better proposition than us that night. They were very good, excellent, but we'd have beaten them any other night."

Ritchie Galvin (299), drummer with Earl Preston and the TTs, was on the same bill as the Tornados. "I've never liked using anybody else's drums as every time I do I break something. The Tornados had a No.1 hit with 'Telstar'. They put their gear on stage and said, 'We'd rather you didn't bring your gear on.' Clem Cattini said, 'You can use my drums – brand new Ludwig, so you'll have a good workout on them.' I said, 'Okay' and when we did our first number, I put his snare drum through his bass drum skin."

Faith Brown (300), then with the Carrolls: "I didn't much care for performing in the Cavern myself as it was so smoky and sweaty and you would finish the show looking like a drowned rat. I enjoyed seeing the Beatles but what I remember most is John Lennon breaking a string and swearing. We had no swearing at home and so this was something new to me – I had never heard anyone swear on stage."

The Bachelors' double bass almost touched the ceiling. **Dec Clusky (301)** recalls, "It just said in our diary, 'The Cavern, Liverpool'. We didn't know anything about the place. It sounded like another night club. When we found it in a little back street, we couldn't believe it. The sound was sensational, because anyone sounds good in a place like that. However, we were a pretty sane and rational act and I don't think the crowd wanted that."

Alan Price (302): "We came down from Newcastle to Liverpool in a little van in 1963 and we carried our own gear into the Cavern for a lunchtime session. We were very nervous about playing there and I said to a girl in a duffle coat who was watching us, 'Do you think they'll like rhythm and blues here?' 'Like it?', she said, 'We invented it.'"

Ray McFall (303): "Sonny Boy Williamson came to the Cavern at lunchtime and did a lunchtime show and the first thing he said was, 'Who will go out and get me a bottle?' He wanted a bottle of Scotch and two bottles of Coke and he sat in the bandroom, with bottles in each hand, simultaneously swigging Scotch and Coke. He wasn't a young man and I thought he mightn't get on stage, but he played for an hour. He came off stage and finished the Scotch, and went to his hotel and got another one and drank that in the same manner, and I remember saying to Bob that he was going to be flat on his back when he is due to come on stage in the evening, but I couldn't have been more wrong. He was there on time and he sang and played for the best part of two hours. He must have had a cast-iron stomach and he was marvellous."

Jimmy Justice was popular in 1962. He'd had hits with 'When My Little Girl Is Smiling' and 'Ain't That Funny'. He was booked to appear at the Cavern in July 1962 on the same session as Billy Kramer and the Coasters. **Tony Sanders (304)**, drummer with the Coasters: "Jimmy had a record in the charts and so the Cavern was packed. The changing room was tiny and Jimmy Justice was standing talking to Billy J. Kramer. I was setting my drums up and I stopped for a second and looked at the two of them. Kramer looked every inch a star, but Jimmy Justice didn't, although he was then the big event and Kramer was a nobody."

By this time, Billy was being managed by **Ted Knibbs (305)**. "Billy had pride in his appearance. He was an apprentice engineer on the railways and you'd see him coming in with his dirty hands and dirty face. When you met him half an hour later, he'd be immaculate from head to toe, clean in every respect, thanks to his mother who took pride in her lad."

Looking back, **Billy J. Kramer (306)** admits that he overdid things. "I was known for being the guy who dressed nice, the boy-next-door type of image. Now that I'm older and can look back, I think that if I'd gone on in a pair of jeans and a T-shirt or a denim jacket and rocked them, they'd have loved me. I must have been a bit crazy to appear in the Cavern in a gold lamé suit or a mohair jacket."

Cilla Black (307) never had her own band, but she sang as a guest vocalist with several groups. "I was very shy and I would never ask anybody if I could sing with them. For a start, the groups would look at you as if you'd gone berserk. Why should they let some daft bird sing with them? All my mates knew I could sing and it was they who said, 'Let Cilla have a go.' Rory Storm and the Hurricanes were the very first group I sang with. I sang Peggy Lee's 'Fever' and they were quite impressed and asked me to sing again. It was a bit of light relief and it let Rory and Wally have a rest. Ringo thinks that I was a bit flash and that I really wanted to sing. I did, but I had to be persuaded. I never rehearsed and used to say 'What do you know?' or 'I'll do what you know in your key.' That was difficult in Rory's band 'cause they could only play in one key, and it certainly wasn't mine."

This is the booking sheet for the Kansas City Five in May and June 1962. They were a hybrid of jazz and rock and got bookings on both counts. They had day jobs and with commendable restraint, they only accepted bookings at weekends and bank holidays.

Friday May 11 – Iron Door with Ian & the Zodiacs and *Operation Big Beat* at Tower Ballroom, New Brighton

Saturday May 12 – All night rock show at Iron Door

Thursday May 17 – Iron Door with the Invaders

Saturday May 19 – Parish Hall, Wallasey with the Pressmen

Saturday May 26 – Odd Spot with the Druids Jazz Band and then Iron Door

Sunday June 10 – Whitsun Jazz Festival at the Palace Hotel, Birkdale and then Iron Door

Monday June 11 – Newton Amateur Football Club, Greasby with Merseysippi Jazz Band

Friday June 15 – Iron Door with the Crescent City Stompers and *Rockerama* at Tower Ballroom, New Brighton

Saturday June 16 – Iron Door with Lew Bird and his New Orleans Jazz Band

Friday June 29 – *Operation Big Beat 3* at Tower Ballroom, New Brighton. Freddie Starr sings with the Kansas City Five

Saturday June 30 – All night rock show at Iron Door. Freddie Starr sings with the Kansas City Five

Tommy Hughes (308): "Freddie Starr used to run up and down the stage at the Iron Door. Derry Wilkie used to come down and they would do 'What'd I Say' with two microphones and they would be two good showmen. They would do the *Oh Boy!* show and Freddie would be Elvis and Billy Fury. He was always mad. He stopped a motorist once and said, 'Would you mind me giving me a push?' and he went into a garden and sat on a kid's swing. On an all-nighter at the Iron Door, it was about four o'clock in the morning and the hot dog stall had closed down. He went round the back, got a roll, split it open, put his willy in it, put a whole pile of tomato sauce on it and came out and said, 'Anybody fancy a hot dog?' He was doing things like that all the time."

The Cavern's all-night sessions would feature several groups, most of which would be performing elsewhere on Merseyside on the same night. **Bobby Thomson (309)** of the Dominoes explains, "I was an apprentice plumber and the work bored me stupid. I badly wanted to get on the road. We had some great times around the clubs. We'd play at the Orrell Park Ballroom from eight to nine and then tear up to St. Luke's Hall in Crosby and play from quarter to ten to eleven. Then we'd pile into our house in Seaforth and sleep in the front room. We'd get up at half-past five and go down to the

Cavern for the end of their all-nighter. We'd play there from seven till eight. We'd done three gigs in one night with a couple of hours sleep in between. Remember that most of us had day jobs."

Eric London (310): "When I was with Faron's Flamingos, we were all playing Burns guitars and so Rushworth's used us in an advertising campaign. They put a huge photo of us in their window. I worked for the Halifax Building Society and my boss passed the shop and saw the display. He came back to the office and immediately wrote to my father to find out what I was doing in the evenings. As it turned out, I was earning more from the gigs than from my job. My dad wasn't worried as he had been the guarantor when I bought the guitar for £85."

Dave Williams (311): "Dale Roberts and the Jaywalkers came from Ellesmere Port. I worked in Bowaters and I had the further distance to travel to get to the Cavern. I bought a scooter and I would ride with the guitar between my legs. I spent two years with the band and we did 270 gigs and I was still working five or six days a week."

It was all too much for **Les Braid (312)** of the Swinging Blue Jeans. "We were working six nights a week. We were resident in the Cavern, and in the Downbeat, and in the Tower Ballroom in New Brighton. I worked for the Corporation and I had to be at work at quarter to eight in the morning. Very often I never got home until half past one. We did this for two and a half years before we went professional and I was so tired during the day that I don't know how I managed to get through the work. One day I was sent to the Town Hall to do a job on the door of the main ballroom. I was half asleep as usual. The door was catching on the carpet, and so I had to kneel down to repair the bottom hinge. I thought, this carpet feels nice and comfortable and I fell asleep on the floor. When I woke up, I finished the job and went home."

IV. The Eppy-Centre

Cilla was managed by Brian Epstein, signed to Parlophone and her records were produced by George Martin. **Cilla Black (313)** tells me, "Others had wanted to manage me but they were turned down by my father, a docker who didn't trust managers. He liked Brian because he'd once bought a piano from the Epsteins."

Dave Lovelady (314) recalls, "We were the second group that Brian Epstein asked to turn professional but we turned him down because we were students. Brian was studying accountancy, I was studying architecture, Billy was with the Atomic Energy Authority and Mike was with a solicitor. We turned Brian Epstein down three times. Six months later he asked us again. By this time Gerry and Billy had had No.1s. We realised that this wasn't a flash in the pan, so we agreed. If we'd said yes immediately, we would have been second in line and maybe we would have been given the songs that Gerry got."

Billy Kinsley was 15 and Tony Crane 16 when they formed the Merseybeats in 1962, taking their name from the *Mersey Beat* newspaper. **Billy Kinsley (315)** says, "We were the third band to be signed by Brian Epstein but we left him because he wouldn't buy us suits. He bought the Beatles suits and we were jealous."

Bob Wooler (316) recalls being with Brian Epstein in the Majestic Ballroom in 1962: "Clay Ellis and the Raiders came on and BE went into one of his transfixed states. After he had gone home, BE asked me if I knew where he lived. I said, 'Bromborough', and he said, 'Is there any chance of meeting him?' 'Tonight?' 'Tonight.' It was 11.30pm, the end of the dance, and I agreed to take him. The Nemperor stayed in the car while I knocked on the door of an ordinary council house. His mother said he was in bed: he had a day job and had to be up for work in the morning. When I did see him again, he said, 'I wish I hadn't gone to bed.' and I thought, 'Just as well you did. God knows what would have happened in the back of the Nemperor's car. Brain wasn't only interested in your tonsils.' Brian did have ideas for signing the lad but it would have been instead of Billy J. and the lad kept asking me about it. The Nemperor said, 'I am in a dilemma. I want to sign Billy Kramer, he has great potential, and so what can I do for Clay Ellis? I would like to take the Bromborough lad on, but I can't have two similar artists.' It was heads or tails between Billy J. Kramer and Clay Ellis, and Billy won. Clay Ellis became disillusioned and he stopped performing."

Dave Lovelady (317): "Brain Epstein knew we would always turn up on time and give a complete cabaret act. He'd have great reports coming back but we were never pushed any farther. My parents said we were Brian Epstein's reserve group. If Billy J. Kramer had to back out of a booking at the last moment, Brian knew he could send for the Fourmost."

John McNally (318) recalls, "Brian Epstein wished he'd signed us and he gave us a Lennon and McCartney song, 'Things We Said Today'. He wanted us to record it but there were so many problems with our management and with him that, in the end, the Beatles put it out as one of their B-sides."

Tony Bramwell (319): "Brian was only a few years older than the Beatles but he was smart and educated and always wore suits. Nowadays people slag him off for his business decisions but he was setting the precedent. I know he got frustrated by all he had to do and he did unfortunately employ a few inept people. They disappeared out of the business when Brian died, which shows that they weren't up to much. The Beatles impressed me – they didn't crack up under pressure. They accepted that it was expected of them. I am amazed that they could be so productive when they were so busy."

V. I Call Your Name

William Howard Ashton lived in Bootle with his parents and performed with his friends. They couldn't decide what to call themselves. **Billy J. Kramer (320)**: "We were thinking along the lines of Billy Ford and the Phantoms, and Tony Sanders came up with the Billy Kramer name. Floyd Cramer was big at the time and we thought that spelling it with a K made it sound more masculine and aggressive. John Lennon added the J to make the name more American and give it a better ring. I asked him what the J stood for and he said, 'Julian'. I said that I didn't like that, that it was a queer's name. I didn't know that he had a son called Julian."

Earl Royce (321) of Earl Royce and the Olympics is back to being Billy Kelly again; "Royston Earl was the name of someone's uncle and we took the Olympics from a drum kit. I didn't really want my name out front as I felt we worked as a team. I'm glad that I didn't use my real name as I can keep it quiet about it now and not have people asking me for a song."

According to the *Liverpool Echo,* Priscilla White was renamed Cilla Black because "the darker shade suits her singing so perfectly". This sounds good, but it was an accident. Bill Harry, the editor of *Mersey Beat*, was working late one night and, being tired, he wrote Cilla Black for Cilla White. Cilla thought it looked better, so she kept it.

Stu James (322) of the Mojos: "Stu Slater is my real name. I changed it to Stu James because I didn't think Stu Slater sounded much like a pop star's name. It is just James Stewart reversed."

The Searchers took their name from the title of a John Wayne film, and were originally the backing group for the singer Johnny Sandon, originally Billy Beck, and he had taken his name from the Sandon Hotel. **Tom Earley (323)**: "There had been a TV series, *The Pathfinders*, about a wartime bomber squadron and we thought it was a pretty good name. It was also connected with Longfellow as the Pathfinders were something to do with buckskins and coon hats. We had a business card with a drawing of a pathfinder that I did, so it became a trademark."

The Liverpool group the Nomads were forced to change their name because it had already been registered by a London group. They picked the Mojos as a tribute to Muddy Waters and his record 'Got My Mojo Working'. Peter Flannery became Lee Curtis by reversing the name of the American singer Curtis Lee. Brian Tarr became **Denny Seyton (324)**: "My name really did come out of a hat. We had a pieces of paper with Christian names and pieces with surnames and we put them together. I was the singer because I was the poorest guitar-player and I had the loudest voice. There were no microphones when we started. We called the band, the Sabres, because that was the name on the drum." John Boyle who was with Denny, added, "And when we got microphones, we realised our mistake!"

Kenny Johnson was Sonny Webb, the name being an amalgam of the American country singers, Sonny James and Webb Pierce. The Cascades' bass guitarist **Joe Butler (325)** recalls, "Merseybeat worked both ways. We were not a soft and gentle country band. We brought our natural environment to Nashville music. I think it worked well and we scored because we had a following from both the beat and the country audiences."

The Undertakers acquired their name by accident. **Brian Jones (326)** recalls, "We were called the Vegas Five and there was a misprint in the *Liverpool Echo*. We were playing at the Aintree Institute and we looked to see if we were listed. The name 'Undertaker' was advertised for the Aintree Institute and then we found the name 'Vegas Five' in the Deaths column. We phoned Bob Wooler and he said, "You might as well be called the Undertakers." We learned 'The Dead March' in the dressing room before we went on."

In 1964 **Geoff Nugent (327)** was not happy with the decision to drop the coffin-shaped amplifiers and their undertakers' dress. "Tony Hatch and our manager said that we weren't selling records because our name was sick. I totally disagreed with them and I reckon our downfall was changing our name to the 'Takers. The A-side of the 'Takers single was an old Drifters' song, 'If You Don't Come Back'. It was a good number, but they stopped plugging it as soon as it was starting to move."

The Undertakers became the 'Takers and got involved in a ridiculous scheme. **Brian Jones (328)** recalls, "A publicity company had an idea for 'If You Don't Come Back'. They asked us to go to East Berlin and get arrested at Checkpoint Charlie. The guitarist and I did get arrested and spent 24 hours being interrogated. They threatened to send us to Siberia for currency smuggling. The record sold reasonably well but it didn't make the charts and we decided to go to America, except for Geoff Nugent who stayed here."

Faron's Flamingos emerged from a band formed at the Liverpool Mercury Cycling Club. In the winter they preferred skiffle to cycling. The group, the Hi-Hats, became Robin and the Ravens, Robin wearing a yellow silk suit and the band pink jackets. They were booked to play some American bases in France, but before they went, Robin left the Ravens and **Faron (329)**, who had split with the TTs, took his place. "Paddy Chambers and Nicky Crouch played guitars. Trevor Morais played drums and I was on bass. I hadn't played bass before and I asked Billy Kinsley to show me how. He only had time to give me one lesson, how to play in the key of E. For the first few weeks I played everything in E. As regards our name, Bob Wooler thought it was a good idea to stick with the bird thing of Robin and the Ravens, so we became Faron's Flamingos."

Faron had a dynamic stage personality, as **Trevor Morais (330)** recalls. "Faron wore sunglasses and T-shirts on stage long before anybody else. He'd jump up in the air and land on his knees. I thought he was a great, exciting performer."

The film *Violent Playground* was shot in Liverpool in 1957, and Freddie appears in the cast under his wonderfully apt, real name of Freddie Fowell. As a singer, he intended to go to Germany billed simply as 'Freddie'. He learned that there was already a German singer of that name and as he didn't want to use his real name, he borrowed Ringo's surname and became Freddie Starr.

Mike Byrne (331): "Rory Storm inspired the name of my first band. They did the summer season at Pwllheli and I went there as a holidaymaker. They did a talent show every week and I got up and did 'Whole Lotta Shakin''. When I got my first band, I kept in touch with them and I worked at the Grosvenor Ball Room for the first time, Rory gave me the name, Mike and the Thunderbirds."

Ian and the Zodiacs recorded their version of the Marvelettes' 'Beechwood 4-5789' in London. **Charlie Flynn (332):** "I wrote the B-side, which was called 'You Can Think Again'. I didn't want to put my own name on the label and as I'd been repeating the line from a western film, 'Remember the name Wade', I put Wellington Wade on the label. I put a pair of doll's wellington boots on the end of my bass guitar. Oriole released 'Let's Turkey Trot' as a single under the name of Wellington Wade. It didn't get much push, but the magazine *Reveille* said I was a star of the future."

Ralph Ellis (333) didn't appreciate the gimmick in their name as the Swinging Blue Jeans didn't live up to their name: "It would have been better if we'd worn jeans from the beginning, but at that time smartness was the vogue. Later on we did a link-up with a jeans manufacturer in Liverpool, Lybro. They invented one that was blue on the outside and green on the inside. When it rained your legs turned green and they weren't the best of designs and they always seemed to be a bad fit. You were meant to put them on in a hot bath, zip them up and sit there for about an hour and then they would shrink to the shape of your body."

6 WORKIN' FOR THE MAN

I. Travel and Lodgings
II. Tony Sheridan
III. The Hamburg Throat
IV. Mach Schau
V. Speed Recordings
VI. Star time
VII. Mean streets

"Those little old ladies in the toilets, man – without them, we were dead."
(Roy Young)

I. Travel and Lodgings

A young Hamburg resident **Frank Dostal (334)** recalls: "My brother went to South Africa and he sent me the Little Richard single of 'Tutti Frutti' and from then, I was very interested in rock'n'roll. Until 1962 I was very interested in modern jazz, but the two or three clubs where rock'n'roll happened in Hamburg were in a no-go area for people like me. They were in rough areas and lots of seamen went there. I did go when the Star-Club opened. By then I was so interested in the music that I had to see it live."

No other bands played the Indra after its restraining order, but the Kaiserkeller and the Top Ten did brisk business throughout 1961 with one Liverpool band following another. The Star-Club at Grosse Freiheit 39 opened on 13 April 1962. By the standards of the area, this was a plush club – and a big one, accommodating 2,000 patrons. The Beatles are the only band to play in all four clubs.

Günter Zint (335): "The Star-Club had been a cinema and then it was a dance hall for working people. It was for the poor people in Hamburg: the young ladies who wanted to get married went there on Saturday nights. Then it was a cheap cinema, Stern Kino. Manfred Weissleder had a sex club in the same building and the guy who ran the cinema said that the people going to the sex club were disturbing his business. He said to Manfred, 'You must move out or take the cinema as well.' Manfred took the cinema but it was too big for a sex club, it was not intimate enough, and so he decided to make it a night club with live music. He met Horst Fascher, who spoke English and knew something about rock'n'roll and said, 'Horst, you get me groups and we will make it a music place'. Stern means Star and so when Manfred opened the club, he called it the Star-Club."

Adrian Barber (336): "Manfred Weissleder was all right. He respected your ability if you were a musician but there were certain rules. If you showed him any disrespect, you had to go and if you insulted him in front of a woman, you would be lucky if you were left alive."

Frank Dostal (337): "The Star-Club was our temple, the best place you could think of. It was also a great place to go to as you would rarely hear crap there. The management knew what they wanted. If an agent persuaded them to take a band which wasn't any good, they wouldn't use them anymore. You were surrounded by interesting musicians, so it was a constant party. It was open 12 hours a day and on Saturday 14 hours, so you had a great party every night with very good music. Its energy was fantastic."

Horst Fascher (338): "Our concept was four bands in a night. That meant they were playing one hour before midnight and one hour after midnight. If a band was unlucky, it did the first hour, eight till nine, and the last hour, three till four. We usually opened at 8pm and finished at four in the morning. That was eight hours playing time with four bands. Later on we had more bands, sometimes six and eight and even ten bands in a night. The bands had to stay around, drinking beers and staying awake, but they had girls and they had fun. They were very very disciplined and I never had any trouble with any of the bands. All the musicians loved me and I loved them. It was like a big family."

And how did you become part of that big family? **Sylvia Saunders (339)** of the Liver Birds: "My friend Valerie played guitar and I asked her to show me. She did show me but my fingers were too small for the frets. I got a drum-kit instead. We went to Rushworth's and my mother signed the HP contract. We then advertised for more girls to join the band, and that was Mary and Pam."

Mary Dostal (340): "At first we made the mistake of wanting to look very feminine and we had black dresses with chiffon sleeves but when we saw the photographs, we realised that it didn't look right with the music. We started wearing trousers which was much better for moving about on stage. It was definitely an attraction for people to come and see these four strange little girls on stage. We had bad luck in England with our manager and we found out that we were receiving a lot less money than we were getting for the gig. Our parents were getting very worried about us as we were travelling a lot and not earning any money. Henry Henroid put an article in *Mersey Beat* that he was looking for groups for the Star-Club so we went to the audition. He said immediately that he was interested but Sylvia was only 17."

After the fiasco with the Beatles in December 1960, the clubs and the authorities were insisting on the appropriate paperwork. **Allan Williams (341):** "To get the Beatles back to Germany, the German Consulate said, 'You have to be registered as a licensed theatrical agent', that is, I had to prove I was a person of good character. You had to get permission from the local council that you were a man of good standing and did not have any criminal convictions. You couldn't give the address of a club because you would be accused of being under the influence of alcohol when you signed artists up. There had to be no alcohol on the premises, and once I got my agency, they allowed the Beatles to go over. I had to sign a fidelity bond, and, if they got into trouble again, I would be held responsible. Likewise, Peter Eckhorn at the Top Ten had to guarantee their good behaviour."

A court order was needed if you were under 18. **Mary Dostal (342):** "The court permission with Sylvia took longer than we thought. Manfred Weissleder arranged for us to stay in a little hotel in London as it had to take place there. Jimmy Savile, who was staying at the same hotel, said, 'Girls, I will get *The People* to write an article about you as that will get you a bit of money to help you out.' A photographer asked us to sit on the steps outside the hotel and look happy and then sad. On Sunday, there was a big article on the front of *The People*, 'Parents, don't let this happen to your daughters.' Our parents wanted us home right away and we needed someone in the music business to say that they would take care of Sylvia while she was in Hamburg. That was Mickie Most, although he never came to Hamburg, and the next day they put us on the train. The next night we were playing and the audiences went hysterical."

Beryl Marsden (343): "I was 16 and I had to have a special licence. I had to go to the Bow Street Magistrates Court and have a chaperone, and I went there when I was 17. It was not a lot of fun to see everyone else partying to all hours of the morning as I had to be out of the club and back in my room by 10.30. When I was getting up for breakfast, the others would come rolling in from being out all night, but it was probably for the best."

Günter Zint (344): "Stevie Winwood was only 15 or 16 when he came here and twice I had to pick him up from the police station because he was arrested. He did not know what his money was worth. The first time he had some money, he walked to the city to buy some trousers and when he came to pay, he took a bundle of 100 mark notes and put them on the table. When they saw a young boy with so much money, they thought something must be criminal and called the police. He told them that he played in the Star-Club. They called the Star-Club and Manfred Weissleder asked me if I would go to the police station and get him out. They put him in again for something similar."

Joe Fagin (345): "I was driving to Litherland Town Hall for a gig one night and I knocked the door off a huge Chevrolet Impala. A massive guy of six foot four got out and I thought that he was going to kill me. Luckily, Johnny Fanning, who roadied for Kingsize Taylor, was able to calm him down. I was lucky because it was Manfred Weissleder. He was looking for bands to go to Hamburg and he watched us perform. It was a Wednesday and he told us to be there on Monday. We packed our jobs in and we drove over in that same Chevy, which had had the door repaired. We were given 24 hours to recuperate and the next night we worked one hour on, three hours off from 6pm to 4am. I lost my voice and so the rhythm guitarist took over. He lost his and so the bass player had to sing."

Going from Liverpool to Hamburg is easy enough today but not back then when money was tight. **Fred Marsden (346):** "We had to drive from Liverpool to Hamburg. We had our own van and I did most of the driving. We got to Hamburg about two in the afternoon and the manager of the Top Ten said that we were going to play at seven o'clock. We had gone 36 hours without sleeping, so Peter Eckhorn, the manager, gave us Preludins to keep us awake."

Mike Pender (347) of the Searchers: "The first time we went Tony Jackson took his bass cabinet with him, and we went the difficult way – the train down to Harwich and then by boat to the Hook of Holland and train to Hamburg. We didn't mind, we wanted to make it and when we got to Hamburg, we thought we had made it. We had no big ideas or dreams about recording or having hits. We had no idea what was going to happen to us."

Lee Curtis (348): "We went from Liverpool to the Hook of Holland. We were going by car, boat and train. We set off a day late because little Davy, Mushy, our bass player, disappeared. He was having problems with his girlfriend because he was going away for a month. By the time he turned up, we had to rebook and we went the following day. We got on the boat train and we ended up at the Hook of Holland and then got on the train to Hamburg. The German police came on board and asked for our passports and visas. They were in their green uniforms with their belts with guns on, which was quite scary. 'Achtung, achtung', and we didn't understand what they were saying. We had to leave the train and we were put in the hands of the Dutch police as they wouldn't let us through. Because of little Davy, the visas were one day out of date. The police looked after us very well, but they put us in a cell and we stayed the night there, trying to contact the Star-Club to verify the fact that we did have work there. We didn't have a contract with us as that was with our manager. The next day the police took us back to the Hook of Holland and we were put on the boat train with no money and nothing to eat. Don Alcyd was our drummer and he was as close to being a hippie as you could get. He knew a beatnik who was on the boat and called John the Road, who was living on his wits. John the Road managed to wangle a big meal in the restaurant and we got some sandwiches for ourselves. We got off at Harwich and when we got to the train station, our tickets were invalid. Our manager had to telex the station we were leaving from and we were going to spend the night on the station until a policeman moved us on. A railway worker invited to his home and gave us a meal. We got to the station the following morning and our tickets were there. We got home, obtained new visas and then set off again for the Star-Club."

And what happened next? **Lee Curtis (349)**: "We went through it all again, this time with a van, and driving on the wrong side of the road. I was the only driver and we eventually got to the Star-Club and that place was pulsing as we walked in with the solid beat of drums and bass. I remember the hanging Chinese lanterns over the dance floor and it had so much atmosphere. I can't remember the band that was on but they were really good. Anybody who played there had to be good. No one played there who hadn't been vetted by Horst Fascher or Manfred Weissleder. They saw and heard them and if they thought they were good enough, they booked them. Pete Best phoned Manfred Weissleder and we got there on his say-so."

Roy Young (350): "I was on *Drumbeat* and *Oh Boy!* and I was invited to go to Hamburg. I had no idea what it was all about but it felt cool because it was getting out of England. I got out of my cab at the Top Ten club on the Reeperbahn and some guys were loading amplifiers and guitars into an old van. Two of them invited me for a coffee so that they could tell me about Hamburg, and it was John and Paul. I was told that Horst Fascher would take care of me: he had been a professional boxer who had killed a guy and had had his licence taken away. When I got to the club to open up, the Germans were shouting out to me, 'Beatles! Beatles!' and they wanted their songs. I didn't know what they did. I went into 'Long Tall Sally', 'Tutti Frutti' and 'Lucille' and luckily for me, Little Richard was popular there too. I didn't know that Paul was into Little Richard like me. If I had not been as strong a singer as I am – and I do have a powerful, rock'n'roll voice – they would have thrown me out."

Mary Dostal (351): "The man who picked us up at the hotel took us to the Star-Club in a taxi. It had a Catholic church next to it and the taxi dropped us off by the church. I was so happy to see this church as I was planning to play in the Liver Birds for two years and then become a nun. We walked round and we saw all the clubs and we couldn't believe it. If my parents had seen it, they would have brought me home right away. Instead, I was telling my mother about the church and how nice it was."

Chris Curtis (352): "We finished at five or six o'clock on Sunday mornings and going to church was a good way of winding down. It was a convent church so there were a lot of nuns there. It was great, but the whole area was seedy and awful. There were transvestites standing in the doorway of the clubs, and because I had very long hair, a lot of people thought I was a tranny, and I wasn't. Manfred Weissleder, who was a great bloke, and Horst Fascher, who did the announcing, would ask me why I had my hair like that, and I would say, 'Because I use it in the act.'"

Ian Edwards (353): "The first time I went down the Grosse Freiheit to the Star-Club was frightening. We were four young lads from Liverpool and we had arrived in the blue capital of the world, but it was the strippers, prostitutes and gangsters who looked after the bands. We didn't have any problems: they told us where to go and what to do and they were always looking after us. If the girls of the night had a good night, then it was a good night on stage for us as well. The bottles would be sent up. You would lose face if you didn't drink what they sent you. It's fine if they send you beer but it's hard for four people to drink a bottle of Scotch in an hour."

Fred Marsden (354): "Everybody was on our side in Hamburg so we were all right. We saw some great fights in the audience in the Top Ten. Hamburg, like Liverpool, is a seaport and you would get sailors coming in and getting a few beers or champagnes inside them and then they'd be requesting songs. There was one sailor who kept asking us to play 'Lucille' as he was a big fan of the Everly Brothers. We played 'Lucille' and he sent us a bottle of champagne. He asked us to play it again and we got another bottle, and at half-past one I fell off my drums as I was drunk. That's the only time I have ever done that. We also got a crate of champagne off Gene Vincent because we'd been backing him, but I don't think it was very expensive champagne."

Mark Peters (355) ran into trouble the first night he played at Hamburg. "The manager gave me a bunch of flowers, and I threw them back because I thought that he was insinuating that I was a poof. It was hard to calm him down because then he wanted to kill me. Over there, giving flowers is one of the biggest compliments he could have paid me."

Dave Lovelady (356) grew up fast when he went there with Kingsize Taylor. "I hated the whole time in Hamburg. I was a young lad straight from school and I'd never even been to London. It was the biggest thrill of my life to fly to Hamburg. The person who was supposed to meet us at the airport didn't show up, but we had enough money to get a taxi to the Star-Club. It was like Blackpool but with strip clubs everywhere. As we walked up the steps to the Star-Club, the doors burst open. A fellow come tumbling down the steps and the bouncers came out and shot him right in front of our eyes."

The lodgings were grim. **Mike Pender (357)**: "We were met by Horst Fascher who took us to a hotel. The lady of the house showed us our rooms and we went 'Good grief, have you seen the girls here?' Our eyes were popping out of our heads, but we didn't know what a brothel was. But once you'd seen it, that was it: you settled back into the music. I was more excited about Bill Haley and Fats Domino coming to the Star-Club than seeing any of the ladies."

Frank Allen (358), then with Cliff Bennett and the Rebel Rousers: "I had never heard of Liverpool before I went to Hamburg or at least, I didn't know that there was anything special about it. I saw this *Mersey Beat* paper they brought over and I thought this was fantastic. They had a whole little musical world that had nothing to do with anyone outside Liverpool and they had their own local stars. I gravitated towards the Searchers because they were nice quiet lads who didn't drink a lot and I was like that too. I exclude Tony Jackson from that as he was boozing and raving and having a great time with the rest of the bands."

Les Maguire (359): "Initially at the Top Ten, we slept in bunk beds in the attic. When we were playing at the Star-Club, we stayed at the Hotel Germania and then at one of the flats over the clubs. It was rough. The food was pretty basic – cheese, biscuits, bread, corn flakes, coffee, beer, so going to the Seaman's Mission was a treat. It was run by the English and you could get a proper fried breakfast there as well as fresh milk."

Lee Curtis (360): "There was a flat above a strip club across the road from the Star-Club, which was one of the places that we stayed. It had bare boards and four beds, couple of chairs and a table. One of the Beatles had been sick and the cleaning lady wouldn't remove it and it was there for two or three days. She complained to Manfred, who told the Beatles to clean it up and all they did was put cigarette ends in it, matchsticks and what have you. After a few days she went back and told Manfred, and when he went to look, they told him it was their hedgehog."

Fortunately, the Beatles never shared their lodgings with the Liver Birds. **Mary Dostal (361)**: "There was Kingsize Taylor, Lee Curtis, Ian and the Zodiacs and the Remo Four and we were like a family. We lived together on the fourth floor of the Hotel Pacific. Some of the lads from the other groups would ask us to wash their shirts and we would."

Alan Schroeder (362): "I can't remember what we did with our clothes but I know my shirts would be wrecked. We didn't have a lot of money and we would drink Fanta and eat egg and chips and stay at the Pacific Hotel. We had this van outside with a mattress in it. If someone was stuck for a bed, he could kip in the van."

Bob Conrad (363): "We went to play at the Star-Club for a month but we were conned because it was one of those five week-months. We hardly got any money and at the time we were breaking open sandwich machines to get something to eat."

Spencer Lloyd Mason (364): "Preludins could be bought like sweets in the shops and all the bands were on them. I don't think they would got through the hours without them. I would fly out to Hamburg most Friday nights for £7 return and I would collect the bands' money which was not always easy. Horst Fascher was Manfred Weissleider's right-hand man and minder. I would ask him for the money for the three or fours bands who were working there and once he said to me, 'Come back Monday.' I said, 'No, I want the money now. The boys have to eat.' 'Come back Monday,' he yelled. The third time I asked him, he pulled out a shooter and stuck it on the end of my nose and I got the message: 'Okay, I'll come back Monday'. The bouncers were very violent and they would beat anyone who was out of order to a pulp."

II. Tony Sheridan

Sam Hardie (365) from the Dominoes: "The first few times I saw Tony Sheridan, it didn't register, but then I became a confirmed addict. I do think he is the greatest singer ever. He was Mr. Soul, the musician's musician."

Les Maguire (366) of Gerry and the Pacemakers: "Any group that came back from Hamburg would say, 'Tony Sheridan, fabulous, he's a knockout.' He influenced so many people that the Liverpool sound should be called the Tony Sheridan sound. He did more for Liverpool and the Beatles than anybody else."

Johnny Hutch (367) of the Big Three: "It was like going out with an old banger and coming back with a Rolls-Royce. The Beatles owed everything to Sheridan because they copied him to a T. They copied his style on guitar. Sheridan was a fantastic guitarist, the governor."

Bobby Thomson (368) of the Dominoes: "When John Lennon came back from Hamburg, he stood with his legs wide apart and he held the guitar like a machine gun. He didn't stand like that before and once I saw Sheridan, I knew whom he'd copied. Sheridan became one of my heroes, one of the first good white blues singers."

Chris Curtis (369): "Gerry Marsden was doing an impression of Tony Sheridan. No one gives that man enough credit. He was great. If you impersonate someone singing, it is never the same as your own throat doing the job. He was the man who instigated 'You'll Never Walk Alone' (sings). Gerry must have heard Tony singing it."

The reason why Gerry and the Pacemakers started performing 'You'll Never Walk Alone' is one of the mysteries of Merseybeat. Chris Curtis could be right but Gerry maintains that is through seeing the film, *Carousel*, which is again possible but there were beat recordings before Gerry Marsden's – Roy Hamilton (1954), Gene Vincent (1957), Conway Twitty (1959) – all of which he might have heard, not to mention Frank Sinatra, Bing Crosby and Judy Garland. Les Chadwick told me that he had the Gene Vincent LP and that there is where Gerry got it from.

Sam Hardie (370) of Kingsize Taylor and the Dominoes saw the change in Gerry and the Pacemakers: "I'd heard Gerry in Liverpool before I went to Hamburg. I thought he was pretty good but I'd say now that he imitated Tony Sheridan. He wasn't the only one and Tony Sheridan hasn't been given enough credit."

And what does **Gerry Marsden (371)** say to this? "Tony Sheridan was a genius, a great guitar player. I used to watch Tony every night and he influenced me a great deal, not so much in his singing as in his rhythm. He drove like mad and I nicked a lot of his ideas. He also wrote nice songs. While we were there, he wrote a song called 'Why (Can't You Love Me Again)?' I wanted to record it and he said, 'Hang on, I've got a better one.' He sang 'Please Let Them Be'. I recorded it sometime later. It was one of the biggest flops in the history of records, but it's a lovely song."

Sheridan's most significant contribution was his radical approach to familiar songs. **Ian Edwards (372)** of Ian and the Zodiacs was impressed: "We used to copy a record as best as we could and then we came across Tony Sheridan who didn't give two hoots as to how somebody else had recorded it. We realised that we shouldn't be carbon copies and we got a lot more adventurous."

Roy Young (373): "Tony Sheridan had a little book that he would put on his amplifier and he would jump from one song to another and you had to follow him: it was quite chaotic really. It was eight hours a night, it sounds ridiculous today. At 10, there was a half-hour break and then you would go on until 4 in the morning. Many times gangsters would come into the club, and the patrons would have to vacate the table if they were sitting at the front because they would want to sit there. The waiters would give them drinks and they would throw 50 marks onto the stage and that meant they wanted 'What'd I Say', which could go on for an hour. Once I left Tony, went down the road, had something to eat and he was still playing the same song when I got back. You hear guys today saying that they have to play two shows in one night and they are complaining. Even today, I will more likely go out there and not realise what time it is and just go on and on until I am carried off."

Fred Marsden (374): "Hamburg changed the guitarists more than the drummers 'cause Tony Sheridan was a fantastic guitarist and singer, although he was unpredictable. He was a god to the guitarists as he was so good. All the guitarists were sliding their finger down the frets but it didn't affect my drumming as I was always the same type of drummer. I played with Tony Sheridan a few times and he told me to get lost, I wasn't good enough for him. He said, 'Come on Fred, you're dragging, get going.'"

Lee Curtis (375): "I remember Tony Sheridan being cruel to Billy J Kramer when we all went back over there in the Nineties. Billy got changed into this sequined blue suit and he looked superb. Tony went, 'Umm, nice, wow, but you know something, Billy, that ain't gonna help you out there.' Out there it didn't matter what you looked like, you had to have the talent. You had to be able to sing or play and you had to be able to put up on a show, and Tony was right, you didn't do the show by painting yourself up. They would appreciate a beautiful costume: they would think, 'He's made the effort, but can he sing?'"

Tony Sheridan had his detractors. **Dicky Tarrach (376)**: "I was always happier when Tony Sheridan was not playing. The Beat Brothers came on stage and played about 15 minutes alone and then Tony Sheridan came on as the big star and I didn't like that. The Beatles worked very well with Roy Young but with Tony Sheridan, it didn't work for me. Sheridan was like the old world and they were on the way to the new."

Mary Dostal (377): "You never knew with Tony Sheridan whether he was going to be his nice self or his horrible self but he was always very good with the audience. He could speak German because he was married to a German girl."

But Tony wasn't alone in appearing a little different to the audience. **Frank Dostal (378)**: "What I liked about some of the bands is that they weren't polite, they seemed to be playing for themselves, rather than playing for the audience. Mike Hart of the Roadrunners was a very weird guy and he was singing and playing for himself, not even for the rest of the band. He did make announcements but he was only talking to the in crowd. He did it because somebody told him to, not because he wanted to make announcements."

Tony Sheridan left his mark on the local German bands, although they weren't always to know it. **Sam Hardie (379)** recalls: "A German magazine used to publish the

English words to rock'n'roll hits and they asked Tony Sheridan to write down the words to 'Skinny Minnie'. He made the whole thing full of obscene and disgusting swear words. It was a load of nonsense, complete and utter rubbish. The paper published the words and German groups blithely started singing them."

Bobby Thomson (380): "A German group called the Four Renders wanted to change their name. Kingsize Taylor told them that the word for 'friend' in Liverpool was 'skin' and a week or two later, we saw an ad for the opening of a new club by the Four Skins."

You may wonder why Tony Sheridan didn't become a superstar. Unlike the Beatles, he couldn't adapt his uninhibited performance for British audiences. Does the public fall for someone who is sweating before he even goes on stage? He was also temperamental and his disagreements with the pianist Roy Young can even be heard on record. Like P.J. Proby, Tony Sheridan possessed a self-destructive streak that ruined his opportunities. **Paddy Chambers (381)** of Paddy, Klaus and Gibson described one occasion, "We'd been backing Sheridan for months. We were booked for a live broadcast of the BBC's *Saturday Club*, but he started doing strange songs that we'd never heard him sing before. We couldn't believe it."

Another reason for Tony Sheridan's lack of chart success was that he was still based in Germany when the hits were happening in the UK. There's little doubt that lengthy stays in Hamburg affected the chances of several performers, including Kingsize Taylor and the Dominoes, Lee Curtis and the All Stars, and Ian and the Zodiacs. But perhaps, most important of all, was the way **Tony Sheridan (382)** viewed success: "The Searchers were a group who worked very hard to make it and stay there, but I was someone who didn't really care. If it happens, it happens and if it doesn't, it doesn't."

Günter Zint (383): "Tony Sheridan always thought, and he still thinks, and that is a tragedy, that he was the big star. It turned out differently. Tony made some records and the Beatles made the backing music as the Beat Brothers. He said, 'You are my backing group', and he was the star. History has shown that he was wrong. He is still making good music but he works in clubs for the same sort of money that he got in the Sixties. I organised some concerts for the St Pauli Museum and I gave him some engagements but we always had trouble – we had trouble with the time schedules, we had troubles with the payment, we had troubles with everything. Sometimes he gives a fantastic concert but another time he makes a song 25 minutes long and the room is almost empty. Sometimes he is great and sometimes he is boring."

III. The Hamburg Throat

A feature of the Merseyside groups is that many of them had two or three good vocalists. It's essential for harmony work and also if you're performing for hours on end in Hamburg. You could end up with the Hamburg throat: for some vocalists, Hamburg was more about oral wrecks than oral sex.

Lee Curtis (384): "You didn't really avoid the Hamburg throat but once you got over it, you didn't get it again during that visit. Hamburg, like Liverpool, was full of salt air and that affected everybody, and of course, we were all singing a lot. I didn't have much trouble with it, but I did come home to England to have my tonsils out at Walton Hospital. Some people thought they had something really nasty with the Hamburg throat, but it was just wear and tear and you ended up with a stronger voice. The Germans always used to say to me, 'My god, such volume' and they were right – Hamburg enhanced my voice: it got muscles."

Frank Dostal (385): "I don't know if anyone went to a doctor or took any singing lessons, but I never heard of anybody doing that. What we were doing wasn't supposed to be sensible, and it wasn't sensible. The charm of what made people love this music wasn't because it was sensible. It was because it was everything else but that. You were part of a counter-culture, so you didn't want to have a trained voice: you wanted to have an expressive voice."

Kuno Dreysse (386): "Yesterday I heard an early recording by the Beatles where John Lennon sings 'Memphis Tennessee'. I find it hard to believe that it is John Lennon. In Hamburg, he got the roughness in his voice and the power to scream. At the beginning it was 'Did I get the chords right?' but in Hamburg they found their way."

Les Chadwick (387) from Gerry and the Pacemakers: "Playing in Hamburg made all of the bands. We played from 7pm to 4am in the Top Ten with a 10 minute break every hour and another half hour at midnight. You really get to know each other when you do that, but it was hard on Gerry. He was the only singer but we did break it up by doing some instrumentals and also every song had about four instrumental breaks."

Fred Marsden (388): "When Gerry was 12 or 13, he was in the church choir and his voice was absolutely brilliant. Gerry was a very good singer but he was never as good after Hamburg as it battered his voice. We would go on at seven, do an hour, have a ten minute break, do another hour, have a ten minute break right through until two o'clock. It wasn't so bad for the Beatles as John, George and Paul all sang and even Pete did a couple of numbers. They could spread it out. Gerry was our main singer and the smoking and the singing battered his voice. He got lots of coughs and chest colds after that, and that's why he sounds husky now."

IV. Mach Schau

It wasn't enough to stand there and perform your songs: you had to *mach schau*. **Lee Curtis (389)**: "In Hamburg they expected you to do a show. The Beatles were doing silly and hilarious things to make time pass. You could do anything in Germany and it was accepted, like standing up on the piano or jumping into the audience. Nobody wanted the Shadows' walk there."

Les Maguire (390) of Gerry and the Pacemakers: "There was a Swedish group which was immaculately dressed and could do all the Shadows' fancy walks. They were very good. Then the Beatles came on and I've never laughed so hard in my life. John, Paul and George were doing the Shadows' walks, but all distorted and disjointed. Later we were very embarrassed for the Swedish group."

Dicky Tarrach (391): "The Beatles were the first guys I had seen who talked to the audience. All the other bands said, 'Thank you, the next song is…' The Beatles made jokes on stage, they were very intelligent and they had German girlfriends and so they were learning the language, and they spoke these mixed German and English words to the audience. John Lennon had a toilet seat round his head. They were laughing about these things and that inspired us to do little stories and be talking with the audience."

Chris Curtis (392): "We would start with a speedy number to get them up dancing. That way the club would sell more beer. They called it mach schau. We would race around and I would shake my head and they really liked that. For some unknown reasons, the Germans liked me better with short hair and I thought it would be the other way round. I looked like an ordinary English chap when I had my hair cut."

Günter Zint (393): "The Remo Four was a fantastic group. When Tony Ashton came on stage, there was one song, 'But I Was Cool', he did with a hat. He pulled it over his ears and eyes, and he was singing it and acting it so fantastically. It was theatre. Sometimes the groups had fun by dressing as women or they would ask the waitresses to come on stage to make music together with them. A lot of funny things happened there: they had their own comic fashion shows and it was like music theatre."

Lee Curtis (394): "I remember the Pretty Things who were jumping about and the drummer was on his knees where he had knocked this vase of flowers over and broken it. The drummer was drumming in the water, just gone, *mach schau* was *mach schau*. I was maching schau from the word go. I wanted to make an impression but I never wanted to make a fool of myself. I was never a shrinking violet on stage. I would give the people what they wanted."

Chris Curtis (395): "You could ask Pete Best to play for 19 hours and he'd put his head down and do it. He'd drum like a dream with real style and stamina all night long and that really was the Beatles' sound – forget the guitars and forget the faces – you couldn't avoid that insistent whack, whack, whack! The rhythm guitar went along with it and the bass chucked in the two and four beats and George was wonderful on the guitar. His little legs would kick out to the side when he did his own tunes. He'd go all posh and say, 'I'd like to do a tune now from Carl Perkins, 'Everybody's Trying To Be My Baby', and it's in A.' Who wanted to know what key it was in? But he always said that."

Günter Zint (396): "John Lennon made jokes about his boss, Manfred Weissleder, and one time he was almost thrown out of the club. Betty who was working on the bar went to Manfred and excused John and said, 'Please let him stay here: it was a joke and it wasn't like you thought.' It was because the English humour is much more sensitive and intelligent than German humour. You have *Monty Python* and we have nothing like that."

Dicky Tarrach (397): "The Rattles were inspired by the Beatles. The Rattles had their own style and today we are more modern but we play the old songs with a new sound. In those days we had our own style and our own way to look and move. We rehearsed all these things. Manfred Weissleder was our manager. He wanted his own band and a guy from England called Henry Henroid stayed for six months in Hamburg and looked after us at the end of 1963. It would be our first tour of England so what should we do?

Most German musicians only played around here, they were very keen on playing the songs right and were always watching their guitars, looking down. Henry said, 'Boys, this is a show, you must always smile and it is better to play something wrong than be looking down, and you have to look at the girls and shake your head'. We worked in the Star-Club for two or three hours every afternoon, we looked into the audience and we were the first in Germany to do all these little things, and when we came to England, we got a fantastic reaction."

Once the Swinging Blue Jeans, still largely playing traditional jazz, reached Hamburg, they soon realised some changes were necessary. They played their first night disastrously as a trad band and returned to the Star-Club as a rock'n'roll outfit the next day. **Ralph Ellis (398)**: "When we were in the Star-Club, we were doing 'Down By The Riverside' and we had to change to rock'n'roll. The audience stopped dancing and they said, 'What are you playing? We don't understand this music.' We had to change completely to rock'n'roll within a couple of nights. When we started playing 'Johnny B. Goode' and Buddy Holly stuff, a banjo didn't fit in so Pete Moss decided to leave."

Lee Curtis (399): "In Germany they say that I am the ultimate professional. I am never late and always clean and always on time and never drunk and always do a good show and I always do more than I'm paid for. If I am booked for two 45 minute spots, you could end up with two one and a half hours. I just love getting on a stage and working. I would watch the other bands. Horst said one night, 'Lee, I think you don't like Star-Club,' and I said, 'I love it.' He said, 'No, you are not like all the other guys, you don't go drunken. You don't like girls.' I said, 'I don't drink a lot, Horst, but I love women. That's my good time, out there on the stage.'"

The Beatles, however, wanted to be paid for their extra time on stage. **Günter Zint (400)**: "The Beatles were working very hard. They had a fight with Horst Fascher and Manfred Weissleder because they had done overtime and not been paid for it. Manfred said once, 'Okay, you get 250 marks for overtime a week, but then you play until you fall from the stage.' They had to work very hard. Last time when Paul McCartney was here, he said that this was a very good rehearsal for them: they were young kids playing with guitars but they learnt how to satisfy an audience in Hamburg." So tell me again – just why did Paul McCartney think the Liverpool Institute of Performing Arts was necessary?

Whilst working in Giessen, near Frankfurt, **Chris Farlowe (401)** found the problems of payment were tackled differently: "The guy that ran our club was a Jew from Auschwitz. Every time I asked him for money, he would show me the number on his arm and he would say, 'I have had trouble; I have seen hardship', so he was really telling me not to ask for any more money."

But **Chris Farlowe (402),** who also worked in Hamburg, found a brilliant, alternative way of supplementing his income: "I come from a military family. When I went to Germany in 1961, I was going into the junk shops down at the sea front and they were selling German uniforms. I bought a few things, Iron Crosses and the like, and I brought them back to England. People bought them from me and so I went back for some more. That is how my business started." Chris started a theatrical costumiers and it is his uniforms (or rather the original German Nazis) that you see in *'Allo 'Allo!*

Mike Pender (403): "We were in the Star-Club for months on end so there was plenty of time to learn songs. There were no Walkmans then and we just wrote down the words and the chords. When you're doing the last spot at four in the morning, no one is taking any notice, so you try them out. We would throw in new songs that we weren't going to get them right the first time. The Star-Club was an excellent place for learning new songs."

Frank Dostal (404): "The Beatles were very relaxed but at the same time very energetic and humorous. They had this very special mix of rock'n'roll and black music that was more or less unknown to German audiences. You could not get records by the likes of the Shirelles in Germany, so nobody knew of them. Some American seamen sold their records to the shop owners. They spent a lot of money here because of the nice young ladies who offered them favours. They needed a lot of money so they sold whatever they could."

Mike Pender (405): "We actually found 'Sweets For My Sweet' in Hamburg. We found it in one of the record shops around Hamburg and we decided to do it because we thought it suited Tony's vocal. We liked all those early American rock'n'roll type of records. It fitted our style, three part harmony and a good sort of sugary, flowery song for the time, but we did it faster than the Drifters. We thought, 'This is something a little bit different, let's do it.' And that's why it was such a good first record. I can remember Tony Hatch when he first heard the song. He come to the Iron Door and we performed it on stage, Les Ackerley was beaming in the background thinking, 'He's gonna love this.' And sure enough, as soon as he heard it, he knew that was the one that was going to happen for us."

V. Speed Recordings

The Beatles played 14 weeks at the Top Ten club from March to July 1961. During May, they were spotted by the German schlager singer, **Tommy Kent (406),** who was produced by the orchestra leader, Bert Kaempfert, for Polydor Records. "Bert wanted to talk to Ivo Robic about some songs that evening and so he told me I could have his car and go to the Reeperbahn and look around. I went in the Top Ten Club. It was dirty and very crowded and you had to drink a lot because if you did not drink very much, they threw you out. The atmosphere was very good. From the first second that I heard the Beatles, I thought, 'What fun they are' and I knew that they were very good. Tony Sheridan was singing with them. I went back to Bert Kaempfert and told him that he must see them. The next night I went to the Top Ten with Bert Kaempfert and his wife, and I said to Paul McCartney, 'Can I make some music with you?' and we did 'Be Bop A Lula', 'Kansas City' and two blues numbers. I enjoyed that very much and then I introduced Paul to Bert Kaempfert and we left. The next day I made a record, 'Ein Mann, Der Nicht Nein Sagen Kann (A Man Who Can Say No)'. I went back home to Munich and Bert Kaempfert made a contract with the Beatles."

The key song at that first session with Bert Kaempfert in June 1961 was 'My Bonnie'. Tony Sheridan had been performing this with the Jets and had included it in their performances during his first visit to Hamburg in 1960. Tony and the Beatles recorded this in alternate versions: one with a slow English introduction and one with a German, although sometimes it is reissued without either. This track has been unfairly ignored: it is a fine example of British rock'n'roll and it demonstrates how exciting Sheridan and the Beatles could be on stage. They tried a similar approach with 'When The Saints Go Marching In', but not so satisfactorily. Sheridan sang the country music weepie 'Nobody's Child' and one of his own songs, 'Why (Can't You Love Me Again)?' The fifth track was the Jimmy Reed blues song, 'Take Out Some Insurance On Me, Baby'. The Beatles also recorded two tracks on their own – John Lennon's version of the oldie, 'Ain't She Sweet', was inspired by Gene Vincent's and their Sixties instrumental, 'Cry For A Shadow', is very creditable. Rory Storm was reading that the Shadows' new single was 'The Frightened City' and George and John pretended they had heard it and wrote 'Cry For A Shadow'.

German bandleader Bert Kaempfert, who produced these tracks, is the only person to have worked with the three giants of popular music. He wrote 'Wooden Heart' and 'Strangers in the Night', No.1 records for Elvis Presley and Frank Sinatra respectively. His new assistant turned out to be someone that the Beatles knew well: the singer **Paul Murphy (407)**: "Mr. Klein, the doorman at Polydor Records, was a German soldier who had been wounded during the war and was a POW in England. I said that I would like to speak to Bert Kaempfert and he told me to speak to Mr. Voigt, which is pronounced 'Fucked' and we had a lot of fun with that name. He said, 'What makes you think you can make records better than our German producers?' and he thought that I had come for a job as a producer and not as a singer. I became Bert Kaempfert's assistant and as he became more popular, I was given more to do. I was given a project with a French singer and as Kingsize Taylor's band was around, I asked them to do the session. Then I recorded Tony Sheridan and things went pretty well for me."

The best album is one recorded by Kingsize Taylor and the Dominoes as the Shakers. **Paul Murphy (408)**: "We did the album right after the Star-Club and so we hardly had any sleep. We took a few happy pills and went in and recorded it. I still think it is brilliant. The Liverpool sound has got a lot to thank Hamburg for: where else could you rehearse, have reasonable living conditions, eat good food and be paid as well?" Come again.

It's doubtful if anyone will discover the extent of Kingsize Taylor's discography. **Bobby Thomson (409)**: "Kingsize would sign anything and I had terrible visions of getting sued. We were signed to Polydor, Fontana, Philips and Decca at the same time. We recorded under different names to cover up what we were doing. We aped Howie Casey's name and came up with Boot Lacey and the Toecaps. The Germans who recorded us didn't appreciate our humour and they called us the Shakers. Kingsize would say, 'Right, we'll do an LP for 500 DM' and so the whole band would do an LP for £40. I don't know how many records we made but it has to run into a couple of hundred individual tracks."

Kingsize Taylor (410) can't remember that many of them himself because they were recorded after a hard day's night at the Star-Club. "70% of our records were done in one take. We made one LP in forty minutes. We once walked straight in at 4.30 in the morning and came out at eight with an LP in the can. That was the Shakers' album that got to No.1 in the German LP charts."

Horst Fascher (411): "Paul Murphy came to the Star-Club, and he got the bands and recorded them without letting us know. When we found it was happening, Manfred said, 'Horst, we cannot allow that. They have to pay some money to us. We bring the bands over and they are just taking them to the studio and only give them 200 DM or 300 DM for a whole LP. That is not fair.' We tried to keep Paul Murphy and some of the other guys out of the club and then Manfred had a brainwave. He said, 'Okay, they want to make records. We will sell our name to Philips.' They started the Star-Club label and we made a lot of records."

Kuno Dreysse (412): "Liverpool was the heart of everything in those days. At the beginning the Searchers were much more interesting than the Beatles because I liked 'Farmer John' and they had a fantastic live album on Star-Club Records. The Londoners were very good, and Kingsize Taylor played the guitar perfectly, probably better than the Beatles. With the Beatles, it wasn't the music that they played: it was the personality that caught you."

In 2002 *The Searchers At The Star-Club was* issued in its entirety. **Chris Curtis (413)**: "I was surprised by its quality. We had been back in England and we had got well known, and we had a contract to go back. We were told that we didn't have to do it, we could be bought out of it, but we said, 'They paid money to see us before we were well-known, so we will return the favour.' They really appreciated it. Look at the crowd on the front of that album. They went absolutely nuts for us."

Adrian Barber (414) "There was so much speed available that you couldn't move. You could buy little 5mg amphetamine tablets in the stores. They weren't as strong as Preludin, but if you kept taking them, you got the desired result, which is you don't sleep and you can work and work and work. If you didn't like what they were selling in the shops, you could go to the bathroom and buy it from the little ladies there. I got close to one of the gangsters and he took me to some place in the country and in his tractor trailer was the entire supply of amphetamine for North Germany for a year. He was feeling good that day and he was giving it to me as he wanted everybody to feel as good as he did."

Some sessions did not work out so well. **Lee Curtis (415)**: "We went into a recording studio in Bremerhaven and the engineers, who were below the stage, told us to go through our repertoire. We were trying things for two hours and then they told us that was the record, we couldn't redo it. The songs didn't have finishes to them and we thought they were getting a balance and we never went for it 100 per cent. It was very laidback. They brought an LP out and put out a single. My brother sent a copy to Radio Caroline North and 'Ecstasy' became their Record of the Week and you couldn't buy it in the UK. In the end, we fixed it that it could be released here but it had died by then."

As 1962 changed into the magical 1963, it's fitting that the Beatles should have been back at the Star-Club, playing with Kingsize Taylor and the Dominoes. Their performance was recorded on Kingsize Taylor's tape recorder and for years, he owned these tapes without realising that he had a potential goldmine. In 1977, with the entrepreneurial abilities of Paul Murphy, the recordings made their way onto the market and EMI and the Beatles took legal action. There was a further court case in the 1990s and the position appears to be, that a company can issue the tapes on vinyl but not on CD. (No, it doesn't make sense to me either.) Quite apart from the quasi-official releases, there have been scores of bootleg issues.

Kingsize Taylor (416): "Adrian Barber made the recording. He set up one microphone but it was my machine and my tapes. Nobody ever objected to the fact that we were recording them, and I could never understand why they later objected to them because they were unique and there was nothing detrimental on them. Anyone who thinks I poached the Beatles' stuff is talking rubbish. The recorder was left on all the time and the tapes also feature the Dominoes, Tony Sheridan and Cliff Bennett and the Rebel Rousers. I showed the tapes to Brian Epstein who offered me £20 for them. He didn't stand a chance of getting them for that, but it was only for sentimental reasons that I held onto them. I think the record was worth bringing out. We offered the Beatles 60% of the total take and they didn't want to know. I wouldn't have put them out if they had been detrimental to the Beatles. The music itself was fine and the tapes had plenty of atmosphere, but by the time the record came out most of the quality had gone. The company tried to improve the sound by mixing it on 24 track machines, but it should have been released as it was. That was the Beatles playing in the Star-Club and it was an absolute gem. Nobody was interested in the records in the way they were released and I made nothing out of it."

So we are deprived of the singing talents of **Horst Fascher (417)** backed by the Beatles: "The day I have never forgotten is New Year's Eve, 1962 to 1963 and it was the Beatles' last time in Hamburg and I did some songs with them, 'Hallelujah I Love Her So' and 'Be Bop A Lula'. I was the singer and the Beatles backed me, and this is unforgettable. Even John Lennon said, 'Thank you, Horst', and so he was satisfied about it."

The Mojos went to Hamburg early in 1964 and, while there, recorded a group composition, 'Everything's Alright'. It was a cold-blooded creation, as the group's guitarist **Nicky Crouch (418)** explains: "We thought of the most popular beat, the most popular riff as an introduction, and the most popular concept for a pop song. We threw the lot together and 'Everything's Alright' came out."

Drummer **Bob Conrad (419)**: "We'd been in a drinking house on the Reeperbahn and we were in no fit state to record. Terry rushed off in the middle of a take because he had to be sick. He came back very red-faced and he played a superb solo. I don't know how he managed to be so inspired. He may have been sitting at that piano but he was definitely not with us."

'Everything's Alright' did well in the UK and on the Continent where the Mojos made a promotional film for the new video juke-boxes. Pianist **Terry O'Toole (420)** says, with typical Liverpool bravado, "'Everything's Alright' was not a great number but it was different from the run-of-the-mill things that were hits. If we'd been more far-sighted, if we'd been more level-headed, if we'd been better managed, we could have got it together and come out on top like Pink Floyd and the Moody Blues."

Stu James (421): "We felt a bit guilty about 'Everything's Alright' because a lot of people thought that we were getting away from the blues and harmonica stuff. We never released any blues as the Mojos. We did record a twelve-bar blues with mouth-harp called 'Spoonful' but Decca wouldn't release it as they wanted something more poppy. However, Decca did put out an EP with some R&B songs on it and I think it's the best thing that we did. That may not be saying too much because we were young white kids and it'd be ridiculous to compare our version of 'Got My Mojo Working' with Muddy Waters' version."

Nicky Crouch (422): "Without a doubt Stu has a fantastic voice, but he's never done the right material. He hasn't tested himself to the full. When he was in the Mojos he sang 'I (Who Have Nothing)', which is a hard song to sing and he sang it really well. When I hear 'Didn't We' or some of Neil Sedaka's numbers, I wish that we could have played them and that Stu had sung them the way he really could sing them. We'd have all been millionaires.

Many of the groups recorded in German, and often the hit records were recorded in German such as 'Ein Tausend Nadelstiche (A Thousand Needlepricks)', which is the Searchers' version of 'Needles And Pins'. **Bernd Matheja (423)**: "When the Searchers recorded 'Needles And Pins', the first line in German was meant to say 'I saw her at night', but the way Mike Pender sang it, it became 'I saw her naked today'. He had a problem with the 'ch' sound. They tried it again and again but it didn't work, so on the German version, he is still singing 'I saw her naked today'."

The Beatles recorded German versions of 'I Want To Hold Your Hand' and 'She Loves You', but made no other foreign language versions of their hits. **Gene Pitney (424)** is very grateful to them. "I had to record my songs in Italian, German, French and Spanish and I was relieved when the market changed and records in English were acceptable everywhere. We have the Beatles to thank for that. They didn't record in all those languages and so people had to accept them as they were. After 1964 the charts in most countries were about 50 per cent English language records, and in some places you had to sing in English or you wouldn't chart at all."

In 1966 the Remo Four made an excellent album, *Smile*, in German, although it was not released in the UK at the time. **Tony Ashton (425)**: "Colin was featured on 'Peter Gunn' and that went down a storm. He would turn his AC30 up and use feedback. Colin and I used to share the singing, and we did a definitive album, *Smile*, which is a cult album in Germany. Hamburg was amazing: to think, we were scrounging off hookers."

Russ Ballard (426): "I've done the five hours a night in Germany and it's the best thing in the world to make a band tight and get them to really know each other. You are stuck there playing, playing, playing and you think it is hell but it is the best thing that can happen to you. That is what made the Beatles great. They had the talent of course but Germany got them tighter."

Joe Fagin (427): "Hamburg was bloody hard work but at home I had been earning £2.10s (£2.50) a gig and now I was on £45 a week and I drank most of it. We were innocent boys in the middle of Sin City. There was circus ring that would give you free booze if you could stay on one of the horses. Of course as soon as you got on, the horse went crazy. St. Pauli was full of gangsters and Manfred Weissleider was the biggest of them all. I got into a fight with a doorman from another club and that guy had to come round and apologise to me or lose his job. Vince Taylor and the Playboys came to the Star-Club on a booking but Vince disappeared after two days – no one knew why. Around that time, I had a fight with Horst Fascher and he sacked me. I teamed up with the Playboys and we went to France and did Vince Taylor's bookings. We had a hit with a French version of 'Sealed With A Kiss'."

VI. Star time

The most successful of the Hamburg night-spots was the Star-Club. In September 1963 the club published a list of the number of appearances in its first 18 months by the various performers. Tony Sheridan is first with 394 appearances, followed by Kingsize Taylor and the Dominoes with 332. There's a large gap until we reach the third act, the German band the Rattles, with 154. The rest of the Top Ten is as follows: Cliff Bennett and the Rebel Rousers, a London-based band – 144, the Undertakers – 140, the Searchers – 126, Davy Jones (a coloured singer who recorded for Piccadilly, not the Monkee) – also 126, Gerry and the Pacemakers – 105, the Bachelors (not the Irish trio but a beat group) – 84, and the Beatles – 79. The Star-Club was dominated by UK performers and a postcard sent home by John Lennon in 1962 states: "All 24 of us sleep in one room but we're English."

The bands also met American stars making one-off appearances. **Mike Pender (428)** of the Searchers commented, "Playing at the Star-Club and mixing with acts like the Everly Brothers, Gene Vincent and Jerry Lee Lewis gave us great confidence."

Gerry Marsden (429): "I got to know the stars whose records I'd bought. Meeting Fats Domino, Jerry Lee Lewis and Gene Vincent was like meeting God, but I found out that they were ordinary, nice people. It was a good lesson because I thought they'd be flash and big-time. They were very down to earth and it taught me to always be the same and not to get too clever."

Roy Young (430): "One time in Hamburg, we were called the Beat Brothers and it was Tony Sheridan, Ringo and myself and a bass player called Colin Bland. At that time Little Richard was a guest and I was performing 'Long Tall Sally'. Tony was looking at me across the stage and there was Little Richard jumping up and down, and I said, 'I'm sorry, man, I forgot you were here. You're the man that's got to do this.' He said, 'No, you sound great, man. You're like me.' It was the biggest compliment that I have ever had."

Sam Hardie (431): "When we were in Hamburg the second time, I had various black magic books and I was trying to get the spells to work. One of them was how to fly, and one of the things you used to make this spell work was a rabbit skin. I tried to get them all together. We were on with Little Richard, and Richard was very religious. He used to hold prayer sessions and when he heard I was learning to fly, he said, 'Sam, you ain't gonna fly nowhere, you ain't no bird'. He was really concerned about it."

Screaming Lord Sutch was a different matter. **Sam Hardie (432)** of Kingsize Taylor and the Dominoes was there. "Everybody was looking forward to seeing Ray Charles at the Star-Club. He was God as far as most musicians were concerned. There were six acts on the show that night including Screaming Lord Sutch, who made a point of saying, 'It'll be a great show tonight with me and Ray Charles.' He was convinced it was a double-billing. Ray Charles went on stage about nine o'clock, did his show and vanished. Screaming Lord Sutch didn't go on until five o'clock in the morning, when the place was empty."

Paul McCartney (433): "Gene Vincent's 'Be Bop a Lula' was the first record I ever bought – one of those big 78s on a purple label with the Capitol Tower on the bag. Great! We got to know Gene when we were at the Star-Club He'd been a marine and he was forever offering to knock me out. He said, 'Marines only have to touch these two pressure points.' I'd say, 'Sod off, Gene' but he'd insist, 'I'll only knock you out for a minute.' He had a few tricks like that but I always resisted them."

VII. Mean Streets

The Big Three were signed by Brian Epstein who sent them to Hamburg. **Johnny Hutch (434)**: "I've no idea why he did it. He wanted to change us and make us conform, and yet he sent us to the Star-Club where nearly everyone became a head case."

Spencer Lloyd Mason (435): "Eppy wanted to sign the Big Three and he bought them orange suits. Adrian Barber cut off the bottom of the trousers at the Star-Club and went on stage like Robinson Crusoe. Eppy realised his mistake and said he had to be replaced immediately. Brian Griffiths stepped in, and Manfred Weissleder gave Adrian a job as stage manager, even though he was off his head on pills most of the time. When Duane Eddy came, Manfred told him that he wasn't to touch Duane's equipment, and naturally he was fascinated by Duane's amp. He took it apart but found he couldn't get it back together. Duane that night had to use the standard AC 40 and he didn't go down too well."

Adrian Barber (436): "If we had done the sort of things we did in Hamburg when we were in Liverpool, we might have been put in a lunatic asylum. You could freak out in St. Pauli. We opened at the Star-Club one Saturday afternoon at 4pm and we went straight through to 6am. We had been playing hot rock'n'roll and we weren't about to go home and go to bed. I went down the fish market and this lady was selling piglets and I bought one. I took it back to the apartment and the thing got into bed with the singer from another group, Buddy Britten, and it had shat everywhere. I got a piece of string and tied it round the pig's neck, and so I'm going to work and the pig has got to come to work with me. We get into the street and I am dragging the pig and the pig didn't want to go and it is putting up a fight. It squealed loudly and I was dragging it through the Reeperbahn with everyone is looking at me. Manfred laughed and said, 'You're pilled again.' There was a butcher's facility at the back of the Star-Club and the piglet went off there and we had pork cutlets that night. (Laughs)"

Groups took drugs to help them through the night. Amphetamines were available from chemists and many of the Germans they met were ready to sell them to the groups.

Most musicians were swallowing Preludin with their beers. **John Gustafson (437)** of the Big Three: "Memories of Hamburg? 'Drunken insanity' sums it up. You were reduced to a physical wreck after four days, but it was enjoyable to be a physical wreck. It was wonderful to be lying in the gutter in a whisky-sodden heap in rainwater. I'll never do it again. Picture it yourself. It was a huge nightclub in the middle of a million pubs and strip joints, there was nowhere to go. You stand in the middle of the road and do nothing or go in one of these places. You're out of your mind the whole time."

Chris Curtis (438): "You can't keep taking things and perform well, at least not for long. I used to take Preludin because of the long nights in Hamburg, just to keep me awake, but all my playing was from the heart. I did take downers 'cause I needed to sleep."

Sam Hardie (439): "John Lennon had had quite a few and was the worse for wear. The curtains opened and the Beatles were on stage. John was sitting on the piano just striking any old note. There was nothing musical coming out and the group carried on playing. Eventually he wandered to the front of the stage and went into his 'Heil Hitler' routine, putting his arm out and all this sort of thing. A gang of lads stood at the front, gazing at the Beatles in wonderment. John kicked one of them in the face."

Lee Curtis (440) remembers, "One song that I took to Germany with me was Marty Wilde's arrangement of 'Jezebel'. I did 7,000 performances at the Star-Club and I sang 'Jezebel' on every one. It has a big long note for me to finish on and it could last for 10, 15 or even 30 seconds. I stop when I feel the steam is running out. There was only one time when I failed to hit it and that was when the guitarist broke a string and the chord came out wrong. It always went down to tumultuous applause. I wish I had recorded it as a single. One night I walked into the Star-Club and Freddie Starr had my gear on and was doing an impression of me and that was one of the greatest compliments that has been paid to me. He was doing 'Jezebel' and he went for the finish but he didn't get there."

Bobby Thomson (441) remembers Paul McCartney's ad-libs as being more educational. "Paul spoke fluent German and I saw him teaching the Germans to speak English. He said, 'Here's a good word – banana.' The whole crowd, all 2,000 of them, went 'Banana'. You can imagine what that sounded like. Then he said, 'Apple' and they went 'Apple'. He said, 'Here's a very hard one – orange.' They all yelled 'Orange', except for this one voice at the back which went 'Banana'."

Kingsize Taylor deliberately upset the clientele. **Colin Manley (442)** was there. "We were backing Teddy one New Year's Eve at the Star-Club and he came out with one of Hitler's speeches. I don't know the exact gist, but when they were in Berlin and surrounded by the Americans and the Russians, Hitler said over the radio that there were 80,000 troops outside when there were only 8,000. Teddy gave this speech out to a packed Star-Club. The reaction was strange. We were expecting bottles to be thrown, but perhaps because of Teddy's enormous size, they saw the funny side and we got drinks instead."

Lee Curtis (443): "It was rough in Germany. A man might pull a gun on you. I've seen someone in the corner with a knife in his neck. We were having a drink and this character started annoying us. Teddy told him to behave himself, but he persisted.

Teddy went to talk to him, and his hand went in his pocket and we saw the top end of a gun. I'd have run, but not Teddy. With no messing whatsoever, he cuffed him good and proper, a wallop around the neck, a karate chop or something. It had the desired effect. We didn't see him anymore."

In the tales about violence in the German clubs, Kingsize stands alone. **Sam Hardie (444)** recalls, "We were playing in Berlin and Kingsize hadn't turned up. We launched into the show and he still hadn't arrived. Later on we learned that he'd been in a bar down the road and had had an argument with the barman. He turned the whole length of the bar over. The owner telephoned the police and he started knocking them all over the place. It took twelve policemen to get him under control."

And was Kingsize and his friends arrested? **Kingsize Taylor (445)**: "Not at all, because we were civilians. They had done a wrongful arrest. They had arrested us and cautioned us as military people, which we weren't."

Hamburg was also too violent for **Tony Sanders (446)** of the Coasters: "'I was there four weeks and I couldn't believe the violence. I saw a guy stabbed one night. He staggered out of an alley, blood pouring everywhere, and the police arrived with sub-machine-guns. Guns and knuckledusters could be bought quite easily in shops. There were also little steel tubular coshes and when they were shaken, a ball bearing on a long string shot out which could knock a hole in your skull. The Reeperbahn was one of the most notorious streets in Europe. We saw prostitutes sitting in windows waiting to be picked up, and lesbians and homosexuals flaunting themselves. I can't understand how the Beatles took all this in their stride. George Harrison was only 17 when he went there. I was 23 and it frightened the life out of me."

Les Maguire (447): "The waiters were very good too. It was a port with lots of Swedish sailors, and the sailors would be out of their mind half the time. There would be lots of fights so the waiters had these extendable truncheons and they would go round beating people. They would say, 'Keep on playing, faster, *mach schau*', as they were beating people."

And yet despite all the violence, the area was law-abiding in one respect. **Günter Zint (448)**: "Everybody under 18 has to leave at 10 o'clock and then at midnight, the people under 21 had to leave. You must have identity cards in Hamburg and so they would be inspected. When the Beatles were on stage and it was ten o'clock, Paul McCartney was making jokes about Weissleder. He knew some German language and he made some jokes about these rules."

Horst Fascher (449): "Manfred Weissleder was always in danger of losing his licence. The government didn't like a rock'n'roll club with young people in the red light district. The authorities were scared that respectable young girls might be asked to do other business."

The Star-Club was open for such long hours that the audience was constantly changing. **Ian Edwards (450)** of Ian and the Zodiacs: "Those that came in up to ten o'clock were teenagers. There was a curfew at ten o'clock, so they had to leave. The older element came in after that. They'd been to the bierkellers and wanted to hear the latest rock'n'roll. They had to work the next morning, so they went home at one o'clock. Then we got the girls off the streets, the common crooks and the homosexual element.

They were the people who looked after us. The people who made their business out of St. Pauli, the red-light district of Hamburg felt that they had to look after us because we were having such a good impact on their trade. We could walk in the St. Pauli streets at four o'clock in the morning and be okay."

Naturally, some youngsters wanted to go to other clubs. **Dave May (451)** of the Silhouettes tried one: "Just up the street from the Star-Club was the Roxy Bar. You'd get men in there who'd had injections and developed women's bodies. They looked really gorgeous. You'd walk in and they'd all have their backs to you, sitting at the bar with their tight skirts on. You'd think, 'Oh, very nice', but as soon as they turned round, you'd see their flattened noses and cauliflower ears."

There was a danger that the lads could be fleeced of their earnings, but no one messed with groups employed by the Star-Club. Manfred Weissleder, the manager, was respected by the other club owners. **Charlie Flynn (452)** of Ian and the Zodiacs recalled: "An Irish show band called the Crickets had just arrived in Hamburg. They were enticed into a strip club on the Reeperbahn and two hostesses came over to the boys and asked for a drink. The waiters brought two bottles of champagne. Next came the bill, which was the equivalent of £120. They had nowhere near that amount, so the waiter took their jewellery and watches and kicked them out of the club. They told Manfred Weissleder about it and he got on the phone. Someone from that strip club must have run a four-minute mile because he just appeared with all the rings and all their money."

Wayne Bickerton (453): "The Star-Club gave you a little badge, which ensured that most people didn't touch you. If they did, the heavies from the Star-Club would descend upon them. I still saw a lot of dreadful things because most of the people who were thrown out of clubs were badly beaten up. One evening just before we went on stage some gentleman who hadn't paid his bills was brought in upside down. He was shaken until the money came out of his pockets. They took his money and his watch and threw him out of the back door. It's a bit disconcerting when you're trying to tune your guitar up."

Considering all this violence, it's not surprising that **Dave May (454)** did a double take when he saw the bouncer. "The doorman at the Star-Club was a one-armed man. You're in a violent city and you think, 'My God, a bouncer with one arm. There's no chance.' I expressed my surprise and he said, 'Oh yes, I am the bouncer, but do not worry. There will be no trouble as I have my friend Tommy with me.' I said, 'Tommy? Where's Tommy?' He opened his jacket and said, 'There.' He had a .45 automatic tucked into his trousers."

Hamburg was an eye-opener for these boys, who had been living at home with their parents – even if Liverpool was considered a tough city. Postcards home couldn't hint at the real story. It changed their lives, and **Ray Ennis (455)** of the Swinging Blue Jeans is glad it happened. "We went over there as raw young lads. For the first week we were petrified and homesick – we hated the place. After a month we cried because we didn't want to come home. It was the most fantastic experience. You saw every degrading thing you could ever think of. Some fellows at 50 have never seen a quarter of what I saw at 17."

The most concise summary of this insane quarter comes from **Lewis Collins (456)** of the Mojos, later a star of *The Professionals* TV series. "My God, I went there a greenhorn and still a virgin at eighteen. I came back an old man having experienced just about everything in the book."

7 DRUMMED OUT

I. Before the Storm
II. John, Paul, George and Pete
III. Enter Brian Epstein
IV. Decca Audition
V. Twist And Out
VI. How good was Pete Best's drumming?
VII. Enter Ringo Starr
VIII. New Drummers for Old
IX. So, why was he sacked?

"Their sentences were read out, their buttons and rank insignia were ripped from their uniforms, their heads usually shaved, and, wearing a sign proclaiming their guilt, they were marched out of the camp. Drummers beat 'The Rogues' March' or, in the Confederate Army, 'Yankee Doodle."
(Civil War Source Book, Philip Katcher)

"I cannot do this bloody thing."
(Macbeth, and possibly Brian Epstein)

I. Before the Storm

By the early 1960s rock'n'roll had lost its initial impetus. Elvis Presley had gone into the US Army, and when he came out of the forces, his music had a new maturity but much of its vitality had gone. Jerry Lee Lewis' success had been cut short by a controversial marriage to a young girl. The wildest rock 'n' roll singer of them all, Little Richard, had found religion. In America, rock 'n' roll had given way to the Bobbies – Bobby Rydell, Bobby Vinton and Bobby Vee. They made pleasant, unadventurous records, but not all the music deserved the Vee-sign. Another Bobby, Bobby Darin, displayed versatility, and Dion's 'The Wanderer' was up to anything from the 1950s. Indeed, Dion and Bob Dylan are the only contemporary musicians apart from the Beatles in the collage assembled for the cover of *Sgt Pepper's Lonely Hearts Club Band.*

Although there was considerable talent around, no British performer had the ability to revolutionise the music industry. Cliff Richard had become a family entertainer. Frankie Vaughan, who came from Liverpool, invested his role as macho man with a humour, suggesting that he didn't take himself too seriously. Anyway, he preferred romantic ballads and show songs to rock'n'roll, leaving the path clear for Tom Jones. Another Scouser, Billy Fury, had a moody charisma, but he turned to beat-ballads and inconsequential ballads when he should have been stretching his talent. Adam Faith's abilities were more as an actor than a singer, and only three British rock 'n' roll records could stand alongside the best American ones: Cliff Richard's 'Move It!', Johnny Kidd and the Pirates' 'Shakin' All Over' and Billy Fury's 'Wondrous Place', which far outstrips the original by Jimmy Jones.

British performers resorted to covering, and in most cases copying, American hits. 'A Teenager In Love' was an American hit for Dion and the Belmonts but there were British cover versions in the same vein by Marty Wilde, Craig Douglas and Dickie Valentine. The American songwriters, often based in New York's Brill Building, came up with polished, carefully crafted work which few British songwriters approached. Ian Samwell wrote some excellent rock'n'roll songs, 'Move It!' and 'Dynamite' among them, but he was not prolific enough. Lionel Bart, who had written early hits for Cliff Richard and Tommy Steele, had switched to stage musicals, and in view of the success of *Oliver!*, who could blame him?

The world was ready for the Beatles. **Tony Crane (457)**: "I don't think anything would have stopped the Beatles. They were ready to come through. The public were ready for singing vocal groups who looked a bit rough and sang a bit rough. Everything else was too soft and nice."

II. John, Paul, George and Pete

Would the Beatles have been a world force as John, Paul, George and Pete? Although many musicians hold strong views, none can say for certain. In 1984, I wrote that I regarded Pete Best as one of the unluckiest men in the world, and, by the same token, Ringo Starr one of the luckiest. Since the first *Anthology* package in 1995, the circumstances of Pete Best's life have changed dramatically in his favour, but my assessment of Ringo remains unchanged: he's a talented but very lucky man. He says the same himself.

There appears to be no specific incident which triggered Pete Best's sacking. Neither the Beatles nor Brian Epstein ever gave credible or consistent explanations as to why they gave Pete Best the boot. I believe Pete Best when he says he himself doesn't know the reason: would he have been party to the discussions? Of course not.

As an example of the confusion, consider the *Anthology* programmes, which were, after all, meant to be the last word on all things Beatle. **Bob Wooler (458)**: "It was very wrong of the Beatles to suggest on the *Anthology* video that Pete Best was unreliable – well, they didn't suggest it, they stated it and it is absolute rubbish to say that. The most unreliable Beatle was Paul McCartney, who had the worst punctuality record, although he was not consistently late for engagements. I would say to Paul at the Aintree Institute, 'You've missed the middle spot and you'll have to go on last', which is going home time. He'd say, 'Sorry, I was busy writing a song.' That didn't impress me at the time as I had a show to put on." Also, on the *Anthology* video, George said it was karma that Ringo was meant to be with the Beatles, hardly a thought he would have had in 1962.

The suggestion Pete Best was sacked because he refused to have a mop-top haircut is also unfounded. Pete Best told me that he was never asked to have one and would have complied if they wanted uniformity. **Astrid Kirchherr (459)**: "All my friends at art school used to run around with what you would call a Beatle haircut. My boyfriend, Klaus Voormann, had this style and Stuart Sutcliffe liked it very much. He was the first one who had the nerve to get the cream out of his hair and he asked me to cut his hair. Pete Best had very curly hair and it wouldn't have worked for him. Even if he had wanted it, I could not have cut his hair that way."

When discussing Pete Best, there are three oft-quoted issues: his personality, his looks and his skills as a drummer. As an outsider, it might appear incredulous that Pete Best's good looks could work against him, but they did.

Geoff Nugent (460) of the Undertakers: "Pete Best put the Beatles on the map. You'd see two or three girls around Paul and George and John, but you'd see 50 around Pete. I very rarely saw him smile and yet he was always pleasant. If you look at any of the Beatles' photographs with Pete Best, the first face you're drawn to is Pete's. I don't care if you're a man or a woman."

The promoter **Ron Appleby (461)** confirms this: "We had a dance at the Kingsway in Southport and we were charging 2/6d (12p) for admission before eight o'clock and 3s (15p) after. Brian Epstein decided that everyone who came into the dance before eight o'clock would be given a photograph of the Beatles, and he was hopping mad because the girls were ripping up the photograph and sticking the pictures of Pete Best on their jumpers."

Pete Best (462) was so popular that girls would camp out in his garden: "I was a bit embarrassed about it, but I thought that it could only help the group. If I got more screams on stage than the others for doing a particular number, then fine. It wasn't a case of 'That's one up for Pete at the back.' For me, it was 'That's good for the Beatles as a whole.' That's all I was concerned about."

Whether the Beatles like it or not, most people think that Pete Best was sacked from The Beatles because he was too good-looking. Pete had plenty of girlfriends, but the others also did well and, anyway, at the time John had only just married Cynthia. It might have annoyed The Beatles that the girls cried out for Pete at their shows, but they weren't stupid and could surely see that it would benefit the group as a whole. Brian Epstein would have been pleased by the reaction and although Pete declined a homosexual encounter, it would not have bothered Eppy as he was knocked back with some regularity. By the same argument, he would never have taken on Billy J. Kramer.

Pete Best was invaluable to the Beatles for two other reasons, which admittedly became less significant once Brian Epstein came into the picture. **Ron Appleby (463)** again. "In the early bookings of the Beatles – this is BE, Before Epstein – the only person you could contact was Pete Best because he was the only one with a telephone. In those days, anyone with a telephone was rich. It was Pete's van, too, so he had both the transport and the telephone."

Another possible factor is the forceful personality of Pete's mother, Mona Best. Although she had never managed the Beatles, she played an integral part in securing their bookings and she wanted to ensure that Brian Epstein would manage the group properly. A case of mother knows Best. Whenever I met her, I found her very pleasant but I sensed that she liked to get her way. When I asked **Mona Best (464)** why she thought her son had been dismissed, she said, "I asked Brian what the reason was and he said, 'I can't tell you'. I said, 'Well, may I give you my reason?' 'It's jealousy, Brian, because Pete is the one with the terrific following.' Peter had to be dismissed at that stage because if they became nationally known, Peter would have been the main Beatle with the others just the props." That is parental pride and there's nothing wrong with that, but what if she had been constantly making similar remarks to Brian Epstein, who had already recognised that the group's main strength would be in their songwriting? Mrs. Best, with the best of intentions, might have sealed her son's fate.

III. Enter Brian Epstein

The promoter Ron Appleby's definitions of BE and AE (Before and After Epstein) are apt. Brian Epstein's involvement with the Liverpool groups, especially the Beatles, led to changes in personnel and presentation. Brian Epstein first saw the Beatles at the Cavern in November 1961 and a few weeks later he had the Beatles under contract. Brian Epstein's personal assistant NEMS, **Alistair Taylor (465)**, remembers: "One day Brian asked me to join him for lunch but he wanted to look in at the Cavern first to catch one of the Beatles' lunchtime sessions. I recognised the Beatles from their visits to NEMS, though I don't remember them buying many records, and we looked out of place in white shirts and dark, business suits. The Beatles were playing 'A Taste Of Honey' and 'Twist And Shout' but we were particularly impressed that they included original songs. The one that sticks in my mind is 'Hello Little Girl'."

Bob Wooler (466): "Allan Williams had fallen out with the Beatles over the payment of commission and he told me to have nothing more to do with them. I said, 'Too late, Allan, I am already totally Beatleised. It's impossible, Allan.' Allan Williams didn't want to know them, but Ray McFall, Bill Harry and Sam Leach all toyed with the idea of managing them. Ray McFall knew they needed someone to manage them, but his personality was so different to theirs and he wouldn't have tolerated their behaviour. I remember him saying to me, 'The Beatles really need a manager,' and I thought, 'Then you'll find out how awkward the sods can be.' Bill Harry was preoccupied with *Mersey Beat* and I think they would have fallen out with Sam Leach. I don't know about Mona Best but she was looking after their bookings at the time and recognised their potential – or at least, Pete's potential! I don't think the other three would have accepted her as she would have been furthering Pete's career rather than the group's. Brian Epstein was obviously the right choice for the Beatles and he was in a different league to the other managers like Joe Flannery and Ted Knibbs."

Brian Epstein didn't want to change the Beatles right away. Quite the reverse. The promoter **Ron Appleby (467)** again: "Brian Epstein was always immaculately dressed, and he stood out against the Beatles' jeans and leather jackets. One night Bob Wooler said, 'There's another Beatle here tonight.' I went up to the balcony to look. There was Eppy. He'd bought himself the full Hamburg rig – jeans, black leather jacket and black polo-neck sweater. He'd emulated the Beatles completely, but whereas their gear was well-worn and travelled, his was brand new."

Brian Epstein was full of tricks to get the Beatles noticed. He had them support Joe Brown and the Bruvvers at one concert. **Joe Brown (468)**: "We were topping the bill and we were the last on, and he put the Beatles on before us. If you're second top, you normally close the first half, but the idea was to get the audience standing up and screaming so hard that the main act couldn't get on. This was before they'd had any hit records, but it was a real hard act to follow. Still, we did it."

IV. Decca Audition

There were no recording studios or music publishers in Liverpool, and Brian Epstein was looking for contacts who could help him secure a record contract for the Beatles. *Liverpool Echo* ran a weekly record review column by Disker, a pseudonym for **Tony Barrow (469)**, a Crosby boy who had moved to London. "I worked for Decca as the only full-time sleeve-note writer in the business. I wrote sleeve notes for all kind of LPs: Duke Ellington, Gracie Fields, and Anthony Newley's *Stop the World – I Want To Get Off*. While I was at Decca, Brian Epstein got in touch with me. He had written to Disker and to his great surprise, he received a reply from London. He wanted me to write about the Beatles in the *Liverpool Echo*. I told him that I only reviewed records but I gave him a contact at the paper and asked him to keep in touch. Later on, Brian played me an acetate of the Beatles recorded at the Cavern. The sound quality was abominable, although it did convey the atmosphere of the Cavern. It wasn't my place to say, 'Don't call us, we'll call you.' I spoke on the telephone to the marketing department and said that I had one of their customers here, a record dealer from Liverpool, and they might want to put pressure on the A&R department for an audition. They said, 'That name doesn't ring any bells. Is 'Epstein' the name of the shop?' I said, 'Good grief, no. The shops are called NEMS.' As soon as I mentioned NEMS they said, 'NEMS, oh yes. Brian Epstein's group must have an audition.'"

The Beatles had their audition at Decca on New Year's Day, 1962. They thought that Decca would sign them. Decca wanted to sign a beat group but they chose the cleaner-looking Brian Poole and the Tremeloes. They also signed the Bachelors, as **John Stokes (470)** recalled: "Dick Rowe might have been trying to make up his mind between us and them because we were around at the time. They released 'Love Me Do' just before we released 'Charmaine'. It was in the charts when ours was released but theirs went out of the charts very quickly and 'Charmaine' really took off. They were to depose us from the No.1 spot twice. We had 'I Believe' and 'Diane' at No.1 and their records would go straight to the top – everything else was shoved out of the way."

The head of Decca's A&R department, Dick Rowe, is castigated for making one of the biggest blunders of all time. However, the Beatles were rejected by other record companies who heard the same tapes, and Decca were to sign the Rolling Stones. Another Crosby boy, **Noel Walker (471)**, had talked his way into Decca and was one of Dick Rowe's producers: "Half of the problem was that Dick Rowe was too old to realise what was happening in teen music. He had done great work with Billy Fury and with Craig Douglas and he was also a country and western fan. He didn't care for black rhythm and blues, and so he turned down the Beatles because he didn't think they would sell records."

The Beatles' Decca tapes became legendary. For a long time, only a few people had heard them, then they were widely bootlegged and now many of the tracks are available on *Anthology 1*. No one has since paid them much attention because they were not, after all, very good. However, the decision to reject them wasn't solely Dick Rowe's. It wasn't Dick Rowe but **Mike Smith (472)**, who had recorded them for Decca: "Someone at Decca had to show some interest in the Beatles because Brian Epstein ran NEMS, which was an important account for the sales people. I thought the Beatles were absolutely wonderful on stage and, in retrospect, I should have trusted my instincts. They weren't very good in the studio and really we got to the Beatles too early. Nothing against Pete Best but Ringo Starr wasn't in the band and they hadn't developed their songwriting. Had I picked up on them six months later, there was no way I couldn't have recognised the quality of their songs. They did black R&B like the Coasters' 'Three Cool Cats' and it wasn't very good. I think they were overawed by the situation and their personalities didn't come across. I took the tape to Decca House and I was told that they sounded like the Shadows. I had recorded two bands and I was told that I could take one and not the other. I went with Brian Poole and the Tremeloes because they had been the better band in the studio. So much in this industry depends upon being in the right place at the right time, and whether I did the right thing or not, I'll never know. In fairness, I don't think I could have worked with them the way that George Martin did – I would have got involved in their bad parts and not encouraged the good ones. When I met them later on, they gave me a two-fingered salute."

Pete Best (473): "At the time, Decca was the company and we thought hard about the material we were going to play at the audition. It was a good cross-section of numbers and we recorded them like a live set with just one or two takes on each number. We were trying to be cool, calm and collected about it, but there were frogs in our throats. We weren't on form and the tape could have been a lot better."

V. Twist And Out

Brian Epstein did not use his family's money to secure the Beatles a recording contract or even to record them himself. Indeed, he worked independently of his father. Brian's brother, **Clive Epstein (474)**, knew the background. "I didn't take much notice at first because we had some very successful stores on Merseyside and we were expanding into the suburbs. It wasn't until the spring of 1962 that I took the whole thing more seriously. Brian and I had dinner at the 23 club in Hope Street and he put forward various ideas for forming an organisation to manage artists and promote concerts. I felt that this could be a useful way of diversifying. It became a family matter and, after careful consideration, my father decided that entertainment activities weren't for him. We decided that NEMS Enterprises would be formed to look after our entertainment activities and would be jointly controlled by Brian and myself."

The Beatles were signed to one of EMI's smaller labels, Parlophone, a label best known for Scottish dance records and comedy albums. **Pete Best (475)**: "We went to Germany in April to open the Star-Club while Brian took a tape of the Decca auditions round the recording companies in London, trying to get us a contract. In May we received a telegram from Brian saying, 'Congratulations. You've got a recording session with EMI. Write your own material.' That was when they wrote

'Love Me Do'. We came back and auditioned for George Martin at EMI. He liked 'Love Me Do' and said, 'Fine. Go away and rehearse a bit more. Then come back and we'll put the finishing touches to it.' Between those recording dates, in August 1962, I got kicked out."

One minute it was 'Twist and Shout', the next it was twist and out. But was it so unexpected? Hadn't **Pete Best (476)** suspected that something was wrong? "I'd been with the Beatles for two years. We'd been through thick and thin together. There were times when the money from bookings wasn't enough to keep things going. There was a strong fellowship about the group and I never thought that they wanted to get rid of me. On Tuesday night I'd been playing at the Cavern and Brian said he'd like to see me in his office the next morning. This was quite normal because, with the family phone, I fixed the bookings and he'd ask me about venues and prices. I went down the next morning without a care in the world and he said, 'The lads don't want you in the group any more.'"

There are several significant facts in that statement – there had been no big row and Pete had no warning that anything was wrong: indeed, he had no inkling that he was to be dismissed. It is fair to assume that the reason or reasons were something that could not easily be corrected. The sacking was handled abysmally but it should be remembered that we are not dealing with ICI or EMI here (although in a sense we are): there was no contract of employment and everyone was young – Brian Epstein was 28 and George Harrison was only 19. The fact that Brian Epstein never gave any reasons for the sacking suggests he was uncomfortable about his role.

The Beatles had sacked people before – John smashed a washboard over Pete Shotton's head to dismiss him from the Quarry Men – so why did they ask Brian to do it? Probably because they were ashamed of what they were doing, but we'll come to that.

VI. How good was Pete Best's drumming?

Several writers have attributed Pete's sacking to the Beatles' record producer, George Martin. He is said to have disliked Pete's drumming and although the release of *Anthology 1* in 1995 did a lot for Pete Best's bank balance, it did nothing for his credibility. His drumming on the demo of 'Love Me Do' from 6 June 1962 is uneven and he loses the plot halfway through. He might just as well have been banging bin lids and it is unfortunate that George Martin heard him on a bad day, a very bad day.

George Martin (477): "I thought Pete was an essential part of the Beatles because of his image: there was a moody James Dean look about him. But I didn't like his drumming. I didn't think it held the band together as it should have done and I was determined that the Beatles weren't going to suffer because of it. I told Brian that I was going to use a session drummer when we made records. I didn't realise that the other boys had been thinking of getting rid of Pete anyway and that my decision was the last straw that broke the camel's back. So Pete was given the boot, poor chap. It was hard luck on him, but it was inevitable."

Hearing the drumming on that demo of 'Love Me Do', it is not surprising that George Martin wanted to use a session drummer. The Beatles and Brian Epstein may not have known it, but there was nothing unusual in that. Inconsistencies in tempo may have been okay on stage, but not on record, and drummers were the most likely to be replaced in the studio. "The reasons were purely financial," elucidates **Clem Cattini (478)** of the Tornados and a session drummer, "You were expected to complete four tracks in three hours. An inexperienced group might need a week to do two titles, not because they were incapable but because sessions are quite different to being on the road. You can't get away with so much. You need more discipline." Having someone ghost Pete Best's drumming might compound the doubts, justified and otherwise, that the others had about him.

Pete Best was a good rock'n'roll drummer and was excellent on their 1961 single with Tony Sheridan, 'My Bonnie', but he lacked versatility and was known to play the same pattern, either slow or fast depending on the speed of the song. John Lennon may not have wanted to stray from rock'n'roll, but Paul McCartney was experimenting with show songs and standards. Furthermore, the drum and bass are closely wedded as the foundation of a band's sound and so he would have noticed Pete's limitations.

Bob Wooler (479) recalled, "The Beatles used to play the Cavern at lunchtimes and sometimes they would stay behind and rehearse, and just myself and the cleaners would hear them. One day I came back from the Grapes about ten past three and the Beatles were rehearsing. Paul was showing Pete Best how he wanted the drums to be played for a certain tune and I thought, 'That's pushing it a bit.' At times Pete would be like a zombie on the drums: it was as though he was saying, 'Do I have to do this?', and that went against him with Paul McCartney, who was all for communication. Pete had no show about him – he always looked bored – but he came alive for photo sessions as he was very photogenic." When Clive Gregson caught the Pete Best Band in Nashville, Pete was looking at his watch – can you imagine how behaviour like that would have gone down with the ultimate showman, Paul McCartney?

Harry Prytherch (480): "Most of us used to do two beats or four beats to the bar which was a bomp-ba-bomp, bomp-ba-bomp. Now Pete Best had the original Beatles sound because he would drum eight – bomp-bomp-bomp-bomp-bomp-bomp-bomp-bomp – and that was lashing out at you and that was half of their sound. You could heard the difference when Ringo took over as Pete was a real pounding rock'n'roll drummer."

Another criticism is that Pete didn't fit in with The Beatles. **Cynthia Lennon (481)**: "They got on okay with Pete but he didn't join in with their jokes and their banter. Ringo was nutty enough to fit in right way. Pete was far more serious."

Sure, he was quiet but so was George and in any event, you can't have four garrulous members in one group. By the same argument, the Rolling Stones would have sacked Charlie Watts. Les Chadwick, like George Harrison, was quiet and studious about his music and an unlikely companion for Gerry Marsden, yet he fitted perfectly into Gerry and the Pacemakers.

Bill Harry (482) had problems whenever he wished to interview Pete for *Mersey Beat*. "Pete Best never said anything; he was a most difficult person to interview. He didn't fit in with the rest of them as a personality. If somebody talked to him, he'd just grunt or nod, but I always liked him. When it was announced that Ringo was taking over, I felt an injustice was being done, but not because he was getting kicked out on the brink of success. That's the luck of the game. I felt there should have been some truth about why he was put out. They should have said, 'We've decided that we get on better with Ringo, and we want Ringo with us.' Instead they suggested that Pete Best wasn't good enough."

Ray McFall (483): "I laboured under the illusion that Pete Best was required to go because he wasn't up to scratch, but I don't believe that anymore and I am surprised that I took that view. Pete Best could have coped equally well, and they would have been equally successful with him. What he lacked as a drummer, if he did, he made up in his good looks and that may explain why Pete left the band. I think they came to the conclusion that he was getting too much attention. And he wasn't really a Beatle, not as you know the others, he was quiet and very sensitive. He was a nice boy and maybe he was too nice for the group. I think he would have acquitted himself very well and I don't think that the Beatles would have suffered by retaining him, but Ringo was a close friend, and it's their prerogative."

VII. Enter Ringo Starr

John, Paul and George knew Ringo (whose real name was Richard Starkey) well and they realised that he'd be right for the group. He had started his career in Eddie Clayton's skiffle group. **Eddie Clayton (484)**: "Ritchie liked gold lamé waistcoats, snappy suits and jewellery and this is what caught Brian Epstein's eye. He probably thought that Pete didn't have the right image and Ritchie, being more flamboyant, particularly on stage, would be just right."

When Ritchie joined Rory Storm and the Hurricanes, he acquired a new name, as Johnny Byrne, also the recipient of a new name, **Johnny Guitar (485)** recalled: "We were offered a contract with Butlin's in Pwellheli and it was fantastic money, £25 a week each, which was a fortune in the Sixties. We had to decide whether we stayed at home with our routine jobs or whether we turned professional. Ringo was very much against it. He was serving an apprenticeship at Henry Hunt's, making school climbing frames. We persuaded him when we mentioned that women were 'available'. Rory said we'd all have to have good stage names. He said, 'You can be Ringo Starr' and Ritchie said, 'No, I like my own name.' Rory insisted and said, 'What can you sing?' We had a spot called Ringo Starrtime. Ringo sang the Shirelles' number, 'Boys'. If Rory hadn't twisted his arm, I don't think he'd have done a lot of the things he did."

Rory Storm and the Hurricanes were playing at Butlin's holiday camp in Skegness. One day John and Paul appeared. **Johnny Guitar (486)**, who was sharing a caravan with Ringo, described what happened. "They knocked on the door of our caravan about ten o'clock one morning and I was very surprised because John hated Butlin's. He thought it was like Belsen. Paul said, 'We've come to ask Ringo to join us.' We went into the camp and Rory said, 'What are we going to do?' because this is mid-season and we couldn't work without a drummer. Paul said, 'Mr. Epstein would like Pete Best to play with you.' We couldn't stand in Ringo's way because we knew the Beatles were going to be big. We went back to Liverpool and saw Pete, but he was so upset that he didn't want to play with anybody. When we got back to Skegness, somebody said he'd play drums for us. We said, 'Are you a drummer?' and he said, 'No, I'm an actor.' He was Anthony Ashdown who had been in the film *The Loneliness of the Long-Distance Runner*. He got us by for a week or two until a relief drummer could come out."

Iris Caldwell (487): "Rory was very happy for Ringo as he knew this was a big opportunity. He did ask Epstein if Ringo could stay the last three weeks of the season but Ringo wanted to go there and then, which was a shame. He could have stayed the last three weeks, and, as a result, Rory didn't get the contract for Butlin's the next year." The Stormy Tempest character in the 1973 film, *That'll Be The Day*, was based on Rory.

Rory himself was a limited vocalist and Ringo's talents on the drums were not fully exploited with the Hurricanes. The Beatles had recognised his potential, but the change from Pete Best to Ringo Starr came as a shock to Merseyside fans. And to **Beryl Adams (488)** , Brian Epstein's secretary: "I had no idea that Pete was going to be sacked – nothing had been building up as far as I could see – and I was shocked to come back from holiday and find out what had been happening. I had called in the shop on the Saturday and Brian said, 'Beryl, are you doing anything tonight?' and he invited me for a meal and said that we would then go and see the Beatles with Ringo at Hulme Hall in Port Sunlight. It was his first appearance with them and it was amazing to watch – half the girls were crying hysterically and half of them were happy because it was Ringo. Bob Wooler was very upset because he was very fond of Pete."

There was an outcry when the Beatles introduced Ringo Starr as their new member at the Cavern. George Harrison was given a black eye by a Best supporter after their first set at a lunchtime session. **Ian Edwards (489)** was there. "They were shouting 'Ringo out, Pete in' and refusing to let them play. There was a big question as to whether this could be the Beatles' downfall. Everyone was talking about it. Ritchie was playing in a group that wasn't taken seriously and suddenly he's in the biggest thing on Merseyside. He was a very good rock drummer, but there were a lot of better drummers around, like Johnny Hutch."

Johnny Hutch (490) told me that Brian Epstein had considered him as Pete Best's replacement. "Brian asked me to join the Beatles and I said, 'I wouldn't join the Beatles for a gold clock. There's only one group as far as I'm concerned and that's the Big Three. The Beatles can't make a better sound than that and Pete Best is a very good friend of mine. I couldn't do the dirty on him."

I find that story hard to accept as Johnny Hutch is a tough character who is likely to have disrupted the Beatles. He considered Paul McCartney 'a grade-A creep' and he laughed when I quoted Nik Cohen's description of John Lennon rampaging through Liverpool 'like a wounded buffalo'. **Johnny Hutch (491)**: "That's a load of rubbish. He only seems a hard case to types like you because you're the sort that's never been in a fight. He wasn't a hard case to me. He was a bully who didn't pick on people his own size. I saw him hit someone once and I told him that if he did it again, he'd have to contend with me. I could tell him to sit there and behave."

At one point too, Brian had thought of adding keyboards to the band. **Roy Young (492)**: "I was playing with the Beatles at the Star-Club and Brian Epstein grabbed me and said, 'I wonder if you would consider coming with the four lads back to England to procure a recording contract.' I had a three year contract with the club with a brand new car written into it every year. I felt comfortable with that, and I didn't want to leave Hamburg. It was such fun and so enjoyable but I loved being with them and John would do so many things on stage. One night I was looking at him on stage and he was chewing gum, and I didn't know how he could chew gum and sing. He spat the gum out and it hit my nose and he fell on the floor laughing. I went back to Brian and said, 'No', but I did appreciate the offer. They are the greatest thing on earth in musical terms, and I wouldn't have my family if I had done that."

The offer to replace Pete Best in the Beatles surprised Ringo. However, he had not been poached from Rory Storm. He had already decided to leave the group. **Dave Lovelady (493)**, then drumming with Kingsize Taylor and the Dominoes, explains: "After we'd been in Hamburg two months, the time came when I had to come home and return to my studies. Teddy Taylor and the rest of the boys wanted to stay professional, so it was decided that I would leave and they would fly out a replacement. Teddy wrote to Ringo and asked him if he would like to take my place. He wrote back to say that he would and he gave Rory Storm his notice. About ten days later, Teddy had a letter saying that he'd decided to join the Beatles instead. I came home and we did a swap with the Four Jays. Brian Redman took my place with Kingsize Taylor, and I joined the Four Jays or the Fourmost, as they were to become."

After Ringo Starr, Rory Storm used Gibson Kemp, another fine drummer who moved on to the Dominoes. **Lee Curtis (494)** asked Rory about his problems. "Rory told me he'd had a new drummer again, and I said, 'Why another one? Gibson Kemp's a knockout drummer.' He said, 'I've lost Ringo and now I've lost Gibson as well. He's joined the Dominoes, so I'm breaking in another one.' I said, 'What's going on, Rory? Why can't you keep your drummers?' He said, 'What can I say? I make 'em and they take 'em.'"

It was some weeks before **Pete Best (495)** wanted to play again. "I wouldn't rate Ringo as a better drummer than me – I'm adamant about that – and when it happened, I felt like putting a stone round my neck and jumping off the Pier Head. I knew the Beatles were going places and to be kicked out was soul-destroying. I never realised that the Beatles would be international stars, but I was sure we'd be a chart group. I wanted to forget about everything. I didn't want to play the drums. I didn't want to meet anyone. The fact that the Beatles weren't at the dismissal hurt a lot more than the fact that Brian was the one who told me that I wasn't a Beatle anymore."

VIII. New Drummers for Old

Chris Curtis (496) of the Searchers: "When Pete Best left, I even thought of turning into a guitarist and getting him to drum in our band. The Beatles didn't hate Pete Best but they didn't want a star on the drums. Ringo was a good drummer but he was more ordinary. At that Decca audition, I think they also realised that Pete had so much power that no-one would know how to record him. That's why so many Merseyside discs are icky, all thin and weedy – except for the Searchers'. Our engineer knew what he was doing, but not always. 'Love Potion No.9' was our biggest seller in America and the drums are so thin on that record. It was right for their radio stations, they like that kind of sound."

Several groups asked Pete to join them. He wanted to be in a band which was not managed by Brian Epstein, so he became part of Lee Curtis and the All Stars, handled by Joe Flannery. **Lee Curtis (497)**: "I was delighted that he joined me because he was such a personality on Merseyside. To have Pete Best drumming behind you was a tremendous attraction. I'd seen him with the Beatles and it was absolutely amazing because the girls screamed like hell for Pete to sing. 'Let Pete sing. Let Pete sing.'"

Lee Curtis' group was called the All Stars because each member had his own following. Pete Best had his fans and Lee shared the vocals with a young girl, **Beryl Marsden (498)**. "We used to rehearse at Peter's house and his mum would be telling tales of how awful the Beatles were and how I mustn't go near them, never speak to them or listen to their music. It was a terrible thing for them to do, but I liked their music and I couldn't stay away too long. I rang up one day and said, 'I'm not very well. I can't come in and rehearse', and I skived off to a lunchtime session at the Cavern. Unfortunately, I got caught out and I got a really bad scolding from Peter's mother. But it was worth it."

Even though the Beatles were acquiring a national following, they sometimes played on the same bill as the All Stars. What were these quasi-reunions like? **Pete Best (499)**: "We played on the same bill as the Beatles on two occasions. One was at the Cavern when we were second on the bill to the Beatles. The other was in the *Mersey Beat* Pollwinners Concert. On both occasions, we were on just prior to the Beatles, and we had to pass one another. We passed face to face, yet nothing was ever said."

The Pollwinners Concert was held after the results of the second *Mersey Beat* popularity poll was published in January 1963. The Beatles were still the top group and Lee Curtis and the All Stars were second. How many of those votes were for Lee Curtis, how many were for Pete Best, and how many were due to the group and its management filling in voting slips? The Top Twenty was as follows, and what a difference a year makes.

1962	1963	
1	1	The Beatles
–	2	Lee Curtis and the All Stars
7	3	The Big Three
19	3	Billy Kramer and the Coasters
12	5	The Undertakers
10	6	The Fourmost
2	7	Gerry and the Pacemakers
3	8	Johnny Sandon and the Remo Four
–	9	Vic and the Spidermen
–	10	The Merseybeats
–	11	The Swinging Blue Jeans

8	12	The Strangers
–	13	Group One
11	14	Ian and the Zodiacs
–	15	Pete Maclaine and the Dakotas
–	16	The Dennisons
–	17	Gus Travis and the Midnighters
14	18	Mark Peters and the Cyclones
4	19	Rory Storm and the Hurricanes
–	20	Johnny Templer and the Hi-Cats

Some big changes had taken place in the 12 months between the polls, and just as Pete Best could have been responsible for the high placing of Lee Curtis and the All Stars, the loss of Ringo Starr could have caused Rory Storm and the Hurricanes' drop in popularity. **Billy J. Kramer (500)** remembers the Pollwinners concert: "The Beatles did 'Please Please Me' and I told George Harrison that they should record it. It was the first time I'd heard them perform an original number. Brian Epstein said in his book, *A Cellarful of Noise*, that the first time he heard the Beatles he knew that they were going to be as big as Elvis. Well, the first time I saw them at Litherland Town Hall I thought that, and my friends thought I was crazy. When I heard them do 'Please Please Me', I knew it."

Because the Merseybeats were one of the younger groups on Merseyside, they were overawed by the Beatles. **Billy Kinsley (501)**: "We played a gig at Liverpool University with the Beatles who'd just entered the charts with 'Love Me Do'. It was the first time they'd sung 'A Taste Of Honey'. Paul had chosen the song, and the others didn't like it. Paul came up to me and said, 'What did you think of 'A Taste Of Honey'?' and I said, 'I was knocked out by it. Superb.' Paul grabbed hold of me and said, 'Go and tell the others that.' He took me into their dressing room and John said, 'Go on then. What do you think?' I was 15 years old and very nervous because there was big JL asking me what I thought of a song he didn't like. I told him that I thought 'A Taste Of Honey' was great. Paul said, 'Ha, ha, John, told you so.' They decided that night to put it on their first album."

Tony Barrow (502) shows how quickly Ringo was accepted as a member of the Beatles: "Muriel Young introduced a series of programs for Radio Luxembourg and the Beatles were there to promote their second single, 'Please Please Me'. She introduced them by saying 'And when I tell you that their names are John, Paul, George and Ringo…' and the crowd in the studio went mad. They were much more interested in the Beatles than they would be in the average pop group who'd had one hit record."

John and Paul shared the composing credit on their compositions. Songs would be listed "Lennon-McCartney" even if it was completely Lennon ('Help!') or completely Paul ('Yesterday'). Although it caused friction in later years, **Tony Barrow (503)** thinks it was the right decision: "Lennon and McCartney shared composer credits equally. This ensured that they derived an equal financial share from everything they wrote. They did collaborate with each other on songs but, creatively, it was never a 50/50 split. It could be 75/25 or even 90/10. One would have a pretty solid idea and the other partner would add the rest."

Johnny Dean (504), the editor of the monthly *Beatles Book*, has an example of that partnership. "I got to Studio 2 in Abbey Road, and Brian Epstein, George Martin and Dick James were hanging around waiting for the Beatles to turn up. I learned that the boys would write a song on the way to the studio. They walked in and they sang it with acoustic guitars and with everyone cocking an ear to hear what it was like. It was 'She Loves You' and it didn't sound very impressive. The song when I first heard it and the song when they'd finished it were completely different. What they did in between was the Beatles' magic."

That magic included Ringo Starr's drumming. As John and Paul's compositions became more sophisticated, Ringo was able to develop new techniques. It's unfortunate that Pete Best never had the opportunity to prove himself, sticking, when he has played, to a rock'n'roll groove. After Lee Curtis and still managed by Joe Flannery, he formed the Pete Best Four which included Wayne Bickerton and Tony Waddington, who have since written and produced hits for the Rubettes, Mac and Katie Kissoon and Liverpool FC. **Wayne Bickerton (505)**: "Pete was a good drummer. All the stories of him not being able to play properly are grossly exaggerated. The problem he fought against was being an ex-Beatle, which worked against the band. Reporters asked him about the Beatles and nothing else. They weren't interested in the future of his new band. It's ironic because Tony and I went on to become successful songwriters and producers. The talent was in the band, but it was secondary."

IX. So, why was he sacked?

Rick Wakeman (506): "When you know what the future is, it's easy to criticise the past. Nobody could have foreseen what would happen to the Beatles and Pete was just unlucky. Who knows why some people leave some groups? It can be something that doesn't have a verbal explanation, something intangible, you know. It just didn't feel right and no-one knows why."

George Melly (507): "I think they were right in getting rid of Pete Best and recruiting Ringo Starr. Pete Best was tremendously popular in Liverpool and undoubtedly it was a great tragedy for him to be sacked at the very moment when they were breaking but, whoever it was, be it Brian Epstein, George Martin or the Beatles, whoever it was, saw that Ringo's personality was the perfect foil. He was plain whereas the others were all rather good-looking. He was thick whereas the others were rather bright. He was working class whereas the others were basically suburban. Ringo completed the Beatles and made them more effective, not just musically but as personalities."

In 1984 I wrote the original 'Drummed Out' chapter for *Let's Go Down The Cavern,* assembling the material from the interviews I had conducted. I concluded that there were several factors at work in the dismissal of Pete Best, but I thought that, unless Paul or George came clean, the matter would never fully be resolved. In the 1990s, I read the chapter and realised that I thought the matter needed closer inspection and so I did further interviews and wrote the book, *Drummed Out! The Sacking Of Pete Best.* I concentrated on that week and tried to find out exactly what had happened.

Neither Pete Best nor his half-brother Roag would have anything to do with the book while it was being researched, the excuse being that they were working on their own project. Fair enough, but after publication, they told Bill Harry, Bob Wooler and several others that the book was riddled with errors. I never learnt what those errors were: Roag told me that "there are too many to mention". Since then, rather like Pete meeting the rest of the Beatles, I have met Pete twice but we have only exchanged pleasantries. As they had not objected to my original chapter in 1984, I assumed that the Best brothers did not care for the fresh research and/or the conclusions.

The *Drummed Out!* book had good reviews but some critics remarked that the book did not reach a conclusion by giving the reason for Pete Best's dismissal. Well, the book did reach a conclusion, showing that many factors were at work. The book concludes that Paul, John, George, George Martin and Brian Epstein all had their reasons for wanting Pete out of the group, and, unfortunately for Pete, everything came to a head in August 1962.

In my view, Paul McCartney had the most reasons to want him out. He thought he was a limited drummer who lacked versatility and preferred Ringo. George Martin's criticism confirmed his thoughts and he didn't want a drummer who might hold back his own ambitions. He and Pete only tolerated each other and possibly the boyish-looking McCartney was jealous of his good looks.

John felt the same way, but not as strongly. He was going through his own personal traumas being forced into a marriage and possibly Paul seized the moment. Did John agree to Pete's sacking while he was distracted?

George considered Ringo the better musician and preferred him in the group as they were good friends. However, he revealed that he also felt vulnerable after Pete's sacking: if they could get rid of Pete, they might also get rid of him. This suggests that George didn't play a large role in the dismissal.

Brian Epstein, I believe, would be glad to be away from Mona Best's comments and as he wanted to impress George Martin with a top class band, Pete had to go. Granada TV were filming the Beatles at the Cavern on 22 August 1962 and it would be all the better if they were seen with a new drummer.

There may be other factors of which we are not aware or able to assess, and here's one. When the Beatles returned from Hamburg in June 1962, Neil Aspinall left his job as a trainee accountant and became their full-time road manager. He was very friendly with Pete Best and had lodgings in Hayman's Green with the Best family. He made Mona Best pregnant and she had his son, Roag, on 21 July 1962. When Pete was sacked from the Beatles, he told Neil he would have to leave the house if he was to continue with the Beatles. Neil was effectively being deprived of seeing his son. This is a situation worthy of *The Jerry Springer Show* and if your best friend was having it off with your mother, surely he wouldn't be your best friend anymore.

What is more, John Lennon was the most provocative person on Merseyside. He couldn't care less what he said to anyone. He once told Brian Epstein that he wished Hitler had finished the job. When the Beatles were on stage in August 1962, I can imagine him making cutting remarks, remarks that only Pete would appreciate, but he would be needling him all the same. He wouldn't be able to stop himself – that's the way he was. For all these reasons, I am convinced that Mona Best's pregnancy was a telling factor in the sacking of Pete Best, but I've no idea how much and nobody is talking.

Dill Harry prides himself on being an investigative reporter so I can't see how he came to accept Brian Epstein's press release. On 23 August 1962, the good readers of *Mersey Beat* were told, "Pete Best left the group by mutual agreement. There were no arguments or difficulties, and this has been an entirely amicable decision." By then, most of the readers must have known otherwise.

Also, musicians are sacked from groups all the time and no one at the time would have thought that the Beatles were going to be the biggest group in the world. Except, of course, Brian Epstein.

8   SECRET AGENT

I. Two Cities
II. Flying Dakotas

"A horse never runs so fast as when he has other horses to catch up and outpace."
(Ovid)

I. Two Cities

Even if the Beatles had moved to Australia in 1961, Liverpool would have become a focal point for the music industry. Something unique was happening in the city. Certainly there were beat groups elsewhere, but nothing to compare with Liverpool. There was camaraderie with little rivalry between the groups. **Derek Quinn (508)** of the zany Manchester group, Freddie and the Dreamers, noticed the difference. "Liverpool groups used to go and see each other, especially at the Cavern. We would be playing at the Cavern and in would walk some of the Swinging Blue Jeans, Gerry and the Pacemakers, the Beatles and the Undertakers. All groups converged on the Cavern, and if you were from Manchester, they wanted to see what you were like. The groups from Manchester didn't spend much time going to see other groups."

Manchester is only 30 miles from Liverpool and yet the approach to music was different. The few beat clubs in the city were lavishly decorated; groups performed in front of a Swiss chalet set in the Jungfrau. Most groups gained their experience in working men's clubs or cabaret, and they might be the entertainment between the bingo sessions. This was very different to the Cavern where the punters wanted nothing but music. **Derek Leckenby (509)** from the Manchester group Herman's Hermits says, "The Liverpool groups had much more aggression. When they played rock'n'roll, they forced it on you, especially the Big Three. I'd go anywhere to see the Big Three. I don't think the Manchester groups had as much energy, although they had the musical abilities."

"I don't think there was a Manchester sound or, if there was, it was a spin-off of the Liverpool sound," says **Freddie Garrity (510)**. "We all played the Cavern and the other Liverpool clubs and the Hollies were very like a Liverpool group with their incessant drumbeat and raucous chords."

The Manchester groups sought bookings on Merseyside. They could find out what was going on, play in beat clubs for themselves and, of course, purloin a few ideas. **Bernie Calvert (511)** later played with the Hollies, but in the early 1960s, he found popularity on Merseyside as a part of the Manchester band, Rick O'Shea and the Dolphins. "We used to do 'I Love How You Love Me' and songs like that. That was the Manchester scene, more polite if you like. We used to play a club in Litherland and we went down well because we were different to the Liverpool bands. We didn't have that R & B attack. The scenes started to merge in 1963 after the Beatles broke through and then the Hollies."

Mike Maxfield (512) of Pete Maclaine and the Dakotas: "We were probably the first Manchester band to play in Liverpool. It was somewhere in West Derby and these girls told us about the Cavern. We went down there and we nagged Ray McFall into giving us a gig. He was reticent at first because he said there were already too many groups in Liverpool."

Some Manchester musicians copied what they had seen in Liverpool. **Peter Noone (513)**, Herman of Herman's Hermits: "Most of us didn't take the bands too seriously. We listened to our parents, who said, 'Put the guitar down and do a job with your hands.' We did it half-heartedly, but the Beatles wanted to make a career out of it from the beginning. Their attitude was, 'We're not messing about up here. We take ourselves deadly seriously.' That rubbed off on a lot of bands, including us.'

Derek Leckenby (514) of Herman's Hermits recalled seeing the Hollies for the first time. "I knew the lads when they belonged to other groups, but when I saw them start out as the Hollies, I couldn't believe it. They did a Sunday afternoon show at the Oasis in Manchester and they were dynamite. I'm sure they'd been scouting round Liverpool, picking up a few ideas."

Don Andrew (515) of the Remo Four has reservations about the Beatles but applauds their originality. The Hollies, in his view, were not in the same class. "A lot of groups tried to copy the Beatles. Faron's Flamingoes, Earl Preston and the TTs, and Rory Storm and the Hurricanes all went down the Beatles' road in terms of the songs they performed and the way they performed them. Some groups even tried to look like the Beatles. The biggest culprits were the Hollies, who copied the Beatles in every way. They suddenly appeared looking like the Beatles and playing the same sort of numbers, but they never got their sound. They shouldn't be classed with the Beatles because they were always second-rate, but in Manchester, they were regarded very highly."

The Hollies had a hit with their first record '(Ain't That) Just Like Me', an American song recommended to them by Johnny Hutch. **Allan Clarke (516)** of the Hollies: "We were playing the Manchester clubs a hell of a lot and doing gigs in Liverpool at the same time. The Beatles were a top-notch group before they even made records, and we were Manchester's equivalent. We played the Cavern quite frequently and they loved us there. The first time that we went on, we thought that we were going to get stoned. Fortunately we didn't, and we went back lots of times. It was a prestige gig, the equivalent of being asked to play the London Palladium. You'd do it for nothing because that was where groups were found by the impresarios from London. We did an audition at the Cavern and we were seen by Ron Richards. We were signed up on that gig and he became our recording manager. When we first made records, we were classed as a Liverpool band. People said, 'This group from the Mersey', and they were right because the Toggery where we originate from is right by the River Mersey in Stockport." Er, yes…

Graham Nash (517): "I hated being called Manchester's answer to the Beatles. I didn't want us to be compared to anybody and certainly not a great band like the Beatles. When I first met David Crosby, he told me that when he was coming to England with the Byrds, some promoter had billed them as America's answer to the Beatles. You can't do that, it's just not on."

Mark Lewisohn (518): "One of John Lennon's first controversial remarks was when he blasted the Hollies for being Beatles copycats. He thought that they had only come along because of the Beatles. He remembered the headline, 'Lennon blasts Hollies', all through his life."

C.P. Lee (519): "The Manchester band, the Imperials, appeared in the Cavern in 1961 and they wore matching jackets which were red with gold braid. They did their first set and said, 'We'll be back later on.' One of the Scousers shouted out, 'What time do you feed the elephants?' and that was it. They never want back after the interval."

II. Flying Dakotas

The Dakotas, another Manchester group, found success backing Billy J. Kramer. The circumstances behind the teaming give an insight into how Brian Epstein worked.

Pete Maclaine and the Dakotas were one of the most popular groups in Manchester. **Pete Maclaine (520)**, a confident lead singer, remembers how they started. "We played in a talent contest at the Plaza in Manchester and the manager said, 'Why don't you all dress up as Indians and call yourselves the Dakotas?' We liked the idea of the Dakotas, but we didn't like the idea of dressing up. Most Indians don't drink pints of bitter. We used to do standards like 'Lover Come Back to Me' and we also did impressions. My impression of Gene Vincent went down very well at the Cavern. I did it once singing 'Baby Blue', which calls for 16 bars of very heavy drumming. Tony Mansfield collapsed and fainted over his kit because it was so hot in the Cavern."

Although **Pete Maclaine (521)** and the Dakotas had regular bookings at the Cavern, their paths never crossed with the Beatles. "I told Brian Epstein that we never saw the Beatles. Every time we were at the Cavern, they were working elsewhere, but then we did a booking with them. We did the first half hour and came off very sweaty and damp and sat down in the small dressing room. All of a sudden, the door opened and in walked Lennon, McCartney, Best and Harrison. I remember sitting in the corner and feeling the atmosphere change. The Beatles took off with 'Long Tall Sally' with McCartney singing in some ridiculously high key. From then on, the Dakotas were never the same. I picked them up the morning after and they'd changed their hairstyles. They'd started to comb it forward. They even started talking in Liverpool accents, and I said, 'What are you talking like that for? You're from Manchester.' They wanted to do songs like 'Money' and 'Twist and Shout'. I could feel that they didn't want me out front. They wanted to be a four-man group like the Beatles, so it was goodbye Pete Maclaine."

Mike Maxfield (522): "Pete Maclaine says that we copied the Beatles, and that didn't happen. It was a business thing really. We had been working with Pete for a long time and we had been going down to the Cavern a lot, and Brian Epstein wanted us to back Billy Kramer. He wasn't the best singer in the world, but he did have a very pleasing voice. We had a meeting with Brian at the Playhouse Theatre in Manchester and I remember his blue Ford Zephyr. We negotiated a deal and there was a side deal with Pete Maclaine, but I don't know the details and nothing came of it. Mind you, we signed a separate recording contract and Billy had his. When we made the records, we got a session fee of £7.10s (£7.50), which was not such a good deal, but we did share the appearance money."

Tony Mansfield (523), drummer with the Dakotas: "We were an unusual band for the time because we could all read music and so when Rolf Harris, Bert Weedon, Vince Eager or Mike Berry was booked into the Oasis in Manchester, we could pick up the music and have it together in half an hour. Pete Maclaine was somebody we played with and he was very good but we really wanted to be on our own. The deal was to back Billy Kramer and I am sure if Pete had an offer to go out on his own, he would have taken it. There was no animosity between us and when I left the Dakotas five or six years later, Pete and I bought a boutique *Pygmalia* off Tony Hicks and Graham Nash of the Hollies and we had that for a while."

In 1962 Billy Kramer and the Coasters were managed by 59 year old Ted Knibbs. They often worked for Brian Epstein, as their drummer **Tony Sanders (524)** recalls: "The Beatles liked working with us because we didn't clash with them and we didn't pinch their songs. A lot of bands were copying them. Sometimes they'd find the first group on would be going through their numbers. We were completely different. We aped Cliff Richard and the Shadows. Now and then Epstein sent us as guinea-pigs to a place. We were playing in Colwyn Bay once and the stage was made up of snooker tables with hardboard over them. Our gear was rocking around everywhere. Epstein asked us what the place was like. We told him and it was all sorted out when the Beatles arrived the next week."

Tony Sanders (525) discovered that working for Brian Epstein had its drawbacks. "We were getting less cash than before because Epstein didn't know the score. Whereas we were getting £18 a booking under Ted Knibbs, we were doing the same bookings for Epstein for £12. He wasn't robbing us. He ran it straight, but people were pulling the wool over his eyes. I don't think he was as good a manager as people think. Rather than him pushing the Beatles along, I think they towed him along. Any other man could have done it. They could have done it on their own."

Would Billy J. Kramer have made the charts had he continued with Ted Knibbs? **Ted Knibbs (526)**: "I think Billy would have made it with me if I'd had a couple of hundred pounds. I could always see the possibilities in Billy so long as he stuck to ballads."

Ted didn't have £200. He'd given up his job and forgone his pension rights to manage Billy and the Coasters full time. The change in management was a traumatic time in Billy's life. His parents were older than those of his friends. **Billy J. Kramer (527)**: "I was a fitter and turner for British Railways and I was told to go to Crewe for a year. I said, 'I think I can learn as much in Liverpool and I don't want to be away from home because my parents are getting on.' They told me that if I didn't go, I knew the alternative. One Saturday, Ted Knibbs took me to a restaurant to see Brian Epstein. He said, 'It's no good beating abut the bush. Brian Epstein wants to manage you.' I said, 'I do very well semi-professionally and I've got a trade. My only concern is my parents.' Brian guaranteed that, no matter what happened, they would get £10 a week for two years. If I earned any more, it was mine."

Brian Epstein considered the Coasters a good band, but he didn't have the resources to make them a similar offer. Billy told **Tony Sanders (528)** of the conversation. "Kramer was in tears. He came round to our house and asked me what he should do. I said, 'The lads won't turn professional and you can't do it on your tod. You'll have to leave us.' Six weeks later, he was in the charts with 'Do You Want To Know A Secret?' I had mixed feelings over that. I was pleased for Billy, but I was sick inside."

Epstein's initial thoughts were not to team Billy with the Dakotas. The Remo Four were at that time working with Johnny Sandon, but Eppy thought the group was right for Billy. Their lead guitarist was **Colin Manley (529)**: "One night at the Cavern Brian Epstein said, 'Would you like to back someone else?' and we guessed who it was. Billy was on in the last spot and we stayed and watched him. We had Johnny Sandon with us and his diction was perfect and he could sing like Ben E. King. Then Billy came on and, well, he's no Mario Lanza. We said, 'Yes, we'd like you to manage us but not if we have to back Billy. We want to stay with Johnny.' The next thing we knew was that he was with the Dakotas and the Beatles had given him a song."

John Johnson (530): "I remember Billy Kramer playing the Iron Door. Billy had been throwing out postcards of himself at the end of his act, no doubt one of Brian Epstein's ideas, and the Iron Door's toilets were awash with them. The toilets overflowed over the floor and into the club. Even then I don't think it was bad as the Jacaranda. Their toilets were a cesspool."

Billy wasn't even the first choice for John and Paul's song, 'Do You Want To Know A Secret?'. The song was offered to Nottingham's Shane Fenton and the Fentones. They had had hits with 'I'm A Moody Guy' (1961) and 'Cindy's Birthday' (1962). Shane became **Alvin Stardust (531)**. "Brian came up to me at a Sunday concert somewhere and said he had a number called 'Do You Want To Know A Secret?'. He thought it would be perfect for me but I told him that I already had a manager and that I'd have to pass on it. Maybe if I'd gone and done it, I'd have done the things Billy J. Kramer and the Dakotas did, but you can never go back and say what would have happened if you'd done something else."

All this indicates that Brian Epstein enjoyed scheming. **Allan Clarke (532)** of the Hollies was sorry for Pete Maclaine. "Pete Maclaine and the Dakotas were very successful. They had this great guitarist, Mike Maxfield, who played a Gretsch, and their drummer, who was Elkie Brooks' brother, had a beautiful Ludwig kit. Brian Epstein wanted a professional group to back Billy J. Kramer, so he just swiped the group off Pete."

Mike Maxfield (533): "When we turned professional, I played a Guild guitar. I was sponsored by Guild and I got the guitars free, so I can't think of a better reason for playing one, can you?"

Pete Maclaine (534) recalls, "Billy hadn't had half the success we'd had. We were destined for stardom. We were about to leave for the Star-Club and then have a recording test in London, and the Dakotas blew it just to be with Brian Epstein. Brian offered me the Coasters, but they had nothing like the musicianship of the Dakotas. I said, 'No, I'll form my own band and I'll show you.'"

So Brian Epstein had created the group he wanted and, surprisingly, he sent them to the Star-Club to honour the booking for Pete Maclaine and the Dakotas. **Billy J. Kramer (535)** recalled the first rehearsal: "Brian brought in the Dakotas and we had a discussion in Liverpool. They wanted to do their own thing and Brian told them, 'If you back Billy, you can do your own thing as well. Go down to the Cavern, have a blow together and see how it works out.' I had a rehearsal with them and it was great. John Lennon and Paul McCartney came down and said how good it sounded. We decided that we would work together; and then we went to London and failed the recording test. I was dismayed. I'd never been outside Liverpool before. The Dakotas flew to Hamburg but I was stuck in London for three days until my passport arrived. I hardly had any money, but I managed to get out to Heathrow and caught the plane to Hamburg. I was so green that when they came round with the meals, I said, 'No, thank you.' I didn't realise they were free and I thought I couldn't afford it."

The Dakotas were signed by Brian Epstein, and **Robin MacDonald (536)** wasn't sure about the change. "Pete Maclaine was more of a complete entertainer. He'd tell jokes and was very confident. He was like Bobby Darin. Billy was much more reserved. He was shy and he didn't talk much to the audience. He'd just get on with the singing. You could put Pete anywhere, but stick a mike in front of Billy and it was a different story."

Billy J. Kramer (537) himself wasn't happy with the situation. "The Dakotas weren't the easiest people to get on with. Sometimes I wish that I'd been teamed with the Remo Four or another Liverpool band, but they were excellent musicians."

Although Epstein may be criticised for his manoeuvres, he did so with great commercial success. The Beatles scaled the heights with Ringo Starr, and Billy J. Kramer with the Dakotas made No.2 with their first single. **Billy J. Kramer (538)** recalls, "We'd had 'Do You Want To Know A Secret?' on tape from John Lennon. It was just John on acoustic guitar and he'd recorded it in the loo because it was the only place where he could get peace and quiet. We did it every night at the Star-Club and it didn't do anything. I came back and we did a test for EMI and two weeks later Brian said, 'EMI are going to release 'Do You Want To Know A Secret?'' I was a bit sick because the Beatles had had hits and Gerry had just had a No.1 and I said, 'Does that mean that I've finally got a recording contract?' He said yes and I said, 'Well, let's find a good number because I don't think that's strong enough. 'Love Me Do' and 'Please Please Me' were great but I can't see this one happening.' Brian said that EMI were happy with it. The success of 'Do You Want To Know A Secret?' was the biggest surprise of my life."

In order to retain the Dakotas identity, Brian Epstein insisted that the billing should be 'Billy J. Kramer with the Dakotas' rather than 'Billy J. Kramer and the Dakotas'. The Dakotas had a Top 20 hit in their own right with the instrumental 'The Cruel Sea'. **Mike Maxfield (539)**: "I had been writing instrumentals as I was learning the guitar. I used to do them and I used to go to the Oasis and watch the Dakotas and I would get up and play the odd instrumental with them. Their lead guitarist Bryn Jones did not want to turn professional so I joined them and we put 'The Cruel Sea' into the act. I had seen the film and the opening chords gave me the idea of the sea. They called it 'The Cruel Surf' in America because surfing was the thing over there. A band called the Challengers did an awful version of it and the Ventures put it on the B-side of 'Walk Don't Run 64'. Nobody can dance to it so we don't do it all that often now."

We'll return to Billy J. Kramer's life with the Dakotas, but what of the others in this little drama? Billy's former manager **Ted Knibbs (540)** told me in 1984: "I'm 80 now and I was the only one of my age who was able to bridge the gap between their generation and mine. I was getting a bit tired and I said to Brian, 'I'll let you have Billy but it'll cost you £50.' He said, 'I'll be delighted.' I got £25 of it and I'm still waiting for the rest, but the way things have happened, I'd rather be where I am than where he is. I passed the Coasters over as well, but the Coasters didn't care for Brian. They said, 'Will you take us over again, Ted? We want to leave Brian.'"

Brian Epstein offered the Coasters a new lead singer. The new band could have been Pete Maclaine and the Coasters, Earl Preston and the Coasters, or his protégé Tommy Quickly and the Coasters. However, Ted teamed the Coasters with Graham Jennings, who became Chick Graham. He was a young lad, dubbed 'The Mighty Atom' by Bob Wooler. Chick Graham and the Coasters tried a similar approach to Frankie Lymon and the Teenagers, but even their most commercial record, 'A Little You', didn't sell. Chick abandoned the group for a chance of an acting career and then went into medicine. **Chick Graham (541):** "I was very fortunate because the Coasters had a following in their own right and they could be sure of a reasonably full calendar. I wasn't doing the Coasters any favours as I was very inexperienced. I was only 15 and most of the guys were 19 or 20. Amazing as it may sound, it was all over for me by the time I was 17. It was exciting, but I never really liked it."

Pete Maclaine formed a new group, the Clan. They were playing in Wales when their first record was due to be assessed on the BBC's *Juke Box Jury*. **Pete Maclaine (542)**: "I remember the night 'Yes I Do' was on *Juke Box Jury*. We were playing in Prestatyn and I knocked on the door of a complete stranger and asked if *Juke Box Jury* had been on. He said, 'Yes, it's on now.' I said, 'Has the record by Pete Maclaine and the Clan been on?' He said, 'Yes, it was on first and voted a 'Miss'.' I said, 'Thanks very much' and, being good Manchester lads, we went out and got drunk. We went on stage later on, but we still thought the record would do okay. It was released on a Friday and the initial pressing was 4,500 copies. By Saturday night it had sold out completely in Manchester and Liverpool, which was a sign that it would head towards the charts. I phoned Pete Sullivan, our recording manager, at Decca on Monday morning. I told him the good news and he said, 'Fantastic, but I've got some bad news for you. The pressing plant is on its annual two-week holiday. No records can be pressed. As far as I'm concerned, it's finished.' We recorded one or two other things at Decca. One was a new version of Little Richard's 'Good Golly Miss Molly', but all of a sudden, it was in the hit parade by the Swinging Blue Jeans on EMI. Everything was so secret in those days because so many groups were rehashing old songs. The KGB or the CIA couldn't have been more secretive."

I feel as sorry for **Pete Maclaine (543)** as I do for Pete Best. He still works in Manchester clubs, but he never made the big time, saying in 1984: "I don't hold any grudges, but every one of the Dakotas has since said that they were sorry we had to split up. I'm not too bothered. If they came in here now, I'd be pleased to see them, but I wouldn't go out of my way to send them Christmas cards."

9   SHAKE IT UP, BABY

I. Recording in Liverpool
II. Recording in London – Lennon and McCartney
III. Recording in London – Cover Jobs
IV. Recording in London – Original songs

"Whatever I did shouldn't be stressed too much.
The genius was theirs, no doubt about that."
(George Martin)

I. Recording in Liverpool

There were no recording studios to speak of on Merseyside and before the groups secured contracts, there were only primitive recordings in Liverpool. Bob Wooler told me that very little was recorded live at the Cavern as all the tape recorders would be electrical and there were hardly any spare sockets for the plugs. What we have got, therefore, is all the more valuable.

Percy Phillips' studio at 38 Kensington, about one mile from the city centre, was primitive, but cutting edge for a one-man operation in its day. He would record weddings and social events and Ken Dodd employed him to record his radio appearances as they were being broadcast. Percy Phillips made the first recordings by the Beatles (then the Quarry Men), Billy Fury and the Remo Four. The Quarry Men's 78rpm of 'That'll Be The Day' and 'In Spite Of All The Danger' was the first record by a Merseybeat group to be given public airplay: it was lent to the disc-jockey at the Lune Laundry in Crosby and he played it over the address system.

Bernard Whitty (544) of Lambda Records in Crosby fulfilled a similar role and he made the first recordings by Kingsize Taylor and the Dominoes, Gerry and the Pacemakers, the Pathfinders, the Merseysippi Jazz Band and many folk groups. "Drums were always the problem. Anything else I could control quite easily. If I'd had decent studio facilities, it wouldn't be any problem, but often I was recording in private houses and I had to move the drum kit to where you can't hear too much of it. Once I had a tolerable balance, I put it on tape. Whenever possible, I would record the groups at St. Luke's Hall in Crosby, but not in front of an audience. This was quite handy as it was only across the road from my audio shop. It wasn't far to hump my sound equipment and the booking fee was moderate."

In 1961 the promoter Sam Leach asked Bernard Whitty to record a session by Gerry and the Pacemakers, which took place at St. Luke's Hall. **Sam Leach (545)**: "I thought that there was no way that Gerry and the Pacemakers could get a recording contract in London and so I decided to form my own label. I asked Lambda Records in Crosby to record them and there was a quiet bit in 'You'll Never Walk Alone' where Fred's cymbal kept rattling so I grabbed the cymbal when that part came along. I was short of cash because I had lost the Cassanova Club but it would have worked out because I had arranged a month's credit with a plant in Swansea. I could have sold the singles during the month, paid the bills and ordered more. Someone rang up the plant and said I had no money and they cancelled the order, so it was a good idea which never saw the light of day."

Sam Leach never went back to Bernard Whitty who hung onto the tapes. He rediscovered them four years ago and I played them to **Gerry Marsden (546)**: "They are amazing and it's great to hear that early version of 'Pretend'. The production wasn't too good but what could you do in those days? It sounds like us and it shows that George Martin didn't have to do much to us. All he had to do was turn on the mikes and add the strings. The sound was basically there."

Few acts had the initiative or the wherewithal to make demo recordings to send to London for a recording contact, but, prior to 1963, a group would be invited to London for an audition. This happened to the Swinging Blue Jeans when they were still playing their hybrid of traditional jazz, music hall and current pop. The tracks are good but I can understand why Oriole rejected them as there was no pigeon-hole for marketing them. **Ralph Ellis (547)**: "We had the rhythm section of a trad jazz band with the double bass, the drums and Tommy Hughes and then Pete Moss playing driving banjo, which you can hear on 'Yes Sir That's My Baby'. The front line of a normal trad jazz band would be clarinet, trombone and trumpet, but we had three guitars, and Ray and I used to play harmony on our guitars. That was the sound we had – a trad jazz rhythm section with a rock'n'roll front line."

In 1963, the Searchers recorded an album's worth of demos at a Liverpool club, which they sent to Pye Records. In 2002, the tapes were issued as a CD, *The Iron Door Sessions*. Most intriguingly, there is very little difference between their demo of 'Sweets For My Sweet' and the hit recording. **Chris Curtis (548)**: "The Beatles had just hit and Les Ackerley, the manager of the Iron Door club, told us to put some songs on tape He let us have the club for an afternoon and we got a weeny tape recorder and recorded the whole act. That's John McNally singing on 'Rosalie' and he did a really good job on that. He swings on rhythm guitar too: he plays the best rhythm guitar in the world. Les took it to Decca who didn't want it, but then he took it to Pye. Tony Hatch jumped at it as he wanted to be George Martin to the Searchers or at least, he wanted to be on the bandwagon. 'Sweets For My Sweet' was on the tape and he asked us to record that for our first session. Les Ackerley hoped to be our manager but we signed with Tito Burns as we were told he could do more for us in London. I felt very sorry for Les and for us as Tito Burns turned out to be a horrible man. He really worked his artists too – they were always on tour or making records. Whenever you saw the Zombies, they were like zombies."

Nevertheless, the Searchers had a long run of hits. **John McNally (549)** continues, "All the bands were getting signed by Eppy and we knew that we were as good as most of them. We went to the Iron Door and recorded a few of the songs that we did on stage. Tony Hatch at Pye then invited us to the studios in London to record six songs. We recorded them and went straight to the Star-Club. We'd been over there for a month when we heard that Pye had released 'Sweets For My Sweet' and the record was showing signs of making it. We had to buy ourselves out of our contract from the Star-Club and fly back to England. What pushed the record to No.1 was an appearance on *Thank Your Lucky Stars*.'"

134

The two albums *This is Mersey Beat*, which were released on Oriole in 1963, were not recorded at the Cavern, but they capture the spirit of the music. They were produced by John Schroeder, who is best known for his works with Sounds Orchestral. Unlike George Martin, who was fed performers by Brian Epstein, John Schroeder came to Liverpool to record what was happening. He set up a mobile recording unit in the Rialto Ballroom, and recorded several Merseyside groups over two days. The albums sold well but might have fared better had they been released on a major label. A record contract with Oriole, as Russ Hamilton knew only too well, was the kiss of death.

Although the musicians I've met are forthcoming about their careers, no one remembers much about the Rialto. **Paddy Chambers (550)** of Faron's Flamingoes said, "There's not much to remember because it was all done so fast. It was recorded on a one-track machine and done live with the groups singing and playing at the same time. Everything was done in about two takes."

Yet, despite the primitive condition, *This is Mersey Beat* was a success. **Joe Butler (551)** of the Hillsiders was then a member of Sonny Webb and the Cascades. "I played the bass and the recording engineer didn't put a microphone in front of my amp. He just put two crocodile clips on the back of the speaker, which was hilarious, but he got a great sound. Although those albums were made under atrocious conditions, I thought they were tremendous. There was no studio technique but there was a lot of energy."

Mark Peters and the Silhouettes were recorded at the Merseybeat sessions at the Rialto, and then Oriole records invited them to London. **Dave May (552)** recalls, "Their studio was like a living room with soundproofing. We didn't get the sound we wanted on the 'Fragile (Handle With Care)' single because they didn't put any echo on the lead guitar. We were disappointed, but our loyal fans bought it and we ended up with £6 in royalties between all six of us.'

Steve Fleming (553) has periodic reminders of his time in the Mark Peters and the Silhouettes. "Every six months I get a royalty statement for "Fragile (Handle With Care)", as Peter and I wrote it. It tells me that I've earned 10p or 15p during the past half year."

In 1964 **John Schroeder (554)** came back and recorded more groups. These sessions have not been released and his comments in *Mersey Beat* indicate that he was disillusioned. He said, "One strong criticism I have is that groups persist in performing the same material. For example, I have enough versions of one particular song to release an album entitled *Twelve Ways To Get My Mojo Working*." Well, I'd buy that album: whatever happened to the tapes?

It was inevitable that the Liverpool acts would, on the whole, record in London. They recorded for labels in the EMI and Decca groups as well as for Pye, Philips and Oriole. In 1963 a group would be expected to know the songs before attending a session and four songs might be recorded in three hours. This led to a lot of so-called B-sides being recorded in the final ten minutes. The Beatles accepted the status quo, although they were to become the act which first broke with tradition and changed recording practices forever.

II. Recording in London – Lennon and McCartney

At that first audition, George Martin was not impressed with either the Beatles' drummer Pete Best or their songwriting. He suggested that they record 'How Do You Do It?', a new song by a young Tin Pan Alley songwriter, Mitch Murray. Well, when I say 'new', it had been around a bit. **Mitch Murray (555)**: "I was doing all right as a songwriter. I had done some B-sides for Shirley Bassey and I had the B-side of Mark Wynter's 'Go Away Little Girl', 'That Kinda Talk'. I wrote 'How Do You Do It?', but Adam Faith's management had not taken it up. The music publisher Dick James had heard 'How Do You Do It?' along with a comedy number, 'The Beetroot Song', and he said, 'I think 'The Beetroot Song' will be a very, very big hit.' A singer called Johnny Angel was going to record 'How Do You Do It?' but he changed his mind and recorded another song of mine, 'Better Luck Next Time', so better luck next time, Johnny Angel. The next thing I heard was that a new group from Liverpool was going to record 'How Do You Do It?' and I said, 'I'd prefer a big artist, but let's see how it goes.' The Beatles recorded 'How Do You Do It?' and I hated it. I felt that something had been screwed up, perhaps deliberately, although it now sounds very evocative of the early Beatles. I can't blame them because they were songwriters themselves and didn't want to do it, but it was a waste of a good song. I thought it was terrible and fortunately, Dick James agreed with me. He told George Martin that the Beatles had made a very good demo record. George Martin took it very well and said that he was planning to redo it with the Beatles later on."

George Martin (556): "The Beatles didn't like 'How Do You Do It?' very much, but in those days they had no option but to do what their boss told them. They recorded it but they came to me afterwards and said, 'Look, this really isn't our scene. We'd much rather have our own material.' I told them that they'd have to come up with something as good as that. They retaliated with 'Please Please Me' and of course I flipped over that. I thought it was a great song and after we'd finished, I told them that they'd got their first No.1. I gave the song that they rejected to the next group coming up, Gerry and the Pacemakers, and 'How Do You Do It?' was their first No.1."

Mitch Murray (557): "It makes me cringe to think that George Martin told the Beatles to come up with a song as good as mine, but he knew that I was a professional songwriter and he liked the song. Brian Epstein then suggested that Gerry and the Pacemakers should do the song and he told me that Gerry was a Liverpool Bobby Darin. George Martin asked me to come and hear Gerry at the Cavern but I said, 'I don't care what he sounds like, it's the record that counts.' Arrogant little sod, wasn't I? They made the record, I loved it and it delighted me when it got to No.1."

Fred Marsden (558): "The 1963 winter was a bad one and we drove down from Liverpool overnight, and we sat in the back of a van for ten hours in the worst weather you could imagine. We reached London about half-past one and we were recording at two o'clock. The road manager fell asleep in the studio while we were recording as he was so shattered. We heard the Beatles' demo, but we decided to put a heavier beat on it. The Beatles would have been better off releasing 'How Do You Do It?' as a single rather than 'Love Me Do' as they would have had a No.1 with their first three records."

Gerry Marsden (559): "We were told that 'How Do You Do It? had been written for Adam Faith and that he'd turned it down. I thought at the time that the Beatles had just made a demo for us, which was sent to us in Germany. We were very surprised when we recorded it because it sounded really good but, blooming heck, we never thought it would be a hit."

Les Chadwick (560): "Ronnie Pilsbury who was our unpaid road manager took the day off to come down with us. We had driven all through the night and it had been absolutely freezing. We got there at midday and poor old Ronnie fell asleep in the reception area. When we were called in to make the record, we were so excited that we forgot about him. When we came out at 4pm, he was still asleep and he had missed the whole thing."

Maybe Gerry and the Pacemakers were surprised to be with EMI as they had been expected at Decca. **Noel Walker (561)**: "Dick Rowe knew I was from Liverpool and after that business with the Beatles, he asked me to contact Brian Epstein about any other groups he might have. Brian was going to send me the next group he was going to promote, Gerry and the Pacemakers. It was a cold Monday morning in Decca No.2 studio and we were all set up for Gerry and the Pacemakers but got the Big Three instead. Brian never phoned me and said he was sending a different band: they just turned up. Fortunately, I thought they were fabulous and I still think they were fabulous. Their records epitomise the Mersey sound better than any others, and at that original session we did 'Some Other Guy'."

John Gustafson (562) of the Big Three recalls, "I hated all our singles. The first one, 'Some Other Guy', was a demo tape for Decca. My voice was completely gone. We'd come back from Hamburg that very morning and we were thrown into Decca's No.2 studio in the basement. It was horrible. We were croaking like old frogs. Eppy wouldn't let us do it again and we went berserk. The bass sound was non-existent and the drum sound was awful. The only thing in evidence was the strong guitar line. The solo was reasonable for Griff although he was knackered as well."

The Big Three's 'Some Other Guy' is now regarded as the archetypal Mersey Beat record, but it barely made the Top 40. Gerry and the Pacemakers, however, were at No.1 with Mitch Murray's 'How Do You Do It?'. **Mitch Murray (563)**: "When you have a No.1, you think, 'Phew, at last': it's not bottles of champagne, but relief. Then you think, 'Maybe it's a fluke' and you spend your whole career trying to prove yourself. I wrote 'I Like It' for Gerry's follow-up but John Lennon had given him 'Hello Little Girl'. John threatened to thump me if I got the follow-up and I thought it was worth a thump. 'I Like It' had the same cheekiness and innuendo and it also went to No.1. I didn't get a thump."

Fred Marsden (564): "It was always the Beatles No.1 and Gerry No.2 and because of that I don't think that Gerry really wanted to do any of the Beatles' songs."

'Hello Little Girl' was passed to Brian Epstein's latest signing, the Fourmost. **Brian O'Hara (565)** recalled, "We had nothing original to offer George Martin for a single. I asked John Lennon for a song and I've still got the tape he gave me. He says, 'I wrote this one while I was sitting on the toilet.'"

The Fourmost followed 'Hello Little Girl' with the romantic 'I'm In Love'. **Billy Hatton (566)**: "As opposed to the Beatles doing a song on an album and people saying 'Can we have this one?' or 'Can we have that one?' before it's released, 'I'm In Love' was written by Lennon and McCartney for the Fourmost. That was a big NEMS Enterprises operation."

Similarly, Cilla Black was given 'Love Of The Loved'. **Cilla Black (567)**: "Paul McCartney wrote it and I'd heard the Beatles do it many times in the Cavern. I wanted to do a group arrangement and I was ever so disappointed when I got to the studio and there was brass and everything. Les Reed did the arrangement. He was playing piano and Peter Lee Stirling was on lead guitar. I thought it was very jazzy and I didn't think it would be a hit."

By far the most successful artist to benefit from Lennon and McCartney's songs was Billy J. Kramer with Top 10 hits with 'Do You Want To Know A Secret?', 'Bad To Me', 'I'll Keep You Satisfied' and 'From A Window'. **Billy J. Kramer (568)**:"I think 'From A Window' was the best out of all the Lennon and McCartney songs that I recorded. Paul also offered me 'Yesterday' and I said, 'Paul, all my records have been nicey-nicey. I want a real headbanger.'"

Brian Epstein had been against the American song 'Little Children' being released as a single. **Billy J. Kramer (569)**:"I had to fight a lot of people to get 'Little Children' on the market. Brian wanted me to do another Lennon-McCartney song. I got a big kick when 'Little Children' came out and sold 78,000 in one day. The previous record for the number of singles sold in one day had been the Beatles with 76,000."

Cilla Black topped the charts with 'Anyone Who Had A Heart', a sophisticated Bacharach-David ballad. In the UK her version easily outsold the original by Dionne Warwick. She celebrated her twenty-first birthday with another No.1 record, an English lyric for an Italian song 'You're My World'. She returned to Lennon and McCartney for her fourth single, 'It's For You'. **Cilla Black (570)**: "Paul sounded great on the demo but once we got into the studio, I was again a bit disappointed with the arrangement. It was done as a jazz waltz but I appreciate now that it was fabulous for its time."

In 1968 Cilla's BBC-TV series attracted audiences of up to 16 million. **Cilla Black (571)** recalls, "Paul McCartney said to me, 'What are you going to open your TV series with?' and I said, 'I don't know.' It was a problem because variety shows like *The Billy Cotton Band Show* had dirty big openings with big band arrangements. He said, 'I think you should have a friendly song, a more intimate thing, and I'll write you one.' Paul wrote 'Step Inside Love' and he also had the idea of beginning the show with opening doors. When I first sang it live on the telly, I forgot the words because I was so nervous. I made up some words as I went along and thought it didn't matter because no one had heard the song before. Paul was watching the show and was upset because he thought the producers had been at me to change the lyrics."

Ray McFall (572): "Tommy Quickly is conspicuous as an example of where the Midas touch of Brian Epstein failed. You need to have ability, looks and appeal and everything else but you also need exposure and connections and Brian could arrange that. Any group wanted to be signed by him so that they could join the Beatles tours and so on. Tommy Quickly had all of that and yet it didn't happen for him."

The concept of Lennon and McCartney giving you a hit song did not always pay off. In 1964 Brian Epstein was keen for Tommy Quickly to make the Top 10 and he placed his faith in 'No Reply', which he would record with the Remo Four. Rhythm guitarist **Don Andrew (573)**: "Everything was right for Tommy to have a No.1 hit. The Lennon and McCartney songwriter tag and a reasonable production would guarantee it a place in the Top Ten, if not the very top. We recorded the backing first and we double-tracked the guitars, which was the first time we'd done anything other than a straight one-off. We added extra percussion and Paul McCartney was playing tambourine. John Lennon was clinking Coke bottles together. It was a great rocking backing and all Tommy had to do was add the vocal. It was a combination of nerves and drink, but Tommy couldn't take it. He strained his lungs out but he couldn't sing in tune. Tony Hatch was tearing his hair, and although he must have had some finished tracks, it was never released."

I asked **Allan Clarke (574)** of the Hollies if John and Paul had ever written a song especially for them. "They never approached us. The only Beatles number that we ever did was 'If I Needed Someone'. It was written by George Harrison and we got slated for it. Even George said it was terrible and we didn't like that because it dented our egos. It was a lovely song that had the Hollies ingredients written all over it, but somehow the public didn't accept it. They accepted the Rolling Stones doing a Beatles' song, 'I Wanna Be Your Man', but not us. We made a mistake, but not to worry, we had other hits."

Graham Nash (575): "I thought it was a good song and I was sad that George didn't like it as we certainly didn't want to upset him. We were honouring his songwriting and it was a great song and we did a good job of it. I think we did it a little too fast but the harmonies are pretty good."

Louise Harrison (576): "I never played George's songs first when I got the albums and I never thought that George was any better than John and Paul were. Their strength lay in them being a wonderful team – the blend of their personalities was so magical and no other group has managed to create that sort of magic. The expression about the sum being greater than the parts applied to them."

III. Recording in London – Cover Jobs

Dave Maher (577) of Denny Seyton and the Sabres: "We won the Liverpool heat of the Top Town recording competition at the Crane Theatre and then won the final at the North Pier, Blackpool. We got a recording contract with Philips but unfortunately Brian had to go to hospital, I hurt my back and John broke his foot. While we were off the road, the group that came second, the Four Pennies, got a contract and went to No.1 with 'Juliet'."

The Beatles had been featuring Chan Romero's 'Hippy Hippy Shake' in their stage act. When they appeared on *Juke Box Jury*, they criticised the Swinging Blue Jeans for taking their song. As it wasn't their song, they could hardly complain and it was probably because they were so surprised to hear the Blue Jeans doing rock'n'roll. **Ray Ennis (578)**: "We had to fight like hell with EMI to get 'Hippy Hippy Shake' released. They said, 'No, this'll never make it.' We felt so strongly about it, four little humble lads from Liverpool, that we said, 'If you don't release it, we won't make any more records.' They released it, and Wally Ridley, the A&R man, apologised afterwards. 'Hippy Hippy Shake' sold three million. Then an amazing thing happened: we got a letter from Jerry Allison of the Crickets, who was touring in the States with Chan Romero. Chan had been working in a car factory in Detroit. Our version of 'Hippy Hippy Shake' got into the Top 30 in the States and put him on the road again. He was too shy to write himself so Jerry wrote on his behalf and sent us a demo of another song called 'My Little Ruby' as a possible follow-up. We took it to EMI but they said no. Instead we did 'Good Golly Miss Molly', which was like 'Hippy Hippy Shake, Part 2'.'

Ralph Ellis (579): "I played the guitar solo on 'Hippy Hippy Shake'. Only one minute 57 seconds, but I was exhausted by the end."

The Escorts also took a song from the Beatles' stage act – Larry Williams' rock'n'roll classic, 'Dizzy Miss Lizzy'. According to **Terry Sylvester (580)**, "We just went in and did the song. There was no real thought behind it. We went in singing and shouting our heads off and, to be honest, I didn't think that Jack Baverstock was a very good producer. He was fine at recording orchestras, but when it came to recording a four-piece group, I don't think he had a clue."

Lee Curtis and the All Stars are known for 'Let's Stomp' which featured Pete Best on drums. **Lee Curtis (581)** hates it with a passion. "Let's Stomp' was diabolical. The original by Bobby Comstock was absolutely brilliant and as the Stomp was popular on Merseyside, we'd asked Decca if we could cover it. They wanted us to rave away madly at the end by doing a repeat of the words, 'Let's stomp'. We were green and we agreed and we repeated the words 'Let's stomp' 36 times. I got sick of counting. The record was released and it died."

Tony Crane (582) says, "We recorded our favourite songs because we loved them. I don't think that we improved on the originals, but our versions do have a distinctive sound, even though we were trying to copy the originals. A young lad with a Liverpool accent can't sound like an experienced American R&B singer."

Johnny Hutch (583) of the Big Three: "Brian Epstein gave me Ben E. King's 'Here Comes The Night'. You've got to be fantastic to sing that one and you need a coloured singer's voice. I couldn't do it. I said that I could only do it my way, but he wanted me to sing it like the record. Brian never appreciated that the originals of those songs might be better than anything his groups could do.'

The Dennisons' version of Rufus Thomas' 'Walkin' The Dog' was recorded on a day off from a tour with Gerry and the Pacemakers and Ben E. King. **Ray Scragg (584)** recalls, "'Walkin' The Dog' was played on *Juke Box Jury* and Sid James said, 'If I knew who that fellow was, I'd buy him a drink.' He thought that there was something similar about our voices."

Clive Hornby (585) adds, "'Walkin' The Dog" was our best record but the Rolling Stones released it on an LP at the same time. People said, 'Your record's great but we've just bought the Stones' LP.' We lost a lot of sales because of them."

If you do cover something, you may be beaten to it. **Denny Seyton (586)**: "We made 'Tricky Dicky' which sold 40,000 and we were going to follow it with '(There's)

Always Something There To Remind Me' as we had heard the Lou Johnson record on Radio Caroline. When we got there, our A&R man said, 'This song sounds familiar' and he found out that Sandie Shaw had cut it. We said, 'Okay, we'll do 'I Understand' by the G-Clefs. That'll be great for the New Year as it goes into 'Auld Lang Syne'. He said, 'No, Freddie and the Dreamers are doing that.' Our third choice was 'Wishin' And Hopin'' and the Merseybeats had just done that. In the end, we settled for the old rock'n'roll song, 'Short Fat Fannie' and the A&R man said, 'Great. If it goes well, you can do 'Great Balls Of Fire' next."

Lee Curtis (587) was to continue to have trouble with Decca. "We made suggestions to Decca about numbers that we would like to record. We asked if we could do 'Twist And Shout'. They said no and a few weeks later it was a hit on Decca for Brian Poole and the Tremeloes. We then asked if we could do 'Money'. They said no and it was a hit on Decca for Bern Elliott and the Fenmen. Next we asked if we could do 'Shout'. They said no and it was a hit on Decca for Lulu with the Luvvers. We asked if we could do 'It's Only Make Believe'. They said no and it was a hit on Decca for Billy Fury. We wasted our opportunities with 'Let's Stomp' and that monotonous ending."

Beryl Marsden (588): "The first single was done in an afternoon at Decca with session men. I loved 'I Know' as that was my kind of music, r&b and soulful, but 'I Only Care About You' was intended as the A-side. I don't think I was truly happy with my A&R man at Decca because I was missing out on good songs. I did hear 'Tell Him' by the Exciters and I thought I could do that, but it was given to Billie Davis instead. Obviously, his thoughts weren't on my career."

Pete Frame (589): "Girls didn't aspire to play instruments. Girls of those days had no ideas about careers in music, no ideas about careers anyway. They would read *Roxy* and *Valentine,* which were all geared towards girls leaving school, becoming a typist, looking for the right guy to marry and settling down and becoming a housewife and mother. Women's Lib, forget it, there was nothing there. Women who went into business knew that there was a ceiling. When I worked at the Prudential, women got up to a certain level but they weren't allowed to be promoted above that because they didn't think that the women were competent to do the job or that men would work under them. It was a bit like that in pop music but women didn't learn to play instruments. There are exceptions like Nancy Whiskey, who played guitar, but the only girls around our way were lead singers in groups who did a Valerie Mountain or Carol Deene type thing, and that went on for quite a while."

Faron's Flamingos recorded a single of an original song, the subdued 'See If She Cares', backed by the raving 'Do You Love Me?'. **Faron (590)** recalls, "We thought 'Do You Love Me?' should be the A-side. About 15 people were taken off the street and asked to listen to both sides. Being Londoners, they decided that 'See If She Cares' should be the A-side."

Paddy Chambers (591) comments, "Do You Love Me?' was a Motown song originally recorded by the Contours. I believe it was the first time a Motown song had been covered by a British act."

'Do You Love Me?' was shortly to be covered again. **Faron (592)** was not pleased. "Our record came out and we were playing in St. Helens with Brain Poole and the

Tremeloes. Brian Poole bought me a double scotch and said, 'I like that song you're doing called 'Do You Love Me?'. Can you write down the words?' A couple of weeks later he had the No.1 record with 'Do You Love Me?' and it had only cost him the price of a large scotch."

Faron's Flamingos wasn't the only Merseybeat group to be doing 'Do You Love Me?' **Dave Maher (593)** from Denny Seyton and the Sabres: "There's a bit in 'Do You Love Me?' where the voices go down and there's a stop. Well, at the point our road manager was going to knock off the lights in the Iron Door and I was going to light some flash powder with a cigarette. There would be a big flash and then we would go on with the song. It would be great but we couldn't rehearse it as I only had one lot of flash powder. We get to the part in the song where this is to happen, the road manager knocks the lights off and there is one hell of a flash. There was smoke everywhere and people were thinking that the Messiah had come. When the lights came back on again, they were running up the stairs and Les Ackerley was running down. He was furious, he thought we had nearly blown up his club."

The Escorts were unlucky with 'I Don't Want To Go On Without You', a Drifters' B-side, as **Mike Gregory (594)** explains: "I'm very sorry that the Moody Blues did it as I thought we had a good chance of getting a hit. Our fan club put out some publicity to stress that ours was the 'original English version', if that makes sense."

The Righteous Brothers topped the charts with 'You've Lost That Lovin' Feelin'', but Cilla's version almost got there first. **Chris Curtis (595)**: "Brian Epstein played me 'You've Lost That Lovin' Feelin'' by the Righteous Brothers and said, 'I've got this for Cilla.' I said, 'Do it if you must, it will be a hit for her but the Righteous Brothers will overtake her.' It was heartbreaking as she couldn't sing that song for nuts. Her best record was 'Liverpool Lullaby' where she actually sounds like a Liverpool girl."

Cilla Black (596): "I think their version is better than mine because it isn't really a solo record. They had that great answering thing in the middle, the deep voice and the very high voice, and though I have a very big range, it didn't work as well. Mind you, I'm sounding supercritical. We can talk about my version of 'Anyone Who Had A Heart', if you like. I thought mine was 100% better than Dionne Warwick's. It was a much better arrangement."

The Searchers' close harmony work was distinctive. Their record epitomised musical tidiness and their guitar sound predates the Byrds on 'Mr. Tambourine Man'. **Mike Pender (597)**: "We found that we could do harmonies on 'Where Have All The Flowers Gone?' and we did a few of those folky songs at the time. People talked about the Byrds and the 12-string guitar and that American folk thing and I think we had something to do with starting that. I loved their version of 'Mr. Tambourine Man' and somewhere in there I could hear ourselves. I don't think they ripped us off, but we gave them some ideas. I also think that 'Mr. Tambourine Man' was a very good song and we could have made a real good job of it."

The Swinging Blue Jeans had success with a ballad, 'You're No Good', a song originally recorded by Betty Everett, and timing is everything. **Ray Ennis (598)**: "'Don't Make Me Over' should have been released after 'You're No Good' and, if it had been, I reckon it would have gone to No.1. EMI didn't want us to put out another slow one but we should have stuck to our guns. We'd had a couple of failures by the time it came out. It made the Top 30 but it could have done much better.'

It was hard to contain the Undertakers' high spirits on record. **Brian Jones (599)** recalls, "We wanted 'Mashed Potatoes' as the A-side, but Pye picked 'Everybody Loves a Lover' and it didn't go into the charts. For the second record, they chose 'What About Us?' when we wanted 'Money', and again it wasn't a hit. Tony Hatch admitted that he'd been wrong and said we could choose the A-side of our third record. We chose 'Just A Little Bit', which went into the charts."

Tom Earley (600): "While the Beatles were in Hamburg, the Undertakers were considered the best band on Merseyside. They never got the credit they deserved but that was because of some pretty lousy records. They had a great vocalist in Jackie Lomax and 'Mashed Potatoes' didn't do him justice. They found it difficult to argue with Tony Hatch at Pye, whereas the Beatles through sheer bloody-mindedness did what they wanted with George Martin at Parlophone."

The Chants had a succession of near misses including an up-tempo version of the standard, 'I Could Write A Book'. **Eddie Amoo (601)** told me in 1984: "I'm sorry that 'I Could Write A Book' didn't make it as Tony Hatch had written a very novel arrangement. Unfortunately, none of our singles ever happened and it was a bit sick when I look at groups like Showaddywaddy and Darts. They were doing exactly what the Chants were doing, only not as well. I'm not saying that vindictively, because I've become successful in the Real Thing."

Jackie DeShannon wrote and originally recorded 'When You Walk In The Room', a song that cleverly rhymes 'nonchalant' with 'me you want'. Jackie was the first to record 'Needles and Pins', which was written by Sonny Bono and Jack Nitschze. The Searchers heard Cliff Bennett and the Rebel Rousers perform it at the Star-Club and realised it would make a great single, but not with Tony Jackson singing lead. **Chris Curtis (602)**: "I didn't like Tony Jackson much, even from the start, and if I'd had the nous, I would have had someone else in the first place. I never had any rows with him though: if he started arguing, I would just walk away. He wanted to sing 'Needles And Pins' and he threatened to reveal something about me if I didn't let him. I said, 'You can tell them what you like, but you're not singing on 'Needles And Pins'. You're singing the words off a page – it sounds much better with Mike.' Then I said, 'Can you count to 50?' and he said, 'Of course I can count to 50.' I said, 'Start counting, and by the time you've reached 50, I'll have phoned Tito Burns to tell him you're out of the band.' He was shocked 'cause all of a sudden he was losing his source of income. The first thing he did when he left the Searchers was get a nose job, and guess where his singing voice had come from? His first solo record though, 'Bye Bye Baby', was a good one."

John McNally (603): "It's a myth that there is a 12-string guitar on 'Needles And Pins'. Mike played a Burns Sonamatic and I played a Hofner Club 60. Our engineer, Ray Prickett, put a little reverb on both guitars and suddenly, we had this harmonic. When the reviews came out praising us for our 12-string sound, we nipped out and bought a couple. From 'When You Walk In The Room', we used them on nearly everything."

Mike Pender (604) says, "A lot of people thought 'Needles and Pins' was way out. The producer of *Crackerjack* said the song was too heavy for his programme. It was a very intimate song and many people relate to it."

Chris Curtis (605): "If you haven't got the listeners in the first few seconds, you haven't got them, and we had certainly got them with that. The opening A chord on 'Needles And Pins' will never be topped. It must have been a good riff as the Byrds have used it countless times – upside down, this way, that way."

'Needles And Pins' went to No.1 at a time when Gerry and the Pacemakers were going for their fourth chart-topper. **Fred Marsden (606)**: "When we did the first three No.1s we were looking for a fourth and Dick James brought in a demo of 'Sha La La La Lee', but it was too bouncy. The Small Faces did it much better and they put more of an off-beat on it. I liked 'Pretend' very much and we used to get a lot of requests to play it. I think it could have been our fourth single, but we did 'I'm The One' instead."

Whatever, the fourth single was Gerry's own song and a good one, 'I'm The One'. **Gerry Marsden (607)**: "I got very drunk when we got three No.1s. It was nice to have achieved something that nobody else had done. We then wanted to get our fourth record to No.1. It was funny because the Searchers had 'Needles and Pins' out, and that made No.1. 'I'm The One' was No.2 for about five weeks. I used to ring John McNally up and say, 'John, will you get off the top?' He'd say, 'We're trying, Gerry.' Every time we did a television show to plug 'I'm The One', the boys would be on another show plugging 'Needles and Pins'. The Searchers kept us from having four records at No.1. I'll never forgive you McNally, you bugger!"

Frank Allen (608): "Chris Curtis and I were having dinner at a trendy little restaurant in London and he said, 'I suppose you're happy with Cliff Bennett' and I realised what was coming. I said, 'Yes, we've signed with Brian Epstein and things are looking good.' I didn't want to rock the boat but a week later we were in Ireland and I was going through purgatory – you know, it's the week when you're being picked on – and I was very fed up. I told Moss the sax player that I had been invited to join the Searchers and I didn't know what to do. He said, 'Don't be mad, take it, and ask them if they want a sax player too!' I rang Chris and I said, 'If you haven't got someone else, then I'll take it.'"

Chris Curtis (609): "Pat Pretty, the publicist at Pye Records, was a lovely lady, who was married to Jack Bentley from *The People*. She had come across a song on the B-side of an American hit by the Orlons, 'Don't Throw Your Love Away' and I thought it was a great title. The guitar riff came out similar to 'Needles And Pins', so again it was following a hit with a semi-copy of a hit. Mike Pender's voice was brilliant on that, just like a little boy wandering through the streets, and I joined in with that very high harmony, and it really worked. It was one of the nicest tunes that the Searchers ever did. The B-side, 'I Pretend I'm With You' was pretty good too, one of my little gems. I also like the B-side of 'Someday We're Gonna Love Again', 'No One Else Could Love Me'. Dusty Springfield went for 'Someday We're Gonna Love Again', she loved it! We'd been working in the ice-rink at Blackpool and we had to fly back in a two-engine plane for the session and they said I wouldn't be using my own drums. I said, 'Get those drums on the 'plane.' We flew down in the night, recorded in the morning and flew back in the afternoon. I thought it was a good intro and the harmony is so high, it's like Graham Nash."

IV. Recording in London – Original Songs

After the uninhibited 'Some Other Guy', the Big Three had their most successful record with 'By The Way' (No.22), but this Mitch Murray song would have been better suited to Freddie and the Dreamers. **John Gustafson (610)**: "It was arms up the back, 'Do it, boys, or it's all over.' We didn't like it, but we tried our best. We all hated 'By The Way' and 'I'm With You' because they were poppy, horrible, three-chord Gerry-and-the-Pacemakers-type songs. We did sneak in some songs we liked on B-sides such as 'Peanut Butter' and 'Cavern Stomp', which was more towards our real direction. We would have much rather have played Little Richard songs, but they wouldn't have been commercial."

Noel Walker (611) justifies what he did with the Big Three: "We had a hit with 'Some Other Guy' and that was the pure Liverpool sound. When the Searchers and Gerry were having hits, it seemed to me that we had to dilute that sound a bit, which was something I didn't particularly want to do but the Mitch Murray song was the way that we had to go with the Big Three. I didn't especially like it but it sold a lot and established them as a name act. Being what they were, they were anxious for success and they trusted Brian Epstein, and it was Brian who wanted them to do that song. It was published by Dick James, incidentally. Tony Hiller was a promotions man at Mills Music and after the success of 'By The Way', he approached me and wrote one for me, 'I'm With You', but that bombed because the public by then knew that this was not the music that the Big Three played."

Noel Walker (612) also cowrote the ferocious B-side of 'By The Way', 'Cavern Stomp'. "We wrote 'Cavern Stomp' in a transit van somewhere in Scotland, and that's earned me a few bob over the years. It was just a B-side. In my view, 'Peanut Butter' was the best record they made, that is just fabulous: Johnny Gus is playing fantastic bass lines on that, and they are creating a rhythm that I hadn't heard from three pieces before. They were difficult to record as you were living on your wits, trying to fill out that sound and make it viable for what was selling at that time. We had that full rich sound from the Searchers and the Blue Jeans and of course the Beatles, who were in a class of their own. Getting the pure Liverpool sound was something we rarely achieved. We got it once on 'Peanut Butter' and also on the EP, *Live At The Cavern*."

Noel Walker must be praised for his initiative in recording the EP, *The Big Three At The Cavern*. George Martin had, after all, decided that the Cavern was not an appropriate venue for recording the Beatles. **Noel Walker (613)**: "EMI had sent round the men in white coats who had told George Martin, 'No, you can't possibly record here.' I was only 22 or 23 and I felt that we could do anything we wanted. Dick Rowe was away as otherwise, he would never have let me do it. We brought up a huge mobile recording unit and arranged to do this live recording, with the screaming audience which was so much a part of the EP. All the people who said it couldn't be done were wrong because we did it."

Rory Gallagher (614): "The great guitarist from Liverpool was Brian Griffiths from the Big Three. He was a dangerous player and extremely good. That was different from George Harrison who had some unusual phrasing but he was working within the song. The Big Three did a great version of 'Reelin' And Rockin'' on their *Cavern* EP and that original song, 'Don't Start Running Away' is also extremely good. Griff plays a great solo on 'Don't Start Running Away', but I don't want to detract from Hutch and Gus – they were great players and great singers."

John Gustafson (615): "It's very nice when somebody as good as that like something you've done. That song was written very quickly. It was following on from 'Some Other Guy'. I turned it upside down, changed the chords a bit and nicked half the intro. I wrote any old words, and we didn't really rehearse it as we never rehearsed. Somehow it found its way onto the EP because it was one of the tracks that they didn't erase or lose. That EP should have been an album."

Johnny Hutch (616) recalls, "Over 1,000 people were screaming and shouting, and I don't think there had ever been so many people in the Cavern. The sweat was pouring off the walls. I was here and the crowd was there and I couldn't hear what I was playing. However, the EP didn't turn out too badly."

John Gustafson (617) continues the story: "The cover of *The Big Three at the Cavern* is quite ramshackle. We looked like rain-sodden idiots. Anyone who was at the Cavern will know it was a sweaty hole. Our suits were wringing wet. We took them off and slopped them in a corner. The photographer had forgotten to take our picture and we were told to put our wet rags on again as though we were playing."

The Big Three's EP was followed by a live album, *At The Cavern*, featuring the Big Three and several other acts. **Noel Walker (618)**: "The EP did wonderfully well but the album bombed. I suspect it was Dick Rowe's fault as he made me put on Heinz, who had nothing to do with Merseybeat. I hated the idea and I think that took the essence out of the album, but there is some bloody good music on it. Beryl Marsden was marvellous and I don't know why she never had hit records. I would like to have produced Beryl Marsden in the studio as I don't think Decca did Beryl justice. I would have liked to have produced the Dennisons as well, but I wasn't allowed to. Straight after the *Cavern* LP, the Fortunes' contract came up for renewal and Decca didn't want them. I said, 'Hey, they sing wonderfully and they should be recorded like they are on the *Cavern* album.' They gave the Fortunes another lease of life and I did 'You've Got Your Troubles'. I added an orchestra and I wanted to get the singing right. When I heard the counterpoint on that song, the jazz musician in me woke up and I liked it very much, and I also knew that it was a beautiful, fragile song. It was one of the few records that turned out exactly as I wanted it and it sold a million. Dick Rowe didn't like it, so he was wrong again. The Monday morning production meetings at Decca were like a geriatric hospital. I had my pulse on the music and they had to listen to my records, but they mightn't want to release them. I left Decca two or three times but they always took me back."

Beryl Marsden (619): "The Cavern album was recorded on a hot, sweaty day. It was really good fun because it was a great atmosphere for recording. I preferred doing live performances, recording as opposed to going into a studio. I used to be a little bit scared of studios."

Lee Curtis ~ Teenage Idol turned Matinée Idol.
At The Cavern Club, April 2004
(photo by Ron Ellis)

Karl Terry ~ still rocking.
At the Cavern Club, April 2004
(photo by Ron Ellis)

Freddie Starr and The Midnighters
(fourth from left is John Cochrane, ex Wump & His Werbles)

Ex-Searchers drummer, Chris Curtis in his new jacket, 1996
(photo by Spencer Leigh)

A young Faron with his Flamingos

Kenny Johnson and Tony Crane, 1992
(photo by Spencer Leigh)

Allan Williams and his longtime partner Beryl Adams in front of Peter Grant's portrait of John Lennon
at Liverpool Academy of Arts, 2001 (photo by Spencer Leigh)

Sam Leach, raconteur, at The Cavern
Club, April 2004
(photo by Ron Ellis)

Billy J. Kramer, Tony Crane and Gerry Marsden make a
nostalgic visit to the Cavern re-opening.
(photo by Spencer Leigh)

The Bootles at The Cavern Club, April 2004
'Arguably the best Beatles sound-alikes'
(photo by Ron Ellis)

EARL PRESTON and The Realms

Representation : Jim Godbolt Agency Ltd
145 Wardour Street London, W.1
Regent 8321-2

Management : Jim Ireland
Mardi-Gras, Mount Pleasant, Liverpool 3
Royal 4448

Faron's Flamingos 1961 line-up in Paris
(l-r) ~ Paddy Chambers, Trevor Morris, Faron and Nicky Crouch

The Dennisons
— Decca Records

Kennedy Street Enterprises Ltd.
Kennedy House,
14 Piccadilly, Manchester 1.
CENtral 5423

Tex Carson, Ray Scragg, Eddie Parry, Clive Hornby and Steve McLaren

The Merseybeats groom Billy Butler

Diana Ross, Martha & The Vandellas and Johnny Moore of The Drifters backstage at Wigan ABC,
April 9th, 1965

Gerry de Ville and The City Kings

A selection of Business Cards

BIRCHALL PROMOTIONS

for

Rock Group, Jazz Bands, Dance Bands, Comperes,
Entertainments, etc., etc.

'Phone:-

SOUTHPORT 57298   **BURSCOUGH 2388**

POSTER & DANCE TICKET SERVICE!

Posters in Flourescent Colours, and Tickets Optional.
Prompt Delivery — Satisfaction Assured

Promotion through the whole range of Entertainment

Presenting . . . .

KINGSIZE TAYLOR
AND THE DOMINOES

WITH SWINGING CILLA

J. DULGARN,   S. K. HARDIE   GRE 2363,
61 GLASSONBY CRESCENT,
WEST DERBY, LIVERPOOL 11.   D. LOVELADY   WAT 4338.

THE SWINGING
BLUEGENES

★ ★ ★ ★ ★ ★

164 KINGSWAY
HUYTON
N.: LIVERPOOL
Tel. HUY 5827

Stuart Enterprises

Artistes Representatives
& Promoters

50 STUART RD
WATERLOO
LIVERPOOL 22

TELEPHONES
Day— WAT 7554
Night—ORM 2868

SKIFFLE   COUNTRY-n-WESTERN   POPS   BLUES-n-BALLADS

AL CALDWELL

and his raving

TEXAN

RHYTHM-n-BLUES GROUP

*National Finalists Liverpool
Empire 1958 and
People £5000 contest finalists
Butlins 1958*

54 Broadgreen Road,
Liverpool, 13.
Phone: STOneycroft 3324

Stuart Enterprises

ARTISTE
REPRESENTATION & PROMOTION

50a STUART RD,
WATERLOO,
LIVERPOOL 22.

Phone:
Day WAT. 7554
Night ORM 2868

John Lennon holding baby Julian

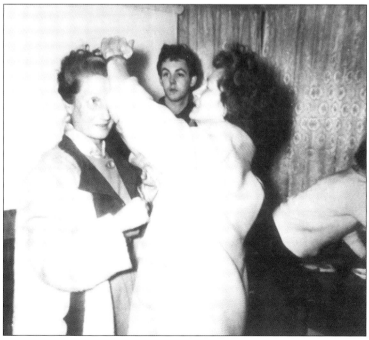

Julia Lennon (John's mother) does her sister Harriet's hair as Paul McCartney looks on

Dance Tickets

BEAT WAVE

7-45 — **PALACE HOTEL** — 11-45
- SOUTHPORT -

Saturday, January 25th, 1964

THE   THE   THE

CLANSMEN ★ COSSACKS ★ RAVE-ONS

LATE BAR   **TICKETS 5/-**

ORGANIZED BY SOUTHPORT YOUNG CONSERVATIVES

SCOUT & GUIDE HEADQUARTERS
Mosley Street, Birkdale

Twist and Shake

with

THE TOLEDO 4
(*Southport*)

SATURDAY, 7th DECEMBER, 1963

8-0 till 11-0 p.m.

TICKET 3/-   *Refreshments*

PALACE HOTEL, BIRKDALE

"BIG BEAT NITE"

SATURDAY, 8th FEBRUARY, 1964

7-45 till 11-45 p.m.

THE KARACTERS   **THE 4 MUSKETEERS**
THE 4 CLEFFS   **JOHNNY RINGO & THE COLTS**

TICKET 5/-   Late Bar

Organised by Southport Y.C.'s

One of the best known venues of the 50s & 60s, the now demolished Palace Hotel, Southport

The original Remo Four line-up at Don's 50th (1992)
(l-r) Harry Prytherch, Keith Stokes, Colin Manley, Don Andrew

Vince Earl of the Connoisseurs with agent Dave Forshaw, 2002

More Dance Tickets

Merseycats members photoshoot (old musicians never die…)

*Barry Womersley and Pete 'Kin' Kelly of Rhythm & Blues Inc.,
October 1990 at a Reunion Night at Southport's Floral Hall*

Billy Butler (ex Tuxedos and now BBC Radio Merseyside presenter) chats to Sonny Curtis of The Crickets

Reunion Night
Ray Marshall (Berry Pickers), Alex Paton (Mersey Boys), Ronnie Malpass (Mocambo Club),
Barry Womersley (Ro Blue), and Alan Menzies (Bootles), in 1999

P. J. Proby (introduced into England on Jack Good's Beatles show) with 50's rocker Wee Willie Harris
and Merseybeat writer, Ron Ellis

The original Swinging Blue Jeans

Spencer Leigh with legendary D.J. Dr. Rock and original Beatles manager Allan Williams, 2002

Old Merseybeat stars at The Cavern Reunion of 1984

The great 1984 reunion. (Clockwise from top left) 1 Charlie Flynn (Ian and the Zodiacs), 2 Joe Walsh (Lee Curtis and the All Stars), 3 Barry Womersley (Rhythm and Blues Inc.), 4 Jimmy Tushingham (Silhouettes), 5 John Cochrane (Wump and his Werbles), 6 Frank Connor (Hideaways), 7 Joe Butler (Sonny Webb and the Cascades), 8 Joey Wall (Cavern DJ), 9 Fred Knibbs, 10 Kenny Johnson (Sonny Webb and the Cascades), 11 Brian Hilton (hill-siders), 12 Dave Maher (Denny Seyton and the Sabres), 13 Gus Travis, 14 Les Braid (Swinging Blue Jeans), 15 Colin Manley (Remo Four), 16 Tony Marsh (Coasters), 17 Brian Jones (Undertakers), 18 John Frankland (Dominoes), 19 Ray Ennis (Swinging Blue Jeans), 20 Sam Hardie (Dominoes), 21 Rod McClelland (Silhouettes), 22 Denny

Alexander (Undertakers), 23 Bob Evans, 24 Brian Johnson (silhou-ettes), 25 Jack Curtis (Vic Grace and the Secrets), 26 Ritchie Galvin (Coasters), 27 Tony Sanders (Earl Preston and the TTs). (Elsam, Mann and Cooper Ltd.)

The Fourmost had their biggest hit with 'A Little Loving'. **Dave Lovelady (620)** says, "We went into Dick James' office one day and he played us some songs. There was nothing suitable, and we were about to leave when he said, 'Hang on. There's something in this morning's post. I'll open it and play it.' Sure enough, 'A Little Loving' had arrived in the post. It had been written by Russell Alquist, Juliet Mills' husband. Brian O'Hara and I hated it, but we were outvoted."

The Searchers topped the charts with the Drifters' 'Sweets For My Sweet', which was produced by Tony Hatch. They followed it with something similar, 'Sugar And Spice'. **Chris Curtis (621)**: "Tony Hatch tricked us good style with that. We were looking for a follow-up to 'Sweets For My Sweet' and I was going on the American idea: if that's one a hit, follow it with something similar. He sensed that was what I wanted, so he told us that he had heard this bloke, Fred Nightingale, in a pub singing 'Sugar And Spice'. (Sings first verse, then sings it again somewhat differently.) Tony Hatch used to be in the Coldstream Guards and you can see he wrote it himself from a marching tune. I said, 'It's an icky title. Who in Liverpool will go in a shop and say, 'Have you got 'Sugar And Spice'?' In the end, we said we'd do it but guess who isn't singing harmony? I said I'd do the 'oo-ee-oo' bits just to carry it through but I wasn't going to sing those idiotic words – (sings) 'Sugar and spice and all things nice, Kisses sweeter than wine.' I'd rather sing Paul McCartney's 'Mary Had A Little Lamb'."

Tony Hatch (622): "The Searchers didn't have anything that would be good enough to follow 'Sweets For My Sweet' and I did think that if they knew I'd written something, they might not record it. I said I'd got this very simple song from a friend of mine called Fred Nightingale, and we tried it out and it worked very well. 'Sugar And Spice' went to No.2 and when I told them it was me, they said they'd known it all along. Some years later the producers of *Good Morning, Vietnam* wanted 'Sweets For My Sweet' and when they couldn't get it, they settled for 'Sugar And Spice'. I was on a plane coming back from Australia and that was the feature film. I told a few people that I had a song in the film, but I had forgotten that I'd put that bloody name on it, so when the credits rolled at the end, it said, 'Sugar And Spice – Fred Nightingale'. Everyone was saying, 'Well, we didn't see your name there.'"

The Searchers had an original hit in 1964 with 'He's Got No Love', which was written by Chris Curtis and Mike Pender. **Chris Curtis (623)**: "Ah, but you know what that tune is. You play that and then play 'The Last Time' by the Rolling Stones. We were naughty boys as I stole the tune. I can give you another example. Aretha Franklin had an album track that I loved called 'Can't You Just See Me'. We did the backing track and I loved it, but then I thought, 'I'm not getting enough out of this', and I put a whole new set of lyrics to it called 'I'm Your Lovin' Man'. The lyrics are rubbish but I got the money."

John Gustafson (624): "'Really Mystified' is the first song I ever wrote when I was 16 and the lyric content was very low in those days. It was called 'Baby Please Don't Go' and I changed the lyrics for the Merseybeats. I wrote it but Tony got his name on it because we thought we were Lennon/McCartney, that we would split everything like that."

'Alfie' was inspired by the film starring Michael Caine and was written specially for Cilla by Burt Bacharach and Hal David. Bacharach wrote the arrangement and played piano on the record and there is a film of the session, showing Cilla doing take after take and Bacharach eventually saying, "I think we got it that time". The producer George Martin responds, "I think we got it on Take Two, Burt." **Cilla Black (625)**: "I used to think I was very soulful and sang in an American accent, but if you listen to my early records, you will notice that 'there' and 'where' are two words that I couldn't lose my accent on. I thought I had total accent control on 'Alfie' but I hadn't. I still said 'thur'."

The most pronounced example of a Scouse accent on record occurs on the Merseybeats' 'Wishin' And Hopin''. Hal David wrote "Wear your hair just for him" for Dionne Warwick: with a change in gender, the Merseybeats sing "Wear your hur just for hur."

After the Big Three, **John Gustafson (626)** joined the Merseybeats: "Marty Wilde did 'My Heart And I' as a B-side and Duffy Power picked up on it and did it in his act. We got the idea from Duffy and when we were recording it, Jack Baverstock who was about 60, brought an Italian opera singer into the studio to meet us. We told him we were about to do Richard Tauber's 'My Heart And I'. 'Ah yes,' he said, 'and we started singing it.' He was shocked when he heard our thundering noise."

Mike Pender (627) of the Searchers: "I always felt I could make a better job of almost every track I ever recorded, yet you can't do that because it's down to time and money. You can't sit in the studio all night and day trying to perfect the thing. You can go so far and once the producer is satisfied, that's it, whether it's got mistakes on it or what. If he's pleased with it and he doesn't think the public are going to hear anything, that's it. I don't think I'm ever singing flat and in fact, I always prided myself in being on key. What I'm trying to think of is being out of sync when you double track or something like that. Sometimes you don't just get it quite right, but I was pretty good at double-tracking."

Although they found national fame, the Liverpool folk band, the Spinners, haven't had any hit singles, but one member, **Cliff Hall (628)**, rescued Wayne Fontana and the Mindbenders. "We were recording in London and Wayne Fontana and his band were in another studio making 'The Game Of Love'. They got stuck for a deep bass voice and their producer said, 'I'll go and ask the Spinners and see if Cliff will do it.' So he said to me, 'Would you like to take part in a Top 20 record?' I said, 'No, we're doing an LP which is going to hit the charts for us anyway.' He said, 'Wayne Fontana would like to hear your deep bass voice on a special part of this song.' I said, 'What's in it for me?' and Jack Baverstock said, 'If it hits No.1 in the UK, we'll give you £2,000.' I said, 'All right, you're on.' I went and did it, and that deep voice in 'The Game Of Love' that says 'Love' is mine. The record got to No.2 in this country. It made No.1 in America, but I didn't get anything out of it. I wish I'd told him that I should get something if it got to No.1 anywhere in the world."

Tom Earley (629): "We were a Wirral group, Birkenhead boys not Liverpool boys, and we played regularly at the Krall Club in New Brighton. We were approached by Barry Lloyd, who worked in the Caroline Sales Office in Liverpool, with the idea of writing a song dedicated to Radio Caroline. He saw it as an opportunity to promote a band using Radio Caroline as he would manage us too. We wrote the song and took it down to Caroline in London and got a publishing contract with Roar Music in Dean Street. I remember loading the gear into the van in the Wirral and going down the motorway in a beaten-up Bedford van and arriving at this very lavish studio in St. John's Wood and setting up the equipment, and it was miked from the front of the amps. It was only one or two takes, and we didn't have the luxury of overdubbing but we managed to achieve a reasonable sound. We were hoping that it would be adopted as the Caroline North's signature tune, but we were pipped by the Fortunes' 'Caroline' down South, and when they integrated the two stations, our record died out. It was played on Radio Luxembourg and we did a programme for them. We also got airplay on the BBC and it even got played on *Juke Box Jury*. There was a record shop in Birkenhead called McKenzie's and the same week that the Beatles' 'I Feel Fine' was top, we were No.11."

Gerry Marsden proved himself a good songwriter, particularly with poignant ballads. A group composition, 'Don't Let the Sun Catch You Crying' was Gerry and the Pacemakers' biggest selling single in America, reaching No.4. **Fred Marsden (630)** recalls, "Unfortunately we didn't realise that it had the same title as a Ray Charles song and we were sued for breach of copyright. We ended up having to pay for the use of the title." (I'm surprised that they gave way over this as you can't copyright a title and I can write a song tomorrow called 'Strawberry Fields Forever' if I want to.)

Gerry and the Pacemakers starred in the film *Ferry Cross The Mersey*. It was written by Tony Warren, the creator of *Coronation Street*. Its locations included Birkenhead Market, the Locarno Ballroom, the Adelphi Hotel, the Pier Head, the Mersey Tunnel and the Cavern. **Fred Marsden (631)**: "There is not a strong story-line to *Ferry Cross The Mersey*. We were supposed to have a script by Tony Warren but he opted out at the last minute and most of it was done during the filming itself. In the film, there are three lads riding motorbikes or Pacemaker scooters. I fell off in the studio and damaged my arm and as I wouldn't go on it after that, I had to ride pillion. I didn't mind the film too much as there were some decent shots in it. Usually, I tried to be the funny chap with hand motions and smiling to the crowd and joking with Gerry, and that is what they tried to do on the film itself."

It may have a feeble plot, but there was an original score and **Les Maguire (632)** of the Pacemakers points out one unusual feature. "We spent three days shooting in the Locarno for a ballroom scene. All of a sudden a fight broke out and there were bodies going everywhere. The director was so pleased that he used it in the film. It's not often that you see a real fight on the screen."

The film includes some of the also-rans in cameo appearances: the R&B group the Black Knights, the Blackwells, who wore skin-tight leather and were known as 'the blond bombshells', and Earl Royce and the Olympics, with 'Shake A Tail Feather'. Earl also recorded an all-embracing version of 'Que Sera Sera' which included riffs from 'Sweets For My Sweet' and 'La Bamba' as well as a football whistle. I didn't know you could be offside in a recording studio.

The title song, 'Ferry Cross The Mersey', was another Top Ten hit. Gerry's brother, **Fred Marsden (633)**, says, "There were a lot of songs about different places round the world like Chicago, Broadway and London, but nobody had ever mentioned Liverpool before." The song is relevant today – consider "We don't care what your name is, boy? We'll never turn you away," What is it but a comment on asylum?

10   TICKET TO RIDE

I. The NEMS Organisation
II. TV appearances
III. Package Tours
IV. Touring Around
V. Starr Wars: The Backside Strikes Back

"The life I love is making music with my friends."
(On the Road Again, Willie Nelson)

"Hell is other people"
(Jean-Paul Sartre)

I. The NEMS Organisation

Many writers have suggested that Brian Epstein was incompetent but this is unfair. NEMS may not have been managed as well as ICI, but it was well run for an entertainment company. The musicians had itineraries and wage packets, and hotels were booked in advance. Although Epstein had his faults, he wasn't a gangster, unlike some of the UK impresarios.

Sid Bernstein (634): "Brian Epstein had a lot of virtues. In our business, it is very rare that you meet people who have the kind of elegance that he had, the integrity that he had, the depth of understanding that he had and the honesty that he had. The music business is not glamorous: it is very rough and it is not the art, love or beauty that the lyrics profess. Brian Epstein was very rare. Our agreements were done without contracts. They were done over the phone."

At one time it looked as though Epstein was going to sign up the whole of Merseyside. The Beatles, Cilla Black, Gerry and the Pacemakers, Billy J. Kramer, the Fourmost, the Big Three and Tommy Quickly were all on his books. He went to clubs to see the opposition and to find new talent. He turned down Freddie Starr, considering him too much like Billy Fury.

Epstein himself was rejected by Kingsize Taylor and the Swinging Blue Jeans. Some performers resented this wealthy businessman. **Ray Ennis (635)** of the Swinging Blue Jeans: "He wanted to manage us, but we thought that he had enough groups. That was a good decision from our point of view because he only really concentrated on the Beatles and Cilla Black. We wouldn't sign with him so he wouldn't let us be photographed with any of his groups, let alone do any of John and Paul's songs."

As the Eppy-demic spread, NEMS needed to expand. Brian took on more staff and moved his operation to London. **Tony Barrow (636)** worked as a publicist and he recalls one of Brian's first remarks: "From the very first, Brian had been telling everyone that the Beatles were going to be as big as Elvis but I took that with a pinch of salt. I personally liked what I'd heard of the Beatles and could see that there was a lot more to them than just their music, but I didn't class them alongside Elvis." Brian

Epstein was undeniably a man of vision, but if he really believed in what he was telling Tony Barrow, why did he bother with the other acts?

Johnny Rogan (637): "There was a degree of hyperbole about his statement that the Beatles would be bigger than Elvis. If he really believed it, he's an even bigger visionary than we give him credit for. I see him as a businessman. He knew that Liverpool was a happening place for beat groups, he knew that it was going to take off, and so he signed up as many groups as he could. He was an excellent manager and he's only been criticised from the money aspect – he should have made more money from the Beatles. He had integrity as he didn't get involved with tax avoidance schemes, although, admittedly, there was some trouble with *Help!* There are so many different functions which a manager has to perform and many of the qualities are mutually exclusive – some pamper their artists and others have them like frightened schoolchildren. Being a good manager is about getting success for your artist to accord with your personality, and that's what he did."

In analysing Epstein, it's hard to get away from his homosexuality. The book *The Love You Make* suggests that Brian's involvement with the Beatles was triggered by a deep affection for John Lennon. Peter Brown, the author, was an insider, but it is surely a simplistic view of a complex man. Although there were several performers with whom Epstein wanted a sexual relationship, his main concern was to build up a powerful agency. Nonetheless, you can divide the performers with NEMS into groups: those he considered talented and those he fancied. John Lennon fell into both groups.

Shane Fenton aka **Alvin Stardust (638)** was not managed by Epstein, but he saw how the business was run: "Brian was the first of the new kind of manager, although these days the industry is run by accountants and people who are very cold in their attitude towards the 'product'. Brian was very sensitive and put his heart into things he believed, but he wasn't interested in anything unless he was convinced it would be financially successful. He had a very astute business mind and he saw the Beatles as capable of making him a fortune. If they'd done something that he thought was uncommercial, he wouldn't have let them release it. He wouldn't say, 'We'll release that because it's a nice song and your playing is good.' If it was out of tune and the playing was rubbish, he'd still want to release it if he thought it would be a hit. He'd got a perfect combination with himself, George Martin and the Beatles.'

Brian Epstein appeared on the panel of *Juke Box Jury* to assess new records and was very conscious of being a celebrity. **Colin Manley (639)** recalled how he worked: "Going in his office was like being in a comedy sketch. I always remember one phone call when he said, 'I want Prince Charles for the première. I *want* him!' He put the phone down and said, 'Yes, Colin, what do you want?' He always had time for you and he'd ask you to put songs on tape for him to listen to. He was a decent sort but the job was too much for him. He wanted to do it all himself and wouldn't delegate."

The London promoter Larry Parnes had built up a stable of pop artists in the 1950s, including Tommy Steele, Joe Brown and Billy Fury, and Epstein wanted to emulate this. He was in a position of power that sometimes got the better of him. Once when judging a talent contest he announced that he would sign the winners. The Rustiks had a short-lived career but they were with NEMS as a result of that whim.

1963 was a remarkable year for Brian Epstein and also for record producer **George Martin (640)**. He turned Epstein's impulses into gold records and his productions held the No.1 spot on the British charts for 33 weeks in one 39 week period. "Brian kept bringing me new acts. He had access to all the talent in Liverpool, and he brought me Gerry and the Pacemakers, Billy J. Kramer, Cilla Black and the Fourmost. In the end I had to tell him to take them elsewhere because I couldn't cope. I was working so hard that I practically drove myself into an early grave. I was running a conveyor belt for the hits and, as soon as I had one record slipping from the No.1 spot, I had another one waiting to take its place. It was like being in a relay race, only I was doing all the running."

Brian Epstein was a fastidious employer. His secretary **Freda Kelly (641)** remembers one occasion: 'We worked till six and I missed a comma out of the date. I should have put 24th, comma, space, March. Normally I would have rolled the letter back into the typewriter and put the comma in, but Eppy had put a big circle round it in ink. There was no way I could fit that comma in and I would have to retype the letter. I looked at him with hatred in my eyes. I never opened my mouth but he got the message. He said, 'You learn by your mistakes.'"

As to whether Brian Epstein was a good manager, it depends on whom you're talking to and whom you're talking about. When he first saw the Beatles perform in November 1961, they looked uncouth in their black Hamburg gear, but he channelled the excitement of their music, gave them stage suits and moptop haircuts and made them more presentable.. The forcefulness of their music was combined with a slick presentation. Ironically, the Beatles were rough lads who were smoothed down, whereas shortly afterwards, down south, the Rolling Stones were well-educated youngsters who were encouraged by their manager, Andrew Loog Oldham, to be controversial.

Epstein's Svengali act extended to other performers, as **Bill Harry (642)** explains. "Brian Epstein liked to control an artist's image, and when he took them over, he smoothed them out. The Big Three is one example and Cilla Black another. Cilla would sing belting rock songs like 'Boys' with Kingsize Taylor and the Dominoes, but Brian didn't like this. He put her in pretty dresses and had her sing Bacharach and David ballads. Before Brian Epstein took her over, I had imagined her becoming a rock singer and she became a modern Gracie Fields."

He pushed **Billy J. Kramer (643)** into doing something against his wishes: "I remember doing *Sunday Night at the London Palladium* when I hadn't slept decently for a month. I said to Brian, 'You're telling me to do it and that it'll be good for my career, but I'm not ready. You can't take a kid, get him a couple of hits, and put him on a stage where Frank Sinatra, Bing Crosby and Judy Garland have performed.' I didn't have the experience. Anyway, we rehearsed for the show. 'I'll Keep You Satisfied' was No.4 and they were saying, 'Take 24 bars out of this and eight bars out of that', and I have to own up, I went to pieces. It didn't sound so bad in the theatre but, on the TV in close-up, people could see how nervous I was. The following week my record sales went straight down and I thought I'd blown it, that my career was over."

One testimonial to Brian Epstein's management is that the other managers were found wanting, and most performers now wish they'd been handled by NEMS. **John McNally (644)** of the Searchers: "One of my regrets is not having been managed by Epstein. We'd have been a better band for it and he always wanted to sign us. He came to the Cavern to see us just before Johnny Sandon left and we knew he was coming with a view to managing us. We took our gear down the steps to the Cavern and then went to the Grapes for a drink. That was fatal because Johnny got drunk, Tony got drunk, and when we came on stage it was chaos. Johnny pulled all the wires out. Everything went flat. We died a death and Epstein wasn't interested."

II. TV appearances

ITV's *Thank Your Lucky Stars*, which started in 1961, shared the youth market at Saturday tea-time with the BBC's *Juke Box Jury*. Stars and hopefuls would mime their latest releases, and several American performers appeared on the show. *Thank Your Lucky Stars* was to be upstaged by *Top of the Pops*, which began in 1963, and by *Ready, Steady, Go!*, which included live performances and captured the teenage lifestyle. The most memorable edition of *Thank Your Lucky Stars* was an all-Liverpool one in December 1963, the first national programme to bring the Merseyside groups together. There was a great reaction, but it wasn't very exciting as performers simply mimed to their latest records.

Lee Curtis was not managed by NEMS and perhaps this explains his second-class ride on the programme. Not that things were very much better organised for the star turn, as **Lee Curtis (645)** explains, "The stage was set for the Beatles. Out they came with their guitars and the director said, 'Right, gentlemen, just take your places and we'll see that the lighting is right.' They jumped on the stage and stood there, motionless, waiting for the next instruction. The director held his head in his hands and started gesticulating. He said, 'We've got a left-handed bass player and the shadows are going across everybody's face. Why doesn't anybody tell me these things?'"

Billy Hatton (646) of the Fourmost has the secret of plausible miming. "We always sang the song anyway because otherwise you're mouthing the words and your throat isn't expanding and contracting. Your veins aren't sticking out on high notes, and it's like a ventriloquist's dummy opening its mouth. A lot of groups said, 'What are you singing for? You're supposed to be miming,' and we'd say, 'You don't look as though you're singing otherwise.' A lot of groups followed us by singing live when they were miming."

However, that's no help if your record isn't played properly. **Ralph Ellis (647)** of the Swinging Blue Jeans recalls an early *Top of the Pops*: "We went on to mime to 'Hippy Hippy Shake', but instead of it being played at 45rpm, it was accidentally played at 78rpm. When they realised what had happened, they slowed it down and we mimed to that. This caused a great deal of embarrassment as it was a live show. Later we had a good laugh about it, but there was also a hell of a row at the time. After that, they put the records on tape so there was no chance of them being played at the wrong speed."

Juke Box Jury survived from 1959 to 1967. The records were played by David Jacobs, who didn't seem to care for the more progressive ones, and the panellists included the ultra-camp comedian Kenneth Williams, the grumpiest of grumpy old men, Gilbert Harding, and David Jacobs' sparring partner, DJ Pete Murray. My favourite moment occurred when Katie Boyle said of Freddy Cannon's 'The Urge', "It's obscene but I loved it." The Beatles became the entire panel for one edition, and **Cilla Black (648)** was also in demand. "I was very good at it because I'd come from working in an office and buying records each week. I was 19 years old and I knew what was going to be a hit, but I finished a lot of careers when I did *Juke Box Jury*. I'm ever so sorry about Heinz. I said his record was terrible, and he was sitting behind the barrier. He was ever so nice to me, and I felt so bad about it. I realised that I couldn't appear on *Juke Box Jury* once I knew people in show business.'

Freddie Garrity (649) can vouch for Cilla's honesty: "Cilla said that 'You Were Made For Me' sounded like Freda and the Dreamers, so that speaks for itself. Nevertheless, that became my biggest selling record. It sold 750,000 copies in the UK alone…and I've still got them in my garage."

It was valuable exposure to have a record played on *Juke Box Jury*. It could have helped Johnny Sandon and the Remo Four into the charts. **Don Andrew (650)** recalls, "Bobby Rydell's manager was at the first session we did at Pye and he was knocked out with Johnny Sandon's singing and our backing. He told Tony Hatch that we sounded like Ben E. King backed by the Ventures, which was a tremendous compliment. 'Lies' almost made the charts but what could have made the difference was *Juke Box Jury*. We were told that it might be played and we watched other records being discussed. Right at the end, a caption came up on the bottom of the screen: 'Lies' by Johnny Sandon and the Remo Four. David Jacobs said, 'Sorry, but we've run out of time,' and wished everyone good night."

III. Package Tours

A popular group found itself constantly touring. Motorways in Britain were only in their infancy but young lads found the travelling exhilarating. Many came from working-class homes where their parents couldn't afford a car, and so travelling was an adventure. **Billy Hatton (651)** toured in a coach with the Fourmost: "All the seats were ripped out and it leaked exhaust fumes. Mike, who was six foot four, used to lie across the luggage compartment with a tarpaulin over him; the water would leak through the roof and run off down the side into a drain that we put in. *New Musical Express* said, 'The Fourmost travel in a specially converted luxury coach.' It was a tip."

The Undertakers had some unusual but appropriate stage props amidst their luggage, as **Geoff Nugent (652)** recalled: "We were on the A41 route through Whitchurch to London. We came down this 1 in 10 hill and all of a sudden I heard a bang. I stuck my head out of the window and said, 'We'd better go back. The coffin's fallen off.' When we got back, two fellows from a baker's van were staring, completely bewildered, at the coffin. We said, 'That's our coffin. Thanks very much,' and put it back on the van."

Frank Townsend (653): "The Easybeats were the only surf band in Liverpool. We did the Beach Boys' songs and we had a contract with Bilbo in Cornwall to supply us with surfboards and so we always had them on the van. We drove to Rimini in Italy one Christmas for a show and we went over the Brenner Pass with surfboards on the rack while everybody else was going the other way with their skis."

Package shows were very popular. Six or seven acts would perform for 20 minutes each and the bill-topper would have half an hour. **Gerry Marsden (654)** contrasts it with Hamburg: "It was a holiday. In Hamburg we went on stage at seven and came off at two in the morning, with a 15 minute break every hour. When we made records we were sent on national tours and told to do 20 minutes on stage. That was only five numbers, so it was dead easy."

Nicky Crouch (655): "The Dave Clark Five were a business band and that was something I'd not seen too much of in Liverpool. If anyone criticised Dave Clark for the records he was making, he'd pull out a wad of fivers and say that was his justification."

The package tours were possible because groups had very little equipment: they would use the house PA, and solo performers could be backed by the same musicians. The Remo Four backed Gene Pitney on one tour. **Colin Manley (656)**: "He had recorded 'Town Without Pity' and brought the music over with him. He didn't have the record, which had a complicated chord structure. I've since taught myself to read music, but then we couldn't make head or tail of it. He kept asking us to play 'Town Without Pity' and we used to say, 'There's no point. The audiences don't know it here.' That was true, but we couldn't play it anyway. We must have done all right as he bought us all suitcases at the end of the tour. He'd seen our battered cases and thought we needed new ones."

Ray Scragg (657) of the Dennisons remembered a tour with Tommy Roe and Billy J. Kramer. "The itinerary wasn't well planned. We played Liverpool one day, Taunton the next, and zipped back to Blackpool the day after that. We didn't mind because we had a good laugh together. No matter who was on, the rest of the outfit would go into the orchestra pit. Nobody from the auditorium could see us. They'd be singing a serious ballad and we'd be throwing things at them and pulling faces."

In 1963 **Kenny Lynch (658)** toured on a memorable package with the Beatles, Helen Shapiro and Johnny Tillotson. "We were all swapping songs on the coach. I wrote one and gave it to Johnny Tillotson. I later had a hit with it myself – 'You Can Never Stop Me Loving You'. The Beatles offered 'Misery' to Helen Shapiro who said, 'I don't want to do it. I don't like the title.' She was only a kid of 15, so I said, 'I like the song. I'll do it.' They said, 'Great' but John Lennon gave me the greatest rucking in the world because I had Bert Weedon play on it. He'd been booked for the session and I'd been told that he was very good. I played the record to John in Dick James' office and he said, 'Who's that on guitar?' and I said, 'It's Bert Weedon.' He said, 'Why didn't you tell me? I'd have done it for you.' I said, 'What can I do? Do you like the record or don't you?' He said, 'Well, I quite like it.' He didn't pin any medals on me, but it was the first song recorded by someone else from that great catalogue. It sold about 10,000, but it didn't get anywhere near the charts."

Iris Caldwell (659): "I dated Paul for sometime on and off as everybody dated everyone in Liverpool – there was nothing in it – and one night he said to me, 'Do you want to hear the song we've written?' and he sang, 'Last night I said these words to my girl, Why don't you even try, girl, Come on, come on, come on, come on, come on, Please please me like I please you.' I burst out laughing and I said, 'That's not a song, don't be silly.' I was also dating Frank Ifield and I told him about the Beatles and sang 'Please Please Me' to him, and he said, 'Well, I don't have to worry about that.'"

Sonny Webb and the Cascades sometimes found themselves on the same bill as the Beatles. **Kenny Johnson (660)** says, "We did a show at the Grafton when 'Please Please Me' was up in the charts and 'She Loves You' was just coming in. We were on stage before them and nobody was listening to us. They were shouting 'Get off' and the ones closest to is were taking the mickey by saying, 'Isn't he gorgeous?' and laughing. It was awful to go on before the Beatles because the audience couldn't wait for us to get off."

Harry Prytherch (661): "It was a Bank Holiday Monday and we went on expecting to get a reasonable rapport from the audience and all the girls didn't want to know: they all brought their butties and their sandwiches and they are sitting there eating lunch. They were waiting for the Beatles to come on, and they weren't interested in anybody else. They ate their food and then out came the curlers and then the Beatles came on. We were like a fill-in."

John Lennon said that the 'woo woo' in 'She Loves You' was taken from the Isley Brothers' 'Twist And Shout' and the 'yeah yeah' from Elvis Presley's 'All Shook Up'. **Kenny Lynch (662)** recalls, "I was on a coach with the Beatles and they played me a song which included 'woo woo'. I said, 'You can't do that. It's horrible and you sound like a bunch of fairies.'"

Being a compère on a beat show was an awful job but several of today's top comics (Des O'Connor, Little and Large, and Larry Grayson) cut their teeth that way. However, no compère could compare to Tony Marsh. **Derek Quinn (663)** of Freddie and the Dreamers had tears of laughter in his eyes as he related this story: "Tony Marsh was on every tour until he got banned by Granada, EMI and every other venue on the circuit. It was because of a Rolling Stones show when Tony was bevvied. Well, he used to drink a bit but he was fine on stage. He'd never slur his words. He'd say in his tremendous deep voice, 'Ladies and gentlemen, I'd like to introduce the Rolling Stones.' When he came off, we'd say, 'What did you say, Tony?' and he'd burble, burble, burble. He was at the side of the stage on this particular show and he dropped his pants and showed Brian Jones his backside. A mother was in the front row with her daughter and she complained to the management. Tony was taken to court and the summons said that 'Tony Marsh is charged with showing his person to persons in the audience'."

Derek Quinn (664) recalls another incident: "Our first tour was with Roy Orbison, Brian Poole and the Tremeloes and the Searchers. We were going to Scotland and we got through Newcastle with Tony Marsh giving us a lecture on whatever was his subject of the day. He said to Roy Orbison, 'By the way, Roy, I hope you've brought your passport.' Roy said, 'What do you mean, Tony?' He said, 'We're coming to

Scotland soon and you'll need your passport to get in. We're all right because we're British.' Roy's drummer said, 'Gee, Roy, what'll I do? I ain't got my passport.' We stopped at a pub on the border and Tony had it organised. He came back with the landlord who said, 'Are there any foreigners in here? Can I have your passports, please?' Roy Orbison said, 'Gee, man, I've got to get to Glasgow to do a show.' He said, 'You can't come over the border without your passport.' The two of them stood there with the drummer saying, 'What are we gonna do, Roy?'"

Freddie Garrity (665): "I had a house in Manchester, a two-up, two-down with an outside toilet, which cost me £600. I'd also bought an E-type Jag which was three times the price of the house! I wanted Roy to come for a meal before the show. He had a ranch with acres of land and it was like taking him to *Coronation Street*. I served him salad because I didn't know how to cook."

Mark Peters and the Silhouettes toured with Gerry and the Pacemakers. Drummer **Brian Johnson (666)** told me, "We were on tour in Ayr and Gerry had been playing tricks on us, such as pulling on Mark's microphone wire from the side of the stage. We wanted to get our own back and we found a huge cut-out of John Wayne pointing his guns from the film *Rio Bravo*. We placed it above the stage and gently lowered it behind him while he was singing 'You'll Never Walk Alone'. Gerry wondered what the audience were laughing at."

Eddie Parry (667) from the Dennisons recalled: "The first tour we did was with Billy J. Kramer and Tommy Roe. It started out from Cambridge and we were doing Finsbury Park in London the next night. We didn't stay in five-star hotels. It was one star, with no pressing services. My father used to put his trousers under the mattress to press them and that's what I did with my stage trousers. I forgot to pack them when I left. They were still under the mattress and had to be sent down to London by courier before I could go on stage."

Spencer Lloyd Mason (668): "The Mojos and the Kinks were at the bottom of the bill on a package tour and they would take it in turns to open the show. 'Everything's Alright' came out and went up to No.4 and so we thought, 'No more bottom of the bill for us.' Then the Kinks went to No.1 with 'You Really Got Me' and we were at the bottom of the bill again."

In 1964 Kingsize Taylor and the Dominoes were on tour with Chuck Berry. **Bobby Thomson (669)**: "The first gig was at the Finsbury Park Astoria. The first show was at ten past six and at six o'clock we had never even met Chuck Berry and we were backing him. We were worried sick, it was our first major tour, and then he came in with two minutes to go, and we said, 'What songs are we doing?' and he said, 'Chuck Berry songs.' We said, "What keys?" He said, 'Don't worry, we'll have a party.' The gig started and Carl Perkins, the Animals and the Nashville Teens did the first half and we closed the first half, and the second half was Chuck Berry backed by the Dominoes and we hadn't played a note with him. Everything was rocking and the whole thing took off and all the nerves went."

Kingsize Taylor (670): "The Swinging Blue Jeans jumped on the bandwagon with 'Hippy Hippy Shake', and a lot of the crowd didn't appreciate it at all. Someone even went to the trouble of bringing a Christmas pudding and running down the aisle with it. He threw it and it hit Ray straight in the chest. That was in the middle of June and he was not amused."

At Christmas, many pop stars played in pantomime, and they trotted out their hits at the appropriate moments. With his theatrical background, Brian Epstein devised entertainments which were a cross between a package show and a pantomime. It looked like a good idea, but the non-musical items were under-rehearsed, and the fans screamed over the dialogue. **Don Andrew (671)** of the Remo Four was on one of the shows: "*Gerry's Christmas Cracker* was a pop show put on in Liverpool and Leeds. There was Gerry and the Pacemakers, the Hollies, Danny Williams, the Fourmost and Tommy Quickly. Everyone stood inside a giant cracker that had been built across the stage. It was in two halves and it was pulled open by Gerry Marsden with help from the audience. He shouted, 'Who have we got in the cracker? The Hollies!' They'd pull the cracker and there was a big flash and a cloud of smoke. Out came the Hollies while the Remo Four behind the curtain played their latest hit in instrumental form. The first week was at the Odeon, Liverpool. Gerry said, 'Who have we got in the cracker? The Fourmost!' and we started playing 'Hello Little Girl'. The cracker, which was a giant thing and made out of timber, stuck. The explosion went off inside the cracker where the performers were. They staggered out eventually, really shocked."

The Fourmost appeared in a Christmas show with the Beatles, Billy J. Kramer, Cilla Black, Tommy Quickly, the Barron Knights and Rolf Harris at the Finsbury Park Empire in 1963. That, too, was a catalogue of disasters, as **Joey Bower (672)** of the Fourmost relates: "Dave Lovelady was on a rostrum about ten feet high and on rails. It came from the back to the front of the stage when we came on, and was pulled back again when we finished. One night, it rolled forwards and came off the rails and didn't stop. Dave and his kit ended up in the orchestra pit. Another time the stagehands were pushing it forward, and our guitar leads were lying over the rails. The rostrum cut the guitar leads in half, so everything went off.'

And again, **Joey Bower (673)**: "Tommy Quickly sang 'Winter Wonderland' and one of his props was a life-size snowman. One night Brian O'Hara got inside it. Brian walked towards him as he was singing and Tommy nearly died of fright."

The Remo Four turned down an offer to back Billy J, but after lack of progress, they agreed to back another of Brian Epstein's signings, Tommy Quickly. Quickly, whose real name was Quigley, had worked with his sister Pat in a band called the Challengers and Epstein was determined to make him a star. **Don Andrew (674)**:"Looking back on it, it's a crying shame that he wasted his opportunities. Whoever was on top of the bill, be it Billy J. Kramer, Gerry and the Pacemakers or Cilla Black, Tommy used to steal the show for sheer personality. He was mobbed outside the theatres. He had a raucous singing style which was mixed up with his pop image. He was half soul and half Herman's Hermits."

Colin Manley (675):"Tommy Quickly had terrific stage presence and he could have been very big if he'd been handled correctly. Whereas most groups would stand completely still, Tommy would work the stage and do a tap dance. He'd be spruced up in patent leather shoes. He was a pro, but it never came across on record."

And **Colin Manley (676)** also had this insight into John Lennon. "We went on with Tommy Quickly for a short spot just before the Beatles. We couldn't hear the music we were playing because the fans had been whipped into a frenzy. They made almost the same noise for Tommy as they did for the Beatles. I could have played in a different key to everyone else and nobody would have noticed. John Lennon let me use his 12-string Rickenbacker for the introduction to 'The Wild Side Of Life'. When we finished our spot, we'd come off and I'd give it back to him. I could tell by the look on his face that it was all too much for him. I don't think the Beatles had any interest in what they were doing. Nobody could hear what they were playing. It was like being in the bird house of a zoo, greatly amplified. They threw their guitars on the floor when they · had finished. Police appeared from the back and they fled as fast as they could into limousines to get away. They weren't enjoying it."

Another problem was when jelly babies were thrown on stage. Fans came armed with bags of sweets although they meant no harm. They didn't hold fire until the Beatles came on, as **Geoff Nugent (677)** of the Undertakers remembers: "George Harrison had said that he liked jelly babies, and so the audiences started throwing them on the stage. Brian Jones thought it was great fun to catch them in the bell of his sax. The heat was so great that they congealed in the bottom of the horn. He had about a pound and a half of jelly in the bottom of his sax." The Beatles found sweet-throwing a hazard when they went to America. Jelly babies aren't available in the States and fans threw the nearest equivalent, jelly beans, which are painfully hard.

The hysteria for the Beatles was unlike the reaction for anyone else. The DJ **David Hamilton (678)**, remembers, "I was compèring a show in a marquee in Urmston. Brian Poole and the Tremeloes were in the same bill and we all took our lives in our hands. The Beatles arrived in a van and they were to be secreted into the show. There was pandemonium as they leaped out of the van. The marquee was nearly pulled to the ground. It was the most ecstatic audience that I've ever witnessed and I don't know how we all got out in one piece."

The Fourmost appeared for seven months in a variety show at the London Palladium with Frankie Vaughan, Tommy Cooper and Cilla Black. Guitarist Mike Millward became seriously ill, as **Billy Hatton (679)** explains: "Just before the Palladium season he developed cancer. He had growths in his neck and he needed radium treatment, which made him go bald on the back of his head. Before we went on the stage, we used to stick his hair down with Sellotape. He improved after treatment, but then he found out that he had leukaemia and he had to go into Clatterbridge Hospital on the Wirral. We had an idea that he was dying and he asked me if he should leave the group. I said yes, and it's the hardest yes I've ever had to say in my life. He died a short while later."

Considering how much was written about Brian Epstein's and the Beatles' involvement with drugs, it is surprising how little this affected other performers. According to **Dave Lovelady (680)**, "None of the Fourmost took drugs. We were staying at these digs with Joe Cocker and the Rockin' Berries, and there was a big party one night. Some of them rolled cigarettes and passed them round. I was baffled by this and I said to Joey Bower, 'I thought they were all doing well but they're rolling their own ciggies.'"

Chris Curtis (681) fell out with the Searchers in Australia: "I hated Australia. I thought it was a country of dreadful people and I was off me cake. I fell off the stage and I still have the scar on my leg. (Chris pulls up trouser leg to show me.) I went out with an Australian girl who said, 'You need some sleep, darling: come home with me.' She had this marvellous flat, more like half an apartment building, with a wonderful view over the harbour. During the night I was drinking coffee and thought I would leave before she woke up. The windows were open and it was a heavy door. I opened it but it came back and smashed my finger. Nearly took it off, but I went back to the rest of them with my bad leg and my bad finger. I went to my doctor's bag to find something for the pain in my finger, and I found that they had emptied the entire contents, all my tranquillisers, down the lavatory. They thought they were doing me a favour, and I told them that was it and I couldn't take anymore. They forced me to finish the tour. On the way back home, I wrote a Searchers' song on a sick bag but it wasn't used as I left the group. When I got back to Bootle, they tore the nail out at the hospital.'

IV. Touring around

Brian Epstein was fighting a losing battle in trying to transform the Big Three into a happy, smiling pop group. He couldn't control their live performances, as **Johnny Hutch (682)** explains. "A load of thugs used to follow us around. They'd start fights, but Griff was very good at starting fights himself once he'd had a few drinks. He'd hit someone with his guitar and bugger off, leaving us to sort it out. At one gig in South Wales there were about 50 hoods at the front of the stage. They'd annoyed Griff, so he grabbed one of my drumsticks and threw it at them. The next minute all 50 of them were on stage chasing us. I got a broken rib but Griff was all right. He'd rushed around the back and locked himself in the toilet."

Kenny Johnson (683) of Sonny Webb and the Cascades recalls another embarrassing incident, "We went to Ireland on a ten-day tour and people were saying to us, 'Sing 'Rhythm Of The Rain'.' We didn't know it, but the promoter said, 'If you don't learn it quick, you don't get paid.' We found out that we'd been booked as the Cascades, an American group who'd had a hit with 'Rhythm Of The Rain'. We had to learn it and, honest to God, we went on television singing 'Rhythm Of The Rain'."

Spencer Lloyd Mason (684): "Beryl Marsden was unreliable before she even had a record deal. I fixed up an appearance on Border TV and she didn't turn up. She had met Keith Richards along the way and had disappeared off the face of the earth for a fortnight."

Joe Fagin (685): "The worst gig we did was in a dance hall over the Co-op in Hull. We sat in the foyer watching the crowd come in and they were ugliest women we had ever seen. We were going to have an award for the one of us who pulled the ugliest bird, but gave up. We were almost reduced to pulling the fellers that night."

There was also trouble when the group played in the UK. **Dave May (686)** from Mark Peters and the Silhouettes says, "My girlfriend ran our fan club and we didn't want anybody to know that we had girlfriends or were married. Her name was Wendy, but we gave her the fictitious name of Bobbie. If we were on tour, I might take a girl home, and they'd write to the fan club saying how much they particularly liked Dave because he'd taken them home and given them a goodnight kiss. I had to face Wendy's wrath whenever I came home."

Nicky Crouch (687): "We were out with Helen Shapiro one night and just as a joke I put a piece of string around her finger. Spencer Mason got a photographer to take some pictures of us and the next thing we knew our 'engagement' was in the morning papers. We went along with it for a couple of days but the whole thing was very embarrassing for both of us. My girlfriend back home wasn't too pleased to read about it."

Spencer Lloyd Mason (688): "Helen Shapiro's career was on the wane and we were looking for publicity so I announced that she was getting engaged to Nicky Crouch. I saw her father, a delightful man, and told him that it was just a story for the music papers. It made every single front page including *The Times.* As it happens, Nicky was already engaged and I met his fiancé a few days later in Bold Street. She came at me with a shoe in her hand shouting, 'You bastard!'"

Jim Turner (689): "The wrestler Shirley Crabtree, Big Daddy, was a nice guy and a tremendous publicist. He ran dances around Halifax and at the time we were having trouble with Them Grimbles owing to disputes within the group. That night we asked the Tabs to do this gig for them. All went well but previously one of the girls had fallen for a Grimble and things had gone too far. She appeared with her father to see the drummer and, of course, she saw the drummer from the Tabs. There was a row and Shirley saw how this could be brilliant publicity. As a result, *The People* exposed us and said that another group was going out as Them Grimbles."

Ron Ellis (690): "I had sent the Tabs to Leeds for Jim and a few days later, somebody came into Southport Library where I was working and asked if I managed the Tabs. I thought, 'Great, they're being discovered,' but he said, 'Why are they going out as Them Grimbles? Is there a fraud going on?' I said, 'Ah, when I say I am their manager, I mean their acting manager. You will have to ask Jim Turner.' The story was in *The People* and they had really embellished it. They maintained that there were eight groups going out across the country as Them Grimbles."

Dave Crosby (691): "We were told to say that we were Them Grimbles but we had the Tabs written all over our van and our equipment. When we were asked about this, we said that our own van and equipment had been stolen and we had borrowed all this from the Tabs, but then our drummer revealed that we were the Tabs."

Dicky Tarrach (692) from the Rattles: "We are the only band to play the Cavern for a whole week and we played lunchtime and evening and it was amazing, so many people came to see us. I have never sweated so much in my life, you even sweat when you come in. It was very very nice and on the last day, the girls had presents for us like cakes with our name on and the stage was full. *Mersey Beat* wanted us to pick the girl who gave us the best present and she spent a day with us. We recorded one or two songs in German but we didn't like them and we sang in English. They loved our German accent on (sings) 'There is a rose in Spanish Harlem'. We couldn't get the 'r' right and the girls would scream. All the girls were after the band. We asked why and some girls said, 'We want to sleep with a Nazi, maybe it is different from an English guy. The German Ziegfried, is he bigger or not?' It was a nice experience, okay. We were kept pretty busy. (Laughs)"

V. Starr Wars: The Backside Strikes Back

I first encountered Freddie Starr at BBC Radio Merseyside in the early 1980s when he was a guest on Bob Azurdia's afternoon programme. Janice Long was reading the news in another cubicle and Freddie went up to the glass, unzipped his fly and pretended to masturbate. Janice started to laugh and the station manager, Ian Judson, hearing this, ran downstairs and ordered him out. "He's my guest," Bob protested. "Well, you just sit there, zip yourself up and behave yourself," ordered Ian.

My own interview with Freddie was arranged for six o'clock and on the way out, Freddie grabbed my cock and said, "Okay, see you at six. Come on time – I'm into bondage and that takes time. If you do come late, we'll only have time for a wank." When I got to the Atlantic Tower hotel, Freddie was having his hair styled. He saw me and stroked his stylist's leg, "He likes this," he said. When the hair-drier was switched on, he said, "Let's do the interview now. We'll tell the listeners we're talking in a hurricane." When his hair was ready, he stood in an open dressing-gown and admired his physique in the mirror.

I did wonder whether interviewing Freddie about the Merseybeat years was a good idea. When I asked him about Howie Casey, he said, "I married Howie Casey in 1960. It took him two months to find out I was a woman." Freddie's saner comments about Merseybeat are in this book.

Eddie Parry of the Dennisons had told me that Freddie once borrowed his mac and hadn't returned it. I mentioned this and Freddie said, "It's too late now, I've given it to Columbo." **Freddie Starr (693)** said: "I always knew that my time would come, so I wasn't disappointed in the Sixties. I felt that the groups would blow themselves out as being a rock singer or a rock group is very short-lived unless you happen to be the Beatles."

That evening Anne and I went to the Wooky Hollow to see him in concert. He was backed by a superb band, which included Mick Green from the Pirates, but one musician missed a cue. This was hardly surprising as no one appeared to know, least of all Freddie, what was coming next. He turned to the hapless muso and said, "You're sacked." A wall descended between himself and the audience as we couldn't believe what we were witnessing. Had this guy lost his job or was it a joke that had gone wrong? Freddie finished the show and did okay but he would have had more applause without that incident. Some years later, I asked Mick Green if Freddie really had sacked someone that night: "Oh yes," he replied, "That's typical of the way he was. You look at his musicians from one tour to another. Nobody stays for long."

This manic intensity goes back to the Sixties. **Peter Cook (694)**: "If Freddie Starr clicked his fingers, we would have to stop spot on. If there was a mistake, he would blow up and lock himself in the toilet for an hour. We would knock on the door and say, 'Come on, Freddie, let's go back.' He was so temperamental. You daren't make a mistake on stage: it was that tight."

Jim Turner (695): "The only way to handle Freddie Starr was to pick him on the morning of the gig and lock him in the back of the van. If you left the door unlocked, he'd be gone. Otherwise, he would forget about the show or have the wrong day. We would drive to the show and he would be moaning all the way – he'd missed a date with some girl in the afternoon or something like that. On stage, he was brilliant and he would even have hard rockers falling about, but like a lot of people who are artistically capable, he was not commercially sensible. He upset a lot of people who have long memories."

Despite all his girlfriends, Freddie was married and many Merseybeat musicians sympathised with his wife, Betty. He did not take her to the gigs and effectively lived a single life. **Ted Knibbs (696)**: "I thought. Freddie Starr was uncouth. There was a meeting one day in the Mersey Beat to consider a slander action that was being brought against the magazine. Freddie said that the person bringing the action was a homosexual and had tried to get him into bed, which was irrelevant. Freddie was one-finger typing all the time that the meeting was on. We decided that an apology was needed and I went to the typewriter to see what Freddie had done. He had written 'My wife is a fucking pig' over and over."

John Cochrane (697): "I remember doing a job with Derry Wilkie in a van. He was in the passenger side and Freddie was in the back. We stopped for some hitchhikers, and Freddie said, 'Hey you black trash, get in the back, make room for a white man', and he said, 'Yes boss, yes boss', and these fellers said, 'We'll wait for the next lift, it's okay'."

Peter Cook (698): "He was an embarrassment to be out with. If you were in the restaurant he would say to the waitress, 'Cup of tea and a quick wank.' We would curl up and he would say this no matter where he was. You couldn't live with him half the time." Suggested title for a Freddie Starr LP, *You'll Never Wank Alone*.

Following a triumphant appearance on the Royal Variety Performance, Freddie Starr became the country's highest paid comedy impressionist, but he was dogged by controversy, usually of his own making. He will always be associated with *The Sun* headline, "Freddie Starr Ate My Hamster". **Freddie Starr (699)** made the Top Ten in 1974 with 'It's You': "Dave Christie told me that he had a great song for me and I thought it was awful. It was about a woman who had died and the guy was going to kiss her goodbye. I thought it was too morbid, but when I heard the record we made, I thought it was quite nice."

I saw the rambunctious boy on stage again at a Summer Pops concert at the King's Dock in 1997. By now, everybody knew how unreliable he was and he had upset audiences and promoters everywhere. Nevertheless, he was being paid £15,000 which seemed an astonishing figure for a charity event in his hometown. On the day before the concert, tickets were being sprinkled around the media to fill out the audience. About 2,000 people were there.

Freddie took the audience by surprise by coming on first and they nosily rushed in from the reception area. Freddie harangued everyone about how bad the sound was: "Fuck this," he said, "I'm going off again and I'm not coming back until they can fucking hear me in the fucking apartments over there." His band played some songs, a comic called Jeff told some pathetic jokes and there was a long interval.

I don't think I have witnessed a more ramshackle performance by a star or even F. Starr. At one stage, he said, "It's getting dark. What do we do?" After an hour he realised he hadn't done any impressions and we got brilliant impersonations of Johnny Mathis singing 'Misty' and Michael Caine doing 'Be-Bop-A-Lula', but such moments were rare. He did 'My Way' while sitting on the toilet and looking down the bowl, he sang, "To think I did all that." Many of his jokes were politically incorrect – "My wife and I have our differences. I'm Jewish and my wife's a pig." (See – that line about his wife being a pig had developed into a joke.) In a typically wild moment, he asked someone if she liked plants and gave her one of the window-boxes lining the stage. This was a ragged show desperately needing a director, but it probably would have been impossible to impose some discipline.

Freddie Starr wrote his autobiography, *Unwrapped*, in 2001 and judging by his comments about Hamburg, I had asked him the wrong questions. He revealed that he joined in porno films being made by Manfred Weissleder – he wanted to show the actors how to do it! He sat at a table in a transvestite bar in the Reeperbahn and he would guess whether it was a man or a woman under the table who was sucking his dick. If he guessed wrong, he'd have to pay for everybody else.

A Channel 4 documentary, *Freddie Starr Ate My Hamster*, had been sanctioned by Freddie to publicise his autobiography, but far from praising him, one associate after another commented on how impossible he was. He appeared to be exiled in Spain with an audience of one, his current wife. Her previous husband had been a dustman but you got the impression that it was her new husband who was bringing the rubbish home.

In October Freddie came to Liverpool for a book-signing and after that, he was live with Billy Butler on Radio Merseyside. He said he had no idea he was going to be set up on the Channel 4 doc, but why did he appear so ridiculous and so manic in his own interview segments and why was his first prank to throw the director into his pool?

When they had finished, I went into the studio with Michael Snow, the Liverpool songwriter who wrote 'Rosetta' for Georgie Fame and Alan Price. Billy was trying to impersonate Al Jolson: "No, no," said Freddie, "You've got it all wrong. You start with the eyes. Watch me." Freddie rolled his eyes like Jolson and sang 'Sonny Boy', and it was at moments like this that you realise he is brilliant.

Michael Snow said, "Freddie, I haven't seen you since you crapped in Graham Nash's guitar." Freddie described how he had carefully taken the strings off, crapped in the hole and replaced them: his comment on the Hollies. Freddie added that it wasn't just Graham Nash: he had done it on a number of occasions. Pleasant man.

Billy Butler reminded him of the time he put his dick in a roll at the Cavern and then complained that his hot dog was stale. "What's wrong with getting your dick out?" said Freddie, "I've done it hundreds of times." This, I think, is a very telling quote. I am convinced that his biggest asset is also his downfall. Having a huge willy has made him an exhibitionist and this has dominated his humour and his work. It is a shame as he is a brilliantly talented comedian. There aren't many impersonators who can sing like their subjects and his Elvis is among the best.

Although Freddie still tours the UK, he must be disappointed at the way things have turned out. However, his life story would make a tremendous film. Marc Warren, who plays the conman Danny Blue in *Hustle*, looks like a young Freddie Starr and what a great role this would be. Providing, of course, that he has the right equipment, although it's amazing what they can do with prostheses these days.

Ted Knibbs (700): "His real name was Freddie Fowell and I remember Bob Wooler coming into the Grapes, totally exasperated and saying 'Freddie gets Foweller and Foweller.'"

Bob Wooler (701): "Freddie worked in the fruit market and he once put an enormous carrot in his trousers and pulled it out very slowly on the Cavern stage. If Ray McFall had seen that, he would have remonstrated with me, 'Why did you allow him on stage?' Ray McFall hated him and that's not too strong a word. I remember being with Freddie in the Grapes once and an attractive girl went into the ladies. He produced his willy and flopped it on the table. When she came out, he shouted, 'Try this one for size.'"

11   AMERICAN DREAM

I. Getting Ready
II. Looking for America

"They've all come to look for America."
('America', Paul Simon)

I. Getting Ready

Rock'n'roll is American music and in the early 60s, the UK acts could only make an impression in the home market. The UK acts did poorly in America. Even when singing original songs, Cliff Richard only made the US Top 40 once, while the Shadows lost out to the Dane, Jorgen Ingmann on 'Apache'. The Tornados had a freak US No.1 with 'Telstar', although it was an excellent record and Frankie Vaughan had an unlikely US hit with 'Judy'.

Geographically, the US dwarfs the UK and it contains four times as many people, that is, four times as many record-buyers. However, with a population of 50 million English-speaking people, it was only a matter of time before a major international act would emerge from the UK. The way it happened could never have been predicted.

Following the success of 'Hey! Baby', the American **Bruce Channel (702)** did club dates in the UK with his harmonica player, Delbert McClinton. They played the Tower Ballroom in New Brighton on 21 June 1962 with the Beatles in support. "I remember getting off the plane and my luggage was lost so I wore what I had on the plane that night in Maidstone. The tour is a blur after that, but I remember playing a big hall in Liverpool that reminded me of a castle. There were lots of kids there, a whole sea of people, and I said to Delbert, 'They can't all have come to see us', and we soon found out that the Beatles were very popular. Delbert was in the dressing-room with John Lennon who was very interested in his harp. Delbert played something for him and evidently John kept the idea and used it for the sound on 'Love Me Do'. We had heard the harmonica on blues records by Jimmy Reed and people like that, and that influenced 'Hey! Baby'. It's a great thrill to know that our record influenced the Beatles, that our music was appreciated by someone of that stature."

'Love Me Do' made the UK Top 20 at the end of 1962, and the following year belonged to the Beatles as they scored with 'Please Please Me', 'From Me To You', 'She Loves You' and 'I Want To Hold Your Hand'. The Beatles didn't make an impact in America until 1964 and so visiting American stars coming to the UK in 1963 were witnessing a phenomenon they knew nothing about.

Brian Hyland (703): "I played in Liverpool when the Beatles had 'Please Please Me' out and I thought it sounded great. It was clear from listening to it that they sang and played their own instruments and were involved with the whole process of making the record. This contrasted with a lot of American performers who made records with session guys they didn't know. I did an American tour with Bobby Vee in 1963 and I remember us sitting in the dressing-room on the opening night singing 'Love Me Do' and 'Please Please Me' together. The others on the tour were amazed. They'd never heard the songs before and they thought they were great."

The Beatles' first national tour was with Helen Shapiro and Danny Williams in February 1963. The following month they did two weeks with Tommy Roe and Chris Montez. **Chris Montez (704)**: "I was touring England with Tommy Roe and an unknown group called the Beatles. They were booked to get the show going and they had such energy and power. They played me their album, *Please Please Me*, before it was released and I was knocked out. I couldn't stop singing 'I Saw Her Standing There'. It was such a great song. I was top of the charts and topping the bill, but when we got to Liverpool, I said, 'This is your town, you close the show, I'm not the headliner here.' They were amazed that I should say that."

Del Shannon (705) recorded 'From Me To You', thus becoming the first person to take a Lennon and McCartney song into the US Top 100. Del was with the Beatles as part of *Swinging Sound 63* at the Royal Albert Hall in April. "'From Me To You' was a big hit here and I told John Lennon that I was going to do it. He said, 'That'll be all right', but then, just as he was going on stage at the Royal Albert Hall, he turned to me and said, 'Don't do that.' Brian Epstein had told him that he didn't want any Americans covering their songs. The Beatles were going to invade America by themselves."

Three days later the Beatles were at the NME Pollwinners Concert at the Empire Pool, Wembley. **John Stewart (706)**: "I was playing the London Palladium and the opening of the London Hilton with the Kingston Trio. We were big fans of the Springfields and we went to see them get an award at some big concert. The Most Promising New Band was the Beatles and they did 'Twist And Shout' and some of their own songs. Nick Reynolds and I both said, 'That's it. When this hits America, it's over for us.' Within a few months, 'I Want To Hold Your Hand' had come out, they had done *The Ed Sullivan Show* and we never had another Top 40 record."

In May, the Beatles were touring with Roy Orbison. **Duane Eddy (707)**: "I was supposed to tour with the Beatles in 1963 but my manager messed that up and Roy Orbison went instead. That was one of the greatest things that ever happened to Roy. It rejuvenated his whole career and he had several more hit records. He always said that he was very thankful to me for not going on that tour."

On 26 May 1963, I caught the tour at the Liverpool Empire, where the Beatles topped the bill. I remember the cries for the Beatles as Orbison stepped out on stage. I wondered how he could cope with it, but he simply whispered, "A candy-coloured clown they call the Sandman" and he was away. The audience loved him and forgot the Beatles for thirty minutes. **Roy Orbison (708)**: "I remember Paul and John grabbing me by my arms and not letting me go back to take my curtain call. The audience was yelling, 'We want Roy, we want Roy,' and there I was, being held captive by the Beatles who were saying, 'Yankee, go home.' We had a great time."

Carl Perkins (709): "I went to England for the first time on tour with Chuck Berry. The Beatles held a party for me as they wanted to meet me and I certainly wanted to meet them. They were down to earth, super-talented, witty people. 'I Want To Hold Your Hand' was very big here and I thought, 'Man, these cats are going to destroy America.' The kids would love their music and their clothes with those spike-heeled boots. I said, 'The only thing wrong is that you need haircuts', and John said, 'Oh no, we don't do haircuts.'"

In November 1963, the Beatles were invited to appear on the Royal Variety Performance at the Prince of Wales Theatre in London. **Buddy Greco (710)** was also on the bill: "When I got to rehearsals, there were thousands of people outside the Prince of Wales Theatre and I had no idea who they had come to see. I didn't think it was me and I didn't think it was Marlene Dietrich, who, incidentally, had a young piano player called Burt Bacharach. The young men were walking around with crazy haircuts that looked like the Three Stooges, and all the magazines and newspapers had the Beatles on the front page. When I saw them at rehearsal and they did a couple of songs, I thought they were just a nice little rock'n'roll band. *Melody Maker* wanted my opinion of the Beatles, and I said very bluntly, 'If I know my business, the Beatles will be out of business in about a year.' Little did I realise that they would turn out to be geniuses who wrote wonderful songs."

Buddy Greco (711) did witness John Lennon's eccentricity: "I knew John Lennon was a little nuts because while we were talking upstairs, he was putting water in balloons and throwing them into the street. When he said that line about the jewellery, I was backstage and I fell on the floor laughing. It was a great line."

Peter Prichard (712): "There were always crowds outside the theatre before the Royal show and the audience was full of people who'd paid a lot of money for tickets. There were only a few young fans in the gallery right at the top yet their reception was very, very good. It wasn't the type of reception that they would have normally at a concert full of very young people. John Lennon was a very humorous man and that remark about the jewellery shows he could have been a comedian if he had wanted to be."

Indeed. The funniest line that people recall from a Royal Variety Performance wasn't even said by a comedian.

II. Looking for America

In February 1964 the Beatles conquered America with their live performances in Washington and New York and TV appearances on *The Ed Sullivan Show*. Those of us in England didn't appreciate the importance of the show because it was not screened in the UK. Ed Sullivan had a UK agent in **Peter Prichard (713)**: "We had great variety shows in Britain. There really wasn't any gap here and the cost of buying American shows would have been greater than staging *Sunday Night at the London Palladium*. Ed Sullivan was originally a sports journalist, who worked out of New York before the Second World War. He realised that these great sportsmen like Joe Louis and Jack Dempsey wanted to be seen in variety, or as they called it, vaudeville. He put on shows in between movies, and he would have a great sportsman giving an exhibition of his talent and being interviewed, along with a couple of other acts. That was the beginning of *The Ed Sullivan Show*. He had such a great reputation that he was sent to Hollywood and became a show business columnist with a daily column and became very important plugging films. When television came along, all the major studios barred their artists from appearing on television as they thought it would take away from the magic of the motion picture. Ed Sullivan was the only one they would trust and he said, 'Look, it'll gain publicity for your movies.' They tried it with Jimmy Stewart and John Wayne. They came on the show, did a short interview and talked up the new movie, and the box office returns shot up. The rules were relaxed and film stars started to appear on TV, and Mr. Sullivan was the man who had started it off."

Sid Bernstein (714): "As well as promoting concerts, I was doing a class about the great democracies of the world, and our professor told us to read English newspapers and see how the British government works. I read about the Beatles and so I had the edge on other promoters who might have been interested. One of your most conservative newspapers, the *Guardian*, said that Beatlemania was sweeping the UK, so I thought I must bring them over. We did Carnegie Hall in 1964 and the box office manager said, 'Sid, you could have sold 200,000 more tickets.' I did consider doing Madison Square Garden two nights after Carnegie Hall for the kids who were turned away, but Brian Epstein said no. He thought they would want the Beatles all the more the next time. They came back for a big tour and they did Shea Stadium."

Peter Prichard (715): "The Beatles got on *The Ed Sullivan Show* through appearing on the *Royal Variety Performance* in November 1963. Communications were quite difficult then and I sent their photographs, their records and the clippings from the Royal show to Mr. Sullivan and I suggested that we use them on *The Ed Sullivan Show* as the first long-haired young man to appear before the Queen. It was long for that era, but nowadays it's much longer. Brian Epstein was in New York and I'd rung him and told him that I was getting Ed interested. He was very pleased because if he could get *The Ed Sullivan Show,* the records would follow. I did a deal with him, which was for three shows at scale, which was very, very little money. It was $750 for each show, not for each person. I used to go to the show every weekend. I would fly over on a Friday and the Beatles were phenomenal. We immediately put their money up to the top price, which Mr. Sinatra would have been getting, which was only $1,500. We created a new contract for the extra shows, so Ed did a lot with them. Their success was helped by appearing on Ed's show, though nothing would have stopped them anyway."

How did the Beatles find appearing on *The Ed Sullivan Show*? **Peter Prichard (716)**: "I think success was hitting them from so many angles that it was just another show. What they loved was being in New York. They'd never been there before. I remember talking to them on that weekend and they were more interested with the sights they'd seen and going to the record shops, which were huge places, and finding that restaurants were open all night, which were all amazing to four young men out of Liverpool. They knew the prestige of the show but this all was just coming along with the rest of the success that was hitting them so quickly."

Louise Harrison (717): "Their appearance on *The Ed Sullivan Show* was great or, at least, what you could hear of it – and I was immensely proud. Cynthia Lennon was with me and a couple of nights later they were on Carnegie Hall. Normally, we travelled in the same car as the boys but this night we had our own limousine. The hall was so full that seats were placed at the back of the stage for the entourage. At the end of the night, we found that someone had commandeered our limo. We took a taxi to the hotel and we didn't have any money with us. We persuaded a cab driver to take us to the hotel and then we ran upstairs to get the money to pay him."

Rodney Crowell (718): "I had heard them a year before *The Ed Sullivan Show*. There was a radio station in Houston, Texas that somehow got hold of 'Please Please Me' and I heard it every morning when I was on the school bus. The record slayed me but it was an import so I couldn't buy it in the shops. When the Beatles released their album, *Introducing The Beatles*, I saw it there and I knew it was the music I was hearing. I missed them on the first *Ed Sullivan Show*. The next day the kids were talking about nothing else. The Beatles were really smart as they went on it three Sundays in a row. I was cued in front of the television for the second one and I was mesmerised by so much inspiration and energy from people so close to my age."

Ray McFall (719) was invited to go to America for the Carnegie Hall concert: "Brian booked me on the flight and into the same hotel, the Plaza. I was on the fifth floor and they were on the seventh floor and the place was like a fortress. It was crawling with detectives in addition to the hotel staff because the fans were trying to get in. One young lady packed herself in a laundry basket and got delivered to the hotel but they rumbled her right away. I have still got the programme from their gig at Carnegie Hall and it was extraordinary. The entrepreneur took a chance, and everyone in New York wanted to be there – high society people, politicians, everybody. The audiences went mad and it was unforgettable."

Sid Bernstein (720): "Carnegie Hall has a capacity of 2,870 and the head of the box office had never seen anything like it. The two shows, matinee and early evening, sold out in 24 minutes. People were restricted to a maximum of eight tickets, so it only took 700 people to clean out the box office. The tickets were then scalped. The $3.50 seats in the upper balcony were going for $75, the $4.50 ones for $100, and the $5.50 ones for $150. This is a lot of money and the scalpers had a field day."

The Beatles made No.1 with 'I Want to Hold Your Hand'. Five million of its 12 million copies were sold in America alone and the Beatles had five more No.1 singles before the year was out. The US charts for 4 April 1964 shows the Beatles holding the top five positions with 'Can't Buy Me Love' on top, followed by 'Twist and Shout', 'She Loves You', I Want To Hold Your Hand' and 'Please Please Me'. They had another seven entries in the Hot 100, and in Canada they did even better by having nine records in the Top Ten at the same time.

Paul Gambaccini (721): "The first Beatle song I heard was 'I Want to Hold Your Hand'. I was on the couch on the porch of our house in Westport, Conn. I was listening to Stan Z. Burns on WINS, New York and he introduced this song. I was impressed by it but I had no idea that it was going to be as huge as it was as quickly as it was. I have my own theory on this, which Paul McCartney doesn't agree with, but he needs an American perspective to judge. The country had been in deep mourning over the assassination of John F. Kennedy – deep, deep mourning and it really needed an up. It was such mourning that the Singing Nun was No.1 – this was like penance. Everyone wanted to be happy again and the Beatles with 'I Want to Hold Your Hand' were the first positive thing to come along. They had been very unsuccessful at first, so much so that their previous records had been with different labels. 'Love Me Do' was with

Tollie, 'She Loves You' was with Swan, the *Please Please Me* album and single were with Vee-Jay, and Capitol had 'I Want to Hold Your Hand'. They all reissued them and so the Beatles had the whole Top 5 that famous week in April 1964. No-one had ever done that and that was just the beginning of the whole thing."

Tony Barrow (722): "There were fan problems from the word go. It wasn't so much fear that the Beatles would be damaged, though if a large number of hysterical kids had got on the stage, that could have happened. The real fear was that the fans would damage themselves, that they would fall into orchestra pits or off airport balconies. On one American tour, the top of the limousine the Beatles were in was severely dented by kids climbing all over it. We arrived in one Texas city on a charter flight in the middle of the night. Kids appeared from nowhere and they were climbing over the wings before the engines had stopped. It would have been very dangerous if one of those kids had lit a cigarette. Fan control wasn't solely to keep these kids away from their idols; it was also to protect them from damage to themselves."

American fans were more persistent than British fans. **Les Maguire (723)** of Gerry and the Pacemakers explains, "Americans are very confident. Twelve-year-old girls walk into hotels and demand to see people. They say, 'You can't throw me out. My daddy will get his lawyer on you.' You can chase kids away over here but American kids are more aggressive.'

Bobby Vee (724): "There was such an influx of British records after the Beatles made it that anyone with an English accent was in demand. It was absolutely essential that the disc-jockeys should be Beatle crazy and English mad. It made a major dent in the careers of so many American pop singers."

One presenter who was certainly Beatle crazy was Brian Epstein. He was a guest presenter on *Shindig*. **Chris Curtis (725)**: "We did 'Love Potion No. 9' on *Shindig*. Brian Epstein introduced *Shindig*, dressed very British but just right for what he was doing – he was a Keith Fordyce for America."

The concerts in America were often held in stadiums, the most famous being the Beatles at Shea Stadium in 1964 and 1966, both Sid Bernstein productions. **Sid Bernstein (726)** on the first date: "There had been no mention of time and I didn't realise until years later that they only did 28 minutes. You could not hear the music: Shea Stadium is in Queens and you could hear the roar of the crowd in the Bronx. There were 56,000 people there – 1,000 press and 55,000 pays. It was all so new but in 1966 I had more control of it: we had better amplifiers and you could hear some of the music. I also underestimated what my profit would be. I made a profit of $6,500 on a gate of $304,000. Brian Epstein was upset when he heard how little I made and he wanted to give me a gift. I said, 'Your gift was in giving me the boys, Brian.'"

The UK performers had no experience of such large audiences, although **Billy J. Kramer (727)** didn't object. "Show business in my opinion is about communication. I remember the first time girls screamed at me in Liverpool, and afterwards Brian Epstein gave me the rollicking of my life. He said, 'There were half a dozen girls at the front grabbing your feet. You were playing around with them and ignoring the other thousand people who came to see you.' He was quite right, but playing the big concerts in America was just going through the motions. The audience is so large that it becomes impersonal. I still get nervous in a small place, but the 30,000-seaters I've done in America didn't bother me at all."

Billy J. Kramer (728) is also proud of a song he recorded in concert. "I've seen a reference to me in an American book which said that I was a pretty-faced crooner who sang nicey-nicey songs and was lucky to be buddies with the Beatles. That irritates me because there was a different side to me. I recorded a very wild version of 'Sugar Babe' in California with Mick Green on guitar."

Gerry Marsden (729) with his Pacemakers planned to record an LP in concert. "We were asked to do a live LP while we were in Long Beach, California. They got everything lined up and tested the sound two days before. We went on stage to do the show and we didn't realise that when there's 35,000 kids screaming, you tend to play faster. All the tracks came out weird. We only salvaged four and made an EP called *Gerry in California*. One of the tracks I still like although it's too fast is 'Dizzy Miss Lizzy'."

If you can't beat them, join them. The American record producer, **Huey P. Meaux (730)**, jumped on the bandwagon. "I produced several big records in the early 60s but the Beatles came along and knocked me off the charts. Doug Sahm had been bugging me to make some records with him and I told him, 'Doug, we gotta figure out where the Beatles are coming from. If we don't, we'll starve to death.' I got a case of T-bird wine – it was $1 a bottle and it'd get you drunk in a hurry and keep you drunk for days – and I bought some Beatle records. I went to the Wayfarer Hotel in San Antonio and the clerk said, 'Why do you want three rooms?' and I said, 'I'll be playing these records pretty loud.' I realised that it was all so simple: the Beatles had a beat and we were not catching onto that. I called Doug, who was also in San Antonio, and I said, 'C'mon over, man, I'm drunk but I've figured it out.' I told him to write some songs with that beat and to grow his hair. He came up with 'She's About A Mover' and 'The Rains Came' and we recorded them at the Goldstar studios in Houston. American DJs would play anything from England, so I called up London Records in New York and I said, 'Put this out. Leave my name off and we'll call Doug something else.' I thought about knighthoods and the Sir Douglas Quintet sounded perfect. The record made the charts and Doug kept bugging me, 'I want to go on the road, man. When will you tell them it's me?' I told him to keep quiet until the record made the Top 40. Doug was booked for the *Hullabaloo* TV show in New York City, which was mc'd by Trini Lopez. Freddie and the Dreamers were on the show but there was also Doug and me, Vikki Carr from El Paso and Trini himself. Trini said, 'I can't believe so many people from Texas are on the same show. You've got to let me tell the people.' I said, 'Go ahead,' and that was the night that America learnt the identity of the Sir Douglas Quintet."

Joe Butler (731) of Sonny Webb and the Cascades recalls, "When the Beatles first went to the States, they went down great. We were chuffed to think that some of our lads had rammed new music down their throats and got away with it. They were in the Blue Angel one night when we were playing, and Paul said, 'You want to get your band over there. Country music is big in the States and you guys would kill them.' It was good advice, but we didn't appreciate what a gimmick we would have had as a country band from Liverpool."

Naturally, the promotion has to be right. The Remo Four got a booking in America but it wasn't what they wanted. **Colin Manley (732)** explains, "NEMS got us a gig in America playing for two weeks in a department store in Minneapolis. It was called *Liverpool Week* and they wanted a Liverpool group from NEMS Enterprises. We were playing in an auditorium at the top of this huge department store, and we were four monkeys for people to ogle at. At interviews with local radio stations, we had to lay on the Beatles business a bit thick and emphasise our Liverpool accents. It led to nothing, totally nothing, because we didn't have a record out in America to promote."

The Merseybeats had a record to promote but it was the wrong one. **Tony Crane (733)** explains, "We went to America as the Merseybeats on a promotional trip. We played all around New York State for five days. We did 72 radio shows, seven television shows and lots of personal appearances, and we aged three years. We were shattered when we came back. It wasn't a success because instead of promoting one of our hit records, we went over with our latest single in Britain which was 'Last Night (I Made A Little Girl Cry)'. It didn't become a big record. We should have gone over there with 'Wishin' And Hopin'' or 'I Think Of You'."

Ian and the Zodiacs had some regional success in America with 'The Crying Game'. **Charlie Flynn (734)** describes what happened when Ian and the Zodiacs went there to promote their next record, 'Good Morning Little Schoolgirl'. "After we'd had a hit in America with 'The Crying Game', arrangements were made to send us there to promote our next record. Unfortunately it was at a time when the Beatles, the Bachelors, the Dave Clark Five and Herman's Hermits were taking huge amounts of money out of America. The authorities were clamping down on British groups by introducing 'exchange deals', and our manager couldn't find a band to swap with us at short notice. We got visas after a lot of trouble but they wouldn't allow us to play any shows. We were supposed to be doing a three-week tour but we finished up going to radio stations. We couldn't even talk on the radio. We were reduced to saying hello to the DJs and asking them to plug our record. In the first week we went to New Jersey and mimed to our record in Palisades Park. We didn't get paid for it but the immigration authorities threatened to throw us out if we did that again. We had some minor successes – 'Good Morning Little Schoolgirl' made the Top Ten in Boston – but it was three weeks wasted. We went back to Germany and stayed there for two years. When we came home for a holiday in 1967, all my equipment was stolen, so I packed up."

Mark Lewisohn (735): "The Beatles never played in South Africa and I can only presume it was because of their feelings towards apartheid as they were offered £1,000 a night on two occasions. I do recall that in 1964 when the Beatles were in America, they learnt that a concert in Jacksonville was going to be for a segregated audience and they told the promoter that they would not play until it was desegregated. The promoter would have been lynched by thousands of girl fans if he had not acceded to the Beatles' wishes. Incidentally, the one place they wanted to play, and couldn't, was Israel. The Israeli government felt that they would be a bad influence on the youth of the country."

12   HOMEWARD BOUND

I. Back at the Cavern
II. Some Other Guys
III. Some Other Guise
IV. Let's Do The Time Warp Again

"Everyday's an endless stream of cigarettes and magazines."
('Homeward Bound', Paul Simon writing in Widnes, 1965)

I. Back at the Cavern

Beatlemania spread throughout the country. You could buy Beatles caps and Beatles capes, Beatles wigs and Beatles hankies, Beatle boots and Beatle suits. In one day Sayers, a chain of Merseyside bakery shops, sold 25,000 guitar-shaped caked incorporating a photograph of the Beatles. In January 1964 small pieces of the Cavern stage, so-called 'Beatle-board', were sold for charity.

Paddy Delaney (736) found he was as busy outside the Cavern as inside. "Tourists were coming to Mathew Street and snapping this hole in the wall. It was only a doorway with no big sign and as I had to stand on the door, people from all over the world were asking me questions. One American girl wanted to see the bandroom. I pointed to where Ringo Starr always sat. She got down on her knees and she kissed the spot and then broke down crying. There were scenes like that every day of the week.'"

Mike Hargreaves (737) was another of the Cavern's doormen: "Georgy Downs and I were once invited to accompany a local group to a dance hall in Southport as the last time they went some equipment was damaged. We went along in our dress suits, clip-on bow ties and toetexers, that is, the steel-capped shoes. All we did the whole night was stroll around. We heard someone say, 'Watch out, here's those bouncers from Liverpool' and they went as quiet as mice. We also worked on the riverboat shuffles on the Royal Iris and that was a bit difficult as you couldn't throw people out. The only lock-up facilities were the toilets."

On 3 August 1963 the Beatles made their final appearance at the Cavern, bringing their total number of appearances to around 285. The place was packed and the condensation was at its worst. The Beatles were hampered by a loss of power and light, but they gave a memorable performance. **Paddy Delaney (738)** was on the door. "The last time the Beatles appeared at the Cavern was for £20. The booking had been arranged months before. In the meantime, they had risen to the top. They were making thousands of pounds. The crowds outside were going mad. By the time John Lennon had got through the cordon of girls, his mohair jacket had lost a sleeve. I grabbed it to stop a girl getting away with a souvenir. John immediately stitched the sleeve back on. They may have altered their style elsewhere, but they didn't do it at the Cavern. They were the same old Beatles, with John saying, 'Okay, tatty-head, we're going to play that number for you.' There was never anything elaborate about his introductions."

The Beatles encountered difficulties wherever they performed, but Liverpool presented special problems. **Freda Kelly (739)** says of their appearance at the Empire Theatre on 5 December 1965, "I went backstage at the last concert they gave in Liverpool, but I was in the Moody Blues' bandroom for most of the night because I couldn't get into the Beatles'. It was chocka and I realised that Liverpool was the *worst* place for them to play. They couldn't relax because all their cousins and aunts and uncles kept coming backstage."

Mick O'Toole (740): "We used to go to the Locarno on a Friday night, and I remember buying a *New Musical Express* and the Searchers were No.1 with 'Sweets For My Sweet'. Here's a band that was on the Locarno and the No.1 band in the country. And they were awful. They looked the part, sharply suited and well-dressed, but they had such a thin, weedy sound and they seemed to mess about so much. They had very enthusiastic dancers there, and I remember them going into 'What'd I Say' and they got the crowd response thing, but when they stopped, they cleared the floor. We thought they finished and everybody cleared the floor. They started up again and everybody ran madly back on the floor again, and they did this three times, and that time people had thought, 'To hell with this', and they were playing to an empty floor. I thought, 'How can they be the top band in the country and be so bad at communicating with the audience?'"

The Chants were championed by Merseyside MP, Bessie Braddock. **Eddie Amoo (741)** recalls, "'She came into the picture after we signed out first recording contract with Pye Records. Our first single, 'I Don't Care', came to her notice and she started to take an interest in the group. It was mainly because we were a black group from a depressed area of Liverpool and we were the only thing that was happening there. Bessie Braddock took a big interest in the poorer part of Liverpool. She wanted us to do well."

The Spinners created a party atmosphere whenever they appeared at their folk club at Gregson's Well in the city centre. As the pub could only house a few hundred and the Spinners could fill theatres, they weren't doing it for big money. **Hughie Jones (742)**: "We made a determined effort to stay in Liverpool because we had a very successful club and it wasn't until 1965 that we turned pro. We had a long time not to be overawed by the music business and we could see through those wonderful pie-in-the-sky offers. A lot of the beat groups fell apart when they went down to London. It was a shame because what kept the music together had a lot to do with the vitality of Liverpool itself."

The Merseybeats played at the Cavern after becoming nationally famous. **Tony Crane (743)**: "Even after we'd had hit records, we played at the Cavern for a small fee because we owed the place a lot and we owed Liverpool a lot. We didn't want the Liverpool fans to think we had deserted them. We tried to play there for 12 hours non-stop. We played in Bridlington one Saturday evening, drove through the night and started this marathon session at the Cavern at four in the morning. We were shattered when we started, but ended up playing for eight and three-quarter hours. It was five hours before we repeated a number. The only reason we stopped was because our drummer John Banks collapsed. He fell off his drum stool and had to be carried off stage. Billy, Aaron and I carried on without him for another hour and then called it a day. People were coming in at eleven o'clock on the Sunday morning and were cheering us along."

When successful performers came back to Merseyside, they could find themselves regarded rather strangely. **Billy Hatton (744)** of the Fourmost: "Within six months I went from a Ford Prefect to a $17^1/_2$ foot, left-hand-drive, convertible Mercury Monterey. The first Canadian car I got was a black saloon, a $16^1/_2$ foot Ford Fairlane. It was parked outside our terraced house in the Dingle. Brian O'Hara's dad was waiting at the bus stop to go down to the docks. Two other men were there and one said to the other, 'He's got a car parked outside the house that takes up the whole street. It's a big black thing like a hearse. He paid £20,000 for it and he won't even buy his own mother a house.' I'd paid £540 for the car in 1963 and I didn't buy my mother a house because she already had one. She was happy where she was and didn't want to move."

The Liverpool comic **Jimmy Tarbuck (745)** recalls his mother taking an irreverent attitude to his success: "I'd been on *Sunday Night at the London Palladium* a couple of times and Brian Epstein asked me to make three appearances in his shops – one in Walton, one in Allerton Road and one in Whitechapel, all in one day. I started out in Walton and everyone was very nice and friendly. The second one was in Allerton Road and as we only lived round the corner, it was packed with people we knew. I was signing autographs when a voice at the back said, 'Let me in, I'm his mother.' The policeman said, 'Oh, come through, Mrs. Tarbuck,' and she's saying good morning to all the people who wanted my autograph. I'm all dolled up and I said, 'What do you want, Ma?' She said, 'Your father's forgotten his sandwiches. Will you pop them into his office?' I said, 'Mother, do you mind? I'm signing autographs.' 'Oh, listen to him,' she said loudly, 'signing autographs. I'll give you a belt. Take them to your father.' Well, I took them to my dad, who was a bookie in London Road. I was furious but he roared out laughing and it became a great family joke."

Your ego could be dented in other ways. After their bookings, the musicians would meet at the Blue Angel, a club owned by Allan Williams. The Liverpool compère **Chris Murray (746)** recalled, "Billy J. Kramer was in the Blue Angel one night. Allan Williams said, 'And now we're going to listen to the best singer in the club' and everybody looked at Billy J. Kramer. Allan Williams announced Les Arnold and I've never seen anyone look so embarrassed. Billy J. Kramer automatically assumed that it would be him, but the unknown Les Arnold was a tenor and he had a superb voice."

Merseybeat had so engulfed Merseyside that country and western music lost ground. **Chris Murray (747)** relates how one show became successful. "Nobody would buy tickets for a show I was running. One night I was in the Blue Angel and in came Ringo Starr. I said, 'Ringo, please sign some tickets.' He sat there for an hour signing the tickets with 'Best wishes, Ringo Starr', 'Lots of love, Ringo Starr', and we kept taking scotch over to him. I'd offer people tickets and they'd say, 'Oh no, not for a country and western show,' and I'd say, 'Ringo Starr's signed the back,' and they'd buy them. We had the only country and western show that was a sellout, but nobody came."

Ringo Starr was considerate. **Jimmy Tushingham (748)**, who inherited the suit Ringo wore with Rory Storm and the Hurricanes, says, "When Ringo made it with the

Beatles, he had to declare everything to the Inland Revenue. We got hit with a tax bill which stemmed from Ringo having to declare his bookings with Rory Storm and the Hurricanes. He sent a cheque to Rory to pay the bill and a note saying that he was sorry about what happened."

Rory's real name was Alan Caldwell. **Alvin Stardust (749)**, then Shane Fenton, married his sister Iris. Alvin remembers, "His group was a bit like the Stones were later on. Listen to them in concert and it's totally exciting. Listen to the tape afterwards and there's a fair amount out of tune. The drums are out of time and the guitars are off key, but it doesn't detract from the magic."

Most of the people I've interviewed have likened Rory Storm to Rod Stewart, **Alvin Stardust (750)** among them. "If I didn't know how Rod Stewart had developed over the years, I would have sworn blind that he copied Rory. They even look alike. If you see old pictures of Rory and compare them with ones of Rod, you will see that they are slim, tall and athletic. Rory was very unlucky. None of us could really sing but some got the breaks and some didn't."

Ringo's red suit was passed down the line of drummers who replaced him. One was **Jimmy Tushingham (751)**. "They were a show group. They created a brilliant atmosphere, but when the vocal harmony came in, it was a different kettle of fish. They were limited in the chords they could play in that they couldn't play sevenths or eighths or whatever. Johnny Guitar was a brilliant rhythm guitarist as far as his right hand would go. He'd turn to me and say, "You're swinging like a brick, Jimmy. Will you get it up?""

Rory Storm never wanted to leave Liverpool. He didn't like to miss Liverpool's football matches and was captain of the Merseybeat XI. Other musicians joined the team and it evolved into the Merseyboots, with John McNally, Mike Pender and Billy Kinsley. **Billy Kinsley (752)** thought that the Merseybeat XI was a one-man show: "Rory Storm took all the penalties, all the free kicks, all the throw-ins and all the corners. He wanted a record kept of everything, so his dad was constantly taking photographs. Rory got the ball, lined it up and made sure that his dad was ready with the camera before he kicked it. Once, while he was doing this, the promoter Sam Leach ran from the back of the team and took the penalty instead. Rory was raging because Sam Leach had taken the penalty – and missed. To make matters worse, his dad had taken a photograph of Sam Leach. Rory chased Sam round Prescot and we had to continue the game with nine men."

Iris Caldwell (753): "Everything about Rory was outrageous, he had a massive gold comb that he would comb his hair with on stage, and he would play with the Showbiz XI and he always had his top hat and gold comb by the side of the pitch. If he scored a hat trick, he would put his hat on and do a few cartwheels. Everything he did was totally over the top."

Rory captained a team of extroverts and, for starters, he had to give orders to Freddie Starr. **John Kennedy (754)** of the Dominoes remembers one incident: "We were playing the referees in Southport and Rory Storm and Freddie Starr had a row. They both stuttered, so it took ages for the matter to be settled."

The opposition could cause problems, as **Tony Crane (755)** remembers. "Some of the teams we played were really hard and took it very seriously. If you were a pop star, they wanted to cripple you. Nobody inspected the studs on the boots, and in Pwllheli I got a gash in my leg that was six inches long."

II. Some Other Guys

Clive Epstein (756), Brian's brother, says, "There was a wonderful occasion when the Beatles came back to Liverpool for the première of *A Hard Day's Night*. The streets of Liverpool were lined all the way from the airport to Castle Street. It was exactly the same as if Liverpool had won the Cup Final."

This was great for the Beatles, but what about the others? 'Some Other Guy' is an apt song for Merseyside groups as there were hundreds of other guys – groups who didn't have chart success. Some simply didn't have the talent, but there were many other reasons: poor or unscrupulous management, songs nicked by other performers, unsympathetic production and the unwillingness to go fully professional. And for some groups, making it wasn't the be-all and end-all.

Even the groups having success felt that the bubble was going to burst. **Mike Pender (757)** of the Searchers: "It's hard to say when things started to go wrong, but we weren't taking enough care in choosing strong songs. Complacency had set in. We were over the hard times and we had become too satisfied with the good life."

Tony Crane (758) says, "Every band that came after the Beatles was in their shadow. We tried to get our own style by recording ballads for our A-sides. We also didn't want to copy their dress. We liked the way Spanish dancers dressed in bolero jackets, frilly shirts, tight trousers flared at the bottom with little vents, and high-heeled boots. The girls laughed at us at first, but it became our trademark. Lots of people copied us, including Tom Jones, and you can still see the outfits in cabaret bands." The Merseybeats were managed by the fabulously named Alan Cheetam. He owned an outfitter's and although the Merseybeats didn't become rich, they got some decent clothes.

'Trains and Boats and Planes' developed into a chart race between Billy and the song's composer Burt Bacharach, which Bacharach won by going to No.4. 'Trains and Boats and Planes' became Billy's last hit single. **Billy J. Kramer (759)**: "Lots of people turn bitter when their records stop selling. I'm very grateful because I've been to places that I would never otherwise have gone. Critics may think my records were bad, but they did give enjoyment to a lot of people. I've done more in my life than millions and millions of other kids, including those who were in Liverpool at the same time as me."

Lee Curtis was a solo singer who was out of time in the early 1960s – too late for Elvis and too early for Tom Jones. He was resident at the Star-Club when Liverpool acts were making the charts. He recorded some big ballads in Germany but commercial success eluded him as well as financial rewards. **Lee Curtis (760)**: "I wish I had all the money that was owing to me. I've been involved in seven or eight LPs, but I've never been paid a penny in royalties. We'd do gigs and find that the guy responsible for paying us had been called away. We were told we'd get a cheque and if we did it was a rubber one. I am owed thousands of pounds."

Billy J. Kramer (761) describes his problems: "To come from a family of seven, brought up in a council house, and suddenly to have thousands of kids round the house day and night created a lot of pressure. I would sit at home all day and go out about midnight. I'd come home at seven in the morning and I'd be drunk. Brian Epstein used to lecture me but that only made me worse and I became very fat. I reached sixteen and a half stone. I went to see Liverpool FC one night. Ian St. John introduced me to a girl who said, 'Billy, you used to be a nice looking guy. What the hell have you been doing with yourself?' I walked out and I didn't drink for five years. I went down to ten and a half stone and people would walk into the dressing room and say, 'Where's Billy?' I still get people saying, 'Oh, I liked you better when you were chubby.'" When Billy completed the 1984 London Marathon he was described by the media as a reformed alcoholic.

Brian Jones (762) is lucky to be playing his saxophone at all. "I had a very bad dose of flu and I went to see a doctor in New York. He gave me a penicillin injection but the needle froze the nerves in my arm. I couldn't play at all and my arm was paralysed for four and a half years. I left the States and came home and I had three years of complete hell. Eventually I saw some doctors who said it would take 18 months for everything to grow back. After eighteen months, the nerves hadn't grown back so they operated and transplanted the tendons round the other way. My left arm works in a rather odd way, but I can play the sax again."

His sister, **Iris Caldwell (763)** doesn't think it bothered Rory Storm that he never made the charts. "He never wanted to make it nationally as he was happy being King of Liverpool. He didn't want to give up running for Pembroke Harriers and he'd never want to miss a Liverpool match. I've known him come home from Germany for them."

The circumstances of Rory's death in 1972 are tragic. His father had died a few months earlier and neither Rory nor his mother recovered from the shock. Both were found dead, as **Alvin Stardust (764)** remembers, "Rory became very ill. He had a chest infection which meant he couldn't breathe properly. He found it difficult to sleep so he'd take his pills with a drop of Scotch which doped him completely. At the post mortem it was established that he hadn't taken enough pills to kill himself. It had been nothing more than a case of trying to get some kip, but because he was so weak, his body couldn't handle it. He died in the night and his mother found him. She must have felt she'd lost everything. I think she took an overdose, but I'm convinced Rory didn't. When you've known somebody that long, you know whether they're going to do it or not. The whole thing was an accident."

Bob Wooler (765): "His father died and he and his mother were in Hurricanesville on their own. I think this plus his stammer plus the fact that he was no longer a success made him disillusioned and depressed. His world had fallen to pieces, and his mother may have thought the same way too. No one knows for certain what happened, but the outcome was that they both died, and it looked as though they had made a suicide pact – Rory in one room, his mother in another. I am certain his failure as Rory Storm the rock'n'roller had a lot to do with it. Shortly after his death, there was the new fad called Glam Rock. Shane Fenton became Alvin Stardust, and Paul Raven became Gary Glitter. Many people have suggested that Rory would have done well as a Glam Rocker, but this is questionable. Alvin Stardust, like Dave Berry, had some menace about him, and I don't think Rory could have adopted such techniques."

Groups lost their individuality as they tried to emulate the successful sounds of others. They knew that big money was at stake and yet this was their undoing. They became greedy and were no longer content to play for a few pounds, but this is all Merseyside promoters would pay since so much talent was available. Inevitably, the groups disbanded. Many musicians took regular employment and so many took to selling insurance that it would have been possible to form a new group, the Men from the Pru.

Tony Marsh (766) describes how his club act began: "We'd got some new equipment in the Coasters and I'd signed my life away on HP. When we split, I still had these debts hanging over my head and I decided to try a solo career in clubland. I got a booking for £3 10s (£3.50) on a Saturday night in Netherton and they must have been impressed because they gave me £5. When I was with the Coasters, it was a six-way split because there were five members and one manager. We would have to do a £30 booking for me to end up with £5. We'd need to travel to Manchester or Middlesbrough to earn that kind of money and yet that Saturday I'd only travelled two miles up the road. I was my own boss and this was a much easier way of getting the equivalent money. The social clubs are full of guitar/vocalists but I was one of the first. As the groups split up, lads were left with amplifiers and guitars that had to be paid for and some went into the clubs like me.'

Johnny Guitar (767) from Rory Storm and the Hurricanes got a shock in 1984 when he went back in the Eighties to Butlin's, where he had once backed hopefuls in talent competitions: "There was one fellow who always used to get up at these competitions. He wore a long raincoat and hobnailed boots and he'd try to sing 'Swanee River'. We weren't keen because 'Swanee River' was too hard for us anyway. Everybody would roar with laughter and the poor fellow would never win. I went back to Butlin's and who should be playing with the band but the same guy with the same mac and the same boots. Twenty years on and he's still up there. He's been going longer than any of us."

Tony Sanders (768) of the Coasters knows one of the unluckiest case histories. "Arthur Ashton was Billy J. Kramer's cousin. He first worked with Mike Pender and left to join Billy Kramer and the Coasters. Mike's band became the Searchers so Arthur missed the boat. Arthur joined us, and as he'd got a couple of months left to finish his apprenticeship, he wouldn't turn professional. Epstein put Kramer with the Dakotas and Arthur missed the boat again. He went to Germany with Ian and the Zodiacs. They were offered 'Even The Bad Times Are Good' and turned it down. The Tremeloes recorded it and it made the Top Ten. That was the third time, and the fourth came when Shane Fenton was getting a new band together. He asked Arthur to play guitar. Arthur declined. Shane Fenton became highly successful as Alvin Stardust.'

Sometimes there's an opportunity to bask in past glories. **Pat Clusky (769)** of the 1960s group Rikki and the Red Streaks: "Paul McCartney said in an interview in the Seventies that he'd like to appear as an ordinary group in an ordinary club and have a name like Rikki and the Red Streaks. People phoned me from different parts of the media asking me if I'd like to take his place. I thought about it, but I don't think I'd like to be famous. I loved singing and still do, but I can go into a pub and no one wants to disturb me. I find it very embarrassing to say 'Rikki and the Red Streaks' now because everybody laughs. At the time I thought it was a fantastic name."

Earl Preston (770) split with the TTs and worked with the Realms for four years and recorded an LP for Ember. Then he left the business. "In the 1970s, I was sitting over the road in a friend's house. I didn't see *The Old Grey Whistle Test* that night but Bob Harris introduced some old film of Earl Preston and the TTs. The phone never stopped ringing. My mother rang and so did all sorts of relatives and friends, I went to work the next day as usual and was treated like a hero.'

Mike Evans (771) applied his experience to helping others in the Musicians' Union: "I played with the Clayton Squares, Liverpool Scene and Deaf School, and right through 15 years of playing, I found that the people who got the worst deal out of the music business were the musicians themselves. I became the Rock Group Organiser and I serve the membership which hadn't been given much attention in the past. The music business rips musicians off just as viciously as it did in the 1960s. Musicians aren't as naïve as they were but they still accept lousy money and sign ridiculous contracts. I hope I helped some of them to avoid the worst pitfalls." That was in 1984. Mike now works as a publishing editor and he wrote and compiled the best-selling photograph book, *Elvis – A Celebration* (Dorking Kindersley, 2002). I met him the day it entered *The Sunday Times'* best-selling lists and he was ecstatic – his first chart hit.

In contrast to the UK, **Colin Manley (772)** of the Remo Four discovered rock 'n' dole in Germany. "I went to the Arbeitsamt, which means 'work service'. I'd sit on the bench as though I was in Renshaw Hall and see a chap who had a sign meaning 'Show Business'. He dealt with films and music and he'd say, 'Ah, Mr. Manley. Next week you like Munich, Saturday, yes and perhaps Wiesbaden, Sunday.' He'd fix me up with gigs. It was a government service with no middleman, and tax deducted at source. Travel expenses and accommodation were paid for and the landlord would allow you to eat and drink all night on the house. Germany was an amazing place to work. I hate to say it, but it was much better than here."

The term 'country rock' wasn't coined until the mid-Sixties, but with hindsight that term might describe Sonny Webb and the Cascades. **Joe Butler (773)**: "When the Merseybeat thing died, we were out of work and we thought that we might as well be out of work playing the music we wanted to play. We scrapped the name Sonny Webb and the Cascades and started afresh as the Hillsiders. We rehearsed solid country music and made our debut at a country club that had never seen a country band with a drummer and electric bass before. The audience didn't know what to make of us at first, but we built up a following."

III. Some Other Guise

After the Mersey Beat boom, some musicians found success in unexpected ways:

Lewis Collins (774) has become the best-known Mojo as a TV tough guy in *The Professionals*. "I went from band to band after the Mojos and ended up on the cabaret circuit. When that came to a close, I was doing odd jobs. Finally, I was delivering crisps and lemonade in Warrington. It was snowing and I pulled into a lay-by. I thought, 'There's got to be something better than this. I know: I'll be an actor.'"

Many musicians rate **Trevor Morais (775)** of Faron's Flamingos as the best beat drummer on Merseyside. "It was pretty boring after Faron's Flamingos. All the bands in Liverpool were playing the same tunes and there didn't seem much point in continuing. I went to Manchester and played there and then teamed up with Roy Phillips and Tab Martin as the Peddlers. We made some albums but possibly it was a mistake to move from R&B into jazz, but that's how it goes. I got a lot of session work and I've played with Elkie Brooks, Bryan Ferry and David Essex. I am on Art Garfunkel's 'Bright Eyes' single."

Roy Dyke (776), the drummer with the Remo Four, became part of Ashton, Gardner and Dyke, who had a Top 10 hit with 'Resurrection Shuffle': "When the Remo Four disbanded in 1967, I wanted to stay with Tony Ashton as I felt that he had a great sense of direction. We met Kim Gardner in The Ship in Wardour Street which was a great pub for musicians and we formed a trio – organ, bass and drums. That was fashionable then: the Peddlers were contemporary with us and also Emerson, Lake and Palmer. When we were playing around in the studio, we came up with 'Resurrection Shuffle', which was a good party number but it didn't represent the band as we were more into jazz, rock and blues. To our great surprise, it was a hit."

Tony Ashton (777): "Roy and I found Kim Gardner in the Speakeasy and he was a bass player. We got signed up by Deep Purple's management. We did one album and then during the recording for the second album, we came up with 'Resurrection Shuffle'. We became a pop act and we ended up doing the cabaret circuit when we wanted to be an underground band. I can see now that 'Resurrection Shuffle' stands up as a classy rocker but I wanted it on a B-side. It went to No.2 and George Harrison was No.1 with 'My Sweet Lord.'"

Joe Fagin (778) of the Strangers had a Top 10 hit with 'That's Living Alright', the theme from the original *Auf Wiedersehen, Pet.* "When the series was written, Dave Mackay and I were asked to submit some songs for the series and we wrote three, and Dave also wrote 'That's Livin' Alright' with an American he knew. We had the plot, and I must say that the song was perfect for the series, which was wonderfully scripted and acted. However, having that hit record put me out of work as people started thinking, 'Oh, he's got a hit record, he'll cost a fortune' and I lost out on a lot of my bread and butter work doing commercials: I've done Nivea ("Nivea knows how to treat a lady"), Mars and the "Everybody needs bottle" for milk. If they wanted someone who sounded like Joe Cocker or Bob Seger, they would give me a call. I don't know why – I don't think that Joe Cocker and I sound close." Well, I said when I met him on his houseboat, you've both got lived-in voices. "Oh, this voice has been lived-in alright." Joe also crops up in films and TV series and he appeared in the gangland movie, *The Long Good Friday*.

David Garrick (779) had hits in Germany and has maintained his career: "I had the penthouse, I had the Rolls-Royce, but they belonged to the management, and a lot of people had the same problems as me and I had lost everything by 1970. Around 1992, someone from Holland wanted me to do a TV special and when I went on stage in front of 20,000 people, it was incredible. The work has been piling up since. There is so much work since the Berlin Wall came down that I don't need to work in the UK at all." Not one for standing still, David Garrick released a CD of arias, *Apassionata*, in 1999. Bob Wooler was impressed but added, "I didn't like his unshaven look. Designer stubble is only okay in young people."

John Kinrade (780) of the Escorts: "We were a limited company and it had got down to about £5 a week each. We thought it was time to call it a day. If we weren't playing in Liverpool, we had to pay for the road manager and the hotel and the expenses, and we weren't making anything out of it. In the months before we split up, we were playing in Liverpool more because we didn't have those expenses. It was also the one place where we were really popular."

Mike Gregory of the Escorts joined Terry Sylvester in the Swinging Blue Jeans, but Terry then had an opportunity to join the Hollies. **Mike Gregory (781)** left the Swinging Blue Jeans in 1972. He told me in 1984, "I worked with Clodagh Rodgers and played bass on some tracks on the Bay City Rollers' *Once Upon A Star*, which was a No.1 album. I've been playing for some time in Big John's Rock'n'Roll Circus, which is now called the Rock'n'Roll Circus. We do old rock 'n' roll songs, although we don't dress like Teds, and we've made three albums. When I see some of the tripe that gets in, I'm amazed that I haven't made it somewhere. Never mind, I've been plodding on for the last 20 years, and I'm ready for the next 20." It's now 2004 and Mike still leads the Rock'n'Roll Circus around the UK. Their latest CD is a tribute to the Beach Boys.

John Gustafson (782) became a noted session guitarist, playing with Roxy Music and being featured on the original cast album of *Jesus Christ Superstar* and he wrote Status Quo's 1982 hit 'Dear John'. "I had a pub band in London called Rowdy. I saw Status Quo's manager and he asked me if he could play some of our songs to Quo. They recorded 'Dear John', which did well in the charts. I liked the way they did it. It was rock'n'roll for sure, and I'm a dyed-in-the-wool rock'n'roller."

Clive Hornby (783) of the Dennisons appeared in the Liverpool Playhouse's production of John Lennon's *In His Own Write* in 1968 and then found national fame through playing Jack Sugden in *Emmerdale:* "I enjoyed my time in the Dennisons, but I've never regretted going into *Emmerdale*. I've had some great storylines and we've had 10 million viewers. When they had the plane crash in *Emmerdale* in 1993, Jack Sugden had to speak in the pulpit and it was a lovely speech about how he had lost his family and friends."

Billy Kinsley of the Merseybeats has had hits as part of Liverpool Express with his compositions 'You Are My Love' and 'Every Man Must Have A Dream' and he has produced many records at his studio in Crosby. Several of them involve the Class Of 64, a fluid group of Liverpool musicians from the Sixties who perform songs written by Kinsley, Alan Crowley (Tuxedos) and Frankie Connor (Hideaways). **Billy Kinsley (784)** is a jobbing musician with lots of jobs: "We backed Chuck Berry on a TV special in 1972 and everyone was wondering about the delay. We were all plugged in and the cameramen were cheesed off. Then after about two hours, it was all of a sudden, 'Let's go' and we were off. Chuck Berry was being paid £2,000 for the show and he wouldn't play a note until he got the money in cash and in advance. If you watch the show, you can see the money in his back pocket." In 2003 I chaired a radio discussion on the future of Liverpool music. When Paul Hemmings said that he had left the La's because he was fed up with doing the same songs, Billy said, "Well, I've been doing the same songs since 1962."

Jud Lander of the Hideaways found a career in the music business in London and he has been involved with the promotion of Abba, Buffy Sainte-Marie and many other acts. He played harmonica on Culture Club's 'Karma Chameleon' and several other hit records.

Jackie Lomax (785) of the Undertakers made several solo records including 'Sour Milk Sea', produced and written by George Harrison, for the Apple label. He added backing vocals to Rod Stewart's 'Foolish Behaviour'. "Apple released its first four singles on the same day – there was 'Hey Jude', 'Those Were The Days', 'Sour Milk Sea' and something by the Black Dyke Mills Band. It was not a good move as they couldn't expect airplay for all four singles at once. The other labels would have complained to the BBC, so I lost out there." Jackie has made several solo albums, coming to Liverpool to promote *The Ballad Of Liverpool Slim* in 2003.

George's sister, **Louise Harrison (786)**: "Our parents were never overly impressed by Frank Sinatra and Tony Bennett recording George's songs, but then nothing much impressed them – they were Liverpudlians. They were always in control and they answered the thousands of letters we were getting as best they could. They took it in their stride really well. Lots of Beatle fans got letters from my parents and they have kept them. I am always coming across letters that my parents have written as fans have them as their most treasured possessions. I am so proud of what they did. I have lots of photos of my mum and dad and they are always smiling at each other. They were always laughing and poking fun at each other."

Beryl Marsden (787): "The Gunnell agency ruled the London clubs and everything else down there They had Georgie Fame, Geno Washington, Chris Farlowe, you name it: they were managing them. They had the best clubs there, so you'd play at the best clubs. They wanted a band to mould into a supergroup and it was Shotgun Express. They didn't consider the different personalities because there were very strong personalities in that band. I don't think that Rod Stewart was quite confident enough to go solo at the time. The records could have been tons better, but it was a brilliant band with so much going for it. We were very young, very vibrant and quite fiery, and could have done great things, but the record company didn't know what to do with us and chose bland songs and our records were only average. It wasn't a reflection of what we were doing live. Peter Green wanted to form a band and asked me if I was interested but I decided to come back to Liverpool."

In the 1970s Beryl Marsden returned to Liverpool and worked with Paddy Chambers in the soul band, Sinbad. She has made cutting-edge singles like 'I Video' and has also made new age music as part of Beautiful World. She is featured on the soundtrack of *Tarzan And The Lost City* (1998) and released her first solo album, *One Dream*, in 2004. Many Merseybeat musicians think it is unfair that Cilla Black should be a big star and Beryl Marsden is hardly known. **Beryl Marsden (788)** doesn't see it that way.

"We're totally different types of singer with completely different approaches to music. Cilla is a family entertainer while I'm more of a singer. People ask me why I didn't make it and Cilla did, but such questions are ridiculous. Making it isn't about making a million pounds, but about being happy with what you do."Like her friend Sandie Shaw, she is a Buddhist and says that "it keeps me centred, gives me hope."

None of the Mersey Beat musicians became politicians, although Mick Groves of the Spinners became a councillor on the Wirral. However, some of their audience became MPs – Steven Norris, Edwina Currie – and Peter Sissons became a TV newsreader.

IV. Let's Do The Time Warp Again

One of the first indications of a 60s revival was the *Liverpool Explosion* tour of 1979. It was a silly title because two of the seven acts weren't from Merseyside, but **Tony Crane (789)** of the Merseybeats was glad that it happened: "There was ourselves, Gerry and the Pacemakers, Wayne Fontana, the Swinging Blue Jeans, Dave Berry, the Fourmost and Billy J. Kramer. The promoters wanted everybody to travel separately but I said, 'We hardly see each other these days. Why don't we travel together in a big, coach?' We had a fantastic time reliving all the old days and the tour was just as successful as it would have been in the 1960s. A lot of people who remembered us came along, but there were a lot of teenagers too. Groups like the Jam have modelled themselves on bands from the 1960s and the teenagers wanted to see what the originals were like."

Many of the key performers from the Sixties were happy playing cabaret clubs, doing a fly-past of their 60s singles. **Andy Roberts (790)** of the poetry-rock band Liverpool Scene raises a very significant point. "If you go right back to the beginning of the Beatles' recording career and listen to their audition tape for Decca, you'll hear things like 'Besame Mucho'. They were doing cabaret songs and I've since realised that all a lot of the groups wanted to be was a good cabaret band. That's what was acceptable to their parents in the early 1960s and it was regarded as real singing. If you played cabaret, you got good money, wore good gear and stayed in nice hotels. It was only peripheral for such groups to have records in the charts." Maybe *Phoenix Nights* is as much as a documentary as a comedy series.

Paul Du Noyer (791): "Bands of that generation saw themselves as entertainers first, and the Beatles are the exception that proves the rule. They were the first to accept that the recording studio was the medium where they did their best work. Also, most of the Liverpool musicians were working class lads and they were much more earthy and not college boys like the southern groups. It was the southern groups who moved into psychedelia first as it was more intellectual and well away from the beer and football culture that most groups belonged to."

John McNally (792): "The Tremeloes went through a stage where they refused to do their hits on stage. They played rock'n'roll and they lost work because of it. Contracts now stipulate that you must play your hits – the contracts say, 'Searchers as known'. If you deviate from that, they can dock your pay. Most of our hits stand up reasonably well but there are couple that I am not happy playing. We usually throw 'Sugar And Spice in a medley!"

Billy May (793): "I alternated between the Pathfinders and the Valkyries then and they have come together as the Pathfinders now. I took voluntary redundancy from Vauxhall in 1980 and took a chance on playing in pubs at £10 a go and it was a success. I am the only solo act to do 'Bohemian Rhapsody' without backing tapes. It's a scream as everybody joins in with the bit in the middle I get a sheet out which has got hundreds of songs on and people can choose from that. The set never seems to work if you plan it. I go round for a few minutes before each performance and get their requests off them and that gives a start to the night and they start shouting them at me. If it's one of their favourite songs, they can get up and sing with me too. I don't mind, I just do them off the cuff."

Mike Pender (794): "Good old 'Farmer John'. We've seen him a number of times over the years. You always get somebody in the audience, especially when you're playing down in Torquay, out in the sticks. You always get a few farmers in. I always say, 'Is Farmer John in tonight?' and they love the song."

Billy J. Kramer (795) became a highly paid club act. By the 1980s, his voice has considerably deepened and his greasy quiff has been replaced by fluffy blond streaks. Permanent wave rather than New Wave, he had his life in perspective. He told me in 1980: "I've got as much enthusiasm as I used to have, but I've reached the stage where I can go on, take a suit out of a bag and become Billy J. Kramer for an hour. After that hour I take the suit off and I put him away for the night. I don't want to lead a show business life. I prefer to do normal things such as digging my vegetable patch. I've been offered handsome sums to give my autobiography to newspapers but I'll never do it because I know what they want. I've been quite sick at what some people have said. I know a lot about some artists' lives and they know a lot about mine, but no matter how skint I become, I'll never talk about those things to make myself a few quid." Billy said that to me in 1980 and he is a man of integrity as there is still no sign of a book.

The Fourmost were a very popular cabaret act during the 1970s, but eventually singer Brian O'Hara was the only original member left. When he left, the Fourmost continued with no original members, but resisted a name change to the Fraud Most, the Fourleast or the Four Almost.

John Gustafson (796): "Keep moving on, got to make a living. It's partly luck. If you strike the right set of personalities, it can go on for years like Dire Straits and the Who. I've just been unlucky with some volatile personalities. It's a combination of that and being fired and getting fed up with it or whatever. For example, the Merseybeats fired me because they wanted Billy Kinsley back. The old pals' act, I guess. Tony Crane was friends with Billy Kinsley long before he was friends with me. I was never really a Merseybeat, I was just a hired hand, a mercenary. I became the eternal sideman but I've liked it. I have no problem with that at all."

Howie Casey (797): "Paul asked me to work on *Band On The Run* and he wanted me to do a solo on 'Bluebird'. Then I was told that they wanted to film me learning the solo to 'Bluebird', which was a load of cods as I gone to the studio, played a take and that was it. I wanted to do something more technical but Paul said he liked that little slurpy thing. I had to stand in the middle of Abbey Road studio and Paul is going (sings) and I have to follow him. When we did 'Silly Love Songs', Paul was at the piano and knew exactly what he wanted me to play. He is open to suggestions. I put a few extra licks in 'Silly Love Songs' when they sing 'I love you'. I was messing about, but they kept it in. The chord at end of 'Silly Love Songs' is also something I suggested."

After leaving the Roadrunners, Mike Hart released two highly personal collection of songs, *Mike Hart Bleeds* (1969) and *Basher, Chalky, Pongo And Me* (1972). Typical of the waywardness of his career, the CD reissue on See For Miles calls him Mark Hart down the spine. **John Cornelius (798)**: "I place Mike Hart on the same pedestal as Bob Dylan and John Lennon, I thought he was that good. He let himself down in the way that he conducted himself but in my opinion he was the genuine article, a Woody Guthrie who led a rolling stone lifestyle. It is typical that nobody knows where he is today. He was a very gifted songwriter, great singer and a great performer, and charismatic as well, but he didn't give a damn. He was happy playing to a handful of people and some of the most stupendous performances I have seen from anybody have been from him performing to five or six people in Jesse's in Hope Street or O'Connor's on an off night. It made no difference to him that there was only a handful of people there. On a bigger, more organised show, he might fail to turn up or give a very desultory, perfunctory performance, but he was a genius."

I always enjoy meeting Kenny Johnson. It may be just me but I always feel that if John Lennon hadn't become a superstar, he would have ended up like Kenny. Their personalities seem to be very close. **Brian Linford (799)**: "I was at a firm's dance and Kenny Johnson's band was on. As we danced around the floor, he shouted, 'There's that bloke who sacked us from the Mardi Gras.' We had sacked him because country music didn't fit in with the music policy of the club, but I didn't think he'd remember this."

It's a long way from being all over, baby blue. **Bob Wooler (800)** was a keen supporter of local charity such as the Roy Castle Foundation and Merseycats: "I applaud Don and Lin Andrew – Don was with the Remo Four – for setting up the Merseycats charity in the 1980s. Many groups like the Fourmost, the Dennisons and Earl Preston and the TT's have reformed for Merseycats events. So many musicians have come out of retirement and when they announced the Big Three at the Philharmonic Hall, nine musicians came out to play! I admire them for the thousands they have raised for charity, but I didn't attend when they made me an honorary member of the Merseycats at a show at the Grafton. They offered me a lift, but I do hate a fuss being made of me."

The reformed Big Three did not include Adrian, Gus or Hutch. **Johnny Hutch (801)** may not have made it to the top, but he knows he was the best. He said in 1984, "I haven't played since the Big Three broke up, and I think most of the Merseybeat revivals are a load of rubbish. I've still got my drums, I'll never let them go, but the only way I'd do it now is to go back with a couple of musicians who are as good as Griff and Gus. I'd practise for six or eight months and then I'd go out and knock everybody flat." It's 2004 and it hasn't happened.

Tommy Hughes (802): "In the Sixties, we wanted the other groups to be rubbish so we would sound good. Now I want everybody that plays to be brilliant. I wouldn't like younger people to hear them and say, 'That's a load of rubbish.' We are playing better now than we ever did as we have got better equipment now and we are more experienced. There are many good musicians in the Merseycats."

Bob Wooler (803): "I was very impressed with the Mersey Beat edition of *Rock Family Trees* on BBC-2 during 1998. They picked a very positive bunch of people, some of whom were comfortably well off and some of whom like Mike Pender of the Searchers looked extremely good for their age. I did, however, detect a degree of sadness about the whole thing, and I rather liked that undertone. Even Geoff Nugent of the Undertakers who is normally very enthusiastic came out with penetrating observations."

John McNally (804): "I'm not proud of it but there is a bad side to me that says we must always be the best act on the bill. We're often on with Gerry and I'm proud to say that 'When You Walk In The Room' can beat 'You'll Never Walk Alone' as it is a really strong song. We also have the lights and pyros which gives us an advantage over Gerry."

Pete Shotton (805): "John Lennon never changed fundamentally, and I knew him since he was seven years old. The fame, the money, the status he achieved, never affected the fundamental person that he was. He was a classic example of what Kirk Douglas said, 'Success doesn't change you, it changes the people around you.' A lot of people do change and become full of their own self-importance, but that never happened to John, maybe because he was pretty self-important from the time when I first met him. He had a great belief in himself and he always had enormous confidence in himself. People were always attracted to him because of his great confidence and terrific humour which everybody likes. Very quick, you didn't banter words with him as you were on a loser before you started."

Billy J. Kramer (806): "I met Paul McCartney a couple of months age and he said to me, 'What are you doing now, Billy?' I said, 'I'm thinking of learning to play the piano.' He said, 'Go on and do it. The time you spend thinking about doing it could be spent doing it.' That's how positive a thinker he is."

13 PHOENIX RISING

I. The Cavern
II. The mourning of John Lennon

"If they make all this fuss about John Lennon,
what's going to happen when Ken Dodd goes?"
(Scouser in a pub to Alan Bleasdale, 1980)

I. The Cavern

In March 1964 Radio Luxembourg started *Sunday Night at the Cavern* hosted by Bob Wooler and capturing its hectic pace. The Cavern's owner, **Ray McFall (807)**, recalls, "It was a weekly show on Radio Luxembourg lasting half an hour and it would be of typical Liverpool groups, which Bob would arrange. He would also write the script and present the show. They decided to do it fortnightly with two shows in a night and Bob didn't like that. He would write one script and be doing the other during the first show. He suffered from last minuteitis, but it all went off well and the programmes were very enjoyable."

Some of the second-generation Liverpool groups were very good. The Clayton Squares, the Roadrunners, the Kubas (who made an LP as the Koobas) and the Hideaways were all popular at the Cavern. The Hideaways performed 'You've Got To Hide Your Love Away' as 'You've Got To Love Your Hideaway'. They made 412 appearances at the Cavern between 1964 and 1970, over 120 more than the Beatles and not topped by anyone else. A live EP included with the German book *Beat In Liverpool* and featuring the Hideaways and the Clayton Squares shows how enthusiastic Merseyside audiences were as they joined in the singing, but the recording quality is abysmal.

Dave Jones (808): "The Escorts and the Hideaways were my Beatles and my Pacemakers. I followed them both round Liverpool for about two years. The PA and the band equipment were rudimentary but it didn't matter. You were listening to their numbers and wondering if their rendition was better than Earl Preston's or anybody else's."

Ozzie Yue (809): "John Shell was born in Dallas and because his mum was married to an American serviceman, he had American citizenship. He got his conscription papers and he came here for six weeks leave before he went out to Vietnam. He was only out there three months before he was killed in action. It was just a week after he got the purple heart for being wounded in action. He had wanted to get out and see the world, he had seen it as an opportunity, but it was the wrong way of doing it."

Mike Evans (810): "We did the Blue Angel for Allan Williams and then Bob Wooler gave us 15 bookings in a row at the Cavern. Allan Williams wanted to be our manager but we had signed with Bob. He received a telegram from Allan which said, 'Congratulations on signing the Clayton Squares. Now take this knife out of my back.' They took it much more seriously than we did." Being Allan Williams, he messed that up too as he sent it as a Greetings Telegram.

Frankie Connor (811) of the Hideaways: "We played the Cavern nine times in the same week when we went full-time in 1965. We came on the second wave, we were 16 and 17, and we found Bob very trustworthy, and he was putting an agency together with Duggie Evans, the keyboard player from the Blue Angel. They had ourselves, the Clayton Squares, Michael Allen and the Masterminds and they were building a stable like Epstein. They got us work in Carlisle, we were going there once a month for three or four days at a time, and we did well on the east coast of Scotland. We were very visual and we were playing R&B, and we weren't a Beatle group. Bob had stopped his 'hi-fi high' stuff by then and simply introduced us by saying, 'R&B as you like it with the Hideaways'. Paddy Delaney had a wonderful voice too and they used to fight in a mock way about introducing us. Bob gave us some advice: he said, 'I don't think you should learn too many difficult chords because the girls don't come to watch you play diminished chords and augmented chords. They are interested in what you are wearing and how your hair is cut. The image is important and should come first.'"

Mike Evans (812) of the Clayton Squares says the problem lay in getting the right line-up. "Arthur Megginson, our bass player, was completely tone deaf. I had to tune his instrument for him by turning the machine heads while he plucked the strings until it came in tune with a note I was simultaneously blowing on the sax. This became intolerable, but he was such a nice guy and we were such bastards that we couldn't tell him he should go. We devised this dreadful scheme whereby we convinced him he was going deaf by talking gradually quieter and quieter in his company until it got to the point where we mimed whole sentences in the van. We'd suddenly stop our conversations and he'd put his finger in his ear and shake his head and then we'd carry on as normal. He became convinced that something was going wrong with his ears and he went to a doctor who said, 'It's because you're playing all this loud music. You'll have to give it up.' He said, 'I'll have to leave the band because it's doing my ears a lot of harm.' We said, 'That's a shame, Meg.' I saw him about a month later and I said, 'Hello, Meg, how's your ear trouble?' He said, 'The doctor was right. Since I left the band, I've had no problems at all.'" It's a pity that the Beatles didn't dream up such a scheme for removing Pete Best.

A programme in the ITV series *The Sunday Break* was broadcast from the Cavern featuring the Dennisons, but the most prestigious feature was a live show for French television on 1 April 1965 starring Petula Clark. **Ray McFall (813)**: "That was a daring enterprise as there was no satellite television then and connecting the Cavern in Liverpool with a French studio was a monumental task, and the Post Office engineers needed two or three days to set up the landlines. Happily, it went well and Petula Clark sang 'I Know A Place', which could have been written about the Cavern."

Well, it was. Songwriter **Tony Hatch (814)**: "Absolutely, I wrote it about the Cavern. It may be coincidence but Brian Epstein's autobiography was called *A Cellarful Of Noise*, which is a line directly out of 'I Know A Place': 'It is a swinging place, a cellarful of noise.' Brian must have liked that song and borrowed the title."

Mike Evans (815) of the Clayton Squares: "Being managed by Bob Wooler meant that we appeared in every big event at the Cavern including the live programme for French television. Gene Vincent, Manfred Mann and Gerry and the Pacemakers also took part.

Don Arden came to the Cavern because he was managing Gene Vincent and he'd heard about the following we had in Liverpool. Girls were screaming and shouting and we went down better than anyone else, even though we were at the bottom of the bill. Don Arden offered Bob a 50-50 stake in the management of the Clayton Squares and he'd see that we recorded with Andrew Loog Oldham, the manager and record producer of the Rolling Stones. Even though I say it myself, we recorded an amazing version of Otis Redding's 'I've Been Loving You Too Long'. Andrew Loog Oldham was in his Phil Spector phase and we double-tracked and treble-tracked our saxophones. He recorded the keyboards six times and plastered them on top of each other. He recorded the drums three times and it sounded like a huge soul orchestra. There was a tape with all this on, but Oldham had a bust-up with Don Arden and it never got released."

For some years, there had been a need for good recording facilities in Liverpool and Ray McFall's plans for his own, Cavern Sound label, were ill-fated. It was a low key operation with only 2,500 copies of its first single 'An American Sailor at the Cavern' by Phil Brady and the Ranchers being pressed, and by 1965 it was running into debt as **Ray McFall (816)** explains. "A lot of people were still coming to the Cavern but our profitability suffered because we were not licensed. Also, unlike some promoters, we always paid our groups and that can be expensive. We had opened a recording studio, which we should not have attempted without taking professional advice, particularly about marketing. I had taken over the premises next door and the studios were in the basement. For altruistic reasons, the Cavern financially supported *Mersey Beat,* which was a long haul for no return at all. We also had sanitation problems." Yes, well…

A drain on the resources if nowhere else, sanitation had had been a problem from the outset as there were only three toilets and a urinal in the Cavern. A club of comparable size opening today would have to provide three times that number. An appalling discovery meant that the toilet facilities had to be drastically improved.

Liverpool has an underground railway connecting it to Birkenhead and the Wirral. Underneath the city centre was a spot that the drivers used for changing carriages. They complained that water was dripping onto them and their clothing. An analysis was made and the liquid was identified as sewage. The trouble was traced to the Cavern.

After the war, 10 Mathew Street had been used by an importer of Irish bacon. Blocks of ice were used for refrigeration and any melted ice ran off down a drain into a sump. When the Ministry of Food took over the premises, it was assumed that the drains ran into a sewer and so toilets were also installed. Few people were working there and the toilets were flushed only 20 or 30 times a day. When the Cavern opened, 600 people in a single session could be served with soup and Coca-Cola. The sweaty atmosphere would make them drink more, and there would be over 600 patrons using the facilities twice a night in a single session. A gigantic cesspool collected and its squalid contents seeped through the brickwork and onto the hapless railwaymen.

The public authorities had no choice: the Cavern was ordered to close until the pool was cleared and new toilets connected to proper drainage were installed. The cost would be £3,500. The closure was delayed when a company on the ground floor allowed the Cavern the use of their toilets at night. However, the arrangement was doomed to failure. The Cavern's staff grew tired of cleaning the toilets at midnight, and the workers coming in the next morning were horrified by the mess.

Bob Wooler (817): "The Cavern needed a lot of money to correct its drains and ventilation. The whole place was like a Turkish bath as we believed in BO, and that's Box Office and Body Odour. It was the sweat smell of success. The ventilation was State of the Ark and had packed in long ago and this is why I thought I was going to get TB because we were breathing each other's breath and everybody smoked. It was primitive and really terrible. I'll never forget Ted Knibbs saying to me when the Cavern was failing in 1965, 'You know the trouble with the Cavern: it's suffering from fallen arches.' I wish I'd said that." When I repeated this line to Ray McFall, he said, "Bob might have improved upon it and said, 'McFallen arches'.

Bob Wooler (818) continued: "Ray was very lucky and escaped criticism until a disaster happened at some club in Blackburn. The civic authorities thought they'd better take a look at the Liverpool clubs and unfortunately for Ray, the Cavern was the club in the news. They said, 'You've got no back exit, so you'll have to do something about it. Where's your ventilation, and where's all the waste from your toilets going?' These, as it happens, were very good questions. We learnt that the sewage was just going into the ground and I thought, 'My god, not only am I going to get TB, I'm going to get the plague as well.' You can't blame me for popping a few pills now and then to help me make it through the night."

The Beatles played the Liverpool Empire on 5 December 1965 on what was to be their last Liverpool appearance. **Bob Wooler (819)**: "The Beatles were accosted by the press when they were playing the Liverpool Empire. They had just done *Help!*, but they weren't giving any. The press were asking punchy questions such as 'The Cavern is on the ropes, so what are you going to do about it?' They said they couldn't help out but they could have done, they were rolling in cash. The key is in something Ringo said. He said, 'We owe nothing to the Cavern. We've done them a favour and made them famous.' You can't argue with that, but where was their generosity? It would only have been £2,000 a Beatle."

The Cavern closed on Monday 28 February 1966 and I've recorded different accounts of the weekend. **Billy Butler (820)**: "We were told on the Sunday night by Ray McFall that this was going to be the club's last session. My first thought was that we can't shut without a fanfare and Chris Wharton, who was a partner of mine at the time, and myself went round the Liverpool clubs and said that the Cavern was shutting, 'If you want to come down and play, this could be your last chance.' The momentum built up and about half-past eleven, I said, 'Let's block the stairway with chairs and stay here as long as we can, and anyone who wants to leave can go down the side alley. The bailiffs came at nine in the morning and couldn't get in. I went down the alley and went to work at one o'clock because I was working during the day, and, as far as my boss knew, I was at Gladstone Dock doing customs work. I phoned up a few mates, did a little bit to show I'd been there, and then went back to the Cavern, but by then the bailiffs were in."

The club's doorman, **Paddy Delaney (821)**: "It was a typical Sunday night at the Cavern. Ray McFall came to the club about 9.30 and said, 'The bailiff will be here tomorrow morning at ten o'clock.' I was bewildered as I knew he had spent a hell of a lot of money on extensions. He said, 'Instead of finishing at 11.15, let's stay open all night and let everybody in for nothing.' So we carried on. The girls started crying and going into hysterics, and we didn't know how we were going to get them out. At six o'clock they put the chairs on the steps leading down to the club. They intertwined the chairs with each other so that no one could get up or down. The front door was shut and we blockaded ourselves in. I gave instructions that the kids could resist the bailiffs, but not the police. We let the police in when they arrived and the kids were escorted outside. I was kept back because the kids felt I should be the last one to leave. I made my way out of the Cavern into Mathew Street and that was it: the Cavern was officially closed."

One of the groups at that final session was Rory Storm and the Hurricanes. **Jimmy Tushingham (822)** recalls, "As soon as we had finished our show, Rory went up to Bob Wooler and said, 'Have you got the money, Bob?' He said, 'I'll get it for you.' Next minute chairs and tables had been stacked at the bottom of the stairs and nobody could get in or out. Ray McFall had gone bust and we were one of the creditors trying to obtain our £15. We never got it."

Ray McFall (823): "I had nothing to do with the siege. I was outside looking like a bloody undertaker. I went down in the morning and I was dressed immaculately in black. From my personal point of view, I made a dreadful mistake by not making the Cavern a limited company so that the creditors came after me personally, but it's history and very personal too. My solicitor was surprised that the lease fetched as much as it did. If he had taken a lien on it, he could have defrayed his costs, but instead he had to stand in line with everybody else."

Billy Butler (824) organised a protest march. "I remember us all walking up Lord Street singing 'Still I'm Sad', the Yardbirds' song which was popular at the time, and we laid a wreath over the Cavern's doorway. Everyone got down on their knees for a minute's silence and that wreath stayed over the doorway until the flowers died. A few weeks later we handed a petition to Harold Wilson at Lime Street Station, and this led to him reopening the Cavern."

The Cavern was sold by the court receiver after bankruptcy proceedings. The new owners were Joe Davey, the owner of the popular Joe's Café in the city centre, and Alf Geoghegan, a butcher who had been on the boards as Alf, the Lightning Cartoonist. They gave the club a facelift without destroying its atmosphere and some poor souls resolved the drainage for the toilets.

Bob Wooler (825): "Bessie Braddock MP was jumping on the bandwagon by saying she would get the Prime Minister, Harold Wilson, to reopen the club if the necessary work could be done. She was true to her word, but she was annoyed that we now had a liquor licence. She saw the Cavern as a youth club, which in a way it was."

Even now, well into Tony Blair's premiership, there can't be many beat clubs that have been opened by Prime Ministers, but on 23 July 1966 the Cavern was officially reopened by Harold Wilson. For his trouble, he was presented with a pipe made out of wood from the Cavern's original stage. Ken Dodd and MP Bessie Braddock were present. The musicians included the Carrolls, a family of brothers and sisters which included Irene Carroll, now better known as impressionist and actress Faith Brown. The Hideaways, who had been the last group to play at the Cavern, were the first on stage. Harold Wilson suggested that each group booked by the club should agree to appear annually for the next 25 years for the same fee. Obvious, I suppose, from the man who coined the phrase, "the pound in your pocket".

Alf Geoghegan would have approved as he held tight to the purse strings. **C.P. Lee (826)**: "St. Louis Union was a Manchester group who had a hit with 'Girl'. They were with Kennedy Street Enterprises and they split up leaving Kennedy Street with some future bookings. Rather than cancel them a few of us were asked to become St. Louis Union and we had a booking for £50 at the Cavern where, amongst other things, we did a shambolic version of 'Girl'. We were booked for two 45 minutes sets and the person who was running the evening was at the side of the stage with a stopwatch. He said, 'You were tuning up for four minutes. You introduced the numbers for so long and we pay you to sing and not talk, and you had the audience laughing instead of dancing.' He made all these deductions and we ended up with £16."

The Cavern continued to be successful under another new owner, Roy Adams, but the underground railway led to another problem. The network was to be extended and the Cavern's site was needed for an extraction duct. The notice to quit was incorrectly addressed and Roy Adams found he had only a week to vacate the premises. He was granted a stay of execution until 27 March 1973. Then the bulldozers moved in, the Cavern was buried in rubble, and after the railway was completed, the site became a car-park.

Across the road in the old Fruit Exchange, Roy Adams opened the New Cavern Club which held 2,000 people. He booked heavy metal chart names. The Radio City DJ, Pete Price, organised the funding for a Beatles statue, the work of the ardent Communist and Catholic sculptor, Arthur Dooley. The representation of the Beatles on the outside wall of the New Cavern had religious overtones and the inscription, "Four lads who shook the world".

Another sculpture above the door of The Beatles Shop was organised by three fans – John Chambers, Gene Grimes and Leslie Priestley, and in nearby Stanley Street, there is Eleanor Rigby. Tommy Steele charged the City of Liverpool half a sixpence for the placing of his statue in Stanley Street, adjoining Mathew Street. Eleanor Rigby is a Liverpool landmark and she often had flowers in her lap, the gift of 'Mad Margie', who ran the themed café, Lucy In The Sky With Diamonds, the most distinctive café in the area with its juke-box and memorabilia.

The New Cavern Club went through changes of ownership and name. In 1976 Roger Eagle opened the premises as Eric's, which became a leading venue for New Wave music, the Clash making a memorable appearance in 1977. Eric's led to a second Liverpool explosion as more local talent found national fame. Like John and Paul, Elvis Costello would have been successful in any time and any age; and other chart names included China Crisis, Echo and the Bunnymen, A Flock of Seagulls, Frankie Goes To Hollywood, the Lotus Eaters, Orchestral Manoeuvres in the Dark, Teardrop Explodes and The Mighty Wah!.

II. The mourning of John Lennon

Paul Du Noyer (827): "You can take the boy out of Liverpool but you can't take the Liverpool out of the boy. John was very proud of his Liverpool roots, particularly in his last years when he was living in New York. He got very homesick, and he regarded New York as a Liverpool that had got its act together. He was set to come back here and he was going to do a world tour in 1981."

The first Beatle Conventions, organised by Bob Wooler and Allan Williams, took place in the late Seventies. They attracted some fans, but they were not regarded as very successful. They were loath to continue them, and that might have been the end of it but for one thing: the murder of John Lennon in December 1980. Scores of people brought flowers and placed them in the doorway under Arthur Dooley's statue. Mathew Street was a focal point for local people wanting to talk about John. Messages and poems stayed there for weeks.

Bob Wooler (828): "It's extraordinary really but from the moment that John Lennon was shot by a crackpot, the whole attitude towards the Beatles changed. Everyone became Beatleised, and Beatle Conventions have done very well since that date. Sam Leach organised a very big candlelight vigil on St.George's Plateau in Lime Street. I was there helping out and so was Allan Williams. We stood on the steps leading up to St. George's Hall and there were candles galore. David Shepherd, the Bishop of Liverpool, was there with other luminaries. There was a two minute silence, although the traffic didn't stop. The weather was kind to us, it was free, it was extremely well attended and it was very touching. I felt then that there was a rebirth, a renaissance of the Beatles. It got dark very early and then there was a parade of groups throughout the evening."

A Liverpool architect, David Backhouse, was motivated by John Lennon's death into developing the Cavern site. He approached Royal Insurance. Because the group's head office is in Liverpool, it had a long-standing association with the city. Cavern Walks was built and, unlike other precincts in the city, the first shops stocked high quality, designer goods. It is a fabulous building with many intriguing features, not least the floral designs by Cynthia Lennon above the entrances.

Bob Wooler (829): "The statue of the Beatles in Cavern Walks cost tens of thousands of pounds and it is a monstrosity. As Mike McCartney succinctly said when he unveiled it, 'I wouldn't have recognised our kid if he wasn't playing the guitar left-handed.' Perhaps I will meet someone who will put me wise as to why it is excellent and entirely befitting of the global phenomenon it is supposed to depict, but until that happens, I will continue to think of it as pathetic. They don't look like the Beatles and why do they have their backs to each other?" As all four Beatles look alike, I suspect that an Everyman point is being made, but as the four bronze Beatles resemble the sculptor, John Doubleday, it may be wish-fulfillment.

Cavern Walks not only recreates the structure of the old Cavern, but also expands it with a second stage and, most significantly, a fire exit. 15,000 of the original bricks were used in its construction. All the bricks were rescued from the rubble and another 5,000 were sold with plaques for charity. I bought mine for £5 and it is best investment I ever made as a Cavern brick will fetch £300 at a Beatles auction today. I should have bought a wall.

In March 1984 former Merseybeat musicians were invited to sign the wall behind the stage at the new Cavern club. Many of them went to the White Star first, a nearby pub that is as unrefined now as it was in the Sixties. Whenever someone aged between 35 and 45 entered, there was widespread speculation: "Wasn't he in a group?" I had assumed that the musicians would still know or recognize each other but this was not so. Many were actually meeting for the first time because there had been so many groups and venues on Merseyside that they rarely got together. Norman Kuhlke of the Swinging Blue Jeans was stopped outside the club by someone who said, "You'll get free booze if you go through that entrance and say you played in a group." However, all the signatures on the wall did seem legitimate.

Observing all this was like watching umpteen editions of *This Is Your Life* rolled into one. Musicians who hadn't met in twenty years hugged each other, but every conversation was interrupted by another old friend. There was much catching-up to be done, especially as many had brought along their wives, children and even grandchildren. Many of the musicians had married their fans.

After all this time, some had difficulty recognizing old friends. Clive Hornby was at a disadvantage as everyone knew him from *Emmerdale Farm*. Another Dennison, Steve McLaren, looked scarcely twenty-five, while age had taken its toll on others. Gus Travis with his sleek black hair had worked on his appearance, while Lee Curtis in white tuxedo and medallion looked like a star.

Whenever possible, groups assembled in their original line-ups to sign the coloured squares on the wall. The Swinging Blue Jeans went on stage, followed by the Dennisons, the Undertakers, the Merseybeats and the Fourmost. Hank Walters went up with his Dusty Road Ramblers and said, "I've also signed for a couple of the lads who've died. They'd have wanted to be included." Very country.

A young boy blocked the photographers view as Lee Curtis was about to sign the wall. He was asked to move and replied, "It's all right. It's only Grandad."

Roy Brooks of Roy Brooks and the Dions watched quietly as better known musicians signed the wall. When his turn came, he chose one of the larger boxes and in bold lettering wrote "ROY BROOKS AND THE DIONS", close to, but bigger than, the Beatles' name. That sheer cheek is one of the themes of this book.

In March 1984 the Cavern club was opened by the Liverpool defender and new owner, Tommy Smith. Gerry Marsden with his new Pacemakers were the first on stage. **Bob Wooler (830)**:"What does the top part of Cavern Walks remind you of? It is a tall building in a narrow street and it reminds me of the Dakota. You can see it at the beginning of *Rosemary's Baby*, although it had no particular significance then. I asked the architect David Backhouse about it and he said that he had modelled it on a Victorian building, but I think that the Dakota, which is of the Victorian age, may have been subconsciously in his mind. I am impressed by the new Cavern and I appreciate that they have had to add all the trappings and trimmings. I am very glad about the air-conditioning, but the absence of the bandroom with all its fond memories is too much for me to accept."

Part of the Cavern Walks complex was Cavern Mecca, a Beatles' souvenir and information centre run by two dedicated fans, Jim and Liz Hughes. Encouraged by

Allan Williams and Bob Wooler, they were good people who had the right ideas for Beatles festivals but although they appreciated its potential, it affected their health and they left the city. At the same time, although Tommy Smith was a suitably high-profile owner, he did not embrace the club's history and was more concerned with making a success of the Abbey Road pub above it.

Following on from Jim and Liz, a schoolteacher Bill Heckle and a taxi driver Dave Jones discovered how Beatles festivals could work and their annual events have grown and grown. Eventually, they became the owners of the Cavern and they knew what the club needed, organising both contemporary and retrospective events. After Paul McCartney played the Cavern in December 1999, it is easy to find successful acts who want the Cavern on their CV. Lonnie Donegan, Bo Diddley, Wishbone Ash and the Crickets have been among the guests, and when Bill Haley's Comets played, their lead guitarist, Franny Beecher, was 81 years old.

Considering that so many of Liverpool's clubs have been owned by gangsters, it is refreshing to meet Bill and Dave, who are genuine lovers of Sixties music. They also own the Cavern pub in Mathew Street which has valuable rock memorabilia on display and features acoustic-based live music. They have plans for A Hard Day's Night hotel and although Liverpool is overrun with hotels, this one should succeed because of its planned, Beatle-related uniqueness. I think Bill and Dave have escaped the city's gun culture because it is in the hoods' interests that the Cavern should succeed and bring people to the city.

Bill and Dave are the organisers of the annual Beatles festival, which incorporates a one-day festival at the Adelphi Hotel, events at several theatres and at the Cavern. It concludes with the all-embracing Mathew Street Festival where bands play in clubs, pubs and outdoor venues all over the city. There are too many tribute bands for my tastes and it is insulting to have bands representing their countries and not allow them to perform any music from their own culture, but it works superbly and, I suspect, that the audiences wouldn't come any other way. One year I was talking to a Beatles band, A Hard Day's Night, to discover that in the States, they worked as Ohio Express and two of them had played on the original singles.

In October 2003, I was impressed by the International Power Pop festival, based at the Cavern for a week and featuring young bands from around the world playing original music. This, to me, was more like it and I hope this develops and continues.

The first Beatles' exhibition was Beatle City in Seel Street, a lavish museum owned by the local radio station, Radio City. Many of the items were acquired at rock'n'roll auctions at Sotheby's and many of its exhibits were fascinating. I was astonished by the brevity of the contracts for booking the Beatles at the height of their fame. I went around with the pianist, Russ Conway, and he was intrigued by a wall chart listing all the Beatles' gigs. He put on his glasses and wanted to find a show he did with them in Llandudno. While he was studying the dates, an American came up and put his hand on his shoulder: "Gee, you really must love the Beatles," he said, "to be looking that closely."

Beatle City did not last but it has given way to the impressive Beatles Story at the Albert Dock. This was the brainchild of Mike Byrne, a fine vocalist for the

Roadrunners in the Sixties and now singing with Juke Box Eddie's. It is a regular part of the tourist trip and even in the winter, it can attract 500 visitors over a weekend. There is the occasional gig there, notably one with Chas McDevitt and the Quarrymen.

There is a Blue Plaque on John Lennon's house in Menlove Avenue and both that house and Paul McCartney's home in Forthlin Road are National Trust properties open to the public. Many of the sites that the Beatles played are on the tourist trail, and sometimes dedicated fans have taken to putting up plaques when the authorities fall short. In March 2004 a contingent from the Beatles British Fan Club descended on Arnold Grove, Wavertree to erect a plaque on George Harrison's childhood home. Unfortunately, nobody had told the homeowner and in a scene resembling Terry Jones in *Monty Python*, she came storming out and told the group to move on. Blunderwall, indeed.

Fellow musicians who visit Liverpool are keen to see the sites, and this can be a good photo-opportunity for them. When Van Morrison went into The Beatles Shop, the manager, Steve Bailey, went over to say hello. "No, no," said the minder, "No one speaks to Van." "That's a pity," said Steve, "I was only going to offer him staff discount."

Billy Butler (831): "Bob Wooler said that Mathew Street should be renamed Mythew Street and it was only by talking to him that I appreciated the damage that was being done by people not telling the truth. Other people repeat what they say and something that is untrue becomes the accepted fact." In a similar way, Bob has made me wonder about the history I learnt at school. Who's to say that we are not being given the 15th century equivalent of Beatle myths? History, it is sometimes said, is written by the winners, but much of the Beatle history comes from the losers.

Bob Wooler (832): "More than anything, I hate people who do not tell the truth about the past. People take liberties with things, and they think, 'No-one will remember, I can say what the hell I like.' I told Allan Williams, 'You'll be glad when I'm dead. There'll be no-one to correct you when you come out with your ridiculous statements.' He said, 'Well, I won't be the only one.' Of course, Allan is by no means the worst culprit. He may embroider his tales to make them more entertaining, but others do it to make themselves seem more important. Well, I have news for them all. This is my o-bitch-uary: I am coming back to haunt them. I am the Ghost of Mersey Beat Past. My demise will end the lies."

A MERSEYBEAT DISCOGRAPHY

This discography covers all UK record releases by Merseybeat acts up to the end of 1966 Performers who had little or no connection with Liverpool beat clubs are omitted. Hence, the exclusion of Billy Fury, Buddy Britten and Michael Cox, although I have included Johnny Gentle (whom the Beatles backed on a short Scottish tour). Also missing are the Vernons Girls and their offshoots, the Ladybirds and the Breakaways, although the Vernons had success by emphasizing their Scouse accents on 'You Know What I Mean' (Decca F 11450) and also recorded one of the better Beatles novelties, 'We Love The Beatles' (Decca F 11807), if that is not an oxymoron. Other Liverpool acts that recorded during the era included David Garrick, Ken Dodd, Lita Roza, the Spinners, Jimmy Tarbuck, Frankie Vaughan and, god help us, Freddie Lennon, John's father.

The UK catalogue numbers and release dates are given, and the chart statistics are taken from *British Hit Singles* (Guinness World Records), *The Billboard Book Of Top 40 Hits* (Billboard Books) and *Hit Bilanz – Deutsche Chart Singles, 1956-1980* (Taurus Press). A few other chart positions have been included when I have come across them or sought them out. The reason for giving the German hits is twofold: firstly, Germany was the Mersey groups' second home and secondly, so many of the performers told me that they had hits in Germany: in the original edition of *Let's Go Down The Cavern*, I took them at their word – this time I thought this needed to be verified. I confess that the artist whose claims I viewed with the most suspicion was David Garrick, but there it was – 'Dear Mrs. Applebee', a minor UK success, was a German No.1 early in 1967.

Pete Frame (833): "Only a few really stand up as great records, but I love them all because they were the soundtrack of my best years. I was riding around on a Vincent motorbike with a series of very lovely, comely wenches on the back. All we would do is listen to Merseybeat records. Every album that the Beatles released I remember the circumstances in which I first heard it, and you only do that with great records."

Adam, Mike & Tim

Little Baby / You're The Reason Why	(Decca F 12040, 12/64)
That's How I Feel / It's All Too True	(Decca F 12112, 3/65)
Little Pictures / Summer's Here Again	(Decca F 12221, 8/65)
Flowers On The Wall / Give That Girl A Break	(Columbia DB 7836, 2/66)
A Most Peculiar Man / Wedding Day	(Columbia DB 7902, 4/66)

Actually, Peter, Mike and Tim. Peter and Mike Sedgwick were joined by Tim Saunders for a close harmony group somewhere between the Beatles and the Bachelors. 'Little Baby' was an original song written by Les Reed and Barry Mason, but the switch to Columbia and covering US songs from the Statler Brothers ('Flowers On the Wall') and Simon & Garfunkel ('A Most Peculiar Man' with sitar) didn't increase sales.

Steve Aldo

Can I Get A Witness? / Baby, What You Want Me To Do   (Decca F 12041, 12/64)

Everybody Has A Right To Cry / You're Absolutely Right   (Parlophone R 5432, 4/66)

Merseyside manager Spencer Lloyd Mason receives production credit on the first single, a cover of Marvin Gaye's 'Can I Get A Witness?'. Aldo, a bluesy vocalist with lots of personality, deserved more success.

Michael Allen

A seventeen year old with four tracks on the 1965 LP, *Liverpool Today – Live At The Cavern.*

The Beatles

My Bonnie / The Saints (both with Tony Sheridan)
                        (Polydor NH 66 833, 1/62, UK 48, US 26, Germany 32)

Love Me Do/ P.S. I Love You   (Parlophone R 4949, 10/62, UK 17, US 1)
                                    (B-side also made No.10 in US.
                The single reached No.4 in the UK on reissue in 1982.)

Please Please Me / Ask Me Why   (Parlophone R 4983, 1/63, UK 2, US 3, Germany 20)

From Me To You / Thank You Girl   (Parlophone R 5015, 4/63, UK 1)
                       (The US single only made No.41 – curious.)

She Loves You / I'll Get You   (Parlophone R 5055, 8/63, UK 1, US 1, Germany 7)
                     (Both English and German language versions
                made No.7 in Germany, one following the other.)

I Want To Hold Your Hand / This Boy
                  (Parlophone R 5084, 11/63, UK 1, US 1, Germany 1)
                (US B-side, I Saw Her Standing There, made No.14:
              German language version made No.5 in Germany.)

Sweet Georgia Brown / Nobody's Child   (both with Tony Sheridan, the first track
                 having a new vocal to refer to Beatlemania.)
                         (Polydor NH 52-906, 1/64)

Cry For A Shadow / Why (B-side with Tony Sheridan)   (Polydor NH 52-275, 2/64)

Komm, Gib Mir Deine Hand / Sie Liebt Dich   (Germany, Odeon O 22671, 3/64)

Can't Buy Me Love / You Can't Do That   (Parlophone R 5114, 3/64,
                          UK 1, US 1, Germany 24)

Ain't She Sweet / If You Love Me, Baby   (Polydor 52 317, 5/64, UK 29, US 19)
(Polydor realise that they have a John Lennon lead vocal in their back catalogue. B-side with Tony Sheridan.)

A Hard Day's Night / Things We Said Today
                  (Parlophone R 5160, 7/64, UK 1, US 1, Germany 2)

I Feel Fine / She's A Woman   (Parlophone R 5200, 12/64, UK 1, US 1, Germany 3)
                            (B-side also made No.4 in US.)

If I Fell / Tell Me Why   (Parlophone DP 562, 1/65, Germany 25)
        (A Continental single made available in the UK, but hardly anyone knew about it.)

Ticket To Ride / Yes It Is   (Parlophone R 5265, 4/65, UK 1, US 1, Germany 2)

Help! / I'm Down   (Parlophone R 5305, 7/65, UK 1, US 1, Germany 2)

We Can Work It Out / Day Tripper   (Parlophone R 5389, 12/65, UK 1, US 1, Germany 2)
(Both sides listed on UK chart: B-side also made No.5 in US.)

Paperback Writer / Rain   (Parlophone R 5452, 6/66, UK 1, US 1, Germany 1)
(B-side also made No.23 in US.)

Yellow Submarine / Eleanor Rigby   (Parlophone R 5493, 8/66, UK 1, US 2, Germany 1)
(Both sides listed on UK chart: B-side also made No.11 in US.)

Other US hits – Twist And Shout (2. 1964), Do You Want To Know A Secret? (2, 1964), Roll Over Beethoven (68, 1964), All My Loving (45, 1964), You Can't Do That (B-side, 48, 1964), Thank You Girl (B-side, 35, 1964), Why (The Beatles with Tony Sheridan) (88, 1964), Sie Liebt Dich (She Loves You) (97, 1964), I Should Have Known Better (B-side, 53, 1964), And I Love Her (12, 1964), If I Fell (B-side, 53, 1964), I'll Cry Instead (25, 1964), I'm Happy Just to Dance With You (95, 1964), Matchbox (17, 1964), Slow Down (B-side, 25, 1964), Eight Days A Week (1, 1965), I Don't Want To Spoil The Party (B-side, 39, 1965), Yes It Is (B-side, 46, 1965), Yesterday (1, 1965), Act Naturally (B-side, 47, 1965), Nowhere Man (3, 1966), What Goes On (B-side, 81, 1966). Not by Beatles but related: Ringo's Theme (This Boy) (George Martin and his Orchestra) (53, 1964).

Other German hits – Twist And Shout (10, 1963), Roll Over Beethoven (31, 1964), Misery (37, 1964), All My Loving (32, 1964), Do You Want To Know A Secret? (34, 1964), Long Tall Sally (7, 1964), Please Mr. Postman (47, 1964), I Should Have Known Better (6, 1964), Eight Days A Week / No Reply (5, 1965), Rock And Roll Music (2, 1965), Kansas City (18, 1965), Yesterday (6, 1965), Michelle (6, 1966) and Nowhere Man (3, 1966). Up-tempo rockers were favoured in Germany.

Flexidiscs

The Beatles Christmas Record   (Fan Club, 12/63)

Another Beatles Christmas Record   (Fan Club, 12/64)

The Beatles Third Christmas Record   (Fan Club, 12/65)

The Beatles Fourth Christmas Record   (Fan Club, 12/66)

EPs

Twist and Shout   (Parlophone GEP 8882, 7/63)

My Bonnie (with Tony Sheridan)   (Polydor H 21 610, 7/63)

The Beatles' Hits   (Parlophone GEP 8880, 9/63)
(An earlier catalogue number than *Twist And Shout* but its release was held back.)

The Beatles No.1   (Parlophone GEP 8883, 11/63)
(An odd title as there was no No.2, but maybe it means that the Beatles were, simply, No.1.)

All My Loving   (Parlophone GEP 8891, 2/64)

Long Tall Sally   (Parlophone GEP 8913, 6/64)

Four By The Beatles   (Capitol EAP 1-2121, 6/64, US only 92)

Extracts from the film A Hard Day's Night   (Parlophone GEP 8920, 11/64)

201

Extracts from the album A Hard Day's Night	(Parlophone GEP 8924, 11/64)
4 – By The Beatles	(Capitol R 5365, 2/65, US–only 68)
Beatles for Sale	(Parlophone GEP 8931, 4/65)
Beatles for Sale No.2	(Parlophone GEP 8938, 6/65)
The Beatles Million Sellers	(Parlophone GEP 8946, 12/65)
Yesterday	(Parlophone GEP 8948, 3/66)
Nowhere Man	(Parlophone GEP 8952, 7/66)

Evidence of the Beatles' love of EPs are the collections of original material and the superbly packaged *Magical Mystery Tour* in 1967.

Albums

Please Please Me	(Parlophone PMC 1202, 3/63)
With the Beatles	(Parlophone PMC 1206, 11/63)
The Beatles' First	(Polydor 236 201, 6/64)
	(Collects all the Beatles' tracks with Tony Sheridan.)
A Hard Day's Night	(Parlophone PMC 1230, 7/64)
Beatles for Sale	(Parlophone PMC 1240, 12/64)
Help!	(Parlophone PMC 1255, 8/65)
Rubber Soul	(Parlophone PMC 1267, 12/65)
Revolver	(Parlophone PMC 7009, 8/66)
A Collection Of Beatles Oldies	(Parlophone PMC 7016, 12/66)

(Hard to credit that Parlophone didn't issue a collection of hit singles, many of which hadn't been on albums, until Christmas 1966, but hit compilations were not so common then. Indeed, this LP broke the run of the Beatles' chart-topping albums, peaking at No.7.)

Late Arrivals

Probably prompted by the vast number of bootlegs on sale at record fairs, the remaining members of the Beatles began exploring their back catalogue in the 1990s. *Live At The BBC* (Apple CDPCSP 728, 1994) is a double-CD of conversation and songs from their radio broadcasts. 'Baby It's You' was a Top 10 entry, but their cover versions of US songs that had not been officially released before are of most significance – 'I Got A Woman', 'Too Much Monkey Business', 'Keep Your Hands Off My Baby', 'Young Blood', 'A Shot Of Rhythm And Blues', 'Sure To Fall', 'Some Other Guy', 'That's All Right (Mama)', 'Carol', 'Soldier Of Love', 'Clarabella', 'I'm Gonna Sit Right Down And Cry', 'Crying, Waiting, Hoping', 'To Know Her Is To Love Her', 'The Honeymoon Song', 'Lucille', 'Sweet Little Sixteen', 'Lonesome Tears In My Eyes', 'Nothin' Shakin'', 'Hippy Hippy Shake', 'Glad All Over', 'I Just Don't Understand', 'So How Come', 'I Forgot To Remember To Forget', 'I Got To Find My Baby', 'Ooh! My Soul' and 'Don't Ever Change'. Like a night at the Cavern and, proof positive, if any were needed, that the Beatles knew scores of songs.

The commercial success of this CD package was followed by the three double-CDs in the *Anthology* series (Apple CDPSCP 727/8/9, 1995/6/6), which presented all manner of

Beatle outtakes. This included the first private recordings by the Quarrymen, the Decca auditions, 'How Do You Do It?', Lend Me Your Comb' and a fantastic version of Little Willie John's 'Leave My Kitten Alone'.

Another double-CD, *Beatle Bop* (Bear Family BCD 16583, 2001) contains the myriad of released takes from their Hamburg sessions with Tony Sheridan. If you want 'My Bonnie' eight times over, this is the place to go.

Litigation ensured the deletion of the double-CD, *Live At The Star-Club Hamburg 1962* (Lingasong LING 96), but vinyl copies of the album are still around. Now that the tapes have been given to the Beatles, I am confident that they will be released officially one day. No matter how badly the Beatles believe they are performing, it is surely history and should be part of their *œuvre*.

Surprisingly, there have been no official collections of the Beatles' Christmas singles for their fan club members from 1963 to 1969 inclusive, but many bootleg versions exist. The one I have, *The Beatles' Christmas Album*, is on a very convincing Apple label.

Pete Best

(As the Pete Best Four)   (Decca F 11929, 6/64)
I'm Gonna Knock On Your Door / Why Did I Fall in Love With You?

And er, that's it.

Having said that, Pete Best had a stream of releases in the US, all credited to Peter Best, rather than the Pete Best Four or the Pete Best Combo:

I'll Try Anyway / I Wanna Be There   (US, Original Beatles Drummer BEST 800, 1964)
(A contender for the silliest name for a record label)

Don't Play With Me (Little Girl) / If You Can't Get Her   (US, Happening 405, 1964)

If You Can't Get Her / The Way I Feel About You   (US, Happening 1117, 1964)

I Can't Do Without You / Keys To My Heart   (US, Mr. Maestro 711, 1965)

Casting My Spell / I'm Blue   (US, Mr. Maestro 712, 1965)

Boys / Kansas City   (US, Cameo C 391)

Album

Best Of The Beatles   (US, Savage BM 71/2m, 1966)
(Not a double-album, despite the number. Savage gave each side a separate number.)

A curio is the Italian LP, *La Grande Storia Del Rock, Volume 38*, which combines ten of Pete's tracks with two of Lonnie Donegan's. The liner notes concentrate on Donegan, and the supposed cover photograph of Best is of someone else.

The best collection of the Pete Best Combo's work is the 24 track *Beyond The Beatles, 1964-66* (Cherry Red CDMRED 124). All the US single tracks are included with the exception of 'Boys'.

The Big Three

Some Other Guy/ Let True Love Begin   (Decca F 11614, 3/63, UK 37)

By The Way / Cavern Stomp   (Decca F 11689, 6/63, UK 22)

I'm With You / Peanut Butter   (Decca F 11752, 10/63)

If You Ever Change Your Mind / You've Got To Keep Her Under Hand

(Decca F 11927, 6/64)

EP

The Big Three At The Cavern   (Decca DFE 8552, 7/64)

An album's worth of material was recorded at the Cavern, but the other tracks have been lost. The Big Three are also featured in the Faron, Paddy Chambers, Johnny Hutchinson line-up on the compilation LP, *At the Cavern*. They perform 'If You Ever Change Your Mind', which they had previously recorded in the studio. The song is better known as 'Bring It On Home To Me'.

The CD, *Cavern Stomp* (Deram 844 006-2, 1994) included a third version of 'If You Ever Change Your Mind' and the previously unissued 'High School Confidential'.

Brian Epstein sacked the Big Three for "unruly and rowdy behaviour", according to Gus. Then an argument over division of wages caused the band to split up. Hutch worked with other musicians (notably Faron and Paddy Chambers, both of Faron's Flamingos) as the Big Three, but he moved out of music. Griff had a timber yard in Liverpool and now lives in Canada. In 1973 he and Gus made an album called *Resurrection* for Polydor as the Big Three with Elton John's drummer Nigel Olsson.

Cilla Black

Love of the Loved / Shy of Love   (Parlophone R 5065, 10/63, UK35)

Anyone Who Had a Heart / Just for You   (Parlophone R 5101, 1/64, UK 1, Germany 8)

You're My World / Suffer Now I Must   (Parlophone R 5133, 4/64, UK 1, US 26)

It's for You / He Won't Ask Me   (Parlophone R 5162, 7/64, UK 7, US 79)

You've Lost That Lovin' Feelin' / Is It Love?   (Parlophone R 5225, 1/65, UK 2)

I've Been Wrong Before / I Don't Want to Know   (Parlophone R 5265, 4/65, UK 17)

Love's Just A Broken Heart / Yesterday   (Parlophone R5395, 1/66, UK 5)

Alfie / Night Time Is Here   (Parlophone R 5427, 3/66, UK 9, US 95)

Don't Answer Me / The Right One Is Left   (Parlophone R 5463, 6/66, UK 6)

A Fool Am I (Dimmelo Parlami) / For No One   (Parlophone R 5515, 10/66, UK 13)

EPs

Anyone Who Had a Heart   (Parlophone GEP 8901, 4/64)

It's For You   (Parlophone GEP 8916, 10/64)

LPs

Ferry Cross The Mersey   (one track, Columbia 33SX 1676, 1/65)

Cilla   (Parlophone PMC 1243, 2/65)

Cilla Sings A Rainbow   (Parlophone PMC 7004, 5/66)

Several previously unissued tracks are included on the triple CD packages, *1963-1973, The Abbey Road Decade* (EMI CILLA 1, 1997) and *The Best Of 1963-78* (EMI 584 1242, 2003). The first includes an acetate of Cilla performing 'Fever' with Gerry and the Pacemakers.

The Black Knights

I Gotta Woman / Angel of Love   (Columbia DB 7443, 1/65)

Both tracks were written by lead guitarist Kenny Griffiths. 'I Gotta Woman' was included in *Ferry Cross The Mersey* and is on the US version of the soundtrack album.

The Blackwells

Why Don't You Love Me? / All I Want is Your Love   (Columbia DB 7443, 1/65)

The Blackwells, taking a lead from Screaming Lord Sutch's Savages, dyed their hair blond and became residents at the Peppermint Lounge in London Road. **Albie Gormall (834)** of the Blackwells recalls, "We auditioned for *Ferry Cross The Mersey* at the Adelphi. They liked us but thought the song we were doing was copied from something else, which it was. I had some lyrics in the van and so we wrote another song, 'Why Don't You Love Me?' in 20 minutes, which we did in the film."

'Why Don't You Love Me?' was included in *Ferry Cross the Mersey* and is on the US version of the soundtrack album. Unexpectedly, it was covered by Alice Cooper.

The Blue Mountain Boys

Drop Me Gently / One Small Photograph of You   (Oriole 45-CB 1774, 4/63)

The Blue Mountain Boys was one of Liverpool's top country bands, although the record only featured Tony Allen with session musicians. Tony is the father of Ethan Allen, an award-winning performer on the UK country scene.

The Bow Bells

Not To Be Taken / I'll Try Not To Hold It Against You   (Polydor 56 030, 11/65)

Lead vocalist, Nola York

Phil Brady and the Ranchers

(As the Ranchers) An American Sailor at the Cavern / Sidetracked

(Cavern Sound IMSTL 2, 3/65)

Little Rosa / Just One More Time   (Rex R 11011, 9/65)

Please Come Back / Lonesome For Me   (Go AJ 11406, 1965)

Although solely attributed to the Ranchers, Phil Brady was as usual fronting the group on their first single. The A-side was a novelty about the Cavern's popularity, written by Liverpool boatman Timmy McCoy. Bob Wooler wrote the B-side, his other recorded composition being 'I Know' for Billy J. Kramer. 'An American Sailor at the Cavern' was released on the Cavern's own label and many copies were taken by the Official Receiver'

Billy Butler

(Polly Perkins & Bill) I Reckon You / (Polly Perkins only) The Girls Are at It Again

(Decca F 11583, 2/63)

A facsimile of 'Come Outside' with Polly Perkins taking the vocal and BB chipping in from time to time. Polly Perkins wasn't from Liverpool – try Paddington Green.

Billy Butler is a leading broadcaster on Merseyside and has even had a record written about him – 'Mrs. Butler's Eldest Son, Bill' by Bob Pryde (Stag HP 25, 1975).

Howie Casey and the Seniors

Double Twist / True Fine Mama	(Fontana H 364, 2/62)
I Ain't Mad At You / Twist At The Top	(Fontana H 381, 5/62)
Boll Weevil Song / Bony Moronie (Fontana TF 403, 6/63)	
(Also issued in Germany on Philips 267290)	

LPs

Twist at the Top (Fontana TFL 5180, 2/62) (as Wailin' Howie Casey and the Seniors)
Let's Twist (reissue of *Twist at the Top*) (Wing WL 1022, 3/65)

The LP was recorded in a day when the band had a short residency at the Twist at the Top club in Ilford and is fine if you like twisting at 100 miles an hour. Howie Casey played sax and used Derry Wilkie and Freddie Starr as vocalists. The vocalists exchange comments on 'Double Twist', while Derry solos on 'I Ain't Mad at You' and Freddie on Eddie Cochran's 'Boll Weevil Song'. **Freddie Starr (835)** says, "I didn't have to do an impersonation because my voice sounded like his anyway."

Lee Castle and the Barons

A Love She Can Count On / Foolin'	(Parlophone R 5151, 7/64)

Pleasant Shane Fenton sound but dated by 1964.

The Chants

I Don't Care / Come Go With Me	(Pye 7N 15557, 10/63)
I Could Write A Book / A Thousand Stars	(Pye 7N 15591, 1/64)
She's Mine / Then I'll Be Home	(Pye 7N 15643, 6/64)
Sweet Was the Wine / One Star	(Pye 7N 15691, 9/64)
Lovelight / Come Back And Get This Loving Baby	(Fontana H 716, 6/66)

If ever a group deserved an album, it was the Chants: sadly under-recorded. Eddie Amoo found success with the Real Thing in the 70s.

The Clayton Squares

Come And Get It / And Tears Fell	(Decca F 12250, 10/65)
There She Is / Imagination	(Decca F 12456, 7/66)

The Clayton Squares are also featured with the Hideaways on a live EP included with the German publication *Beat In Liverpool*.

The Cordes

Give Her Time / She's Leaving	(Cavern Sound IMSTL 1, 3/65)

Never met a Corde, never seen the single, but the first release on Ray McFall's Cavern Sound label.

The Crescents

Wrong / Baby Baby Baby	(Columbia DB 4093, 3/58)

The correspondence from the record company relating to this single asks if "it might be advantageous to use the word 'Liverpool' in some way." Indeed.

The Cryin' Shames

Please Stay / What's News, Pussycat? (Decca F 12340, 2/66, UK 26)
Nobody Waved Goodbye / You (Decca F 12425, 6/66)

The Cryin' Shames' 'Please Stay', produced by Joe Meek, was an excellent record, but it lent heavily on Zoot Money's arrangement of the same song. **Pete Frame (836)**: "I think the Cryin' Shames' 'Please Stay' is a fantastic record, better than any other version. I was talking to Seymour Stein who was trying to get Chrissie Hynde to do 'Please Stay'. I sent him a tape of the Cryin' Shames and when she heard it, she realised that the definitive version had already been made."

Lee Curtis and the All Stars

(Solo) Little Girl / Just One More Dance (Decca F 11622, 3/63)
Let's Stomp / Poor Unlucky Me (Decca F 11690, 6/63)
What About Me? / I've Got My Eyes on You (Decca F 11830, 2/64)
Ecstasy / A Shot Of Rhythm And Blues (Philips BF 1385, 12/64)

Pete Best plays drums on 'Let's Stomp' single. Lee is featured on the Decca album, *At The Cavern*.

The German releases are:
Ecstasy / A Shot Of Rhythm And Blues (Star-Club 148504 STF, 1964)
Shame And Scandal In The Family / Nobody But You (Star-Club 148542 STF, 1966)
Kelly / Mohair Sam (Star-Club 148553 STF, 1966)
Come On Down To My Boat / Concerto For Her (Star-Club 148590 STF, 1967)
LPs
Star-Club Show 3 (Star-Club 158002 STY, 1965)
It's Lee (Star-Club 158017 STY, 1965)

'Ecstasy', originally recorded for the German market, was a 'Record Of The Week' on Radio Caroline, but Philips missed the boat (literally) by delaying its British release. Lee reckons that the records he made in Germany are his best, especially an album track 'It's No Good for Me'.

Lee Curtis and the All Stars' Decca and Star-Club recordings have been collected on *Star-Club Show 3* (Repertoire IMS 7012, 1994) and *It's Lee* (Repertoire IMS 7013, 1994).

The Cyclones

Little Egypt / Nobody (Oriole 45-CB 1898, 4/64)

In their enthusiasm, the group play the songs too fast. 'Nobody' was a group original, but just as the record was coming out, they changed their name to The Few. Bet the record company loved that – oh, they were on Oriole, no one noticed anyway.

The Dakotas

The Cruel Sea / The Millionaire (Parlophone R 5044, 7/63, UK 18)
Magic Carpet / Humdinger (Parlophone R 5064, 9/63)
Oyeh / My Girl Josephine (Parlophone R 5203, 11/64)
EP
Meet the Dakotas (Parlophone GEP 8888, 10/63)

Solo releases by the Manchester group that backed Billy J. Kramer. Mike Maxfield's 'The Cruel Sea' was a storming instrumental, covered for the US market by the Ventures, the B-side of their US Top 10 single, 'Walk Don't Run, '64'. The title is taken from a book (and film) by Liverpool author, Nicholas Monsarrat.

Rod Davis

Nothing to do with Merseybeat but after leaving the Quarry Men, Rod Davis went to Cambridge University and played banjo as part of the Trad Grads.

Runnin' Shoes / Rag-Day Jazz Band Ball   (Decca F 11403, 11/61)

One of the vocalists was Herb Ellis, the Australian athlete who had won a gold at the Olympics in Rome, hence 'Runnin' Shoes', which was 'Marching Through Georgia' with new lyrics. The Trad Grads performed the song on the BBC news programme, *Tonight*, introduced by Cliff Michelmore.

The Delmonts

EP

Tom O'Connor Meets The Delmonts   (Rex EPR 5003, 1966)

Two solo tracks from Delmonts on EP, 'Sea Of Heartbreak', 'Beyond The Shadows'.

The Del Renas

Featured on both volumes of the compilation *This is Merseybeat*.

The Dennisons

Come On Be My Girl / Little Latin Lupe Lu   (Decca F 11691, 7/63, UK 46)
Walkin' the Dog / You Don't Know What Love Is   (Decca F 11880, 2/64, UK 36)
Nobody Like My Babe / Lucy (You Sure Did It This Time)   (Decca F 11990, 10/64)

Also featured on compilation album *At the Cavern*.

The Dimensions

Tears on My Pillow / You Don't Have to Whisper   (Parlophone R 5294, 7/65)

Anguished A-side, and powerful vocals and thunderous drums on flip.

Jason Eddie and the Centremen

Whatcha Gonna Do, Baby / Come On Baby   (Parlophone R 5388, 12/65)
Singing The Blues / True To You   (Parlophone R 5473, 6/66)

Billy Fury's brother meets Joe Meek.

The Escorts

Dizzy Miss Lizzy / All I Want Is You   (Fontana TF 453, 4/64)
The One to Cry / Tell Me Baby   (Fontana TF 474, 6/64, UK 49)
I Don't Want to Go on Without You / Don't Forget To Write   (Fontana TF 516, 11/64)
C'mon Home Baby / You'll Get No Lovin' That Way   (Fontana TF 570, 5/65)
Let It Be Me / Mad Mad World   (Fontana TF 651, 4/66)
From Head To Toe / Night Time   (Columbia DB 8061, 11/66)

The Escorts sound very young on their first single, 'Dizzy Miss Lizzy' and they were. A few years younger than the Beatles, the group matured in public and their final singles are excellent. They have all been collected on the CD, *From The Blue Angel* (Edsel EDCD 422, 1995).

Paul McCartney played tambourine on 'From Head To Toe'. Paddy Chambers joined the Escorts in the later years, writing an impression of the Impressions with 'Night Time'. The song was revived by Elvis Costello on the 12-inch single for 'Everyday I Write The Book'.

When the group split, Mike Gregory went to the Swinging Blue Jeans and Terry Sylvester to the Hollies.

The Exchequers

All The World Is Mine / It's All Over	(Decca F 11871, 3/64)
Buzz Buzz Buzz / You Are My New Love	(Germany, Ariola 18596)
Mama Didn't Know / Do The Bird	(Germany, Ariola)

Actually a Chester group but when they went to Hamburg, they recorded as the Liverpool Beats. Those releases are:

Memphis Tennessee / Big Bad John	(Vogue DV 14173, 1964)
Boys / Hey Hey Shorty	(Vogue 14201, 1964)

LP
This Is Liverpool – Live	(Vogue LDV 17005, 1964)

Faron's Flamingos

She If She Cares / Do You Love Me?	(Oriole 45-CB 1834, 8/63)
Shake Sherry / Give Me Time	(Oriole 45-CB 1867, 10/63)

Also, four tracks on the compilation albums *This Is Merseybeat*, and both sides of their first single are on *Group Beat '63* (Realm RM-149).

The Fourmost

Hello Little Girl / Just In Case	(Parlophone R 5056, 9/63, UK 9)
I'm in Love / Respectable	(Parlophone R 5078, 12/63, UK 17)
A Little Loving / Waitin' For You	(Parlophone R 5128, 4/64, UK 6)
How Can I Tell Her? / You Got That Way	(Parlophone R 5157, 7/64, UK 33)
Baby I Need Your Loving / That's Only What They Say	(Parlophone R 5194, 11/64, UK 24)
Everything in the Garden / He Could Never	(Parlophone R 5304, 7/65)
Girls Girls Girls / Why Do Fools Fall In Love?	(Parlophone R 5379, 11/65, UK 33)
Here, There And Everywhere / You've Changed	(Parlophone R 5491, 8/66)
Auntie Maggie's Remedy / Turn The Lights Down	(Parlophone R 5528, 11/66)

EP
The Sound of the Fourmost	(Parlophone GEP 8892, 3/64)
The Fourmost	(Parlophone GEP 8917, 8/64)

LP
First and Fourmost	(Parlophone PMC 1259, 11/65)

Also on soundtrack album *Ferry Cross the Mersey*.

Billy Hatton (837): "We had our great friends, Sound Incorporated, in the studio for 'Yakety Yak' so that we could get that sax sound. It's lovely to hear it as we were enjoying it so much. Maybe it's me but I think I can hear the clink of bottles in the background. On the Chipmunky part of 'Girls, Girls, Girls', that is George Martin and Dick James singing along. I couldn't get down to the low notes on 'My Block' as I had a sore throat and so every time we got to the word 'block', the engineer Norman 'Hurricane' Smith filled in for me."

Their 1969 single of 'Rosetta' (CBS 4041) was produced by Paul McCartney. **Dave Lovelady (838)** recalls, "Paul liked the way we could mimic instruments with our voices, our 'mouth music' if you like. Brian O'Hara was the trumpeter and we were the trombones. We used it on 'Rosetta' and the Beatles did the same thing on 'Lady Madonna'. There were proper instruments on our record as well. I was playing the piano at the session and Brian O'Hara told me to play it badly. I soon found out why. Paul said, 'Look, I'll do the piano bit', and so he was played on our record. Unfortunately, it didn't sell."

Their 1975 gig LP, The Fourmost, is worth seeking out. A compilation of their Parlophone tracks, *The Best Of The EMI Years* (EMI CD EMS 1449) was released in 1992. Among the 32 tracks are the previously unissued 'My How The Time Goes By', 'Stop' and 'Dawn (Go Away)'.

Johnny Gentle

Wendy / Boys And Girls (Were Meant For Each Other)	(Philips PB 908, 4/59)
Milk From The Coconut / I Like The Way	(Philips PB 945, 11/59)
This Friendly World / Darlin' Won't You Wait	(Philips PB 988, 1/60)
After My Laughter Came Tears / Sonja	(Philips BF 1069, 10/60)
Darlin' / Pick A Star	(Philips PB 1142, 61)
(as Darren Young) I've Just Fallen For Someone / My Tears Will Turn To Laughter	(Parlophone R 4919, 8/62)
(as part of the Viscounts) Sally / On Broadway	(Columbia DB 7436, 12/64)

EP

The Gentle Touch	(Philips BBE 12345, 1960)

Gerry and the Pacemakers

How Do You Do It? / Away from You	(Columbia DB 4987, 3/63, UK 1, US 9)
I Like It / It Happened to Me	(Columbia DB 7041, 6/63, UK 1, US 17)
You'll Never Walk Alone / It's Alright	(Columbia DB 7126, 10/63, UK 1, US 48)
I'm The One / You've Got What I Like	(Columbia DB 7189, 1/64, UK 2, US 82)
Don't Let the Sun Catch You Crying / Show Me That You Care	(Columbia DB 7268, 4/64, UK 6, US 4)
It's Gonna Be Alright / It's Just Because	(Columbia DB 7353, 8/64, UK 24, US 23)
Ferry Cross the Mersey / You You You	(Columbia DB 7437, 12/64, UK 8, US 6)
I'll Be There / Baby You're So Good To Me	(Columbia DB 7504, 3/65, UK 15, US 14)
Give All Your Love To Me / Skinny Minnie	(Laurie 3313, 8/65, US 68)
Walk Hand In Hand / Dreams	(Columbia DB 7738, 10/65, UK 29)

La La La / Without You (Columbia DB 7835, 2/66)
Girl On A Swing / Fool To Myself (Columbia DB 8044, 11/66, US 28)
(US B-side was The Way You Look Tonight)

The original version of 'Don't Let The Sun Catch You Crying' is not by Gerry but by Louise Cordet (Decca F 11824, 2/64). **Gerry Marsden (839)**: "We were doing it on tour before we recorded it and Louise was on the bill. She asked us if she could sing it but she said was going to do it in French," says Gerry, "She did it in English and took it rather fast. It's not bad but the best version is definitely by Jose Feliciano. The worst is by Trini Lopez who added all this unka-dunka stuff."

Les Chadwick (840): "'Walk Hand In Hand' wasn't a hit but I always thought it was the best that Gerry ever sang."

'Dreams', in which Gerry dreams of Liverpool FC, is the quirkiest record from the Mersey boom. Since then he has recorded both as Gerry Marsden and as Gerry and the Pacemakers and is prone to recording new versions of 'You'll Never Walk Alone'. The Tony Sheridan song 'Please Let Them Be', which is mentioned in the chapter 'Germany Calling', was released in 1967 on CBS 2784 under the name of Gerry Marsden: an excellent ballad which didn't sell.

EPs

How Do You Do It? (Columbia SEG 8257, 7/63)
You'll Never Walk Alone (Columbia SEG 8295, 12/63)
I'm the One (Columbia SEG 8311, 2/64)
Don't Let the Sun Catch You Crying (Columbia SEG 8346, 5/64)
It's Gonna Be Alright (Columbia SEG 8367, 12/64)
Gerry In California (Columbia SEG 8388, 2/65)
Ferry Cross the Mersey (Columbia SEG 8397, 3/65)
Rip It Up (Columbia SEG 8426, 6/65)

LPs

How Do You Like It? (Columbia 33 SX 1546, 10/63)
You'll Never Walk Alone (Regal Starline REG 1070, 1964) (Proof positive that EMI never regarded Gerry and the Pacemakers in the same light as the Beatles. Within a year, Gerry's first LP appears on a budget label.)

Ferry Cross the Mersey (mostly Gerry and the Pacemakers) (Columbia 33 SX 1676, 1/65) (Reissued on EMI DORIG 114, 1997) (The stereo and mono versions are different. For example, the stereo 'Ferry' starts with the drums and Gerry coming in: the mono with just Gerry on his guitar.)

Gerry and the Pacemakers had different album releases in the US, resulting in several tracks which did not appear in the UK:

Don't Let The Sun Catch You Crying (Laurie LLP 2024, 1964)
Second Album (Laurie LLP 2027, 1964)
I'll Be There (Laurie LLP 2030, 1965)
Ferry Cross The Mersey (United Artists UAL 3387, 1965)
Greatest Hits (Laurie LLP 2031, 1965)
Girl On A Swing (Laurie LLP 2037, 1966)

There are numerous Gerry and the Pacemakers CDs on the market, especially at local supermarkets, where 1980s tracks are often packaged with a photo of the original band. The following reissue CDs feature original material:

The EP Collection   (See For Miles SEE CD 95, 1989)

The Best Of The EMI Years (EMI CDEMS 1443, 1992) (31 tracks including their 1963 demo of 'Hello Little Girl'.)

Gerry And The Pacemakers At Abbey Road (EMI CDABBEY 102, 1997) (includes outtakes and studio conversation)

Girl On A Swing (US, Fiesta FIR 151, 2002) (32 tracks, many of them not issued in the UK)

A track from Gerry and the Pacemakers' demos from 1961, 'What'd I Say', was included on *Unearthed Merseybeat*.

Apple own the copyright to *Ferry Cross The Mersey*, but have not done anything with it, nor passed the film over to Gerry Marsden. The film was shot in Liverpool and, although the acting and storyline are chronic, it contains some good musical performances and many Liverpool landmarks. It cries out for a DVD reissue with a commentary from Gerry.

Chick Graham and the Coasters

I Know / Education	(Decca F 11859, 2/64)
A Little You / Dance Baby Dance	(Decca F 11932, 7/64)

'A Little You' became a hit in 1965 for Freddie and the Dreamers.

Johnny Gustafson

Just to Be with You / Sweet Day	(Polydor 56 022, 7/65)
Take Me for a Little While / Make Me Your Number One	(Polydor 56 043, 12/65)

(With John Banks of the Merseybeats and billed as Johnny and John)

Bumper To Bumper / Scrape My Boot	(Polydor BM 56 087, 1966)

Johnny Gus's first solo album, *Goose Grease*, was released on Angel Air SJPCD008 in 1997.

The Hideaways

Despite their enormous following on Merseyside, they can only be found on the live EP included with the German publication 'Beat In Liverpool'. In 1970 they recorded 'The Brandenburg Concerto' under the name of Confucius for RCA.

The Hillsiders

I Wonder If I Care As Much / Cottonfields	(Decca F 12026, 11/64)
Please Be My Love / The Children's Song	(Decca F 12161, 5/65)
Hello Trouble / Every Minute Every Hour	(Rex 11010, 9/65)

LP

Country Hits	(Decca LPR 1003, 11/64)

Emerging from the rockabilly band, Sonny Webb and the Cascades, came the Hillsiders, who for many years were the top UK country band. They made albums with George Hamilton IV and Bobby Bare.

The album, *Liverpool Goes Country* (Decca LPR 1002, 11/64), features the Hillsiders and Phil Brady as well as the Delmonts, Carl Goldie, Tom O'Connor and Hank Walters

Ian and the Zodiacs

Beechwood 4-5789 / You Can Think Again	(Oriole 45-CB 1849, 9/63)
(As Wellington Wade) Let's Turkey Trot / It Ain't Necessarily So	
	(Oriole CB 1857, 10/63)
Just the Little Things I Like / This Won't Happen to Me	(Fontana TF 548, 2/65)
No Money, No Honey / Where Were You?	(Fontana TF 708, 5/66)
Wade In The Water / Come On Along Girl	(Fontana TF 753, 10/66)

Wellington Wade was the pseudonym of Charlie Flynn of the Zodiacs, who took the lead vocal on 'Let's Turkey Trot'. 'It Ain't Necessarily So' was one of three tracks that Ian and the Zodiacs recorded for the albums, *This Is Mersey Beat*.

LPs

Gear Again – 12 Hits	(Wing WL 1074, 9/65)
(As the Koppykats) *The Beatles Best*	(Fontana 700153, 1966)
(As the Koppykats) *More Beatles Best*	(Fontana 701543, 1967)

Ian and the Zodiacs were also one of the first Beatle tribute bands and their two budget albums have been collected by a Hungarian label as *Rarities* (Rock-In-Beat B 000058 AT 9). *Beatlemania!!* (Mastersound MS CD 448, 2002) is a UK collection of 20 of the tracks. **Ian Edwards (841)** recalls, "We admired the Beatles and we were always among the first to do their new releases on stage. Philips asked us to do an LP of their hits. We found that the Beatles were very easy to copy and we think we got the harmonies right. The album came out on a budget label and it did very well, but we'd accepted a fee and didn't get any royalties."

Ian and the Zodiacs' German releases are:

Spartacus / Message To Martha	(Star-Club 148514 STF, 1965)
Bitte Komm Wieder / All Of Me	(Fontana 269235 TF, 1965)
So Much In Love / All Of Me	(Star-Club 148535 STF, 1965)
Leave It To Me / Why Can't It Be Me?	(Star-Club 148543 STF, 1966)
No Money, No Honey / Ride Your Pony	(Star-Club 148548 STF, 1966)
Any Day Now / Na-Na-Na-Na-Na	(Star-Club 148572, 1966)
(As the Koppykats) Help! / Nowhere Man	(Pop Ten Records, 6805 015, 1966)

LPs

Star-Club Show 7	(Star-Club 158007 STY, 1965)
Just Listen To Ian And The Zodiacs	(Star-Club 158020 STY, 1966)
Locomotive	(Star-Club 158029 STY, 1966)

The following US singles, recorded in Hamburg, were not released here:

Spartacus / Message To Martha	(Star-Club 148514, 1964)
The Crying Game / Livin' Lovin' Wreck	(Philips 40244, 1964)
Good Morning Little Schoolgirl / Message To Martha	(Philips 40277, 1965)
So Much In Love / This Empty Place	(Philips 40291, 1965)
Leave It To Me / Why Can't It Be Me?	(Philips 40343, 1966)

Ian and the Zodiacs' Star-Club recordings have been collected on *Star-Club Show 7* (Repertoire IMS 7006, 1994), *Just Listen To Ian And The Zodiacs* (Repertoire IMS 7007, 1994) and *Locomotive* (Repertoire IMS 7008,1994). They feature the original albums with many bonus tracks.

Tony Jackson and the Vibrations

Bye Bye Baby / Watch Your Step	(Pye 7N 15685, 9/64, UK 38)
You Beat Me to the Punch / This Little Girl of Mine	(Pye 7N 15745, 12/64)
Love Potion Number Nine / Fortune Teller	(Pye 7N 15766, 2/65)
Stage Door / That's What I Want	(Pye 7N 15876, 7/65)
You're My Number One / Let Me Know	(CBS 202039, 1/66)
Never Leave Your Baby's Side / I'm The One She Really Thinks A Lot Of	
	(CBS 202069, 5/66)
Follow Me / Walk That Walk	(CBS 202297, 9/66)
Anything Else You Want / Come On And Stop	(CBS 202408, 11/66)

Sacked Searcher backed by non-Liverpool musicians. A succession of singles on Pye and CBS followed but he didn't carry the Searchers' fans with him. An EP, *The Tony Jackson Group*, was released in Portugal on a radio station's label (Estudio EEP 50013, 1977). It contained covers of 'Just Like Me' (Paul Revere and the Raiders), 'Understanding' (Small Faces), 'Shake' (Sam Cooke) and 'He Was A Friend Of Mine' (The Byrds' tribute to John F. Kennedy). Beatles aside, this has been one of the rarest Merseybeat items. All the single tracks and the EP have been collected on the CD, *Just Like Me* (Strange Things Are Happening STCD 10003, 1991). Excellent album – the guy was just unlucky.

Jeannie and the Big Guys

Don't Lie To Me / Boys	(Piccadilly 7N 35147, 10/63)
I Want You / Sticks And Stones	(Piccadilly 7N 35164, 2/64)
(As Cindy Cole) A Love Like Yours / He's Sure The Boy I Love	
	(Columbia DB 7519, 4/65)
(As Cindy Cole) Lonely City Blue Boy / Just Being Your Baby	
	(Columbia DB 7973, 7/66)

Jeannie and the Big Guys were Chester's top group, but they often worked the Liverpool clubs. Jeannie was Rita Hughes, the daughter of a publican from The Mariner's Arms in Chester. She was originally the Miss in Four Hits And A Miss, a versatile band with 'Lullaby Of Birdland' in the repertoire. She worked with Earl Royce and the Olympics when the Big Guys folded and recorded two singles for Columbia as Cindy Cole. She died in 1989 when only 42.

Casey Jones and the Engineers

One Way Ticket / I'm Gonna Love	(Columbia DB 7083, 7/63)

After local success as Cass and the Cassanovas, Brian Casser went to Hamburg and became popular at the Star-Club. He never made it in the UK but Eric Clapton devotees will recognize the name as Eric was an Engineer – albeit only for a couple of weeks and not on this record.

Casey Jones' German hits were 'Don't Ha Ha' (with a Bristol group, the Governors, 2, 1965), 'Candy Man' (30, 1965), 'Jack The Ripper' (9, 1965), 'Yockomo' (17, 1965), 'Little Girl' (25, 1966) and 'Come On And Dance' (39, 1966), all on the Golden 12 label. He also released a German language version of 'Bumble Bee' (1966). Considering that no one on Merseyside thought much of Brian Casser's musical ability, this level of success baffles me, but all attempts to contact him have failed.

The Kirkbys

It's A Crime / I've Never Been So Much In Love   (RCA 1542, 9/66)

Two singles in Finland:

'Cos My Baby's Gone / She'll Get No Lovin' That Way   (RCA FAS 942)
Don't You Want Me No More / Bless You   (RCA FAS 948)

Billy J. Kramer with the Dakotas

Do You Want to Know a Secret / I'll Be on My Way   (Parlophone R 5023, 4/63, UK 2)
Bad to Me / I Call Your Name   (Parlophone R 5049, 7/63, UK 1, US 9)
I'll Keep You Satisfied / I Know   (Parlophone R 5073, 10/63, UK 4, US 30)
Little Children / They Remind Me of You   (Parlophone R 5105, 2/64, UK 1, US 7)
From A Window / Second to None   (Parlophone R 5156, 7/64, UK 10, US 23)
It's Gotta Last Forever / Don't You Do It No More   (Parlophone R 5234, 1/65, US 67)
Trains And Boats And Planes / That's the Way I Feel
                                              (Parlophone R 5285, 5/65, UK 12, US 47)
Neon City / I'll Be Doggone   (Parlophone R 5362, 11/65)
We're Doing Fine / Forgive Me   (Parlophone R 5408, 2/66)
You Make Me Feel Like Someone / Take My Hand   (Parlophone R 5482, 7/66)

EPs

Hits   (Parlophone GEP 8885, 9/63)
I'll Keep You Satisfied   (Parlophone GEP 8895, 12/63)
Little Children   (Parlophone GEP 8907, 5/64)
From a Window   (Parlophone GEP 8921, 11/64)
Billy J. Plays the States   (Parlophone GEP 8928, 2/65)

LP

Listen…   (Parlophone PMC 1209, 11/63) (Reissued on EMI DORIG 110, 1997)

Billy J. Kramer with the Dakotas had different album releases in the US, resulting in several tracks which did not appear in the UK:

Little Children   (Imperial LP-9267, 6/64)
I'll Keep You Satisfied   (Imperial LP-9273, 10/64)
Trains And Boats And Planes   (Imperial LP-9291, 9/65)

Plenty of interest in Billy's later career: 'Colour Of My Life' (1969), 'Is There Anymore At Home Like You?' (1978), 'Blue Christmas' (on blue vinyl, 1979), 'You Can't Live On Memories' (1983) and 'Shootin' The Breeze' (1984). Billy has re-recorded his hits from time to time, which cheapo-cheapo CDs often try and pass as the originals. CD collections of Parlophone material are *The EP Collection* (See For Miles SEE CD 422), *The Best Of Billy J. Kramer And The Dakotas - The Definitive Collection* (US EMI E2

96055, 1991) and *Billy J. Kramer With The Dakotas At Abbey Road, 1963-1966* (EMI 493 4512). Billy was always a bag of nerves and you can hear John Lennon giving him grief on the outtake of 'I'm In Love' on *The Definitive Collection*. The track was not released at the time and the Lennon and McCartney song was passed to the Fourmost.

The Kubas

Magic Potion / I Love Her   (Columbia DB 7451, 1/65)
(As The Koobas) Take Me for a Little While / Somewhere in the Night
                                                                              (Pye 7N 17012, 11/65)
(As The Koobas) You'd Better Make Up Your Mind / A Place I Know
                                                                              (Pye 7N 17087, 4/66)
(As The Koobas) Sweet Music / Face   (Columbia DB 7988, 8/66)

A very good second generation group, but the spelling change didn't help their record sales. They appeared on the Beatles' final UK tour in 1965 and made a fine album of their own songs, *The Koobas* (Columbia SCX 6271, 1969). This was reissued with singles cuts on *The Koobas* (BGO BGOCD 487, 2000), but the original LP sells for over £100 today.

The Liverbirds

The four Scouse girls known as Liverbirds had no UK releases, but they performed in Germany, mostly at the Star-Club, and had the following releases:

Shop Around / It's Got To Be You   (Star-Club 148508 STF, 1964)
Diddley Daddy / Leave All Your Loves In The Past
                                                          (Star-Club 148526 STF, 1965, Germany 33)
Peanut Butter / Why Do You Hang Around Me?   (Star-Club 148528 STF, 1965)
Loop De Loop / Bo Diddley Is A Lover   (Star-Club 148554 STF, 1966)
LPs
Star Club Show 4   (Star-Club 158003 STL, 1965)
                                       (Reissued with bonus tracks, Repertoire IMS 7009, 1994)
More Of The Liverbirds   (Star-Club 158020 STL, 1966)
                                       (Reissued with bonus tracks, Repertoire IMS 7010, 1994)

One of Pam Birch's songs, 'It's Got To Be You', was recorded by Johnny Kidd in 1966.

The Liverpool Beats

German pseudonym used by the Exchequers.

Mark and John

Walk Right Back / Karen   (Decca F 12044, 12/64)

The Mark Four were signed to Decca, but the group became Mark and John because of an American act with the same name. The B-side, 'Karen', was written by Bob Pryde and Joyce Hopkinson, who played club dates around Merseyside as Pryde and Joy. 'Karen' was recorded but not released by Denny Seyton and the Sabres and also was an outtake from Bill Kenwright's first recording session in 1967.

Beryl Marsden

I Know / I Only Care About You	(Decca F 11707, 8/63)
When the Lovelight Starts Shining Through His Eyes /	
Love Is Going to Happen to Me	(Decca F 11819, 1/64)
Who You Gonna Hurt? / Gonna Make Him My Baby	
	(Columbia DB 7718, 10/65, UK 29 on NME chart)
Music Talk / Break-a-way	(Columbia DB 7797, 12/65)
What's She Got / Let's Go Somewhere	(Columbia DB 7888, 4/66)
(As part of Shotgun Express):	
I Could Feel The Whole World Turn Around / Curtains (instrumental)	
	(Columbia DB 8025, 10/66)

Beryl has been described as Gerry's sister, but they weren't related. 'Break-a-way', a Jackie DeShannon song, was revived in 1983 by Tracey Ullman. Beryl did not have the hits, but she has had a very varied life, being part of Shotgun Express with Rod Stewart, Peter Green and Mick Fleetwood. Peter Green said in 2003 that he should have married her and if he had, the course of rock history might have changed.

Beryl Marsden (842): "The only hit I ever had was hyped into the lower reaches of the charts and so, as far as I'm concerned, I've never had a hit record." And that's called sad.

Spencer Mason and his Orchestra

Till The End Of Time / The Way Of Love	(Decca F 12235, 10/65)
Flugel In Carnaby Street / Albuferia	(Parlophone R 5555, 1/67)

Delusions of grandeur here. The Mojos' manager wasn't conducting anything. The orchestrations were arranged and conducted by Johnny Harris and the vocals were by the Mike Sammes Singers.

The Masterminds

She Belongs To Me / Taken My Love	(Immediate IM 005, 9/65)

The only Liverpool band to record a Bob Dylan song and they are trying hard to sound American. The single was produced by Andrew Loog Oldham, but why didn't he record a follow-up or listen to their original material?

The Merseybeats

It's Love That Really Counts / Fortune Teller	(Fontana TF 412, 8/63, UK 24)
I Think Of You / Mr. Moonlight	(Fontana TF 431, 1/64, UK 5)
Don't Turn Around / Really Mystified	(Fontana TF 459, 4/64, UK 13)
Wishin' and Hopin' / Milkman	(Fontana TF 482, 6/64, UK 13)
Last Night (I Made A Little Girl Cry) / See Me Back	(Fontana TF 504, 10/64, UK 40)
Nur Unsere Liebe Zählt (It's Love That Really Counts) /	
Nur Du Allein (I Think Of You)	(Germany, Fontana 269 310, 1964)
	(German language single)
Don't Let It Happen to Us /	
It Would Take A Long, Long Time	(Fontana TF 568, 5/65)

I Love You, Yes I Do / Good, Good Lovin'	(Fontana TF 607, 9/65, UK 22)
I Stand Accused / All My Life	(Fontana TF 645, 12/65, UK 38)
(As The Merseys) Sorrow / Some Other Day	(Fontana TF 694, 4/66, UK 4)
(As The Merseys) So Sad About Us / Love Will Continue	(Fontana H 732, 8/66)
(As The Merseys) Rhythm Of Love / Is It Love?	(Fontana H 776, 11/66)

EPs

The Merseybeats On Stage	(Fontana TE 17422, 3/64)
The Merseybeats	(Fontana TE 17423, 3/64)
Wishin' And Hopin'	(Fontana TE 17432, 11/64)

LP

| *The Merseybeats* | (Fontana TL 5210, 6/64) |
| | (Reissued as a budget LP, Wing WL 1163, 1965) |

Their first recording, 'Our Day Will Come', was for the compilation *This Is Merseybeat, Volume 1*. Tony Crane and Billy Kinsley became Liverpool's response to the Walker Brothers with the Merseys. The Merseybeats remain a hard-working touring band, but their 12-inch tribute, 'This Is Merseybeat' (Tudor CD 12 23, 1981), was more disco than 1960s beat. All the Merseybeats' singles together with four EP and album tracks can be found on the mid-price CD, *The Very Best Of The Merseybeats* (Karussell 552 102-2, 1997). Plans for John Lennon to produce 'I'll Be Back' never materialised, but Pete Townshend did write them a song, 'So Sad About Us'.

The Mojos

Forever / They Say	(Decca F 11732, 10/63)
Everything's Alright / Give Your Lovin' To Me	(Decca F 11853, 3/64, UK 9)
Why Not Tonight? / Don't Do It Anymore	(Decca F 11918, 6/64, UK 25)
Seven Daffodils / Nothin' At All	(Decca F 11959, 8/64, UK 30)
Comin' On To Cry / That's the Way It Goes	(Decca F 12127, 4/65)
Wait a Minute / Wonder If She Knows	(Decca F 12231, 8/65)
Goodbye Dolly Gray / I Just Can't Let Her Go	(Decca F 12557, 2/67)

(Okay, 1967, and an example of a group not having a clue what to do next)

EP

| *The Mojos* | (Decca DFE 8591, 8/64) |

As the Nomads, they have one track on This Is Merseybeat, Volume 2.

The complete Mojos can be found on *Everything's Alright*   (Deram 820 962-2, 1994)

The Nocturns

| 'Carryin' On'/'Three Cool Cats' | (Decca F 12002, 10/64) |

The group appeared in the Catacomb Club in the West End musical *Maggie May* and are included on the EP 'Carryin' on with More Songs from *Maggie May*' (Decca DFE 8602).

Tom O'Connor

EP

Tom O'Connor Meets The Delmonts (Rex EPR 5003)

Solo tracks on EP –'Pretty Pictures', 'I Can't Imagine What Went Wrong'

Paddy, Klaus & Gibson

I Wanna Know / I Tried	(Pye 7N 15906, 7/65)
No Good Without You / Rejected	(Pye 7N 17060, 2/66)
Quick Before They Catch Us / Teresa	(Pye 7N 17112, 5/66)

Formed in Hamburg by two Liverpool lads (Paddy Chambers, Gibson Kemp) and one German. Klaus Voormann subsequently played with Manfred Mann and the Plastic Ono Band and designed the LP sleeve for the Beatles' *Revolver*.

The Pathfinders

I Love You Caroline / Something I Can Always Do	(Decca F 12038, 12/64)
Don't You Believe It / Castle Of Love	(Parlophone R 5372, 11/65)

Their theme for Radio Caroline was ousted by the Fortunes' 'Caroline'. **Tom Earley (843)**: "The first one was aimed at pirate radio, and I wish 'Something I Can Always Do' had been an A-side as it was a good, upbeat song." Billy May comments that the second single was meant to be in the Motown vein but it didn't have the right atmosphere.

Mal Perry

Lollipop / Love Me Again	(Fontana H 125, 4/58)
Make Me A Miracle / That's When Your Heartaches Begin	(Fontana H 133, 5/58)
Who Are They To Say? / Too Young To Love	(Fontana H 149, 9/58)
The Things I Didn't Say / The Girl Next Door	(Fontana H 157, 11/58)
Willingly / Richer Than I	(Fontana H 172, 1/59)

Mal Perry was a Liverpool singer on that first beat show at the Liverpool Stadium in 1960. Fontana gave him five chances in a year, then he came back to Liverpool and got a regular job. Still working and often eats in Keith's Wine Bar.

Mark Peters and the Silhouettes

Fragile (Handle with Care) / Janie	(Oriole 45-CB 1836, 8/63)
Cindy's Gonna Cry / Show Her	(Oriole 45-CB 1909, 6/64)
Don't Cry For Me / I Told You So	(Piccadilly 7N 35207, 10/64)

Also featured on *This is Merseybeat, Volume 1*. 'Fragile (Handle with Care)' is included on *Group Beat '63* (Realm RM 149).

Earl Preston

(With the TTs) I Know Something / Watch Your Step (Fontana TF 406, 7/63)

Earl Preston and the TTs also appear on both volumes of *This Is Merseybeat*, but although they were one of the top groups on Merseyside, they are poorly represented in this discography. Several tracks were recorded but never released. According to the record label and some of the group, the TTs backed Eden Kane on his chart comeback with 'Boys Cry' (Fontana TF 438, 1964, UK 8), but it sounds too orchestral for them.

(With the Realms) Raindrops / That's For Sure	(Fontana TF 481, 6/64)
(Released as 'Realm') Hard Time Loving You / A Certain Kind Of Girl	
	(CBS 202044, 3/66)

After the TTs, Earl Preston formed the Realms. The group performed five tracks, including two originals, on the LP *Liverpool Today – Live at the Cavern* (Ember NR 5028, 9/65), and also featuring The Richmond and Michael Allen. Earl Preston regards the Gordon Mills song, 'Hard Time Loving You' as his best record.

Tommy Quickly

Tip of my Tongue / Heaven Only Knows	(Piccadilly 7N 35137, 7/63)
(With the Remo Four) Kiss Me Quick / No Other Love	(Piccadilly 7N 35151, 11/63)
(With the Remo Four) Prove It / Haven't You Noticed?	(Piccadilly 7N 35167, 3/64)
(With the Remo Four):	
You Might As Well Forget Him / It's As Simple As That	(Piccadilly 7N 35183, 6/64)
(With the Remo Four):	
The Wild Side Of Life / Forget the Other Guy	(Piccadilly 7N 15708, 10/64, UK 33)
(With the Remo Four) Humpty Dumpty / I'll Go Crazy	(Piccadilly 7N 15748, 12/64)

The first single was total pants: few people bought it but because it is a Lennon and McCartney song (well, just McCartney really), it is sought by collectors and a mint copy could fetch £200 at auction. Buy it, but don't play it.

'Humpty Dumpty' was also included in the 1965 film *Pop Gear*. The single was recorded live at the Liverpool Empire on 8 November 1964. 'Kiss Me Quick' is also on the compilation *Package Tour* (Golden Guinea GGL 0268).

Derek Taylor killed off Tommy Quickly in his book, *Fifty Years Adrift*. This is not true. Tommy still lives on Merseyside but he does not want to have anything to do with the business.

The Rainchecks

My Angel / Something About You	(Solar, 1965)

Wallasey group whose single was played on Radio Caroline.

The Remo Four

(With Gregory Phillips) Everybody Knows / Closer To Me	(Pye 7N 15593, 1/64)
Wish I Could Shimmy Like My Sister Kate / Peter Gunn	(Piccadilly 7N 35175, 4/64)
Sally Go Round the Roses / I Know A Girl	(Piccadilly 7N 35186, 6/64)

As well as making singles with Tommy Quickly and Johnny Sandon, the Remo Four backed a southerner, Gregory Phillips, a children's TV presenter. Gregory Phillips, incidentally, was the first person to cover a George Harrison song, namely, 'Don't Bother Me' (Pye 7N 15633, 4/64).

The Remo Four had the following German singles:

Peter Gunn (different version to above) / Mickey's Monkey	(Star-Club 148 522, 4/66)
Live Like A Lady / Sing Hallelujah	(Star-Club 148 577, 12/66)

Their 1966 album, *Smile!* (Star Club 158 034), was reissued twenty years later on CD under the Star-Club imprint on Line Records 9.00196. The Star-Club version of 'Peter Gunn' with Colin Manley on lead guitar and Roy Dyke on drums was played to Duane Eddy in 1996 who said, "That is absolutely wild, I love that. It took guts to play it without the sax. I found the drums very interesting, great drums, and a big sound."

The Remo Four play George Harrison's music on the soundtrack of the film, *Wonderwall* (Apple SAPCOR 1, 11/68). George produced their own song, 'In The First Place', which was issued as a single to coincide with the reissue of the *Wonderwall* film in 1997.

Rhythm And Blues Inc.

Louie Louie / Honey Don't   (Fontana TF 524, 1/65)

Southport's top group offer a frenzied workout of the ultimate garage classic. Barry Womersley often performs on Merseyside, usually with his brother.

The Richmond

A six-piece R&B band included on the 1965 LP *Liverpool Today – Live at the Cavern.* In 'I Shall Not Be Moved' they sing 'Just Because My Skin Is Black'. The group was white but with the lighting in the Cavern, it was hard to tell.

The Riot Squad

Any Time / Jump	(Pye 7N 15752, 1/65)
I Wanna Talk About My Baby / Gonna Make You Mine	(Pye 7N 15817, 4/65)
Nevertheless / Not a Great Talker	(Pye 7N 15869, 6/65)
Cry Cry Cry / How Is It Done	(Pye 7N 17041, 1/66)
I Take It We're Through / Working Out	(Pye 7N 17092, 4/66)
It's Never Too Late To Forgive / Try To Realise	(Pye 7N 17130, 6/66)
Gotta Be A First Time / Bitter Sweet Love	(Pye 7N 17237, 1/67)

When the Kinks' manager, Larry Page, announced his new signing, he played down their Liverpool origins, making them out to be a London R&B band. By way of contrast, a non-Liverpool band called itself the Wackers.

The Riot Squad's shifting personnel included Mitch Mitchell (later with the Jimi Hendrix Experience) and Jon Lord (later, Deep Purple). The high spot of the group's career was a guest appearance on ITV's *Emergency Ward 10.* The singles from 'Cry Cry Cry' onwards were produced by Joe Meek.

The Roadrunners

EP

Pantomania   (Cavern Sound 2. BSN.L7, 2/65)

George Harrison once described the Rolling Stones as being "almost as good as the Roadrunners", but their only UK release is this EP for Liverpool University's 1965 rag week. They perform a bluesy 'Cry, Cry, Cry' and a jokey rewrite of 'The Leaving of Liverpool' and the EP also contains comedy material from students, Chris Edwards and Clive Woods. 5,000 standard copies were pressed, but 10 copies of a special issue included 'My Husband and I', a sketch about the Royal Family that had been banned by the Lord Chamberlain. *Pantomania* was the first record to be produced by Peter Hepworth and Nigel Greenberg at their Cavern Sound studios.

The Roadrunners were popular at the Star-Club, releasing a Germany single ('Little Ruby' / 'Beautiful Delilah', (Ariola 10794 AT, 1964) and sharing an album with Newcastle's Shorty And Them, *Star-Club Show 2* (Star-Club 158001, 1965). The *Star-Club Show 2* LP is available on CD (Repertoire IMS 7014, 1994) and includes *Pantomania* as well as two tracks for a French compilation in 1967.

After stints with the Roadrunners and Liverpool Scene, Mike Hart became a solo performer, and his 1969 LP, *Mike Hart Bleeds* (Dandelion S 63756), produced by John Peel, is brilliant. The CD reissue (See For Miles SEECD 419, 1995) is included with Hart's weaker second album, *Basher, Chalky, Pongo And Me* (1972).

Paul Rodgers

Four An' Twenty Thousand Kisses / Free To Love	(HMV POP 872, 1961)
Always / Joanie Don't Be Angry	(HMV POP 1121, 1963)
Meine Liebe Wird Niemals Enden (All My Sorrows) / Angela (German language)	
	(Germany, Polydor 52349, 1964)

Actually, the Liverpool singer and record producer, Paul Murphy.

Earl Royce and the Olympics

Que Sera, Sera / I Really Do	(Columbia DB 7433, 12/64)
Guess Things Happen That Way / Sure to Fall	(Parlophone R 5261, 4/65)

'Que Sera, Sera', produced by George Martin, bears little resemblance to Doris Day's original and incorporates riffs from 'Sweets for My Sweet' and 'La Bamba' as well as a football whistle. **Earl Royce (844)** says, "Kenneth Williams was the only one who voted it a Miss on *Juke Box Jury* and he was right."

Earl Royce and the Olympics perform 'Shake A Tail Feather' in the film, *Ferry Cross The Mersey*.

Johnny Sandon

(With the Remo Four) Lies / On the Horizon	(Pye 7N 15542, 7/63)
(With the Remo Four) Yes / Magic Potion	(Pye 7N 15559, 10/63)
Sixteen Tons / The Blizzard	(Pye 7N 15602, 1/64)
Donna Means Heartbreak / Some Kinda Wonderful	(Pye 7N 15665, 6/64)
The Blizzard / (I'd Be) A Legend In My Time	(Pye 7N 15717, 10/64)

'Yes' is also on the compilation *Package Tour* (Golden Guinea GGL 0268). Two versions of 'The Blizzard' were released, the second being slower and featuring Pye's wind machine. During the 1970s, Sandon worked the clubs as a comedian under his real name of Billy Beck, but he returned to performing as Johnny Sandon. He worked as a taxi driver, and, utterly disillusioned with life, he hanged himself on Christmas Day, 1996.

Scaffold

2 Day's Monday / Three Blind Jellyfish   (Parlophone R 5443, 5/66)
Goodbat Nightman / A Long Strong Black Pudding   (Parlophone R 5548, 12/66)

Unlike nearly everyone else in this listing, the hits were to come: 'Thank U Very Much' (1967, UK 4, US 69), 'Lily The Pink' (1968, UK 1, Germany 5) and 'Liverpool Lou' (1974, UK 7).

Roger McGough (845) says, "It was great fun doing *Top of the Pops* and touring with the Hollies, the Yardbirds and Manfred Mann, but I felt outside it. I'd be on stage singing the songs and realising that half the audience could sing them better. I've never been a musician and I knew Scaffold was living on borrowed time."

The Searchers

Sweets for My Sweet / It's All Been a Dream   (Pye 7N 15533, 6/63, UK 1, Germany 44)
Sweet Nothin's / What'd I Say   (Philips BF 1274, 9/63, UK 48)
Sugar and Spice / Saints and Searchers   (Pye 7N 15566, 10/63, UK 2, US 44)
Needles and Pins / Saturday Night Out   (Pye 7N 15594, 1/64, UK 1, US 13, Germany 8)
Don't Throw Your Love Away / I Pretend I'm With You
                       (Pye 7N 15630, 4/64, UK 1, US 16, Germany 37)
Someday We're Gonna Love Again / No One Else Could Love Me
                              (Pye 7N 15670, 7/64, UK 11, US 34)
When You Walk In the Room / I'll Be Missing You   (Pye 7N 15694, 9/64, UK 3, US 35)
What Have They Done To the Rain? / This Feeling Inside
                             (Pye 7N 15739, 11/64, UK 13, US 29)
Goodbye My Love / Til I Met You   (Pye 7N 15794, 2/65, UK 4, US 52, Germany 16)
He's Got No Love / So Far Away   (Pye 7N 15878, 6/65, UK 12, US 79)
When I Get Home / I'm Never Coming Back   (Pye 7N 15950, 10/65, UK 35)
Take Me For What I'm Worth / Too Many Miles   (Pye 7N 15992, 12/65, UK 20, US 76)
Take It Or Leave It / Umbrella Man   (Pye 7N 17094, 4/66, UK 31)
Have You Ever Loved Somebody? / It's Just The Way
                              (Pye 7N 17094, 9/66, UK 48, US 94)

EPs

Ain't Gonna Kiss Ya   (Pye NEP 24177, 8/63)
Sweets for My Sweet   (Pye NEP 24183, 9/63)
Hungry for Love   (Pye NEP 24184, 1/64)
The System   (Pye NEP 24201, 7/64)
When You Walk In the Room   (Pye NEP 24204, 11/64)
Bumble Bee   (Pye NEP 24218, 5/65)
Searchers '65   (Pye NEP 24222, 9/65)
Four By Four   (Pye NEP 24228, 1/66)

LPs

Meet The Searchers   (Pye NPL 18086, 7/63)
Sweets For My Sweet   (German import, Philips P 48 052 L, 9/63)
Sugar And Spice   (Pye NPL 18089, 11/63)
It's The Searchers   (Pye NPL 18092, 5/64)

Sounds Like The Searchers	(Pye NPL 18111, 3/65)
Take Me For What I'm Worth	(Pye NPL 18120, 12/65)

'Love Potion Number Nine', the Searchers' only Top 10 hit in America, was never issued as a UK single. They climbed to No.3 with 'Love Potion Number Nine' (Kapp 27, 1964 – also No.23 in Germany) and reached No. 61with 'Ain't That Just Like Me' and No.21 with 'Bumble Bee' (Kapp 49, 1965). As late as 1971, the Searchers made the US Top 100 with 'Desdemona', admittedly only to No.94.

The Searchers rued the day that they allowed Philips to record their set at the Star-Club as, once they made it, it was milked as much as possible. The German releases, all from 1963/4 are:

Sweet Nothin's / What'd I Say	(Philips 345592)
Sweets For My Sweet / Listen To Me	(Philips 345606)
Sick And Tired / Learning The Game	(Philips 345621)
(The label says 'Led In The Game')	
Sho' Know A Lot About Love / Doncha Know	(Star-Club 148500)

EP

Live At The Star-Club	(Philips 423 469 NL)

LP

Sweets For My Sweet	(Philips P 48 052 L)

In the States, much of the Star-Club performance was on *Hear Hear* (Mercury SR 60914) and the remainder was combined with tracks from the Hamburg group, the Rattles, to make *The Rattles Meet The Searchers* (Mercury SR 60994).

Their German language singles were:

Süss Ist Sie (Sugar And Spice) / Liebe (Money)	(Vogue DV 14116, 1963)
Tausend Nadelstiche (Needles And Pins) / Farmer John (German version)	
	(Vogue DV 14130, 1964)

(The literal UK translation of 'Tausend Nadelstiche' is '1,000 Needlepricks' – lovely!)

Verzeih' My Love (Goodbye My Love) /	
Wenn Ich Dich She' (When You Walk In The Room)	(Vogue DV 14338, 1965)

The Searchers also recorded a French EP *The Searchers Chantent En Francais* (Vogue PNV 24121) comprising 'Mais C'Etait Un Reve (It's All Been A Dream)', 'C'Est Arrivé Come Ca (Don't Throw Your Love Away)', 'C'Est De Notre Age (Sugar And Spice – odd one that)' and 'Ils La Chantaient Il Y A Longtemps (Saints And Searchers)'.

I'm not sure how it's happened but I have 27 CDs by the Searchers, an indication of how their tracks are being endlessly reissued and reconstituted for new compilations. Of particular interest are:

The Iron Door Sessions (Sequel CMBCD 485, 2002) (Tony Jackson had kept their audition tapes for Pye, recorded in Liverpool at the Iron Door club but without an audience. 'Maggie May' and 'Let's Stomp' are amongst the titles.)

The Searchers At The Star-Club (Bear Family BCD 16602 AH, 2002) (1963 LP with additional tracks, containing their full performance from 1 March 1963)

BBC Sessions (Castle CMEDD 938, 2CD, 2004) (31 tracks, mostly from *Saturday Club*. Brian Matthew usually interviews Chris Curtis, who is decidedly off-message).

Swedish Radio Sessions, 1964-1967 (Sequel CMRCD 394, 2001) (This CD contains some songs that they never officially recorded.)

German, French And Rare Recordings (Germany, Repertoire RR 4102 WZ, 1990) (For completists only – the Searchers' foreign language recordings plus their worst ever recordings – 'Kinky Kathy Abernathy' and 'Somebody Shot The Lollipop Man'.)

The 30th Anniversary Collection (Sequel NXT CD 170, 3CD set, 1993) (Third CD includes recordings from BBC's *Saturday Club*.)

The 40th Anniversary Collection (Sanctuary CMEDD 726, 2CD, 2003) (The first collection to bring together the Searchers' recordings for Pye, Liberty, RCA, Sire, PRT and Coconut.)

All their Pye albums have been reissued with their mono and stereo versions on each CD, together with bonus tracks: *Meet The Searchers* (Sequel CMRCD 155), *Sugar And Spice* (Sequel CMRCD 156), *It's The Searchers* (Sequel CMRCD 157), *Sounds Like The Searchers* (Sequel CMRCD 158) and *Take Me For What I'm Worth* (Sequel CMRCD 159).

Denny Seyton and the Sabres

Tricky Dicky / Baby, What You Want Me To Do	(Mercury MF 800, 2/64)
Short Fat Fannie / Give Me Back My Heart	(Mercury MF 814, 6/64)
The Way You Look Tonight / Hands Off	(Mercury MF 824, 9/64, UK 48)
(As Denny Seyton's Show-Group):	
Mir Geht Es Wieder Besser (Just A Little Bit Better) / Hushabye	(Germany, Decca D 19681, 1965)
(As Denny Seyton's Show Group):	
It's All Right / Du Bist Meine Wahre Liebe	(Germany, Decca D 19682, 1965)
Just a Kiss/ In the Flowers By The Trees	(Parlophone R 5363, 11/65)

LP

It's The Gear (14 Hits)   (Wing WL 1032, 3/65)

Denny Seyton and the Sabres were asked by an American record company to cover the hits of their contemporaries for an album called *It's The Gear!*. They were told they could have a percentage of the royalties or £200. They listened to what they had recorded and took the money.

In September 1965 Denny Seyton and the Sabres had their moment of glory when 'The Way You Look Tonight' spent one week in the charts at No.48. **Denny Seyton (846)** remembers, "Mark Wynter was singing 'The Way You Look Tonight' and we asked him if he was recording it. He said no, so we did it. The Everly Brothers were at No.49, so for those few days we were selling more than the Everlys."

Spiegl, Fritz and Barock and Roll Ensemble

EP

Eine Kleine Beatle Music   (HMV 7EG 8887, 1964)

Fritz was in the Royal Liverpool Philharmonic Orchestra and this was one of the first bids to unite the two cultures. Surprisingly good.

Freddie Starr and the Midnighters

Who Told You? / Peter Gunn Locomotion	(Decca F 11663, 5/63)
It's Shaking Time / Baby Blue	(Decca F 11786, 11/63)
Never Cry on Someone's Shoulder / Just Keep on Dreaming	(Decca F 12009, 9/64)

All produced by Joe Meek and not a happy arrangement for either party. **Freddie Starr (847)**: "Things would have worked out differently if I'd had Howie Casey and Brian Griffiths around. I should have stuck to the old material, which I loved doing. It was a pain in the backside doing 'Who Told You?', which I really hate. I sound like a choirboy being sick. 'Peter Gunn Locomotion' is no better. It was commercial rubbish." For all that, Freddie asserts his individuality with some loony sounds at the start of 'Peter Gunn Locomotion'.

There is a German LP by Freddy Starr and the Star Boys (sic), actually the Exchequers who became Liverpool Beat, and the album is called *This Is Liverpool Beat* (Vogue LDV 17006, 1964). It is said to be "Recorded live at the Iron Door club, Liverpool", but it wasn't.

Rory Storm and the Hurricanes

Dr. Feelgood / I Can Tell	(Oriole 45-CB 1858, 12/63)
America / Since You Broke My Heart	(Parlophone R 5197, 11/64)

Also featured on both volumes of *This is Mersey Beat*, but, considering their importance to the development of beat music on Merseyside, very few releases. Rory wasn't on 'Since You Broke My Heart'. The vocals were handled by Lu Walters and Johnny Guitar.

The Swinging Blue Jeans

It's Too Late Now / Think of Me	(HMV POP 1170, 6/63, UK 30)
Do You Know? / Angie	(HMV POP 1206, 9/63)
Hippy Hippy Shake / Now I Must Go	(HMV POP 1242, 12/63, UK 2, US 24, Germany 9)
Good Golly Miss Molly / Shaking Feeling	(HMV POP 1273, 3/64, UK 11, US 43, Germany 35)
You're No Good / Don't You Worry About Me	(HMV POP 1304, 5/64, UK 3, US 97)
Promise You'll Tell Her / It's So Right	(HMV POP 1327, 8/64)
It Isn't There / One of These Days	(HMV POP 1375, 12/64)
Make Me Know You're Mine / I've Got A Girl	(HMV POP 1409, 3/65)
Crazy 'Bout My Baby / Good Lovin'	(HMV POP 1477, 10/65)
Don't Make Me Over / What Can I Do Today?	(HMV POP 1501, 1/66, UK 31)
Sandy / I'm Gonna Have You	(HMV POP 1533, 6/66)
Rumours, Gossip, Words Untrue / Now The Summer's Gone	(HMV POP 1564, 11/66)

EPs

Shake	(HMV 7EG 8850, 5/64)
You're No Good, Miss Molly	(HMV 7EG 8868, 8/64)

LP

Blue Jeans A-Swinging (HMV CLP 1802, 10/64)
(Reissued on a CD with mono and stereo versions together, EMI DORIG 104)

Ray Ennis (848): "We made our first album in a day. We were allowed two sessions – one in the morning and one in afternoon and that included a tea break. We had a late night the night before but we had wrapped it up with about four hours' recording. Wally Ridley rejected a lot of our stuff and we had to find other numbers and rehearse them in the lunch hour. We took 'Lawdy Miss Clawdy' off Elvis' first LP, which we particularly liked. We wanted Les to play piano on it which was difficult for him as he had never heard the song before and it was in a key he never played in. In the circumstances, it turned out rather well."

Badly let down by HMV, really. Why did they only record one album for the UK market? Why was the album, *Don't Make Me Over* (Capitol T 6159, 1966), only issued in Canada?

The compilations below include previously unissued material:

Hippy Hippy Shake – The Definitive Collection (US, EMI 0777 7 80256 2 7, 1993) ('You've Got Love', 'Get Rid Of Her', 'It's True', 'Gotta Draw The Line (Sydney)')

The Best Of The EMI Years (EMI CDEMS 1446, 1992) ('Three Little Fishes', 'Ready Teddy', 'Chug-a-lug', 'You're Welcome To My Heart', 'I Wanna Be There', 'I Want Love', 'Summer Comes Sunday', 'Big City')

The Swinging Blue Jeans At Abbey Road, 1963-1967 (EMI 493 3272, 1998) ('Old Man Mose', 'I'm Gonna Sit Right Down And Cry Over You', 'This Boy', 'It's In Her Kiss')

Their German language singles are:
Das Ist Prima (Shaking Feeling) / Good Golly Miss Molly (German language)
(Electrola E 22734, 1964)

Tutti Frutti (German language) / Das Ist Vorbei (Columbia C 22870, 1964)

A full concert by the Swinging Blue Jeans, *Live At The Cascade Club, Köln*, was released in Germany in 1964 and has been reissued on Repertoire REP 4492.

Kingsize Taylor and the Dominoes

(As the Shakers) Money (That's What I Want) / Memphis Tennessee
(Polydor NH 52 158, 6/63)

(As the Shakers) Whole Lotta Lovin' / I Can Tell (Polydor NH 52 272, 12/63)
Memphis Tennessee / Money (That's What I Want) (Polydor NH 66 990, 3/64)
Hippy Hippy Shake / Dr. Feelgood (Polydor NH 66 991, 3/64, Germany 45)
Stupidity / Bad Boy (Decca F 11874, 4/64)
Somebody's Always Trying / Looking For My Baby (Decca F 11935, 7/64)

"'Somebody's Always Trying' was a cracking single," says **Kingsize Taylor (849)** today, "We had Jimmy Page on lead guitar, Alan Hawkshaw on piano, Red Price on sax and two drummers, Clem Cattini and Ginger Baker. The Breakaways were doing the backing vocals and there was an orchestra as well. I can't understand why it hasn't been reissued.".

EP

Teenbeat From The Star-Club, Hamburg 2   (Decca DFE 8569, 4/64)

LP

(As the Shakers) *Let's Do the Madison, Twist, Locomotion, Slop, Hully Gully, Monkey* (Polydor 237 139, 12/63) (Issued in the US as *Real Gonk Man*, Midnight 2102, 1964)

In Germany the band recorded for Polydor as the Shakers whilst under contract to Philips. The Philips recordings weren't issued in the UK but the German single 'Never In a Hundred Years' (Philips 345 618 PF, 1963) shows Taylor's vocal range. The Polydor single of 'Money (That's What I Want)' was given its true identity once the Philips contract had expired. The LP was repackaged under the same number as *Shakers' Twist Club with Kingsize Taylor and the Dominoes*.

The *Teenbeat 2* EP was recorded live at the Star-Club by Ariola Eurodisc and leased to Decca for UK release. *Teenbeat 1* featured the Rattles and *Teenbeat 3* the Bobby Patrick Six, who came from Germany and Scotland respectively. A full concert from Kingsize Taylor was recorded by Ariola and part of this was released on the album, *Twist Time Im Star-Club Hamburg, 2* (Germany, Ariola 70 952 IT) and the rest on *Star-Club Time With Kingsize Taylor And The Dominoes* (Germany Ariola 71 430 IT). The only way to hear the full recordings together is on one of the CDs on the 4 CD set, *Die Ariola Star-Club Aufnahmen* (Bear Family BCD 16226 DK, 1999).

The Dominoes' first commercial recording was backing Audrey Arno on 'Bitte Bleib Doch Bei Mir (Please Stay With Me)' / 'Limbo Italiano', credit being given to 'Audrey Arno die Tony Taylor band (sic). The singer gives an emotional performance on the A-side, possibly because she'd just been told of the death of her father.

Kingsize Taylor's discography is complicated as he would sign anything. If a record company offered him money, he would sign it irrespective of the fact that he was already under contract. Kingsize is not particularly interested in historical detail, so the details of the names he used or the artists he backed may be lost forever.

Kingsize Taylor and the Dominoes' early years (i.e. pre-Hamburg and pre-1960) are well documented on a 4 LP set prepared and issued in Germany, *Liverpool's First Rock'n'Roll Band* (Merseyside's Greatest MGBOX 801005/6/78, 1990).

Sam Hardie played organ with the German band, the Tramps, and can be heard on their 1965 single, 'Eene-Meene-Ming-Mang-Mo' and 'Sweetheart Goodbye'.

Tiffany

I Know / Am I Dreaming?   (Parlophone R 5311, 8/65)

(As Tiffany's Thoughts):

Find Out What's Happening, Baby / Baby, Don't Look Down

                    (Parlophone R 5439, 4,66)

Cluttered production of 'I Know', previously recorded by Beryl Marsden. 'Am I Dreaming?' is a little known Jackie DeShannon song. The publicity for this first single came from Unit Four Plus Two who thanked her for lending transport when their van broke down.

The Trends

All My Loving / Sweet Little Miss Love   (Piccadilly 7N 35171, 12/63)

You're A Wonderful One / The Way You Do the Things You Do   (Pye 7N 15644, 4/64)

The NME reviewer thought the Trends' 'You're A Wonderful One' was better than Marvin Gaye's.

Cy Tucker

My Prayer / High School Dance   (Fontana TF 424, 11/63)

Let Me Call You Sweetheart / I Apologise   (Fontana TF 470, 5/64)

My Friend / Hurt   (Fontana TF 534, 2/65)

Cy Tucker was the second vocalist and guitarist with Earl Preston and the TTs. His powerful revival of 'My Prayer' was advertised as "Liverpool's latest – Liverpool's greatest – Mr. Emotion."

'My Friend' was recorded with a 40 piece orchestra, conducted by Les Reed, and the Mike Sammes Singers. **Cy Tucker (850)** says, "I was terrified and, to make it worse, the holes in my shoes had let in the rain."

Cy worked for the GPO and press articles described him as a happy-go-lucky, singing postman. Far more street cred than the Singing Postman from Norwich.

Cy Tucker and the Friars are a very popular Merseyside club act with his group, the Friars, and has released several records to sell at gigs. I think his hearing's going though – everything, and I do mean everything, is turned up to 10 when he plays.

The Undertakers

Everybody Loves a Lover / (Do The) Mashed Potatoes   (Pye 7N 15543, 7/63)

What About Us? / Money   (Pye 7N 15562, 10/63)

Just a Little Bit / Stupidity   (Pye 7N 15607, 2/64, UK 49)

(As the 'Takers) If You Don't Come Back / Think   (Pye 7N 15690, 9/64)

Pye thought that the Undertakers' records weren't selling because of their name, and hence, they became the 'Takers for their fourth single. Still didn't work, but their singles were great including Jackie Lomax's lead vocals and Brian Jones on sax. In 1965 the Undertakers, freed from their Pye contract, recorded an R&B album in New York, but it was not released until 1995 when it was combined with the Pye singles for *Unearthed* (Big Beat CDWIKD 163).

Geoff Nugent fronts the Undertakers to this day. He's not as versatile a vocalist as Lomax but to hear him go "Mashed potato, yeah" is always exciting. Jackie Lomax, now living in America, played the Beatles Convention in 2003 and previewed his new album, *The Ballad Of Liverpool Slim*. He performed nothing from his Undertaker days but did several songs from his Apple album, *Is This What You Want?* (1969), now issued with bonus tracks on Apple CDP 7975812.

The Valkyries

Rip It Up / What's Your Name?   (Parlophone R 5123, 4/64)

Sonny Webb and the Cascades

You've Got Everything / Border of the Blues   (Oriole 45-CB 1873, 12/63)

Featured on both volumes of the compilation *This is Merseybeat*. Lead singer Kenny Johnson has presented *Sounds Country* on BBC Radio Merseyside for over 20 years.

Derry Wilkie and the Pressmen

One track on *This is Merseybeat, Volume 1*. Derry never made the big time but he was a remarkable showman. His quest to find the perfect group continued until his death in 2001. Derry was always very keen on Little Richard and Ray Charles. His first son was called Richard Penniman Wilkie after Little Richard and his second son was Ray Charles Wilkie.

The Young Ones

How Do I Tell You (I Don't Love You) / Baby That's It   (Decca F 11705, 8/63)

A Shel Talmy production. Female vocals on A-side, male on reverse.

Compilation Albums

In July 1963 the two volumes of *This is Merseybeat* (Oriole PS 40047/8) were issued. An EP, *Take Six* (Oriole EP 7080), was extracted from the album. The albums featured ten Liverpool groups and they were:

The Del Renas: Sigh, Cry, Almost Die; When Will I Be Loved?
Faron's Flamingos: Let's Stomp; Shake Sherry; So Fine; Talkin' Bout You
Ian and the Zodiacs: It Ain't Necessarily So; Let's Turkey Trot; Secret Love
The Merseybeats: Our Day Will Come
The Nomads (later, **The Mojos**): My Whole Life Through
Mark Peters and the Silhouettes: Someday (When I'm Gone from You)
Earl Preston and the TTs: All Around the World (Cy Tucker, vocal); Hurt (Cy Tucker, vocal), Thumbin' a Ride
Rory Storm and the Hurricanes: Beautiful Dreamer (Lu Walters, vocal); Dr. Feelgood; I Can Tell
Sonny Webb and the Cascades: Border Of The Blues; Excuse Me; Who Shot Sam?; You've Got Everything
Derry Wilkie and the Pressmen: Hallelujah I Love Her So

Decca released a live album *At the Cavern* (LK 4597) in March 1964, but only four of the nine acts came from Liverpool. The outsiders were Dave Berry and the Cruisers, Bern Elliott and the Fenmen, the Fortunes, Heinz and the Marauders. The Liverpool acts were:

The Big Three: Bring It on Home to Me
Lee Curtis and the All Stars: Jezebel; Skinny Minnie
The Dennisons: Devoted to You; You Better Move On
Beryl Marsden: Everybody Loves a Lover

Gerry and the Pacemakers were the mainstay of the soundtrack album, *Ferry Cross the Mersey* (Columbia 33 SX 1676), issued in January 1965. The album includes Cilla Black and the Fourmost, while the Black Knights and the Blackwells are added to the US version. It is rare for a US album to be more comprehensive that its UK counterpart.

Liverpool Today – Live at the Cavern (Ember NR 5028) was recorded by Cavern Sound and released in September 1965. A good record featuring Earl Preston's Realms, Michael Allen, The Richmond and introductions from Bob Wooler.

CD compilations

This Is Mersey Beat (Edsel EDCD 270, 1989) (The Oriole albums, give and take a couple of tracks)

Some Other Guys – 32 Merseybeat Nuggets (Sequel NEX CD 102, 1990)
(Pye and Piccadilly catalogue)

What About Us? – More Merseybeat Nuggets (Sequel NEX CD 204, 1992)
(More from Pye and Piccadilly)

Liverpool 1963-1968, Volume 1 (See For Miles SEECD 370, 1994)
(EMI catalogue. Volume 2 is only on vinyl – CD CM 125 – and covered the Decca catalogue. Strangely, Volume 1's reissue on CD used the cover picture on Volume 2.)

Live At The Cavern (See For Miles SEECD 385, 1994)
(Combines the live Decca album from the Cavern with the Big Three EP)

A Concert For Colin (Pilar 03 CD, 2000)
(The tribute concert to Colin Manley at the Philharmonic Hall with Vince Earl, the Merseybeats, the Searchers, the Swinging Blue Jeans and several non-Liverpool acts)

This Is Mersey Beat, Volume 3 – Blues, Folk And Beatniks

(Mayfield MA CD 201A, 2002)

(Beautiful packaged CD of unissued vintage tracks, but despite the title, little Merseybeat. Solid blues from the Almost Blues, T.L's Bluesicians and the Terry Hines Sextet, all recorded in 1964/5.)

Unearthed Merseybeat, Volume 1 (Viper CD 016, 2003)
(19 previously unissued tracks plus one that had. Fantastic collection, the gems including the Kirbys, the Merseybeats and the Swinging Blue Jeans.)

Despite this activity, there is scope for a multi-label Merseybeat collection. The trouble relates to the Beatles. A definitive compilation without them is unthinkable, and yet Apple are unlikely to give permission for their appearance on a multi-artist collection.. Even if they did, they might want most of the royalties.

UNISSUED TRACKS

When Mark Lewisohn published his definitive book on the Beatles' recording sessions in 1988, I was green with envy. Here was someone writing at length about tracks we would never hear. He described them so well that I was itching to hear them. Then the Beatles changed their minds, perhaps, if I am cynical, because not even Paul McCartney could generate much interest for his new releases. The three double-CD sets which comprise the Beatle *Anthology* series have demonstrated the huge, global market for unissued tracks and alternative takes from the 60s. In 2003 we were given *Let It Be...Naked* and I can see a host of original Beatle albums being reissued with variations.

The interest in the Beatles' outtakes is undeniable, but there is another treasure trove in the outtakes from the other Merseybeat bands. In 2003 a local record company, Viper, which is owned by Mike Badger from the La's and Paul Hemmings from Lightning Seeds, appreciated what was on their doorsteps and issued the CD, *Unearthed Merseybeat, Volume 1*. I hope it sells sufficiently for further volumes to be considered.

This listing gives what I know to be available. I have heard around 80% of these tracks so I know that they exist. Most of them are in good condition too and certainly none are in such poor condition as the Quarry Men tracks on the Beatles' *Anthology 1*.

The Manchester band, Wayne Fontana and the Mindbenders, was recorded live at the Cavern in February 1964. Whatever became of the tapes? Also, *Mersey Beat* reported that both Derry Wilkie and Barbara Harrison were signed to Decca, but I can't trace any releases.

Alby and the Sorrals
Demo of two originals, 'Why' and 'Foolin'', cut in 1963.

The Beatles
Even after *Anthology*, there is still plenty of unissued stuff around.

'Puttin' On The Style' and several other tapes of the Quarry Men rehearsing.

'Love Of The Loved' (1962) – Decca audition

'Cat Walk' (1962) – Practice session at the Cavern – subsequently became 'Cat Call' for the Chris Barber Band.

'A Picture Of You' (1962) – BBC recording with Pete Best.

'Bad To Me' (1963) – John Lennon's demo for Billy J. Kramer.

'One And One Is Two' (1963) – Paul McCartney's demo, also for Billy J. Kramer.

'I'm In Love' (1963) – What happened to John Lennon's demo when Brian O'Hara died?

'Tie Me Kangaroo Down Sport' (1963) – Rolf Harris and the Beatles on a BBC radio show. Perhaps best forgotten.

'Carnival Of Light' (1967) – 14 minute experimental track, written for a psychedelic festival at the Roundhouse in London's Chalk Farm. This has been on the verge of being released several times. John Lennon says "Barcelona" over and over again.

'Anything' (1967) – Ringo, of all people, leading the experimentation on a 22 piece percussion track.

'Etcetera' (1968) – Paul tried to interest Marianne Faithfull in this ballad but no one remembers what happened next.

'Sour Milk Sea' (1968) – George Harrison demo for Jackie Lomax.

'Heather' (1968) – Paul and Donovan dedicate a song to Paul's stepdaughter.

Several rock'n'roll songs from the *Let It Be* sessions including 'Save The Last Dance For Me' and 'Bye Bye Love'.

'Wake Up In The Morning' (1969) – Unknown Lennon and McCartney song from the *Let It Be* sessions.

'Madman Coming' (1969) – Several attempts were made to record this during the *Let It Be* sessions.

The Big Three

Producer **Noel Walker (851)**: "Just out of interest, I would give them songs from a previous era and see how they would work. One of them was 'I Surrender, Dear' and I asked them to do it in their own way."

Other outtakes that might surface – 'Fortune Teller'; 'Long Tall Sally'; 'Walkin' the Dog'. Quite apart from the famed Decca EP, there's a tape of the Big Three at the Cavern but the balance is wrong as it sounds like a long drum solo from Johnny Hutch. Come to think of it, that might be normal.

Cilla Black

'Who Can I Turn To?'; 'You've Got to Stay With Me'.

Paddy Chambers and Beryl Marsden

'Here We Go Again'; 'Take Me in Your Arms Again'; You and Me', produced by the Real Thing's manager, Tony Hall. First rate soul music from early 70s from when they were a soul duo at the She Club.

The Clayton Squares

'I've Been Loving You Too Long', produced by Andrew Loog Oldham.

The Connoisseurs

The Connoisseurs did a recording test for George Martin, who decided not to offer them a contract. A few months later they acquired a new lead singer in Vince Earl, which could have made the difference. The demos recorded with Vince in Stockport feature good harmonies and instrumentation, and their own song, 'Make Up Your Mind', is a good one. "I hadn't heard it in years," says **Vince Earl (852)**, who became Ron Dixon in *Brookside*, "The mixing could have been better but it's not bad."

The Cordes
They recorded two demos at Lambda Records in Crosby, 'Clarabella' and 'In The Evening'.

The Cryin' Shames
'Let Me In' has a driving rhythm with a kitchen-sink arrangement, subsequently added by the producer, Joe Meek. More Meek than Merseybeat.

Chris Curtis
Chris Curtis missed his opportunity when he left the Searchers as he should have concentrated on songwriting. He has written many songs while back in Liverpool, but done nothing with them, apart from recording rudimentary demos: 'Ain't That A Good Dream?','Daydream Of You', 'Don't Make Love In A Doorway' 'Death Wish', 'Down Down', 'Everything You Do', 'Godiva Came From Kentucky' 'If I Could Find Someone', 'Leave Me Alone', 'Love Keeps Fooling Me', 'Love Me Like You Used To Do' (intended for the Righteous Brothers), 'Lover Deceiver', 'Make The World A Better Place', 'She's Still In Love With Me', 'They Say', 'Thinking About You' and 'What Do I Do Now?'.

Chris Curtis (853): "I once went in a snowstorm to the Liverpool Empire with a song that would be brilliant for Cilla Black called 'Another Heart Is Broken (In The Game Of Life)', one I'd written especially for her with all posh chords on the piano. I thought she's got to go for this, she hasn't had a hit in yonks, and she told me, 'I don't do songs from cassettes.' How's she going to hear the bloody thing? Did she expect me to walk in with a 40-piece orchestra? And she hasn't had a hit since."

Lee Curtis and the All Stars
'No Other Love'

Steve Day and the Syndicate
Wump and his Werbles were one of the first beat groups to play the Cavern. The group became Steve Day and the Syndicate and this 1964 acetate features 'The Last Bus Home' and 'You Ask Me Why'. Songwriter Billy May is from another Liverpool band, the Pathfinders. Sign of the times: no-one would write a song about the last bus home these days as everybody goes by car. In 1979, Steve Day won *Opportunity Knocks!* as the comedian Rod McKenzie.

The Delmonts
Demos of 'Reet Petite', 'Blue Moon', 'First Taste Of Love', 'Before You Accuse Me', 'Sea Of Heartbreak'.

The Dennisons
1962 rehearsal tape includes rock'n'roll standards and 'A Picture Of You'.
'Yakety Yak' (Decca)

The Dimensions

Most Merseybeat bands had some Everly Brothers material in their repertoire and their version of 'I Wonder If I Care As Much' version featured some very tight harmonies. After working with Tiffany, the Dimensions became a cabaret band and worked with Dickie Valentine, who encouraged them to get a record contract. Nothing came of it, but their demo of 'I'll Take You Home Again, Kathleen' shows the lead singer's sensational voice, like Karl Denver in overdrive. Of all the unreleased tracks I have played on BBC Radio Merseyside, this one has attracted the most attention.

The Firecrests

A group of Birkenhead schoolboys with a similar repertoire to the Quarry Men, although they would not have known them – demos of 'Come Go With Me', 'That'll Be The Day' and 'I Knew From The Start' exist. Their lead singer, Chris Morris, became Lance Fortune and had a hit with 'Be Mine' in 1960.

The Four Just Men

Demos recorded at Eroica Studios, 31 Peel Street, Eccles, Manchester, 1964 – 'La Bamba', 'Friday Night', 'Sticks And Stones', unnamed instrumental.

Also 'You're So Ugly', 'Nightmare', 'Working Day Blues', 'Blue'.

The Fourmost

'Love of the Common People'

'Running Bear' (when Joey, Dave and Billy became Clouds) – full of war whoops and mad drumming.

Billy Fury

Both Ozit and Sanctuary Records have been issuing demos and unreleased tracks in recent years – *Wondrous Place* (Ozit CD 0052), *Billy Fury Sings A Buddy Holly Song Plus Other Early Demos And Unreleased Rare Recordings* (Ozit CD 0056 – and, yes, that is the title) and *The Sound Of Fury Demos* (Castle Select CD 608). Billy Fury's original demos for Larry Parnes are on all three albums.

In 1961 Billy's road manager, Liverpudlian Hal Carter, wrote 'Please Love Me' for him, very much in the vein of 'Jealousy'. Because Hal fell out with his employer, Larry Parnes, it was never released. "It was a bit bitchy," says Hal, "but that's the way Parnes was."

There are also some excellent performances of Jimmy Campbell songs from the early 1970s that haven't been released – 'Getting Sentimental Over You' (which sounds like an old-time standard), 'Green Eyed American Actress' and 'That's Right, That's Me', an intriguing song about losing at cards (I think). Opening line of the last song: "Judas Iscariot loaned me his chariot / Mad Jack gave me a loan" – and it gets weirder.

Johnny Gentle with Cass and the Cassanovas

Whilst on tour in Scotland, Johnny recorded a demo of 'After My Laughter Came Tears' with Cass and the Cassanovas.

Gerry and the Pacemakers

Gerry told me (on tape) in the early 1980s that there was nothing in EMI's vaults but unissued tracks have been appearing on compilations over the years.

The biggest find has been his 1961 demo recordings for Bernard Whitty in Crosby. 'What'd I Say' is on the Viper CD and there's 'Whole Lotta Shakin' Goin' On', 'Pretend' and 'Why Oh Why' to come.

Chick Graham and the Coasters

'Will You Love Me Tomorrow?'

George Harrison

Let's put a Beatle in here. Madonna's 1986 film, *Shanghai Surprise*, was a disaster in every way but one – the theme song. George Harrison recorded his song with another Liverpool singer, Vicki Brown, the wife of Joe. Because the film immediately sank, the single was cancelled, but it's one of George's best songs and a good companion to his *Hong Kong Blues*.

Bill Kenwright

The *Coronation Street* personality and theatre impresario started as a singer. Bill spent his teenage years going down to the Cavern and performing when given a chance. 'I'll Find A Way' and 'Karen', both written by Bob Pryde, are from around 1964. In the late 60s he cut several singles although none of them made the charts.

The Kinsleys

When Billy Kinsley left the Merseybeats and returned to live on Merseyside with his new wife, he formed the Kinsleys for local gigs and their demo of 'Goodbye' is excellent. 'Do Me A Favour' was later rewritten as 'Promise You'll Tell Her' and recorded by the Swinging Blue Jeans.

The Kirkbys

The Kirkbys' mainstay was their vocalist and songwriter, Jimmy Campbell. His standards were high and I have seen a five track acetate of unissued material where two tracks had been deliberately damaged because Jimmy thought they were substandard.

In 1967 the Kirkbys without Joe Marouth became 23rd Turnoff (that is, the route to Kirkby) and made the psychedelic single, 'Michaelangelo' (Deram DM 150). All the 23rd Turnoff demos are being released as a CD, *The Dreams Of Michaelangelo*, and there is also to be a CD of the Kirkby's work, *Yes It Is*. This band is set for a radical reassessment.

Billy J. Kramer and the Coasters

Audition tapes for The Grade Organisation.

Billy J. Kramer with the Dakotas

'One and One Is Two' – A McCartney song that Lennon didn't care for. He told Billy, 'Release that and your career is over'. The song was released by Mike Shannon and the Strangers. Who?

Johnny Goodison (the co-writer of 'United We Stand') wrote an album for Billy which was never released. I've not heard any of it, but Peter Skellern, who chanced upon the session, later wrote that it was the worst recording he'd ever heard!

The Mastersounds

Some RCA tracks with Dusty Springfield and Marvin Gaye as backup vocalists.

The Merseybeats

Considering that their home recording from December 1962 is of a young, new inexperienced group, 'So How Come' sounds surprisingly good. Someone recorded over part of the tape, but luckily there are couple of false starts and so a completed version can easily be put together. Clearly, the Merseybeats were influenced by *A Date With The Everly Brothers* (released October 1960) as that is their main source of material

The television programme, *ABC At Large*, decided to have a battle of the bands, Liverpool v Manchester, with the Merseybeats and Deke Rivers. The Merseybeats did 'Misery' from the Beatles' first album and a recording exists.

The British beat groups plundered Arthur Alexander's repertoire ('Anna', 'You Better Move On', 'A Shot Of Rhythm And Blues'), but surprisingly no one released the barnstorming 'Soldier Of Love' as a single. The Beatles performed it on *Pop Go The Beatles* but the Merseybeats' version was never released. Strong harmonies and solid drumming from John

'(You Gotta Go Down On Your Knees and) Cry Me a River' – powerful soul ballad.

The Merseys

'Charlie No One' – The coupling of two Fontana acts – the Merseybeats with Bradford's Kiki Dee – was never released but it should have been. It is a novelty song with more whimsy and less humour than 'Come Outside'.

'Nothing Can Change This Love' – This Sam Cooke song is a close cousin to 'Bring It On Home To Me' and the call-and-response between Tony and Billy on this revival is first rate. The Merseys never did much beyond 'Sorrow' but this could have gone Top 10.

The Mojos

'Drive It Home' – early recording for Decca.

'Spoonful' – **Stu James (854)**:"We felt a bit guilty about 'Everything's Alright' because our fans thought that we were getting away from the blues. We recorded a 12-bar blues called 'Spoonful' with mouth-harp, but Decca wouldn't release it as they wanted something more poppy. However, Decca put out an EP of some R&B songs, which is the best thing we did."

'Call My Name'; 'To Know Her Is to Love Her' (for Pye but management problems prevented release)

Paul Murphy and Johnny Guitar

'Butterfly': one-off recording made at Percy Phillips' recording studio in Kensington, Liverpool on 22 June 1957. The other track, 'She's Got It', is on *Unearthed Merseybeat, Volume 1*.

The Newtowns

Very nice, light beat treatment of 'Over The Rainbow', recorded at Unicord Overseas Promotions, 34 Moorfields, Liverpool 2. At the same session, the Newtowns covered Sandie Shaw's 'Tomorrow' (which is on *Unearthed Merseybeat, Volume 1*) and the Drifters' 'Please Stay'.

The Pathfinders

'I'm Ashamed Of You Baby' (written by Billy May) , 'Love Love Love', 'In My Lonely Room', 'Can I Get A Witness?', 'A Certain Girl', 'I'll Always Love You' – all 1964/5.

Earl Preston and the TTs

'Beautiful Delilah' – Shortly before his death in 1989, lead guitarist Lance Railton gave some mildewed tapes with wine spilt over them to drummer Ritchie Galvin. It turned out to be the group's first recording session from May 1963 and once Ritchie had cleaned them, they sounded fine. Lance used to put two banjo strings on his guitar so he could bend them further. This is a good example of his lead guitar work and with a strong lead vocal by Earl Preston, this is a fine track.

'Back Again To Me' – Songwriting by numbers – this catchy song from 1964 contains every element of the Merseybeat sound. Great fun.

'It Had to Be You' – More cheerful Merseybeat and it's surprising that this band only released one single. Even more so when you consider Joey Spruce's good looks. Oh, that's Earl Preston to you.

'Tossin' And Turnin'' – After backing Eden Kane for a Fontana session, there was some time left so the Merseyside band put down some tracks themselves. They weren't released but this energetic cover version of the US hit by Bobby Lewis is as good as any of the records they made. Great high-pitched oo's from Cy Tucker.

'Bony Moronie' – Cy Tucker rasps his way through the Larry Williams classic. Cy is backed by the TTs and it was recorded at the same session as 'Tossin' And Turnin''.

The Profiles

Regulars at Yankel Feather's Basement Club. Decca declined to issue their single, 'My Baby Kissed Me' and 'You Know She's Mine'.

Tommy Quickly

'No Reply'.

The Remo Four

As far as I know, the only group to have two sessions at Percy Phillips' studio. In November 1958 they recorded 'Poor Little Fool' and 'Hoots Mon' and then, in August 1959, 'Charlie Brown' and 'A Teenager In Love'.

Every year the Remo Four's first drummer, Harry Prytherch, sells memorabilia at the Beatles Convention in Liverpool. He has a CD of their Iron Door sessions – 'The Stranger', 'Perifidia', 'Trambone' and 'Walk Don't Run' – dating from 1961. **Don Andrew (855)** remembers, "It was a rehearsal recorded on a little Grundig tape recorder and we did four tracks. My favourite is 'The Stranger'. Colin Manley used to play every note that Hank Marvin played, the way he played it, and if Hank Marvin made a mistake, Colin used to copy that. We used to repeat the mistakes night after night, even if they weren't meant to be there."

'The Honeymoon Song'

'Playboy' (Marvelettes song)

Earl Royce and the Olympics

A frenzied 'Shake A Tail Feather', which the group performed in *Ferry Cross The Mersey*.

They also recorded 'Silence Is Golden', which was produced by Joe Meek.

Johnny Sandon

Chris Curtis recorded him singing Brook Benton's 'So Many Ways' for Pye.

Scaffold

The Scaffold At Abbey Road (EMI 496 4352, 1998) contained some unissued tracks including the witty calypso, 'Promiscuity' (cowritten with a Liverpool doctor), but still unissued are 'Butterscotch', 'Happy Song', 'Hilary Clarissa Sniffleton', 'Jellied Eels', 'The Leaving Of Liverpool', 'Little Song And Dance Man', 'Many People's Home', 'Nig Nog Pig Wog', 'One Man', 'Thanks A Million', 'Woolly Vest', and 'You Can't Hide Away From Me'.

Ray Scragg

When Ray Scragg left the Dennisons, he cut some demos to his own piano accompaniment. Very much influenced by Ray Charles, Ray's gravel voice sounds good on 'Makin' Whoopee'.

The Searchers

'For What It's Worth'

There is a entire concert performance in Stockholm in 1964, which is worth releasing for Chris Curtis' comments alone.

Denny Seyton and the Sabres

'Little Latin Lupe Lu' – 1963, at Percy Phillips' studio.

'Karen' – That Bob Pryde song again.

'Baby, What You Want Me To Do' – Oh dear. Not a good idea to try and turn Jimmy Reed's R&B classic into a comedy song.

'That's What Love Will Do'; (an Impressions number).

'Along Came Jones' – little known German single.

Also an LP produced by George Martin of which a single 'Just a Kiss' was released. The songs were written by Lally Stott from Prescot, who joined the group in 1965 and went on to write 'Chirpy Chirpy Cheep Cheep', a No.1 for Middle Of The Road. Lally was killed in a motorbike accident on the day of the Queen's Silver Jubilee.

The Silkie

Four students at Hull University – Mike Ramsden, Sylvia Tatler, Ivor Aylesbury and Kevin Cunningham – formed a folk group in 1963, and the bass player Cunningham, who came from Bootle, persuaded them to move to Liverpool. They worked at the Cavern with the Spinners and they recorded tracks at Cavern Sound including 'The Great Silkie' (a Hebridian song which gave them their name),'500 Miles', 'Settle Down', 'Fare Thee Well', 'I Am A Rock', 'Well All Right', 'I'm So Sorry Now', 'Linger', 'I Don't Believe You', 'Somewhere To Run', 'Blue', 'All My Sorrows', 'Prettty Boy Floyd', 'Portland Town', 'Darling Corey' and 'Freight Train', which were not released. They had a management contract with Brian Epstein and a record deal with Fontana. They had a single with 'You've Got To Hide Your Love Away', produced by John Lennon and with Paul on rhythm guitar and George tapping the back of a guitar.

Freddie Starr

Several hours of comedy material recorded at Cavern Sound: I wonder what the Official Receiver did with the tapes

Rory Storm and the Hurricanes

'I'll Be There'; 'Ubangi Stomp' (both produced by Brian Epstein).

Rory Storm and the Hurricanes made very few records and even fewer demos are around. 'Lend Me Your Comb', originally recorded by Carl Perkins, was ideal for Rory, who put his blond quiff in place with a large comb. The demo was recorded in 1965 but sounds earlier, and on its B-side, Rory says, "And now it's time for the star of our little show, Britain's answer to Duane Eddy, the magnificent, the sensational, the fabulous Johnny Guitar." On this playing of 'Green Onions', however, Duane has little to worry about.

The Swinging Blue Jeans

'I'm Shy, Mary Ellen, I'm Shy'; 'Yes Sir That's My Baby' – The Blue Genes came up in the trad boom but unlike the Merseysippi and Blue Magnolia jazz bands, they switched to rock'n'roll. In 1961 and still a jazz band, they went to Oriole for a recording test with John Schroeder. It's a lively, energetic performance featuring banjo and an amplified guitar solo. I fail to see why they didn't get a contract.

'Dizzy Chimes' (1961) – An instrumental, written by bass player Les Braid. There is a second demo, possibly destroyed, for producer Joe Meek.

Between 1959 and 1962, the Blue Jeans recorded many tracks in the ladies' cloakroom at the Mardi Gras (whilst the ladies weren't around, I hasten to add.). The repertoire is very varied – jazz tunes ('Alexander's Ragtime Band', 'Coney Island Washboard'), novelties ('Froggie Went A-Courtin''), standards ('Ain't She Sweet', 'April Showers'), country ('Bonaparte's Retreat'), gospel ('Gloryland', 'It Is No Secret (What God Can Do)'), rock'n'roll ('Forty Miles Of Bad Road', 'Just A Little Too Much') and UK hits ('Travellin' Light', 'What A Crazy World We're Living In'). Oddly, the jazz arrangement on 'Isle Of Capri' sounds like 'It's Not Unusual'.

There is a tape of the Swinging Blue Jeans on stage at the Cavern early in 1963. It is not their standard act as Ray Ennis can't sing due to a sore throat. There are rock'n'roll overtones including the Ventures' 'Walk Don't Run' and an impassioned vocal from Ralph Ellis on 'Send Me Some Lovin'', which has some tough rock'n'roll guitar alongside a jazz banjo.

There are very few extended instrumental solos on Merseybeat recordings, but the Swinging Blue Jeans allowed their drummer, Norman Kuhlke, to have full rein on a lively treatment of Glenn Miller's 'In The Mood'.

The Swinging Blue Jeans never wrecked hotel rooms – quite the reverse, when they returned to a hotel they might put on another show for the patrons. Ralph Ellis wrote 'We're Here Again', a pastiche of a music hall song for those occasions. 'We're Here Again' contains the same humour as the Beatles' Christmas records for their fan club. "How much was that suit then?" "25 guineas." "Good god, you could have got a new one for that."

Their unissued tracks span six decades by now and a very good 2CD set could be compiled of unissued material, but Ray Ennis is against this. He feels that it would confuse the SBJ's existing fans. He may be right but where's his sense of history?

Kingsize Taylor and the Dominoes

The 1957/8 private recordings have only had a limited release on a box set in Germany. Just 'Good Golly Miss Molly' has been issued in the UK, but this is History with a capital H. The group was recorded at the pianist's house at 18 Cambridge Road, Crosby. Even before Kingsize joined, they were good. Arthur Baker takes the vocal on 'Great Balls Of Fire' and Sam Hardie's pumping piano is great fun. There's even an original, 'Baby', written and sung by Charlie Flynn.

To get the balance right, the producer, Bernard Whitty, put the drummer, Dave Lovelady, at the top of the stairs, which was a master touch. 'Roll Over Beethoven' is excellent and the young KST's delivery is so confident – on occasion, he almost speaks the lines. Sam Hardie wrote 'Sad And Blue', a cheerful song about someone contemplating suicide.

Timon

This singer-songwriter from Formby was one of the first performers to be signed by Apple. He recorded 'Something New Every Day' (James Taylor, guitar and Paul

McCartney, piano), 'And Now She Says She's Young' and 'Who Needs a King?', all arranged by Mike Vickers and produced by Peter Asher. George Harrison didn't care for the tracks and so they weren't issued. Timon moved to Threshold and recorded 'And Now She Says She's Young', this time backed by the Moody Blues. He is still around, working as Tymon Dogg, and spending several years in Joe Strummer's Mescaleros.

Gus Travis

Gus had not made any records during his 25 year career but an early 1970s concert was professionally recorded. He's introduced as Gus 'Crazy Legs' Travis and, judging by the audience reaction, those crazy legs were working hard. His rock'n'roll act hasn't changed with the years. Neither has he. He hands out his 1963 publicity photographs at gigs. He'd had thousands printed on a bulk order when he was about to make the big-time. I love the Elvis-styled asides on 'Love Me'.

The Undertakers

'Hold On, I'm Comin'', 'My Babe' (Righteous Brothers song); 'Watch Your Step'; 'What's So Good About Goodbye?'

Lu Walters

'Fever'; 'September Song'; 'Summertime' (Wally was a member of the Hurricanes and he made this private recording in Hamburg backed by the Beatles. The only existing copy appears to belong to Wally's former wife.)

BIBLIOGRAPHY

I didn't usc many reference books while writing the original version of *Let's Go Down The Cavern*, simply because there wasn't anything apart from books on the Beatles. The situation has changed now and there are scores of books on the Beatles and their associates, and I have used them off and on to check places and dates. However, there are still no biographies of Billy J. Kramer, the Searchers or the Swinging Blue Jeans. A bibliography of Beatle books is a book in itself and this is a selection, which includes the key ones. (It feels terribly wanky to be including my own books in this list, but they are relevant.)

Adams, Roy: *Hard Nights – My Life In Liverpool Clubland* (Cavernman, 2003)

A colourful history of Liverpool clubland from one of the Cavern's owners. The stories are often told from the bouncers' perspectives and, hardly surprisingly, the book doesn't pull its punches. Far too many bodybuilding photographs for me - these guys look deformed!

Babiuk, Andy: *Beatles Gear* (Balafon, 2001)

And not just the Beatles? Makes of guitars, drums and amps leave me cold, but this is a very well researched book about what the Beatles (and thereby many other Liverpool musicians) were playing.

Barrow, Tony: *Cilla Black Through The Years* (Headline, 1993)

An illustrated romp through Cilla's career, taken chronologically, and although the author is too reverential towards his subject (he was her publicist, after all), it is a very good guide to all things Cilla. Some great photos.

Baxter, Lew: *Allan Williams Is…The Fool On The Hill* (Praxis, 2003)

Allan Williams' second volume of reminiscences and it's good to have an account of his life after the Beatles. Lots of bar-room philosophising and very entertaining, but it includes events I was at and I know that they didn't happen like that.

Beatles, The: *Anthology* (Cassell, 2000)

I know I've not nicked anything from this because I haven't read it. It's hard to psyche yourself to read such a big book when you know so much of it already.

Best, Pete, Roag and Rory: *The Beatles – The True Beginnings* (Spine, 2002)

A beautifully designed book about the Casbah. Good, informative text but the book is hampered by a lack of decent memorabilia. Colour plates of old stools, drum cases and electrical wires are hardly inspiring. Effectively, this is Pete Best's third autobiography as we have had *Beatle!* (with Patrick Doncaster) and *Best Of The Beatles* (with Bill Harry), but none of them touch on life after the Beatles.

Clayson, Alan: *The Quiet One – A Life Of George Harrison*
(Sidgwick and Jackson, 1990)

Clayson has written biographies of all four Beatles and a mark of their success is their availability as talking books. George Harrison's biography is best because the Beatles' story is rarely told from his angle and Clayson has a real empathy with the subject.

Clayson, Alan: *Hamburg – The Cradle Of British Rock* (Sanctuary, 1997)

The first study of British groups in Hamburg but spoilt by nonsensical opinions – "Would it shatter too many illusions" writes Clayson, "to learn than Dave Dee and the Bostons were more adored in Hamburg (and then all over Germany) than the Beatles?" Because Clayson does not want to encourage prurient instincts (he actually says this!), he does not emphasise the sexual side of the city as much as he should. With someone keeping a tight rein on some of his opinions and ordering him to sex it up, this could have been a great book.

Clayson, Alan with Spencer Leigh: *The Walrus Was Ringo – 101 Beatle Myths Debunked* (Chrome Dreams, 2003)

Good fun to write and the fact that we wrote it together gives it a better balance than either of us individually. The contract stipulated 101 myths and you can tell that we got a bit desperate in making up the total.

Coleman, Ray: *John Winston Lennon* (Sidgwick and Jackson, 1984)

Very good account of Lennon's pre-Yoko years. Coleman is on Lennon's side throughout, and I don't think that even Lennon would have viewed his past behaviour so uncritically.

Coleman, Ray: *Brian Epstein The Man Who Made The Beatles* (Viking, 1989)

Very informative book on Epstein and surprising that the more recently biography, *The Brian Epstein Story*, based on the BBC *Arena* specials, should be so disjointed and add so little. Coleman's book is especially strong on his business dealings.

Davies, Hunter: *The Beatles – The Authorised Biography* (Heinemann, 1968)

"Authorised" may mean "whitewashed" but hey, the Beatles were still a working band and they didn't want to ruin their career. Very easy to read and there's a great section where Davies, quite fortuitiously, is around when they are writing 'With A Little Help From My Friends'.

Davies, Hunter: *The Quarrymen* (Omnibus, 2001)

The story of the Quarrymen would never have been written without their famous ex-members and although none of Colin, Eric, Len, Pete and Rod make it in the music business, the story of their ups and downs is riveting.

Du Noyer, Paul: *Liverpool: Wondrous Place – Music From Cavern To Cream* (Virgin, 2002)

At long last, a book about Liverpool's music scene – Cavern, Eric's, Cream – but only 270 pages. The subject needs a 600 page treatment and indeed, the same could be said of just the Merseybeat years. Still, what's there is very good – Du Noyer, the founder of *Mojo*, comes from Liverpool and has plenty of insights. Plenty of interview material too.

Firminger, John: Cavern Stomp – Merseybeat On Record
(John Firminger Publications, 2002)

44 page collection of cuttings from the music press of the Sixties, reprinting record reviews and adverts from *Disc, New Musical Express* and *Record Mirror*. We've borrowed a few for this book – thanks, John.

Frame, Pete: *The Beatles And Some Other Guys* (Omnibus, 1997)

Superbly researched family trees and not as difficult to read and follow as you might think.

Gentle, Johnny, with Ian Forsyth: *Johnny Gentle And The Beatles* (Merseyrock, 1998)

The essential requirement for writing an autobiography or a memoir is a good memory. Yes, well…

Goldman, Albert: *The Lives Of John Lennon* (Bantam, 1988)

John Lennon's second assassination. Goldman had the funds to carry out major research, but he twisted everything to fit his own salacious theories. Quite a different John Lennon book could have been written with the same research. Await Ron Ellis's account of working with Goldman.

Gottfridsson, Hans Olof: *The Beatles – From Cavern To Star-Club* (Premium, 1997)

Too much detail for the casual fan and possibly even too much for me. Every nuance and variation of their Hamburg recordings is discussed lovingly by Gottfridsson, but the organisation of his material defies belief. With judicious ending, this wonderfully researched, 500 page book could have been reduced by a quarter and been much easier to follow.

Harrison, George: *I Me Mine* (Genesis, 1990)

George reproduces the scraps of paper on which he wrote his lyrics. He distances himself from the Beatles, and John Lennon only makes a guest appearance.

Harrower, David: *Presence* (Faber and Faber, 2001)

Well-researched play about the Beatles in Hamburg. Considering John Lennon's fondness for one-liners, it is curious that Harrower should keep him off-stage. The McCartney character assumes his wit and abrasiveness. It may be fiction, but then so are several, supposedly factual Beatle books. Very entertaining.

Harry, Bill: *Mersey Beat: The Beginnings Of The Beatles* (Omnibus, 1977)

Bill Harry's book of reprints from his *Mersey Beat* newspaper should be permanently in print, but it isn't so. This collection comprises 80 key pages with a long introduction from Harry. The musicians often wrote their own copy and there are classic examples of John Lennon's wit. The original ads surrounding the text give a feeling of time and place.

Harry, Bill: *The Beatles Encyclopedia* (Virgin, 2000)

Bill has also written separate encyclopedias for John, Paul, George and Ringo. The main problem is in guessing which letter something might be under. Nothing much wrong with the information but the difficulty is in finding it. I wanted to look up their fan club records for Christmas and found them under B as 'Beatles Christmas Records'.

Leach, Sam: *The Rocking City* (Pharaoh, 1999)

The Liverpool impresario Sam Leach occupies centre-stage and accepts no criticisms in a fast-moving and often very funny account of The Beatles' years in Merseyside clubs. The facts should have been better checked and Leach, who used to call himself 'The Man That Mersey Beat Forgot', now claims credit for everything, but he's not alone in that.

Leigh, Spencer with John Firminger: *Halfway To Paradise*
(Finbarr International, 1996)

The story of British popular music from 1956 to 1962 told by the people who made it. The TV producer, Jack Good, is possibly the best interviewee I have ever had – every single sentence is worth quoting.

Leigh, Spencer: *Drummed Out!* (Northdown, 1998)

The story of Pete Best's sacking, tackled like a whodunnit and inspired, in a funny way, by that book about the day that Abraham Lincoln died. Pete Best didn't care for it, but I think it is fair (and I would say that, wouldn't I?)

Leigh, Spencer: *Sweeping The Blues Away: A Celebration Of The Merseysippi Jazz Band* (Institute Of Popular Music, University of Liverpool, 2002)

The rejection of jazz is an essential element in the development of Merseybeat. This book looks at it from the other side and it was a pleasure to write and research because they are all such thoroughly nice people. The Merseysippis started in 1949 and are still playing, with four original members, every Monday in Sam's Bar.

Leigh, Spencer: *The Best Of Fellas – The Story Of Bob Wooler* (Drivegreen Publications, 2002)

I pick up the book and read Bob's comments and once again, I picture him prodding me in the chest as he made his points. Contains hundreds of his Woolerisms.

Lewisohn, Mark :*The Beatles Live! – Mark Lewisohn* (Pavilion, 1986)

Wonderfully researched book about every known gig played by the Beatles. It is astonishing that someone not connected with Liverpool could write with some detail about the place.

Lewisohn, Mark: *The Complete Beatles Recording Sessions* (Hamlyn, 1988)

Lewisohn heard all the tapes and then wrote, very informatively, about them.

Lewisohn, Mark: *The Complete Beatles Chronicle* (Pyramid, 1992)

Combines the books on the live gigs and the recording sessions with new material. The one essential book on the Beatles and often seen in remainder shops for £10.

MacDonald, Ian: *Revolution In The Head* (Fourth Estate, 1994)

A thought-provoking song by song analysis of all The Beatles' official releases. Don't overlook the 50 page table combining The Beatles' history with other chart music, cultural events and world news.

Marsden, Gerry, with Ray Coleman: *I'll Never Walk Alone* (Bloomsbury, 1993)

Did Ray Coleman question anything that Gerry said? This self-serving autobiography is bursting with life but factual accuracy isn't the first thing on the menu. Gerry wants credit for everything.

Miles, Barry with Paul McCartney: *Many Years From Now* (Secker & Warburg, 1997)

An authorised biography with many first-hand quotes from McCartney. Although McCartney wants to show himself in the best light, revealing facts occasionally slip through as in his childhood story about killing frogs.

Miles, Barry: *The Beatles – A Diary* (Omnibus, 1998)

Great layout and packed with information, but would it have been the same book without Lewisohn's research? Barry Miles was an insider in the mid-1960s and so can add a personal touch. The paperback edition printed in miniature is sheer madness and an insult to both author and reader.

Norman, Philip: *Shout! The True Story Of The Beatles* (Elm Tree, 1981)

There is a feeling throughout this book that Norman would like to have the courage to do a Goldman, but he pulls back. Well-researched and definitely on Lennon's side, but you would expect that in the wake of the assassination.

O'Brien, Ray: *There Are Places I'll Remember* (Ray O'Brien Publications – Volume 1, 2001: Volume 2, 2003)

Photographs, mostly current, and text about the Beatles' early venues on Merseyside. Useful little books that follow on from *The Beatles' Liverpool* (Ron Jones, Ron Jones Publications, 1991) and *The Beatles' Merseyside* (Ian Forsyth, S.B. Publications, 1991). A fully comprehensive work on this subject is overdue.

O'Donnell, Jim: *The Day John Met Paul* (US, Hall Of Fame, 1994)

Excellent hour by hour account of the Woolton village fête. Plenty of details from local and national newspapers about prices, fashions and the weather, and the author manages to construct a captivating book out of nothing very much.

Pedler, Dominic: *The Songwriting Secrets Of The Beatles* (Omnibus, 2003)

800 page analytical study of the Beatles' songs. Unless you have the same musical background as the author, it is difficult to form an opinion about his opinions, but undoubtedly a brilliant, groundbreaking work.

Peebles, Andy: *The Lennon Tapes* (BBC, 1981)

Like the long and rambling *Rolling Stone* and *Playboy* interviews, this book desperately needs an index. Lots of fond memories of home, but John hadn't been back to Liverpool since he showed Yoko around in 1969.

Pritchard, David and Alan Lysaght: *The Beatles – Inside The One And Only Lonely Hearts Club Band* (Allen & Unwin, 1998)

Pritchard and Lysaght have an impressive list of guests for their US radio series and here their interviews are presented verbatim. Some unlikely subjects include George's sister, Louise, and Murray The K, but when one of them is Brian Epstein, you begin to doubt the veracity of their claims. Did Brian Epstein really offer Little Richard 50 per cent of The Beatles? Why on earth would he do that? And why didn't Richard take it?

Sheff, David: *The Playboy Interviews With John Lennon* (Playboy, 1981)

Yoko has her opinions but she doesn't get a chance to say much while John's around. He'd not mellowed as much as some thought.

Taylor, Alistair: *A Secret History* (John Blake, 2001)

The first memoir of The Beatles' Mr. Fix-It, *Yesterday – The Beatles Remembered* (Sidgwick & Jackson, 1988) was irritatingly written as letters to an imaginary fan. *A Secret History* is far better but neither book has an index, perhaps because there are few references to anyone other than Alistair, Brian Epstein and The Beatles.

Thompson, Phil: *The Best Of Cellars* (Bluecoat Press, 1994)

Phil Thompson always strikes me as rather eccentric so it was surprising to find that he had written such a level-headed history of the Cavern. Excellent photographs, too, and a full listing, mostly taken from *Liverpool Echo*, of all the acts that were billed to appear. Sometimes those acts didn't appear and sometimes other performers were added to the bill, but this is superb research. As I discovered when checking dates for this book, the listing desperately needs an index.

Thomson, Elizabeth and David Gutman: *The Lennon Companion* (Macmillan, 1987)

Many excellent newspaper and magazines features are gathered here including contributions from Martin Amis, Bernard Levin, William Mann, Kenneth Tynan and Tom Wolfe. The correspondence in *The Times* over the MBEs is hilarious and Noël Coward describes them as "bad-mannered little shits".

Wenner, Jann: *Lennon Remembers* (Straight Arrow, 1971)

Wonderfully barbed quotes from John and occasionally Yoko. Is this what therapy does for you? Best to read with *John Lennon / Plastic Ono Band* in the CD player.

Williams, Allan with William Marshall: *The Man Who Gave The Beatles Away* (Elm Tree, 1975)

Allan Williams doesn't want to make anyone look good, least of all himself, and even if some stories are fictional, the book does contatin the spirit of Liverpool and Hamburg around 1960.

Willis-Pitts, P., *Liverpool – The Fifth Beatle; An African-American Odyssey* (Amozen, 2000)

Prem Willis-Pitts can't decide whether to write an autobiography, a history of Merseybeat or a study of black life in Liverpool, and the result is rather ramshackle. Lots of insights and anecdotes though and the photographs and memorabilia are second to none.

NOTES ON CONTRIBUTORS

The first-hand quotes in *Twist And Shout* have been numbered and this is a guide as to who the speakers are and where you can find their contributions. This enables you to use the book in several different ways. You can read the Lee Curtis story by going through his quotes or you could look at the different contributions from the Searchers. I hope, though, the first time around at least, you will read it from start to finish.

As well as locating the various quotes, I have used this section to bring things up to date and tell you what the various Merseybeat performers are doing now. As long as they have managed to keep themselves alive (and there are a lot of casualties along the way), they are likely to be playing somewhere this weekend. The Merseycats charity in the 1980s brought a lot of musos out of retirement and now there are three local charities devoted to the music of the era, Merseycats, Cheshire Cats and Sounds Of The Sixties. I'm saddened by some of the divisions that have occurred and the politics which have brought this about, but the great thing is that so many people are making music again. Indeed, the ones who haven't returned to music making like Johnny Hutch are a rarity. Most of them sound fine: some voices have lost their flexibility, some guitarists have slowed down because of arthritis, and some drummers lack their 1960s energy, but all in all they are doing fine.

No other book has interviewed so many Merseybeat musicians (though whether I have interviewed them well is up to you to judge), but even so I am conscious that I have left some musicians and background people out and perhaps for completeness, I should have got to them. For example, I haven't written enough about the Southport musicians and they are really only covered when they impinge onto the Liverpool scene. Still, I don't mind too much. Alex Paton, who was the drummer for the Mersey Boys and the Toledo 4, is writing a history of Southport bands from 1940 to 1980.

Beryl Adams (488) was Brian Epstein's secretary. Then she worked at the Cavern, managed a few groups, and, for a few years, was married to Bob Wooler. She is a Merseybeat history in herself and tragically died of CJD in 2003 before her memoirs could be published. The book has been completed and hopefully will be published later this year.

Londoner **Frank Allen (358) (608)** joined the Searchers in 1964 and is still there today.

Eddie Amoo (88) (243) (244) (601) (741) sang with the Chants, but found fame in the Real Thing with his brother, Chris. They starred at a soul concert at the Empire in June 2004 and Eddie still looks the hippest man in Liverpool. They perform their hits in extended versions with rap sequences.

Don Andrew (212) (515) (573) (650) (671) (674) (855) played bass with the Remo Four and founded the Merseycats charity.

Ron Appleby (237) (461) (463) (467) was a 60s promoter, usually in the Southport area. He gave up promoting concerts a long time ago and enjoys his retirement in Crossens.

Blackburn born, **Tony Ashton (425) (777)** was in the Remo Four and then Ashton, Gardner and Dyke. A man who lived life to the full, Tony died in 2001. Merseybeat collectors are recommended to look for his 1996 CD single, 'The Big Freedom Dance' (Vague 0001), which was a tribute to John Lennon and their days in Hamburg,

Bob Azurdia (20) (231) wrote for *Mersey Beat* and was the first to write about the Beatles in the national press. He joined BBC Radio Merseyside when it opened in 1967 and became its most incisive interviewer. During a live interview, he realised that the leader of the Liberal party, Paddy Ashdown, didn't know the name of the local candidate and he used that knowledge to devastating effect. Bob died in 1996 after completing a half-marathon on a bitterly cold day when he was ill.

Ken Baldwin (59) has played banjo and guitar with the Merseysippi Jazz Band for 55 years.

Russ Ballard (426) was a member of the Roulettes and then Argent. Great songwriter.

Chris Barber (163) has led one of the UK's top jazz bands for 50 years.

Adrian Barber (140) (221) (336) (414) (436) was a founder member of the Big Three and had success in New York as an engineer and record producer for the Allman Brothers and Vanilla Fudge. Now living in Hawaii and writing his memoirs.

From 1954 **Tony Barrow (469) (502) (503) (636) (722)** was the Disker record reviewer in *Liverpool Echo* and he worked as a publicist for NEMS Enterprises from 1963 to 1968. He and Robin Bextor (father of Sophie) wrote the coffee-table book, *Paul McCartney – Now And Then*, in 2004.

Roger Baskerfield (23) was part of the Coney Island Skiffle Group.

Sid Bernstein (634) (714) (720) (726) promoted the Beatles at Carnegie Hall and Shea Stadium. He's now 75 and testimony to the fact that obesity doesn't always kill. In the 1960s, he couldn't even get in the door of Tony Barrow's office and I have never seen anyone eat so much ice cream: to tell you the truth, I didn't even know it was possible. Sid has a lovely, gentle speaking voice and you can imagine him saying every word of his autobiography, *Not Just The Beatles…* (Jacques & Flusster, 2000).

The mother of Merseybeat, **Mona Best (111) (464)** founded the Casbah Coffee Club in 1959 and was Pete Best's mother. She died following a heart attack in 1988.

Pete Best (178) (246) (293) (462) (473) (475) (476) (495) (499) played drums for the Beatles when they went to Hamburg in August 1960 and was sacked in mysterious circumstances two years later. He joined Lee Curtis and the All Stars and then formed the Pete Best Four. In recent years, he has reactivated both his playing career and the Casbah.

Wayne Bickerton (453) (505) played bass and sang with the Pete Best Four. Wayne and Tony Waddington left the band and wrote and produced numerous hits for the Rubettes, Mac and Katie Kissoon and Liverpool FC. Wayne has been the chairman of the Performing Right Society and now runs Reliable Source Music. He is a doctor of law from the University of Liverpool.

Bryan Biggs (120) is the director of the Bluecoat Arts Centre in Liverpool.

Forget Lily Savage, forget *Blind Date*, forget *Surprise, Surprise!* **Cilla Black (8) (259) (307) (313) (567) (570) (571) (596) (625) (648)** once had credibility. Cilla still records but her voice has passed its best. Her husband and manager, Bobby Willis, died in 1999 and she is now managed by their son, Robert.

John Booker (273) was part of the audience at the Cavern. (This is not the John Booker who was the road manager for the Undertakers.)

Joey Bower (117) (672) (673) was in the Four Jays from 1959 to 1962, but at the time did not want to go professional. The Four Jays became the Fourmost and he joined them after Mike Millward died. He ran a very successful decorating business with Dave Lovelady and Joey, his wife Lesley, Dave and Billy Hatton formed the cabaret group, Clouds.

Les Braid (312) joined the Bluegenes on double-bass in 1958. He switched to electric in 1963 and has now been a Swinging Blue Jean for 46 years.

George Harrison's boyhood friend, **Tony Bramwell (201) (319)** worked for Apple and has released Eva Cassidy's records in the UK.

Faith Brown (300) is a fine impressionist and entertainer who has been touring the UK in *Sunset Boulevard*.

Joe Brown (468) had his biggest hit, 'A Picture Of You', with the Bruvvers in 1962 and married a Liverpool girl, Vicki Haseman from the Vernons Girls. In 2004 he toured the UK in a double-header with Marty Wilde.

Billy Butler (820) (824) (831) was part of the *Spin A Disc* panel on *Thank Your Lucky Stars*, a DJ at the Cavern and the lead singer of the Tuxedos. He presents the afternoon show on BBC Radio Merseyside and has had national acclaim for his hilarious *Hold Your Plums* quiz show.

Joe Butler (325) (551) (731) (773) played bass and sang with Sonny Webb and the Cascades and then the Hillsiders. Now plays with the country band, Hartford West, and broadcasts on Saga 106.6fm.

Mike Byrne (331) founded *The Beatles Story* at the Albert Dock and fronts the rock'n'roll band, Juke Box Eddie's.

Iris Caldwell (74) (108) (239) (487) (659) (753) (763) is the very good-looking sister of Rory Storm (Alan Caldwell) and she was married to Alvin Stardust (Shane Fenton). Their son, Adam F, has had his own hits records and worked on the soundtrack for *Ali G Indahouse* (2002).

Manchester musician **Bernie Calvert (511)** played bass and keyboards for the Hollies from 1966 to 1981.

Howie Casey (84) (175) (176) (177) (182) (194) (797) has played rock'n'roll sax with the Seniors and the Dominoes. He was with Wings and is featured on 'Bluebird'. He lives in Bournemouth but often comes to Merseyside. Still rocking and sounding great.

Clem Cattini (478) is the drummer of the Tornados.

Les Chadwick (387) (560) (840) played guitar in Gerry and the Pacemakers and moved to Australia.

Paddy Chambers (381) (550) (591) was lead guitarist and vocalist with several Liverpool groups (Faron's Flamingos, Big Three, Escorts) as well as being a third of Paddy, Klaus and Gibson. He died in 2000.

Bruce Channel (702) had his moment of glory with 'Hey! Baby' in 1962.

Allan Clarke (281) (516) (532) (574) was the lead singer of the Hollies from 1962 to 1999. Had to call it a day as he was struggling with the notes.

Eddie Clayton (484), real name Eddie Miles, had Ringo Starr in his skiffle group before turning to country. He has been very ill with cancer and there has been a benefit night for him.

Dec Clusky (301) was a part of the Bachelors, who found a niche with new recordings of standards ('Charmaine', 'Diane' and 'I Believe').

Pat Clusky (116) (769) was part of Rikki and his Red Streaks.

John Cochrane (64) (65) (223) (697) was the drummer with Wump and his Werbles.

Lewis Collins (215) (456) (774) was with the Kansas City Five, the Eyes and the Mojos before becoming a Professional. His father, Bill, was road manager for Badfinger.

Frankie Connor (811) was in the Hideaways and now presents 60s programmes on BBC Radio Merseyside. Frankie, Alan Crowley (Tuxedos) and Billy Kinsley write and produce contemporary records for Merseybeat performers, known collectively as Class Of '64. Their best known song is 'Poor Boy From Liverpool' for the Merseybeats.

Bob Conrad (363) (419) called himself John Konrad when he played drums in the Mojos. He died two years ago from cancer.

Peter Cook (103) (209) (694) (698) was the lead guitarist for Earl Royce and the Olympics and Kansas City Five. Plays with a variety of local bands but mostly goes out as a solo in country and Irish acts. Excellent blues guitarist.

John Cornelius (798) is a Liverpool singer-songwriter and artist from the late 60s who wrote the witty memoir, *Liverpool 8.*

After being the Mavericks and the Pacifics, **Tony Crane (272) (295) (457) (582) (733) (743) (755) (758) (789)** formed the Merseybeats in 1962 and has been singing lead and playing guitar with them ever since.

David Crosby (691) was a member of the Tabs, owns the Rox record shops on Merseyside and is writing a play about Buddy Holly.

Nicky Crouch (418) (422) (655) (687) is noted for his time in Faron's Flamingos and the Mojos. A superb guitarist, he has played jazz with Gary Potter, but for the last 10 years, he has been running River City Rockers (sometimes billed as Nicky Crouch's Mojos!) with Tommy Hughes, Brian Johnson, Eric London and Les Williams (Dimensions).

Rodney Crowell (718) was a member of Emmylou Harris' Hot Band. He has written many country hits and his latest albums are about growing up in Houston. 'This Too Will Pass' ends with the words, 'Goodnight George'.

Chris Curtis (100) (224) (277) (352) (369) (392) (395) (413) (438) (496) (548) (595) (602) (605) (609) (621) (623) (681) (725) (853) was the drummer with the Searchers. After one interview, he gave me a much-played copy of the Judy Collins LP, *Golden Apples Of The Sun*, which had been autographed, 'To Chris, Best wishes, Judy Collins'. After 'To Chris', he had appended 'and Spen'. Talk about having a collector's item. Occasionally sings on Merseycats club nights.

Lee Curtis (152) (154) (162) (348) (349) (360) (375) (384) (389) (394) (399) (415) (440) (443) (494) (497) (581) (587) (645) (760) was managed by his brother, Joe Flannery, and fronted the All Stars. Now living in Southport, he often works with Nicky Crouch's band, River City Rockers, and is as dynamic as ever.

Arthur Davis (253) played drums for the Four Just Men. He now backs Faron.

Bernie Davis (6) is a noted bluegrass musician on Merseyside. Brother of Rod.

Rod Davis (52) (54) (76) (95) was a founder member of the Quarry Men and became Quarry Bank's head boy. The Quarry Men are back gigging, admittedly without their three most famous members, and Rod has also released a live CD with Tony Sheridan, *Historical Moments* (Beat Archiv, Germany), and a jazz guitar album with Doug Turner, *Numero Uno* (Scorpion).

Johnny Dean (504), aka Sean O'Mahony, was the editor of the monthly *Beatles Book.*

Paddy Delaney (62) (736) (738) (821) was the doorman at the Cavern. He has written his memoirs but not yet found a publisher.

Valerie Dicks (31) was a regular at the Cavern.

Ken Dodd (3) (11) (82) (294) is Liverpool's greatest comedian, if not the UK's. He was found not guilty of tax evasion but all the jokes he incorporates into his act makes me wonder about the verdict. Now in his 70s and not in the best of health, he still works a punishing schedule of one-nighters.

Lonnie Donegan (39) was to skiffle what Elvis was to rock'n'roll. Many musicians in this list started playing because of Lonnie. He died on tour in November 2002 and an all-star tribute concert took place at the Royal Albert Hall in June 2004. Gerry Marsden was one of the star names.

Frank Dostal (167) (334) (337) (378) (385) (404) was a member of the Rattles and wrote 'Yes Sir I Can Boogie' for Baccara.

Mary Dostal (340) (342) (351) (361) (377), then Mary McGlory, was a Liver Bird. Frank Dostal says he was so impressed by the Liver Birds that he married one.

Kuno Dreysse (159) (170) (172) (386) (412), a leading Hamburg broadcaster, was a musician in the 60s and managed the Star-Club in its final years.

Leading rock writer, **Paul Du Noyer (9) (289) (791) (827)**, has written a definitive, one-volume history of Liverpool music, *Wondrous Place.*

Roy Dyke (776) played drums for the Remo Four and then Ashton, Gardner and Dyke. Now plays in a blues band in Hamburg.

Vince Earl (852) sang with the Connoisseurs and became a singer/comedian round the clubs. He found fame as Ron Dixon in *Brookside*, but he is underrated as a singer. Now 60, he works as Vince Earl and the Attractions with Tony Coates (Liverpool Express), Steve Fleming, Charlie Flynn and Dave Lovelady. A word in passing for Dave Fillis (aka Dave Kent) of the Connoisseurs who has lost his hearing and so has had to pack away his guitars.

Tom Earley (92) (323) (600) (629) (843) was in the Birkenhead group, the Pathfinders. Sometimes works with Billy May.

Duane Eddy (707) was the Man with the Twangy Guitar.

Ian Edwards (131) (153) (353) (372) (450) (489) (841) fronted Ian and the Zodiacs. He reactivated the name a few years ago but no longer sings with them.

Guitarist **Ralph Ellis (37) (218) (333) (398) (547) (579) (647)** was a founder member of the Swinging Blue Jeans. He became a very successful insurance salesman and was able to indulge his passion for guitars. In 2001 he recorded with the Canadian tribute band, the Beat Makers. One of his close friends is the guitar legend, John Jorgenson, who rates Ralph's work very highly.

Merseybeat promoter, **Ron Ellis (690)**, now writes the Johnny Ace detective stories.

Ray Ennis (38) (240) (296) (455) (578) (598) (635) (848) was, and still is, the lead singer with the Swinging Blue Jeans.

Beat poet and travel writer **Royston Ellis (124) (125)** came to Liverpool in 1960. Now lives in Sri Lanka and lectures on cruise ships.

Clive Epstein (474) (756), Brian's brother and fellow director of NEMS Enterprises, went to the top of a ski slope in 1988, took a deep breath and collapsed and died.

Saxophonist **Mike Evans (121) (771) (810) (812) (815)** was a member of the Clayton Squares and Liverpool Scene as well as being a founding member of Deaf School. In 2002 his book *Elvis – A Celebration* made the best-sellers.

Joe Fagin (205) (345) (427) (685) (778) was a member of the Strangers. You may well have heard him tonight on a TV ad.

Chris Farlowe (401) (402) topped the UK charts with 'Out Of Time'.

One of the great Liverpool personalities, **Faron (238) (329) (590) (592)** was the extrovert lead singer of Faron's Flamingos. He has had many physical and personal setbacks in recent years, but he keeps on singing.

Horst Fascher (338) (411) (417) (449) was the manager of the Star-Club. In recent times, he has organised Beatle events in Hamburg and other German cities. If anyone from the era should write his autobiography, it's Horst Fascher.

Chris Finley (257) was in the Masterminds. He still plays, getting up at a Merseycats show at the Liverpool Empire in May 2004. The Masterminds' drummer, John Rathbone, played with Karl Terry and the Cruisers for years, but is now in a nursing home.

Steve Fleming (553) played keyboards for his brother, Mark Peters, in the Silhouettes. This guy has been a Cruiser, a Cyclone, a Silhouette, a Reflection, a Cloud and is currently an Attraction. His son, Paul plays keyboards for Echo and the Bunnymen.

255

Charlie Flynn (133) (332) (452) (734) was a founder member of the Dominoes and then played bass and sang backup in Ian and the Zodiacs. Currently with Vince Earl's Attractions.

Salford born **Clinton Ford (60)** has sung with the Merseysippi Jazz Band on and off since 1957. Still in excellent voice, but he looks so like Colonel Sanders that you are tempted to give him your chicken-in-a-basket order.

Promoter **Dave Forshaw (206) (268)** has not organised any events for some years, but he has worked in security and he looked after Litherland Town Hall shortly before it closed in 2004. About to be demolished (the Hall not Dave!), a landmark Beatle site is about to disappear.

Neil Foster (271) used to edit the rock'n'roll magazine, *Not Fade Away* (which did). His memories of playing sax for the Delacardoes in the early 60s have fuelled his novel, *Cradle Of Rock* (Top F, 2004).

The American record producer **Kim Fowley (288)** is noted as much for his eccentricity as his talent.

Pete Frame (90) (228) (278) (589) (833) (836) is known for his meticulous *Rock Family Trees.* He has published a book of Merseybeat ones and works as a consultant for many Radio 2 programmes.

Irish musician **Rory Gallagher (614)** was one of the world's great guitarists.

Ritchie Galvin (299), who was born Richard Hughes, was the drummer with Earl Preston and the TTs and many Merseyside country bands. Very cheerful and outgoing, he was a public service worker and union activist. If he died peacefully in 2001, it was the first peaceful thing he ever did.

Paul Gambaccini (721) is a recognised authority and broadcaster on all forms of popular music.

Clive Garner (160) is an expert on pre-war music, both English and German, and presents his weekly *Music And Memories* on BBC Radio Merseyside.

Merseysider **David Garrick (779)** had few hits in the UK but became big on the continent. His operatic album, *Apassionata*, was released in 1999.

Freddie Garrity (510) (649) (665) led the Manchester group, Freddie and the Dreamers. Now wheelchair-bound and unlikely to perform again.

Johnny Gentle (291) worked with Eddie Cochran, Billy Fury and the Beatles, but missed out on the hit records. Still performs occasionally using three Merseysiders (Raphael Callaghan, Alan Stratton and Geoff Taggart) as the Gentlemen.

Albie Gormall (834) was part of the Blackwells and still plays rock'n'roll as part of In The Mood around St. Helens.

Hans Otto Gottfridsson (183) (188) is a noted chronicler of the scene – see bibliography.

Chick Graham (541) replaced Billy Kramer as the lead singer of the Coasters.

Jazz singer and pianist **Buddy Greco (710) (711)** recorded his finger-snapping 'Lady Is A Tramp' in 1960.

Mike Gregory (594) (781) was bass player and vocalist for the Escorts before moving to the Swinging Blue Jeans. He now leads the good-time Rock'n'Roll Circus.

If you wanted a guitar, you went to Frank Hessy's and bought one from **Jim Gretty (104)**. He died in 1992 at the age of 78.

Brian Griffiths (192) was a member of the Big Three. He manages a *Mr. Music* store in Calgary. When he was in Liverpool in 2002, he brought me some demos of new songs including a poignant 'Waltz For Paddy' to remember Paddy Chambers.

Eric Griffiths (53) (96) (98) played in the Quarry Men and learnt guitar with John Lennon. Owns a chain of dry cleaners in Edinburgh but does occasional gigs as part of the reformed Quarry Men.

Mick Groves (41) was a member of the Spinners who became a councillor on the Wirral.

Johnny Guitar (56) (63) (71) (75) (189) (190) (485) (486) (767), whose real name was Johnny Byrne, played, well, guitar for Rory Storm and the Hurricanes. He died of motor neurone disease in 1999 and as he did not want others to know of his plight, I saw him apologising for a wrist injury and not playing as well as he should.

Paul McCartney has said that **John Gustafson (106) (129) (130) (279) (280) (282) (437) (562) (610) (615) (617) (624) (626) (782) (796)** of the Big Three was the best bass player on Merseyside. A dyed-in-the-wool rock'n'roller but a very versatile player as his list of sessions demonstrates. I saw him perform a rock'n'roll set, backed by the Merseybeats, at the Locarno a couple of years ago and he was excellent.

Cliff Hall (628) was a member of the Spinners.

Now a DJ for Saga (well, we all get old), **David Hamilton (678)** was a TV presenter in the early 60s.

Colin Hanton (48) (73) (77) (99) played drums with John Lennon's Quarry Men. He upholsters furniture but also plays with the reformed Quarry Men.

Sam Hardie (94) (365) (370) (379) (431) (432) (439) (444) played piano for Kingsize Taylor and the Dominoes. Not been well of late which is unfortunate as the new look KST and the Dominoes are getting plenty of work.

Mike Hargreaves (737) was a doorman at the Cavern from 1960 to 1964.

Louise Harrison (576) (717) (786) is George's sister and lives in Florida. Much of her time is taken up with environmental issues.

Bill Harry (171) (230) (232) (482) (642) is the former editor and publisher of the *Mersey Beat* newspaper. Easily the most prolific author on the Beatles and prefers compiling encyclopedias to writing biographies.

Tony Hatch (622) (814) produced Petula Clark, the Searchers, the Undertakers and the Chants and many other artists for Pye.

Billy Hatton (269) (566) (646) (651) (679) (744) (837) was one of the Fourmost. Now works in security and, for the moment at least, has stopped playing. He has been writing plays and is now working on his memoirs.

Bill Heckle (12) (252) has been one of the owners of the Cavern since 1991.

Henry Heggen (149) is a UK blues singer and harmonica player working in Hamburg with Roy Dyke.

Keith Hemmings (16) (24) was the young architect involved in the initial stages of the Cavern. His son, Paul, played in the La's and the Lightning Seeds.

Vocalist **Robbie Hickson (263)** played with the Kansas City Five. He lives in New Brighton and works as a painter and decorator. Sings occasionally and recently recorded with Skiffle John Lomax.

Herbert Hildebrand (184) was a founder member of the Rattles.

Wally Hill (138) (139) (220) was the manager of Holyoake Hall in Wavertree. Lives in retirement on the Wirral.

The manager of the Iron Door, **Geoff Hogarth (179) (226) (242)**, lives in retirement in Aigburth.

Originally drumming with the Dennisons, **Clive Hornby (585) (783)** found fame as Jack Sugden on *Emmerdale Farm.*

Nicholas Horsfield (119) (122) taught at the Liverpool College of Art and has had a retrospective of his life's work at the Walker Art Gallery.

Tommy Hughes (51) (72) (102) (308) (802) played banjo with the Swinging Blue Jeans, and is a fine rock'n'roll pianist. He is now part of the River City Rollers.

Johnny Hutch (367) (434) (490) (491) (583) (616) (682) (801) was the drummer and vocalist with the Big Three. Went into property and won't have anything to do with the Merseybeat days. The quotes in this book are from an interview I did with him in 1980 and I don't know of anyone who has interviewed him before or since.

Brian Hyland (703) had several pop hits in the early 60s ('Ginny Come Lately', 'Sealed With A Kiss') and still tours the UK regularly.

Stu James (229) (322) (421) (854) born Stu Slater, was the lead singer of the Mojos. He is now a commissioning editor at Virgin Books.

A journeyman drummer, **Brian Johnson (666)** played with the Strangers, the Hurricanes and the Tabs and is now in the River City Rockers.

John Johnson (50) (234) (255) (530) sometimes known as Chuck, is Kenny Johnson's brother. He died recently. I didn't see him often but he was always pleasant and genial.

Kenny Johnson (283) (660) (683) led the country-rock band, Sonny Webb and the Cascades, and then became one of the Hillsiders. Now a popular club act, he presents the country programme on BBC Radio Merseyside.

Stan Johnson (85) was a member of one of the first Mersey groups, the Hy-Tones. "I've got a new guitar," he says, "and I intend to play it at Merseycats one week. I want to but it's hard to play chords when your fingers are stiffening."

Since leaving *Brookside*, **Sue Johnston (261)** has starred in a succession of TV dramas as well as *The Royle Family.*

Brian Jones (249) (326) (328) (599) (762) played sax with the Undertakers, but he is so thin, he looks like he hasn't got a note of music in him! By experimenting with reverb, he sounds better than ever. Plays in several scratch bands and, in 1999, his solo album, *Simply Sax*, made the HMV listening posts.

Dave Jones (251) (808) has been one of the owners of the Cavern since 1991.

Hughie Jones (742) was a member of the Spinners and sings at the many maritime events on Merseyside.

Raymond Jones (247) (248) went into NEMS and asked Brian Epstein for a copy of 'My Bonnie'.

Bobby Kaye (78) (144), now a Liverpool comic, started with the Crescents.

Freda Kelly (265) (641) (739) worked for NEMS Enterprises as Brian Epstein's secretary and ran the official Beatles Fan Club. She could write a wonderful book but, with commendable integrity, she does not want to betray confidences. For many years, she was married to Brian Norris from the Bumblies, the Cryin' Shames and Earl Preston's Realms.

A marginal Merseybeat figure, **John Kennedy (203) (754)** was in at the start of the Dominoes.

Tommy Kent (168) (406) is a schlager singer who sold a million copies of 'Susie Darlin''.

The legendary jazz musician **Barney Kessel (287)** died in 2004. He may have had great taste as a jazz guitarist but when I met him, he was wearing the most garish sports jacket I have ever seen.

Lead guitarist **John Kinrade (780)** was one of the few Sixties musicians who did open a hairdressing salon.

Billy Kinsley (292) (315) (501) (752) (784) was a founder member of the Merseybeats and Liverpool Express. Even today, he is an integral part of music in the city.

Astrid Kirchherr (161) (187) (459) met the Beatles in Hamburg, befriended Stu Sutcliffe and took many wonderful monochrome photographs.

Ted Knibbs (105) (305) (526) (540) (696) (700) was Billy J. Kramer's first manager. Died many years ago but spent his later years at Beatle Conventions. To give you an idea of how long all this is: if he had been alive today, he'd be 100 by now.

Billy J. Kramer (306) (320) (500) (527) (535) (537) (538) (568) (569) (643) (727) (728) (759) (761) (795) (806) was first backed by a Liverpool band, the Coasters, and then a Manchester one, the Dakotas. Now lives in Oyster Bay, New York but frequently performs in the UK.

Ulf Krüger (158) (166) (186) runs a Beatles shop and studio in Hamburg and acts as agent for Astrid Kirchherr.

By a few months, cornet player **John Lawrence (19) (29)** is not quite a founder member of the Merseysippi Jazz Band and is still with them today 55 years later.

Sam Leach (109) (110) (112) (145) (208) (214) (245) (256) (545) was a leading Merseybeat impresario and has written his memoirs in *The Rocking City*.

Derek Leckenby (57) (509) (514) played guitar with Herman's Hermits, both pre- and post- Peter Noone. When I asked him why he had split with Peter, he said, "You can only work with a prat for so long." He died from cancer in 1994.

C. P. Lee (519) (826) is a Manchester academic who played in St. Louis Union and Albertos Y Lost Paranoias. He has written a history of Manchester music, *Shake, Rattle And Rain* (great title!), which was published by Hardinge Simpole in 2002.

Cynthia Lennon (266) (481) was married to John Lennon and she has spoken with considerable dignity at many Beatle conventions.

Mark Lewisohn (518) (735) – see bibliography. There's praise enough there.

Brian Linford (799) was the manager of the Mardi Gras and takes a great interest in the local jazz scene.

Jackie Lomax (285) (785) was the lead singer with the Undertakers and he released an album of new songs, *The Ballad Of Liverpool Slim*, over the internet in 2003.

Eric London (310) was a member of Faron's Flamingos and Group One and now is a River City Rocker.

Dave Lovelady (114) (134) (235) (314) (317) (356) (493) (620) (680) (838) played drums for the Dominoes and then the Fourmost. When the group split, he, Billy Hatton and Joey Bower formed Clouds – Liverpool's answer to Sky! – and he is now in Vince Earl and the Attractions.

John Duff Lowe (107) (136) (142) played piano with the Quarry Men and for a time was with the revamped Four Pennies.

Kenny Lynch (658) (662) had eight chart hits including 'Up On The Roof 'and 'You Can Never Stop Me Loving You'.

I interviewed **Paul McCartney (81) (270) (433)** once for 15 minutes and how I've used and reused that conversation. Here it comes again.

Rod McClelland (132) played lead guitar for Mark Peters and the Silhouettes. Came out of the business and lives on the Wirral.

Robin MacDonald (536) played bass with the Manchester band, the Dakotas.

Ray McFall (61) (219) (250) (303) (483) (572) (719) (807) (813) (816) (823) owned the Cavern in those crucial, beat group years. Lives in Surrey but is often seen on Merseyside at Convention time.

Liverpool's poet laureate, **Roger McGough (845)** was one-third of Scaffold.

Jim McIver (236) was a promoter in the Crosby area of Liverpool.

Pete Maclaine (520) (521) (534) (542) (543) was the original lead singer with the Dakotas. Still performing around clubs in Manchester and sounding good.

John McNally (89) (217) (275) (318) (549) (603) (644) (792) (804) was a founder member of the Searchers and still plays lead guitar in the band.

Les Maguire (359) (366) (390) (447) (632) (723) played piano with Gerry and the Pacemakers and now plays with the Zodiacs.

With his banjo and ready wit, **Billy Maher (97)** was a top entertainer in Merseyside clubs. His daughter, Siobhan, was in River City People and is now married to the top Nashville producer, Ray Kennedy.

Dave Maher (227) (577) (593) was a member of Denny Seyton and the Sabres. Dave works as a long distance lorry driver and so finds it difficult to get to Merseycats. He would love to be playing again.

Colin Manley (213) (297) (442) (529) (639) (656) (675) (676) (732) (772) was lead guitarist with the Remo Four and then played with Georgie Fame, Billy J. Kramer and the Swinging Blue Jeans. He died in 1999 and an all-star tribute, *A Concert For Colin*, at the Philharmonic Hall in Liverpool was a celebration of his life.

Tony Mansfield (523) played drums for the Dakotas. He was born Tony Bookbinder and he is Elkie Brooks' brother. He played in the reformed Dakotas for a while but has a busy job in insurance.

Beryl Marsden (241) (343) (498) (588) (619) (787) (788) (842) was unlucky. She never had the hits and yet was an excellent vocalist. In 1966, she was part of Steampacket with Rod Stewart and Peter Green. Had her first solo CD, *One Dream*, released in 2004.

Fred Marsden (254) (262) (264) (267) (346) (354) (374) (388) (558) (564) (606) (630) (631) (633) was Gerry's brother and the drummer in Gerry and the Pacemakers. He runs the Pacemaker driving school in Formby and most days he is reversing his clients around the corner of my house.

Gerry Marsden (127) (151) (260) (371) (429) (546) (559) (607) (654) (729) (839) led Gerry and the Pacemakers, and still does. Performs for numerous Merseyside charities.

Tony Marsh (766) played guitar with Coasters and now performs as a solo act around the clubs.

George Martin (477) (556) (640) was the record producer for the Beatles and many of their contemporaries.

Hank Marvin (298) is the Shadows' lead guitarist.

Spencer Lloyd Mason (364) (435) (668) (684) (688) managed the Mojos and has run a Newton and Ridley's Carpet Emporium in Liverpool for years. He carpeted me when I first asked him for an interview in 1984. He said, "I've got better things to do than talk about Gerry and his fucking Pacemakers." Twenty years on, he has mellowed.

Bernd Matheja (156) (164) (165) (169) (423) is a noted historian of 60s music, compiling several albums of German recordings for Bear Family.

Mike Maxfield (512) (522) (533) (539) is the Dakotas' lead guitarist. The Dakotas often work on Flying Music tours and last time I saw them they were backing Wayne Fontana, Brian Hyland, Peter Noone and John Walker. They make albums for tours – good ones too - and as their keyboard player, Toni Baker, writes the music for *Phoenix Nights*, they are also involved with TV comedy.

Billy May (793) of the Valkyries and the Pathfinders is now a solo performer around the clubs.

Dave May (118) (123) (451) (454) (552) (686) played in the Silhouettes and taught Stuart Sutcliffe to play bass. He has part of a cabaret duo, the Madisons, which has been going 30 years.

Louisiana record producer, **Huey P. Meaux (730)** discovered Barbara Lynn, Doug Sahm and Freddy Fender.

If Liverpool's city of culture could be summed up by one man, it would be **George Melly (10) (286) (507)**, art critic, jazz singer and raconteur extraordinaire.

Let's dance with **Chris Montez (704)**.

Trevor Morais (330) (775) played drums with Faron's Flamingos. Joined the Peddlers and then toured for years with David Essex.

A fine singer, Liverpudlian **Paul Murphy (407) (408)** found himself working as a record producer in Hamburg in the early 60s. Was married for a time to Gordon Mills' widow.

Chris Murray (746) (747) was the compère at Liverpool's notorious She Club.

Mitch Murray (555) (557) (563) was the young Tin Pan Alley songwriter who wrote 'How Do You Do It?', 'I Like It', 'You Were Made For Me' and many other 60s hits.

Graham Nash (1) (517) (575) was a fifth of the Hollies and then a third of Crosby, Stills and Nash.

Peter Noone (513), aka Herman, led Herman's Hermits to a succession of Top 10 hits in both Britain and America. Still looks astonishingly youthful and, seeing him live, I was surprised to find that his songs had also aged better than expected.

Geoff Nugent (327) (460) (652) (677) played guitar and sang with the Undertakers. Still fronts the band.

Brian O'Hara (565) was the front man of the Fourmost. A member of the awkward squad (which sounds like a good name for a group), he nevertheless had a succession of young and very pretty girlfriends. In 1999, he hanged himself, possibly over financial problems.

Mick O'Toole (67) (69) (87) (128) (740) is an expert on 50s music and Liverpool clubland.

Terry O'Toole (420) played piano with the Mojos and then taught art. He has now retired and has not (yet) returned to music. His son, Steve, is a fine local singer/songwriter.

The Big O, **Roy Orbison (708)** is one US star whose career didn't fade with the Beatles.

Eddie Parry (667) fronted the Dennisons and then sold insurance. He drank too much – I saw him 'sing' uninvited lead vocals with the Swinging Blue Jeans and he had to be removed. He died in 1995.

Dr. Ortwin Pelc (146) (147) (150) (157) is the director of the Museum of Hamburg History.

Mike Pender (91) (276) (347) (357) (403) (405) (428) (597) (604) (627) (757) (794) founded the Searchers with John McNally. They fell out in 1985 and since then he has been fronting Mike Pender's Searchers.

Carl Perkins (709) wrote and recorded the original version of 'Blue Suede Shoes'.

Mark Peters (355) fronted the Silhouettes. He has worked for the British Council for many years, first in Sri Lanka and currently in Egypt.

Gene Pitney (424) both wrote classy songs ('Hello Mary Lou', 'He's A Rebel') and sang them ('24 Hours From Tulsa', 'I'm Gonna Be Strong'). He needed to be strong to hit notes like that.

Roger Planche (26) (44) (45), a member of the Coney Island Skiffle Group, became a jazz singer and pianist.

Earl Preston (290) (770) fronted the TTs and often sings with Cy Tucker at Coopers Emporium opposite the Pier Head. From time to time, Earl works with his former TTs, Wally Shepherd (bass) and Dave Gore (rhythm guitar).

Alan Price (302) played keyboards for the Animals.

Peter Prichard (712) (713) (715) (716) is an agent and impresario who has been involved with the Royal Variety Performance for many years.

Harry Prytherch (80) (135) (137) (141) (210) (480) (661) played drums with the Remo Four and often compères Merseybeat shows.

Dark glasses, harmonica and lead guitar, **Derek Quinn (508) (663) (664)** was one of Freddie's Dreamers. Became a publican in Manchester.

Tim Riley (284) wrote a first-rate account of the Beatles' musicality, *Tell Me Why* (1988).

Andy Roberts (790) read law at Liverpool University and was a member of Liverpool Scene and Plainsong. Now writes TV and film music and led the band on the recent tour by the playwrights Willy Russell and Tim Firth.

The most fastidious of authors and researchers, **Johnny Rogan (637)** wrote a great book about pop management, *Starmakers And Svengalis* (Queen Anne Press, 10988). Revealing chapters on Larry Parnes, Don Arden and Brian Epstein.

Earl Royce (321) (844) fronted the Olympics. He lives and works in Kirkby and has not performed for many years.

Lita Roza (7) spent several years with the Ted Heath Orchestra and then found solo success in the Fifties.

Willy Russell (274), a Cavern regular, became one of the UK's top playwrights – *Educating Rita*, *Shirley Valentine* and *Blood Brothers*, among them.

Tony Sanders (207) (304) (446) (524) (525) (528) (768) played drums for the Coasters. If you hear a country singer called George Sands in the Liverpool clubs, that's Tony Sanders. You might also buy some Venetian blinds from him at his shop in Kirkby.

In the early 60s, **Johnny Sandon (216)** sang with the Searchers and then moved to the Remo Four. He worked as the comic, Billy Beck, and then became a taxi-driver. He was depressed and committed suicide at the third attempt on Christmas Day, 1997.

Sylvia Saunders (339) played drums for the Liver Birds. She married one of the Bobby Patrick Big Six and they ran a hotel in Blackpool.

Alan Schroeder (362) was part of the Black Knights. He organises Merseybeat concerts at the Floral Pavilion, New Brighton.

John Schroeder (554) was a record producer for Oriole and then Pye.

Ray Scragg (584) (657) sang and played guitar with the Dennisons. He worked for the Prudential for many years but he maintained his friendship with the group and they did some reunion gigs. He formed a new group called the Dennisons 2001 shortly before he died from throat cancer.

Denny Seyton (324) (586) (846) fronted the Sabres and then worked as a buyer for Littlewoods. He had a club act, Old Gold, with John Boyle from the Sabres and he did reform the band for a few of the Merseycats shows. One of the latter-day Sabres, Paul Stewart, invented the supports that are used to strengthen the handles on plastic bags – he patented the idea and made a small fortune! Denny has now retired from both buying and singing, preferring to spend his retirement on the golf course.

Del Shannon (705) was the first US performer to record a Lennon and McCartney song – in his case, 'From Me To You'.

Tony Sheridan (174) (180) (382) appeared on Jack Good's *Oh Boy!* show and then went to Hamburg, playing there before the Beatles. I always enjoy seeing him play as I am never sure what is going to happen.

Pete Shotton (40) (55) (805) was John Lennon's best friend at Quarry Bank and they maintained their friendship: "When John first met me, he called me 'Penis' because I was long and thin and my initials were P.S." Had to become a tax exile when he sold his stake in the Fatty Arbuckle chain of restaurants, which he had created. He lives in Ireland.

Mike Smith (472) produced records for Decca and then CBS.

He was born Bernard Jewry, then he became Shane Fenton and after that, **Alvin Stardust (531) (638) (749) (750) (764).**

Freddie Starr (693) (699) (835) (847) – madman or comic genius? You decide.

John Stewart (706) was part of the Kingston Trio.

John Stokes (470) was one of the Bachelors. In an extraordinary court case in 1984, the other Bachelors accused him of singing "like a drowning rat".

Alan Stratton (36) (46) (66) (86) (101) (143) (211) played bass with the Kansas City Five and in recent years has been working with Johnny Gentle. Spoke to him today and he had been playing with Merseybillies and the Merseyside Big Band on consecutive days. "People love hearing a double bass," he says.

Guitar and vocalist **Terry Sylvester (225) (258) (580)** was with the Escorts (1962-66), the Swinging Blue Jeans (1966-1968) and the Hollies (1969-81). Now lives in Ontario and does some *Live And Acoustic* concerts featuring his hits in North America.

Alan Sytner (13) (14) (15) (17) (18) (21) (25) (27) (28) (32) (34) (42) (47) (70) was the founder and first owner of the Cavern. You may not agree with all he says but, boy, is he entertaining.

Liverpool comic **Jimmy Tarbuck (745)** came to fame as a host on ITV's *Sunday Night At The London Palladium*.

Dicky Tarrach (376) (391) (397) (692) played drums with the Rattles.

Alistair Taylor (68) (233) (465) worked for Brian Epstein as his personal assistant and became known to the Beatles as Mr. Fixit. He became General Manager at Apple but was sacked in Allen Klein's purge, and he never appeared to hold this against the Beatles. He worked in hotel and catering for some years and then came back into the Beatle world by appearing at conventions from the late 80s onwards. Whenever I met him, he was always involved in some new book or project and when they appeared they were always the same as the last one! An all-round good guy who died in June 2004.

For the record, butcher's boy Teddy Taylor, better known as **Kingsize Taylor (49) (93) (115) (222) (410) (416) (445) (670) (849)**, was 6 foot $5^{3}/_{4}$ inches and 22 stone.

Karl Terry (79) is still fronting the Cruisers and still doing the splits. Amazing! He says, "I know I could get £100 a night by going out with backing tapes but I will never do it. I would never feel comfortable singing to tapes and so long as I'm performing, it will be with a live band." Karl is writing his autobiography – "It's about time one of the also-rans told their story," he says.

Bobby Thomson (113) (204) (309) (368) (380) (409) (441) (669) sang and played guitar with the Dominoes. Because Kingsize was so good, Bobby, who lives and performs around Birmingham, has been overlooked and underrated.

Frank Townsend (653) still can reach those high, high harmonies. I saw him adding his contributions to Tony Rivers and the Castaways at the Cavern in 2003.

Jim Turner (58) (689) (695) ran the agency, Arcade Variety and was the manager of the Odd Spot club. At different times, he has managed the Kansas City Five, Freddie Starr and the Kubas. He is always involved with some new project and the last time I rang his mobile, he answered from the Cannes film festival.

Cy Tucker (850) sang with the TT's and then fronted the Friars. Catch him at Coopers Emporium or any number of Liverpool clubs and you will be impressed by his voice, but be warned, he is loud – very loud.

Jimmy Tushingham (748) (751) (822) took Ringo Starr's place in Rory Storm and the Hurricanes. He also played in the Connoisseurs and then worked in import and export.

Bobby Vee (724) was one of the most successful American stars of the early Sixties.

Steve Voce (30) (33) (35) (43) has written a controversial column in *Jazz Journal* since 1957. His *Jazz Panorama* programme was broadcast for over 30 years on BBC Radio Merseyside. Hates rock music as fervently as most like it.

Photographer **Jurgen Vollmer (185)** met the Beatles when they first came to Hamburg. His work has been displayed at the Mathew Street Gallery.

Since his marriage broke up, **Rick Wakeman (506)** seems to be back on the road for good.

Noel Walker (471) (561) (611) (612) (613) (618) (851) led the Noel Walker Stompers around Merseyside clubs and became a record producer for Decca, having success with the Big Three and the Fortunes.

The hillbilly docker **Hank Walters (5) (83)** is still singing and playing accordion in Liverpool clubs.

Also known as Bags, **Ralph Watmough (22)** formed his first jazz band in Crosby in 1948.

Bernard Whitty (544) ran Lambda Records in Crosby and made some of the first recordings of the Liverpool acts.

Marty Wilde (2) was one of the UK's top rock'n'roll acts. I saw him in April 2004 still singing "Why must I be a teenager in love?" at the age of 64.

Allan Williams (126) (173) (181) (193) (195) (196) (198) (341) ran the Jacaranda coffee bar and the Blue Angel night club. He is known as the man who gave the Beatles away.

Dave Williams (311) was a member of Group One and he regularly goes to Buddy Holly tributes in Lubbock.

As Merseyside's top DJ, **Bob Wooler (4) (197) (199) (200) (202) (316) (458) (466) (479) (701) (765) (800) (803) (817) (818) (819) (825) (828) (829) (830) (832)** introduced the Beatles over 400 times.

Roy Young (350) (373) (430) (492) was, and still is, a rock'n'roll pianist who came up through the *Oh Boy!* and *Drumbeat!* TV shows.

Ozzie Yue (809) was a member of the Hideaways. He regularly appears in bit parts in TV dramas.

Günter Zint (148) (155) (191) (335) (344) (383) (393) (396) (400) (448) worked as a reporter and photographer in the Reeperbahn.

INDEX

269

273

Spencer Leigh was born in Liverpool in 1945. His *On The Beat* programme has been broadcast on BBC Radio Merseyside for 20 years and he has written for several magazines including *Country Music People, Goldmine, Mojo, Now Dig This, Record Collector* and *Word*. He writes obituaries for *The Independent,* which all too often feature Merseybeat personalities, and has compiled and/or written the sleeve notes for hundreds of albums. His website is www.spencerleigh.demon.co.uk.

Spencer Leigh has written *Paul Simon - Now And Then* (1973), *Presley Nation* (1976), *Stars In My Eyes* (1980), *Let's Go Down The Cavern* (with Pete Frame) (1984), *Speaking Words Of Wisdom: Reflections On The Beatles* (1991), *Aspects Of Elvis* (edited with Alan Clayson) (1994), *Memories Of Buddy Holly* (with Jim Dawson) (US only, 1996), *Halfway To Paradise, Britpop 1955 - 1962* (with John Firminger) (1996), *Behind The Song - The Stories Of 100 Great Pop And Rock Classics* (with Michael Heatley) (1998), *Drummed Out - The Sacking Of Pete Best* (1998), *Brother, Can You Spare A Rhyme? - 100 Years Of Hit Songwriting* (2000), *Baby, That Is Rock And Roll - American Pop, 1954 - 1963* (with John Firminger) (2001), *Sweeping The Blues Away - A Celebration Of The Merseysippi Jazz Band* (2002), *The Best Of Fellas - The Story Of Bob Wooler, Liverpool's First D.J.* (2002), *The Walrus Was Ringo - 101 Beatles Myths Debunked* (with Alan Clayson) (2003) and *Puttin' On The Style – The Lonnie Donegan Story* (2003).

He is currently writing the stories behind 1,000 No.1 hits with Jon Kutner. The book will be published by Omnibus shortly after the 1,000 No.1 which should be early in 2005.